IN PURSUIT
OF ADVENTURE . . .

IN PURSUIT
OF TREASURE . . .

In Pursuit
of the *AWA MARU*

Here is the story behind the most intriguing mystery of World War II . . . and the greatest treasure hunt of all time.

Was the *Awa Maru* actually carrying contraband treasure in violation of the Red Cross agreement that it would carry only wounded Japanese?

If so, was the U.S. submarine commander justified in sinking the *Awa Maru* with more than 2000 men aboard?

Can the lost cargo of the *Awa Maru*—lying on the ocean floor off the China coast—ever be salvaged?

In Pursuit of the
Awa Maru

W. Joe Innis
with
Bill Bunton

BANTAM BOOKS · TORONTO · NEW YORK · LONDON

IN PURSUIT OF THE AWA MARU
A Bantam Book / January 1981

ISBN 0-553-12624-5

Published simultaneously in the United States and Canada

PRINTED IN THE UNITED STATES OF AMERICA

0 9 8 7 6 5 4 3 2 1

For China . . . the plundered.

ACKNOWLEDGMENTS

I owe my thanks to those who, in many and varied ways, contributed to the telling of this story: Frank N. Shamer (captain, U.S. Navy, retired); Earl Symonds; Joe Parks; Doug Coleman; William T. Orr; William Lyles; Robert Barth; Wanda Vail; Mr. and Mrs. Ernesto Galliani; Donald A. Innis; Dr. William Cummings; Mary Nugent; Isaac Davies; Donald H. Freeman; Liz Gray; Wallace Jenkins; Jennell McKinney; John E. Bennett (captain, U.S. Navy, retired); and Nancy Kay.

In addition, I especially want to pay tribute to Susan Zimmerman for her tireless research assistance during the preparation of the original manuscript.

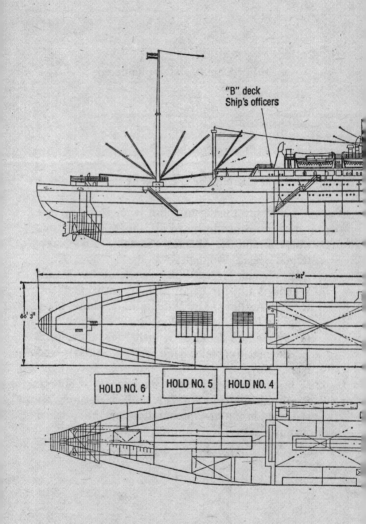

"B" deck
Ship's officers

502'

66' 3"

HOLD NO. 6   HOLD NO. 5   HOLD NO. 4

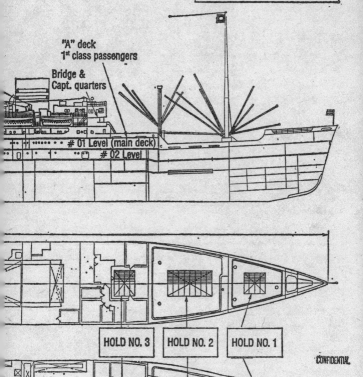

AWA MARU

"A" deck
1st class passengers

Bridge &
Capt. quarters

01 Level (main deck)
02 Level

HOLD NO. 3   HOLD NO. 2   HOLD NO. 1

CONFIDENTIAL

FOREWORD

This story happened. It is based on real events.

It happened pretty much as it appears here. Those who played in it, who made it happen, those who were drawn into the events that culminated in this, the least-known and most deadly sea disaster in naval history, are portrayed here.

Owing to the passage of time and in the interest of fairness, the names of those depicted in the story have been changed. Sometimes a character used here is fashioned from several persons who played parts in the events that occurred more than three decades ago. At other times, characters have been wholly invented. Therefore, this book, though rooted in truth, is a novel: the facts are true, the individuals and the dialogue (except for the court-martial transcripts) are fictitious.

Where the story is consistent with what is known—and the writer has made every effort to make it so—this is something of an historical treatise, the first full account of a naval tragedy neither Japan nor the United States, for different reasons, wants revealed.

To substantiate the story, the writer has drawn on a host of private and public material, personal interviews, classified and unclassified records obtained from official and less than official sources in the U.S., Switzerland and Japan. Wherever possible, the author remained truthful to the data. Where liberties were taken to link what we know for sure with those things we can never know, but fully suspect, the writer did so carefully and hopes, reasonably. Time and circumstances have worked against doing anything else. Some of those still alive would not talk about it. Others, who did talk, had forgotten many of the details. The story they told sometimes did not conform with what others said or with the documentation, or with their own sworn testimony made at the time.

So, like every historical account, presumptions are made and carried forward so that facts match other facts and the whole can be tied together. In this case, these presumptions are the author's and made without prejudice toward any person or government. They are based on the available material and are consistent with it. But they are the writer's presumptions. No one else's.

There were, of course, the Japanese ship, the *Awa Maru*, and the American sub that sank her, the U.S.S. *Queenfish*. Just as there were those in the subsequent court-martial who testified for and against the action taken by the young sub commander. Their statements are public record.

There is a continuing and very real sensitivity about the story presented here. There are national interests, ongoing negotiations, and a good deal of money at stake. Some of the men pursuing these delicate matters are international figures: astronaut-aquanaut Scott Carpenter; Jon Lindbergh, son of the aviation pioneer; Dr. George Bond, formerly the head of the Navy's Man-In-the-Sea Sealab program; presidential adviser and China expert Dr. Harned Pettus Hoose; diving expert and former Sealab aquanaut William J. Bunton. There are others, who cannot, for the moment, be named. Their story will unfold in the years to come. Meanwhile, their interests have been purposely protected.

One of the men, Bunton, has pursued the incredibly intricate story of the *Awa Maru* for more than a decade. He supplied most of the factual background information on which this story is based. His careful attention to detail, his persistence, his ability to win cooperation from a host of diverse personalities, and his willingness to go the extra mile have served to bring to light much of what would have been buried in the recesses of time. He has been the driving force behind the contemporary aspects of this story and the national figures that comprise it. He, who has the most to gain, and the most to lose, has the lasting gratitude of the writer.

Finally, the careful reader who will plot the nautical positions, ships' speeds, times, and compass bearings reported in this chronicle will not be disappointed. The figures are not fictitious and are those supplied by official reports. There has been no attempt to alter them. Even the coordinates that place one ultimate, critical—and highly marketable—sea position stand as reported, publicly revealed here for the first time.

Since these official figures contain a small but significant error, there was no need to change or conceal them. The nature of that error—who knows the correct factor and why?—will be discussed later, when the value of that information, estimated in the billions of dollars, has been established.

Those are the disclaimers.

This is the story. . . .

PROLOGUE

Look. It's been a long time, right? I mean, what?— thirty, thirty-five years now. So I'm not going to sit here and tell you that I wake up every night soakin' wet and screaming myself blue over what went on that night back then. Or that I've spent the last thirty-some years stoppin' every third stranger on the street and sayin': "Hi. I'm radioman third-class Merville Easter, the guy involved in the world's most deadly sea disaster."

I mean, Jesus. We were in war, you know? There are things that go on in war, things that happen. Some, you remember. Some, you forget. Like a lot of things you forget: faces, names, times, the women, when you could find 'em, the blind staggering drunks, and how the poker games turned out. You know.

For the most of it, you're left with damn little. Some impressions maybe. Half-recalled things you'd like to turn to somebody about and say, "Hey, do you remember the time . . . ?" But who are you going to talk to now? I mean, who's around anymore? They're either dead or gone or wishin' they were. It's been a long time.

But sometimes it surprises you, this thing about remembering. You'll be sittin' around with the Sunday papers and sippin' on an ale maybe you haven't tried before, and there's something about the taste of it, something that registers on the roof of your mouth, and you'll get a scene, a flash of something you lived through once and hadn't thought about since. The whole thing.

Maybe it's gettin' old that does it. But you get the whole thing like an eyes-and-ears-of-the-world newsreel runnin' back up behind your eyeballs. Start to finish. And bam. You know? Suddenly there's Old Ox, Boldern, Garrabaldi, Bicca, and the rest of 'em. It's R and R in Pearl and you're at the Tropicana, the smoke-and-beer smell of it, at the back table again, the one under the Uncle Sam Needs You poster that

1

someone has taken a crayon to, changin' the finger pointing at you to a middle finger pointin' up. And you're there, just like you were then, with the same fly workin' its way around a puddle of beer on the table.

You can see all of it. Old Ox at the bar, his enormous ass overhangin' the stool, sort of canted to one side as he leans toward the randy old broad sittin' next to him, fillin' her with war-patrol stories that put Ox second only to Navy Secretary Forrestal. And I'm there at the table, coverin' bets against Ox gettin' in her knickers, right? A bet I got pretty well hedged after watching a cook out of the Seafox crew make Ox's mistake three days before. And sure as hell, just as Bicca and the others were countin' their money and worryin' on my payin', she turns kind of sideways and lets Old Ox have at a great, jagged, yellow-toothed smile that would curl the underbelly of a Jap destroyer.

You get flashes like that, sometimes. But mostly it doesn't come like that. There's a hell of a lot of what went on in three years of floatin' around in a sub that you forget. And, all right. There are some things you remember. Always. Like that night. The last night of the real war.

After that night and the things that happened afterwards, my look at that war changed some. I began questioning things, things that happened then and later, and I didn't like some of the questions. Worse, I didn't like some of the answers.

Look at it this way. Before that night it was an easy war to understand: all the bad guys were bunched up neatly on one side, the good guys on the other. Two teams, right? And you didn't need uniforms to tell 'em apart. The bad guys didn't look anything like the good guys. For a start, they were all midgets. It took stackin' two to make one of us. They had yellow skin, they talked funny, and the whole lot of 'em were issued eyes that weren't set in straight.

But after that night and what they did to the skipper, some of the good and bad of this thing got mixed up. In my mind. In the minds of a whole lot of others. But there wasn't much talk about it. I mean, it's not something you want to bring up. And it's not like we all got together and said, From here on out mum's the word. Nothin' like that, but we talked about it some right afterwards, and tried to tie one thing into another, but when other details became known, the thing got tangled up, what was once clear became not so clear, and pretty soon we didn't talk about it so much, and some of us were mustering out anyway, or being transferred to another sub, and what with the impending invasion of Japan, and then the atom bomb, and finally the capitulation, we didn't talk about it at all.

Like I say, it wasn't something you'd like to bring up. And while we didn't make a pact, we were all sub sailors and through the years we stood together.

Okay. You're sayin' that sounds like so much bullshit, sub sailors staying together. In a way, maybe so. I've never gone for a lot of this stuff either. You've heard the crap: there are two kinds of sailors—sub sailors and those who want to be. Well, at the time, maybe I felt that way. Maybe we all did. You know, you don't just fall into a sub. You had to really want that kind of duty. It's not like they lined you up after basic training and said: "Okay men. You're ready for war. Those of you who want to float around in a submarine, stand over there."

You had to earn those dolphins and it took your volunteering and a hell of a lot of study to do it. On board, each of us had to stand several different watches and know the job in each. And something about how the whole damn sub works: hydraulic systems, air and propulsion systems, those kinds of things. On top of that, you had your specialty. For me, it was sonar. You'd be surprised how much there is to learn in a thing like that, and how much you can tell by the sounds things make under water. There are guys that can all but name the commanding officer of a vessel from the sound the screws of his ship make turning in the water.

Anyway, what I'm sayin' is that it takes a whole lot of wantin' to be, to be a sub sailor. And of course you got to be balls-out crazy to volunteer in the first place. I mean, there was a time at the start of the war when somebody had it figured that the life expectancy of a submariner was twenty minutes at the outside. I mean, you figure it. When they first put us to sea, they had torpedoes that would hit everything but the target you set them for. If you fired four and three didn't broach, come back, and hit you broadside, that was a successful run. Then, of course, you had the whole Jap Navy trackin' the torpedo wake back to where you sat.

So you got crazy guys in a sub: either guys that didn't know better, or did, and didn't give a shit. But on the whole they were proud guys, guys that opted out of all the Navy regulations, protocol, and bullshit aboard a surface vessel. So sub duty attracted the kind of guy who would otherwise be sitting out the war in a brig somewhere for smart-assing an officer or forgetting to shine his shoes, or some damn thing.

And in port they treated us right. Gave us all sorts of

privileges. And when we were anywhere near women—which was damn seldom—we were one up there, for some reason. Maybe it's the danger that turns women on, I don't know. But we had our edge there too. So, whatever else it was to serve in a sub, it was an elite corps, and maybe because of that we stood together.

And when this thing happened, we hung in together about what we'd done, we stood by the skipper and his decision, and we pretty well clammed up about that night and what happened after.

But it's time this thing is talked about. Whether the hell they still got most of this under Navy secret and confidential wraps or not, it's time things were said. It's time we talked.

Who are we protecting anyway? There's a hell of a lot more going on here than one sub, one skipper, and one monumental accident—if that's what it was—that night on the East China Sea.

I mean, Jesus Christ.

I

Date: March 7, 1945
Place: Camp Dealy, Guam
Time: 0730 hours

The silver whistle that hung from the neck of Marine Staff Sergeant Bernard P. Gunderholtz danced brilliantly to his brisk gait as he crossed the asphalt basketball court towards barracks 27-A. The troubles the night before had not diminished his military bearing, and as he neatly skirted the dust of the horseshoe pit in the tropical afternoon heat, he looked splendid: sharply tailored khaki shirt, only just now dampening at the back, a razor-sharp press to his trousers, a barracks cap cocked exactly two fingers above the right eye, boots shimmering from hours of cotton and spit—boots that he now polished alternately on the back of each leg as he faced the three wooden steps to the shuttered barracks. Adjusting the tension on his belt, and being careful not to leave fingerprints on the brass buckle, then shifting his armband so the MP could be read easily, Sergeant Gunderholtz was ready once again to face the crew of the U.S.S. *Queenfish* (SS393).

Aside from the pulsating ache at the back of his head, which had been gathering for the past six hours, Sergeant Gunderholtz felt as beautiful as he looked. His mood could be attributed mainly to the news he had received only fifteen minutes before: the crew had gotten their shipping orders. They were to report immediately to their vessel for a patrol that would commence at dusk. For Gunderholtz, half a dozen Seabees, and some Shore Patrol, this was a banner day. It marked the end of two weeks of R and R for the crew of the *Queenfish;* two weeks in which they had pulled no duty, while their boat, tied to the sub tender at the harbor a half mile away, underwent maintenance by the relief crew; two weeks for the battle-weary crew to experience the diversions of this remote camp. While here, they could eat whatever they

5

wanted, drink beer, sleep as much as they could, drink beer; swim, play baseball and basketball, and drink beer. If they tired of that, they could play horseshoes until they got thirsty.

For Sergeant Gunderholtz it had been a long fourteen days, culminating in a fight on the baseball field at 0130 hours that morning. It had not been the first fight, but in this one he had made the mistake of trying to spare the life of a Seabee who was being throttled by a 265-pound third-class seaman they called Old Ox. Even with the help of his platoon of MPs, Sergeant Gunderholtz had problems. In the dark, he was not sure who or what clocked him.

It took Gunderholtz more than three hours to compose the disciplinary report, owing in part to his headache and in part to his need to describe the complicated altercation.

As near as he could tell, this fight was the last of several and involved one of two cases of whiskey that the Seabees had sold to certain members of the crew when they arrived off their third war patrol. Downing one, the crew elected to bury the other before they lost all consciousness, suspecting, with good cause, that the Seabees would attempt to steal it back. They chose the dead of night to bury it. Waking late the next afternoon, they discovered that the Seabees had graded the area and poured a basketball court.

Sergeant Gunderholtz hoped this report, unlike his many others would prompt his superiors to take disciplinary action against the crew. He did not like the latitude given these sub sailors. He had been in the Marines for ten years and did not believe that one branch of the service should be treated any differently from another. He understood about this R and R, but he was a career military man and he felt there were limits to privileges. He believed in reveille, police calls, and periodic inspections as others believed in church. It was a part of the life he understood. And discipline was part of that. There was, he often said, a war going on.

Camp Dealy, constructed specifically for submariners' R and R, was not a choice assignment for a regular Marine sergeant in the Military Police, and he thought of that as he pushed open the door to barracks 27-A.

The first thing that struck Gunderholtz, even before he focused on the darkened interior, was the overwhelming stench of beer, booze, sweat, and smoke. Coughing once, the sergeant hesitated, then stepped forward. His foot caught an empty bottle and sent it reeling. It bounced off the leg of a metal bunk, then rolled slowly but noisily across the floor and came to rest against the face of a figure clad only in skivvies,

6

sprawled stomach down in the aisle between the cots. Breathing heavily through an open mouth, the figure did not stir. In a corner of the room somebody broke wind in a long, low blast. Few of the men had made it to their bunks; they slept in various positions as though caught in their activities when booze had struck them numb. There had been a poker game, and one of the men, his cards still clutched in one hand, slept face down in a bowl of pretzels. Another snored through a gas mask as he lay face up, nude, on an upturned wall locker. A third had somehow been caught in the process of climbing to an upper bunk; he slept with one leg across the cot, one foot on the floor, clutching the back side of the bunk. On the back wall in foot-long whitewashed letters was the message UP YOUR SEABEE.

Sergeant Gunderholtz blew his official U.S. Marine whistle with a vengeance that morning, and blew it not more than three feet from a man who had made it, more or less, to his top bunk: radioman third-class Merville Easter, the lanky, raven-haired sonarman out of Helena, Montana.

RM3 Easter's first impression was that he had been shot between the eyes by a four-inch deck gun. He dared not reach up to find where his head had been. He was quite content to die in this way, to let quietly slip by whatever remained of life within him. It was not, all things considered, a bad way to go.

When the second blast shook him, he suspected the worst: he was alive and hungover. One does not get shot twice by a four-incher.

Commander Raymond Michael Houffman, skipper of the *Queenfish*, stood at the rail of the submarine tender *Fulton* and watched his men file shakily down the twisting, corrugated steel gangplank to the sub. Though still early, it was already hot. The relief crew, well into their last day of maintenance, gave way to the returning crew with a certain deference and understanding.

Most of the men on maintenance duty had earned their position by surviving five war patrols. The wisecracks they directed to the sailors boarding the vessel were restrained and for the most part good-natured. Even when the 265-pound seaman they called Old Ox was carted aboard by three of his buddies and deposited down the forward hatch, there was only mild laughter. They knew what R and R could do to a man.

Commander Houffman had been through these exercises

before, at Pearl, at Majuro, and he knew his crew needed a couple of days at sea to sober up. Early that morning he had gone through the stack of disciplinary reports that the MPs had filed against his crew members during the last three days; he had noted and dismissed the recommendations. He had fought with ComSubPac to keep this crew together, and he was not going to lose them to a brig.

Aft of the *Queenfish* and also linked to the tender was the *Seafox*, also undergoing last-minute preparations. Houffman could make out the maintenance crew atop the *Seafox* but could not spot Commander Eli Darvies. He suspected Darvies had a similar stack of DRs to contend with. *Seafox* and *Spot*, another sub that was being readied on the opposite side of the tender, together with the *Queenfish*, comprised the wolfpack that would head out under cover of darkness that night. Though the three subs would work as a unit, each of the sub commanders expressed his personality in command of his weapon—for, whatever else a submarine was, it was a single weapon in the hands of a single commander. Some expressed this power cautiously, some recklessly. Those who continued to be operational commanders walked the thin line between caution and abandon.

The tall, angular commander at the rail above the *Queenfish* thus far had survived three heralded patrols. He had won the Navy Cross on his first and second patrols and the Silver Star on his third. On his first two patrols he had bagged 103,000 tons of enemy shipping, a record that had earned the *Queenfish* the Presidential Unit Citation.

Up to now, Houffman knew that thin line and walked it well. Only those who had been with him when the *Queenfish* was commissioned in New Hampshire and who had sailed with him through the Panama Canal and the ensuing three patrols would notice any changes in their skipper: a growing seriousness, a certain tension in the muscles of his jaw, eyes set perhaps a little deeper than before, a growing impatience, a quicker temper. His hair, prematurely gray, had whitened further. And, since the docking at Guam and the string of emergency calls he had received from his wife in the States, there was something else.

Houffman lifted his eyes to the harbor, where the morning breeze had begun working across the light blue water. He tried to piece together the changes three patrols had brought him.

Whatever happens to a man who chooses to fight his wars

from within the belly of a steel shark had happened to Houffman.

There's a kind of man who does that, and although he's prepared for the thing that happens, schooled for it, warned against it, it overtakes him; subtly at first, but inevitably it consumes him. If he's any good at war, it consumes him.

Houffman was good at it. He knew war, knew it as few did, from within the bowels of a submersible killer.

Something happens to a man who fights his wars this way. When he moves within his 307-foot weapon, he does so deliberately, with the graceful, measured economy of one acutely aware of the presence of others, like the stage movement in an overrehearsed play. The give and take of space becomes a kind of dance among the men who fight their wars this way.

Man is a fairly adaptive creature. He loses almost nothing to his environment. In time he learns its restrictions, however severe, and lives within them. In the tiny compartments and cubicles that comprise the submariner's life are the facilities of a fighting surface ship two or three times its size. When a man learns this life and adjusts to it, almost nothing is lost. Almost nothing.

Everyone commands a certain territory, a physical perimeter, a distance that he places between himself and others. Psychologists have studied this phenomenon and noted how threatened and uncomfortable a man becomes when his distance is violated by another. While the distance varies from man to man, a radius of three or four feet seems average. Though circumstances alter the distance at which man can accept others—a crowded subway, for example—he accepts this abridgment of his territory reluctantly, uncomfortably, with averted face, protected posture, a newspaper.

Perhaps one of the hardest things for a submariner to learn is to work within a substantially reduced perimeter, to do so for long periods of time, and to do so comfortably. If it comes to him, this work in a sunken can, and if he's good at it, he can deal with other men almost face to face, and do so as casually as others might at a distance. But there's a price.

If a man is good at his job and learns to forfeit that distance, he will recover the distance in his mind, by re-creating the territory there. A guy at home in a sub is a guy one can easily approach, talk to, joke with, and hardly ever get to know.

9

Commander Houffman was at home in a sub. He had learned the life well. The three patrols had seasoned him for it. He knew his weapon. He knew that within the space of two suburban houses there were living accommodations for a crew of eighty-three, a control room, diesel engines and electric motors, fuel and water tanks, and 252 battery cells, each weighing more than a ton. He knew about that as one feels he knows his own life.

He knew too about the air compressors and high-pressure air banks for blowing ballast and charging torpedo air flasks; the torpedo rooms fore and aft, the ten torpedo tubes, and the stowage space for twenty-four Mark XVIII electric stream-lined missiles of death.

He knew that jammed into the remaining space were refrigerated and dry stores, stills for manufacturing fresh water, air-conditioning and air-purifying equipment, ice machines, shower baths, and main ballast tanks to give neutral buoyancy when running submerged and positive buoyancy when on the surface.

Just as he knew about the variable ballasts for adjusting trim, how the periscope rose and fell from the well, how the bowplanes moved and why. And he knew about the lazaret, the chain locker, the ammunition magazines, and the galley.

Commander Houffman knew his life and the complicated equipment that comprised it, the navigational instruments, the fire-control instruments, the radio, and the radar and sonar gear. He knew that his life and the other lives that were committed to his decisions—right or wrong—depended on how well he understood his weapon, how well he knew each valve, gauge meter, and lever that were part of it.

He had a sense for the maze of oil, air, and water lines that stretched like capillaries beneath her skin. He had a feel for the electric cables that, like ganglia, linked it all together into a responsive nervous system.

And now, standing on the deck of the sub tender U.S.S. *Fulton,* Houffman knew that the thing that happens to a man who chooses to fight his wars from within a machine like this had happened to him.

Restless, he wanted back in.

He wanted every man in his place: his exec, the chief engineer, torpedo and gunnery officer, his seamen. He wanted them ready, tuned, prepared.

He wanted to feel the throb of her diesel engines as she cruised the surface, the dead space when these engines were killed for the dive, the quiet of the electric motors beneath the surface, the throb of her screws thrusting her downward, her bowplanes like huge fins guiding her in the deep.

But Commander Houffman wanted more than the ride. He had emerged from three war patrols with the taste of blood in his mouth. He had acquired a taste for the single-minded purpose of the metal shark being readied beneath him. He had become his war machine, a part of it, and he wanted that taste again.

Below Commander Houffman, the motor macs had laid open the innards of her bowplanes, exposing the cast steel of her joints. The man who watched the operation from above, propped against the rail, hardly fit the "old man" title bestowed on commanders, but then, few of the sub commanders in that war—seldom older than thirty-five—did. It took a young man to accept the odds given a submariner—five-to-one against ever coming out of the war alive.

But for Houffman the title was particularly inept. He was aware of it and managed to maintain a sternness about his boyish face. Only when he relaxed—a condition that was becoming more infrequent these days—and the tight, tense quality that worked his face eased, would the boyishness return and a smile play across his steel-blue eyes.

But as the months at sea worked on him and the sort of electric tension on which he operated mounted, Houffman found fewer moments to relax. Even now, as he watched the general maintenance operation in preparation for his fourth and last patrol on the *Queenfish*, Houffman could not ease the muscles that clutched at the back of his neck.

Houffman had exited an endless, and pointless, briefing from the staff-side at ComSubPac at an ungodly 0700. He and Commanders Lowe and Darvies, of the *Spot* and *Seafox*, had been subjected to better than an hour of rambling war stories. The second feature was an enlightened education on submersible warfare by a guy who was visibly worried at being sent this far forward to deliver the briefing.

Houffman had not made a single note on his pad. There had been no need.

All of it, better than an hour and a half of hearing what he already knew, contributed to the tightness that spread down from his neck to his back.

Until now, it was a tension he'd been able to control. The kind of tight-wire aggressiveness that was part of his character had twice won him the All-American title on the football field at Annapolis. It had also served him well on the baseball diamonds: he had been a highly touted intercollegiate pitcher. In all of it he had played to win.

Just as he played the war. So far, Houffman had come out on top. But war, unlike baseball, was a game in which you either came out a winner or you did not come out at all.

Above the din of the operation below him, Commander Houffman could hear the suck of the grease that the macs were scooping from the buckets near them. Unceremoniously and in huge dollops, they were laying it on the exposed universals, one in each bowplane, working the grease in and around, massaging the joints. There were jokes about the men who did this. Thinking about some of them, Houffman didn't notice the approach of his executive officer, Lieutenant Bill Edwards.

"Captain," Edwards called out, "I've got a man here you've been expecting." As a conversationalist, Edwards was not full of surprises. Yet, somehow, he had a way of attaching the utmost significance to something that one already knew. Perhaps a part of that was in the expression of concern that was etched on his face, lingering in the folds of his mouth and behind his large, brown, serious eyes. Edwards approached the world as though he were about to deliver the announcement of its end.

Only in his mid-twenties, his concern was justified. Although he had had less than one year of submarine duty, his credentials aboard surface warships were impeccable. Severely wounded, and practically single-handedly, he had safely stewarded the crippled cruiser *San Francisco* through a storm of Japanese destroyers and subs in the North Pacific during the Aleutian campaign. It had been more than rough, and it had won Edwards both the Purple Heart and the coveted Navy Cross.

The abdominal pains that gripped him periodically had worsened on the last patrol, his third with the elite submarine service. Some of the crew who knew about it attributed it to the action in the North Pacific; others, to his difficulty in adjusting to the close quarters and charged atmosphere of a sub. While he had been receiving medication from pharmacist mate Harold D. (Doc) Tobey aboard the *Queenfish*, he had, up till now, kept the problem from Commander Houffman.

Acknowledging Edwards, Houffman turned and extended his hand toward the man with him. "I'm Raymond Houffman. I do my best to operate that long black boat down there. I understand you're coming to bat."

Lieutenant Commander Steve Trevor looked very much

like Joe Palooka. He stood over six feet tall, almost as tall as Houffman, but bigger. He had been designed in slabs. Though he had the good-natured look of a football coach in a boys' school, his reputation as a razor-sharp tactician who could stand up to anything the enemy had to deliver had preceded him.

"Well, yeah. And I understand you operate that thing with a little class, judging from what I hear." Trevor's grin consumed his face. "Skipper, for Christ sake, I want you to know right off: I'm comin' to bat all right, but not before I get to watch you take a few swipes at the ball. And I'm looking forward to that. I want to see if everything I've heard about you is true. I just want you to understand that I'm sure as hell no threat to you. I'm going to dry-run this thing with you, and if I can be of any help . . . well, I'll be it."

Trevor was to serve as prospective commanding officer aboard the *Queenfish*. After the run that would begin tonight, he would assume command. It was a way to gain experience before heading off on his own patrols. Among a host of war policies that didn't work, this worked well. A commander knew the idiosyncrasies of his vessel and he learned little shortcuts that saved seconds and, at times, lives. And he knew his crew—in some respects, more than they knew themselves. A lot of these things could be passed on by example during action and by long talks in the dry spells. Trevor welcomed the opportunity, and, sensing a possible conflict in leadership, he had headed it off. It had been the right thing to say.

"Thanks, Steve." Houffman turned back to watching the operation below. "I hope I can provide some adventure on this turn around. Those little slants are makin' themselves pretty scarce these days."

Trevor and Edwards took positions at the rail on either side of the skipper. The two commanders lost themselves for a moment in the work below as a mac jumped clear of the bowplane and signaled the electrician's mate to bring it up. The mac yelled something to a nearby "talker," who relayed the message into his chest-supported mike. The high-pitched whine of the low ratio gears within the guts of the bowplane began to move the great fin upward. Signaling for it to stop, the motor mac jumped back on the fin and began greasing the newly exposed metal.

Edwards was talking across Commander Houffman to Trevor. Houffman tuned him in late: ". . . By God, this man standing here, Steve, well, if there's one guy who's gonna find some action, it's gonna be this guy. I saw some things aboard the *San Francisco* when I was there—I mean some real hell—but this commander here, well, I can tell you, he can find them, and when . . ."

Houffman focused again on the motor mac as he jumped back on the deck of the sub. He wanted the bowplane still higher.

". . . And that's why they call us Houffman's Loopers. See this guy standin' here between us? In Annapolis, the old man was a two-time selection for All-America. Football. Loopers? I mean, Jesus, if being All-America once wasn't . . ."

The report was like a cannon shot, its echo resounding off the hills behind the harbor. For a moment everyone below and on the rail of the tender froze. The report had come seconds after the gears had begun to wind the bowplane still higher. It was the sound of fractured steel. Two of the men nearest the plane scrambled to look, then made way for the chief mate, who, with an exaggerated effort toward casualness, ambled over.

The commanding officer on the rail of the tender already knew what was wrong. Houffman had felt the fracture of the bowplane's universal joint as though it were his own pelvis shattering under strain.

"Skipper, did you hear that?" Edwards' eyes implored first Houffman, then Trevor. "That sounded like . . ."

Houffman did not need to hear Edwards' clarification. He clenched his teeth. The shattered universal would mean they couldn't go out with the pack that night, and if they had to wait for a shipment from Pearl or God knows where, they might not get out for a week.

"I'm not sayin' it is," Edwards continued, "but judging from the sound that thing made when it snapped, that could well mean . . ."

The thing that happens to a man who chooses to fight a war in a submarine had happened to Houffman. He tried to bleed his anger into the rail with a white-knuckled grip.

"So what I'm saying is that it could be a universal joint or it could be—"

"Edwards?" Houffman spoke with a quiet control. There was no edge to his voice. He deliberately eased his grip on the rail. "Edwards, I'd like you to go down there and talk to the man."

"Right, Captain. I'll go down and talk to the chief. I'll get a full report." Edwards turned to head toward the gangplank.

"Edwards?" Houffman took a deep breath, then eased it out.

14

"Yes, Skipper."

"Find out how long it will take him to fix that universal."

Trevor said nothing until Edwards had boarded the vessel below and begun working his way across the deck plates, heading forward between the men. Only then did he venture to change the subject. "I understand you had an 0700 this morning." Trevor had heard about the briefing.

The pause was long enough for Trevor to think that Houffman either had not heard him or chose not to reply. Then Houffman began shaking his head slowly from side to side. "You know..." he said, then drifted back into his thoughts.

Trevor tried again. "Was anything said?"

This time Houffman turned and worked his face into what could have been taken as a smile. "You know," he began again, "these guys have got that rain dance pretty well down pat. They get you up at the crack of dawn to tell you the war's still going on. Then they give you the shot about how important your next patrol is. Implying, of course, that your last wasn't really worth a damn. Then some deskbound lieutenant out of Harvard tells how it really is; and he talks about the need for more tonnage like he's requisitioning Kotex for a squad of Red Cross girls. Then somebody else stands up and tells of the continuing need to be aggressive. Now, understand, he's talking to three seasoned commanders. You've got Darvies in the *Seafox,* you've got Lowe in *Spot,* and me. Now, all of us have been through every kind of action there is, you know. I mean, Jesus. Do you know Eli Darvies?"

"I've heard about him," Trevor replied.

"Well, can you imagine telling Darvies to be more aggressive? It's like telling Attila the Hun he's too circumspect. You know..."

Below them, on the deck of the *Queenfish,* Edwards and the chief mate were in discussion; Edwards, gesturing with his hands, and the chief mate, eyes on his shoes, slowly shaking his head.

"But to answer your question," Houffman said, "you didn't miss a thing in that briefing."

"No special messages?"

"Only one," Houffman said. "Go out and sink something Japanese."

Edwards left the chief below and started working his way across the deck and up to Houffman and Trevor. Watching him move toward the gangplank, Houffman said, "Edwards is going to get up here and tell me two things—that it's the universal and that they're going to have to ship one in from Pearl."

Edwards, his face flushed from the climb, approached the two commanders.

"Skipper, it doesn't look good." This time the concerned expression on the face of the executive officer matched the news he was relaying. "It's the universal joint all right. And they've got to ship one in from Pearl." When his news brought forth only silence, Edwards continued, "According to the chief, they're just not equipped to manufacture a bearing on the tender. They've got to bring one in from Pearl, and you know the problems there. The chief said it's going to take two days, maybe three, to get it over here, and another day, maybe half a day, to set it in. The chief said—"

"Edwards."

"Skipper?"

"I'd like that chief up here in thirty seconds."

When the chief mate of the relief crew reported to Houffman on the deck of the tender, he was out of breath. He was a big man and not given to doing things on the double.

Houffman wasted few words. "You've been on this refit for two weeks, right?"

"Yes, sir."

"You were preparing, I understand, for this boat to ship out with *Seafox* and *Spot*. I believe that was tonight, wasn't it?"

"Yes, sir. But I don't have no control over what happened. These things—"

"And I understand you told my executive officer that you couldn't manufacture a bearing here."

"Yes, sir. We never did nothing like that here. We always send—"

"And that it would take three to four days."

"Yes, sir. First we got to requisition one out of Pearl, and then—"

Houffman cut him short with a raised hand.

"This morning, Chief, I was one of three sub commanders privileged to attend an 0700 briefing by ComSubPac. They discussed the patrol that was to begin for all of us tonight." Houffman paused, and pulled at his face with one hand as though trying to wipe away the fatigue that hung there. "While what was said in that briefing was on a need-to-know basis, I think I can share with you the principal piece of information headquarters passed on to us. It's about this war we've been having."

"Yes, sir?"

"Well, ComSubPac tells me, mister, the damn war is still going on!" The quiet control Houffman had maintained had given way suddenly.

"I'm up to here with this damn war," Houffman continued. "But I'm going to finish my part of it on this patrol and get the hell back home. Then you'll have to deal with this man here." Houffman indicated Trevor. "Until then, and until that boat down there is operational, you're going to deal with me."

Houffman looked down at his feet, then up, clamping his steel-blue eyes on the chief. "The thing in your favor is that you're not going to have to deal with me long. You're going to manufacture that U-joint right here. You're going to have it in place tomorrow afternoon. Because we're casting off tomorrow night! Do you have any questions, mister?" There were those on the boat below who heard this last.

A young ensign had approached the group on the deck just before Houffman's final outburst. When it came, he took two steps back and waited. When nothing more seemed forthcoming, he ventured a hesitant, "Captain Houffman? Uh, sir?"

Houffman disengaged his eyes from the chief and gradually focused on the young ensign. The chief turned and started away.

"Sir," the ensign said, "I've got a message from Comm Section concerning—"

Houffman had his hand up again. He turned to the retreating figure of the chief moving down the passage toward the gangplank. "Chief?" The anger that had been in his face a second before had faded.

The chief turned. "Yes, sir?"

"When you get that U-joint in tomorrow afternoon," he paused to let that sink in, "there are two cases of Black and White for you and your crew. Will you have any use for that?"

A pause, then: "Uh, yeah. Yes, sir. I think we can find a use for that."

"You won't know where in hell it came from, right?"

"It won't be around long enough for anyone to ask, sir."

Houffman, the hardness around the corners of his mouth easing for the first time that morning, turned back to the

17

ensign. "Did you hear anything about cases of Black and White?"

"Uh, no, sir. I didn't hear nothin'. Nothin' like that."

Houffman waited. It took a moment before the ensign remembered why he was standing there. "Sir, there's a call from Stateside for you in the comm shack." Then, in a lower voice, "It's your wife again, sir."

As Houffman turned to follow the ensign through the hatch, Edwards called past Trevor, "Captain, do you want the men off the boat?"

"No. Put them on condition three. They'll need a couple of days to sober up anyway." Houffman stepped over the combing, then turned back. "And tell them we're at sea. They won't know the difference."

Prospective Commanding Officer Trevor and Executive Officer Edwards were left alone at the rail. Below, on the *Queenfish,* the chief was barking orders to the talker, the maneuvering room, and the men clustered at the bowplane housing. Everyone scrambled. They would be setting up the floodlights that night.

Edwards broke the silence between them. "Steve, did you know the skipper before?"

Trevor welcomed the question; it opened up some questions he had. "No. I was four years behind his class. All I knew about him were the trophies he left. He had one hell of a reputation on the gridiron."

Trevor would spend the next few weeks learning everything he could about the *Queenfish,* its crew, its officers, its present commander, and how all of them worked together. He would begin with Edwards: "He seems kind of edgy—the skipper, I mean."

"Well . . . yes." Edwards seemed to think about it. "He's been under the gun, you know."

"What do you mean?"

"Well, we've been out three times. The first two were something. He dropped ten ships, some 87,000 tons. Hell, he couldn't miss. After the second one, our tonnage-sunk rating was ninth in the top hundred patrols of the war. I mean, he was up there with O'Kane on the *Tang* and the rest of them. It looked good going into the third patrol. Unit citations, the whole thing."

"What then? Problems?"

"Yeah. We did all right at first. You know, Houffman operates smoothly. He thinks way the hell ahead of where

18

he's going. We had a couple of good night surface attacks, but then our torpedoes started underrunning. You can't prove something like that, but we all knew that had to be what was happening."

"You were firing the old steam jobs, right?" Trevor had had some experience with the older Mark XIVs. They left a wake and ran erratically, either broaching, porpoising, or underrunning. The new Mark XVIIIs, which the *Queenfish* now carried, were electric, a design, ironically, furnished by the Germans. They were wakeless and far more accurate.

"Yeah, they were steam. Anyway, we got into a lot of trouble. Once we took 139 depth charges, some closer than hell. You know, these two Jap destroyers sat above us all day dropping them on our heads. Anyway, we unloaded our fish, took more misses than hits, and headed to Pearl, then back here."

The sun had moved up over the hills and the breeze that had been moving in across the harbor fell. The men below, while still in the shade of the tender, had stripped to the waist, sweat glistening on the backs of those still wrestling to free the fractured bearing from the bowplane housing. For these men, it would be a long day, a longer night, and an eternal tomorrow.

"Well, that's not what I'd consider a bad patrol." Trevor lifted his arms from the rail, turned, and leaned back against it. "A bad patrol is one you don't come back from."

"But Commander Houffman is different. He likes to win and win big. Look at how he played football and baseball. I'm not sayin' he's reckless. He's not. In my mind he's one of the sharpest commanders in the Pacific. But a guy like that has got to win. And make the win worth talking about."

"So there's that," Edwards continued, "and there's also his problems back home. I don't know what's going on, but he's been hearing from his wife once, sometimes twice, a day since we got here. And it's bothering him. And now the bowplane. He wanted to finish his fourth patrol big and fast so he could get home and solve his problems."

Trevor knew the attrition rate for wives of submariners. When you won those dolphins, you won another woman, and she demanded a hell of a lot more time than your first. A lot can happen to a wife sitting home alone in Backwater, USA.

Trevor had worked out the last of what was bothering Houffman. He volunteered it to Edwards: "And the skipper's got some kind of foot race with Darvies on the *Seafox*, right?"

"Right. Well, you know about the competition in general. It's that . . . well, this thing between Darvies and the old man is something else. Different philosophies, different approaches. Each is convinced he's got the ticket. Between you and me, I wouldn't ride the *Seafox* if they strapped me to the periscope."

"So when the *Seafox* and *Spot* pull out tonight and the *Queenfish* is sittin' cold, the skipper's going to be chompin' at the bit," Trevor said.

"He's going to have that bit chewed in half," Edwards replied.

Commander Houffman trailed the ensign downstairs through the machine shop to the Communications Section office of the sub tender. The communications officer of the *Queenfish*, Mike W. Bass, was propped on the corner of the desk, engaged in conversation with the comm officer of the *Fulton*, when Houffman entered. Bass, holding a clipboard in one hand, eased his weight off the desk and greeted his captain with a broad, easy smile. Like many others aboard the *Queenfish*, he had been in the war long enough to take things in his stride, to do his job effectively, and to do it with the same kind of passion with which he approached a good game of bridge. Houffman and Bass had spent countless hours in that pursuit at slack times aboard the sub. Noting the look on his captain's face, Bass was quick to excuse himself.

"We'll get out of here, Captain, so you can field that call alone. It's coming in on the red phone over there." Bass and the comm officer of the *Fulton* started through the hatch.

"What have you got there, Mike?" Houffman, noting the clipboard of messages, stopped Bass as he was heading out.

"These?" Bass held up the clipboard and fanned through them. "They're all the intercepts, Captain. Everything you ever wanted to know about the war and were afraid to ask." While a sub was linked to a tender, all communications to the sub were routed through the comm section of the tender. For the most part, these communications were of low priority. A good many of them concerned the supplies that had been onloaded to the sub in the last couple of days, so many rolls of toilet paper, so many bars of Lava. Any important messages would be read and signed by the sub officers when under way.

"You're planning on going to direct communications tonight, right?" Commander Houffman said.

"Aren't we sailing tonight?" Bass was puzzled.

"You haven't got the word?"

"Well, Captain, there's always ten percent that don't. What's up?"

"You don't want to know, Mike. But if I have my way, we'll be leaving tomorrow night. So you better leave those here. You can make the pickup tomorrow, God willing."

Alone, Houffman turned to the red phone hanging from the bulkhead. He took a deep breath, exhaled slowly, and after a moment picked up the phone.

"This is Captain Houffman. You can patch me in. . . ."

II

Date: March 8, 1945
Place: Aboard the U.S.S. *Queenfish,* Guam
Time: 1830 hours

Twilight is a long time in coming to the islands in the western Pacific. And, once there, it is reluctant to leave. The sun, melting into the sea, sets fire to the sky in a spectacular, if subdued, blaze of color. It's a fire that consumes itself slowly, yielding its light upward to a night that struggles to snuff it out. It's a long time before the light is quenched and the still begins.

The lifejacketed men on the decks fore and aft of the 2,100-ton submarine know their positions on the maneuvering watch, in light or in darkness, with the kind of certainty that comes with practice, experience. As the night deepens on the black-railed decks, the men responsible for putting the U.S.S. *Queenfish* to sea move with economy and deliberateness; line handlers, anchor brakemen, telephone talkers, and supervisors, all working in a kind of blackout ballet.

The vapor cloud from the diesel engines billows around them as they work in the still air. The smoke hangs between the sub and the towering mother ship, and the smell of it mixes with the pungent perfume of the breadfruit and flame trees on the island. With the fading light, there is no judging distances and, with the experienced crew working the lines, no need to.

The process had taken nearly forty-five minutes, and now, with a roar of her forward and after engines, an echo that reverberates across the quiet harbor, she's ready. The first of her links, her bow line, is flung free, followed in close succession by her fore and aft moorings. And she's alone.

Free, her bow nuzzles inward toward the mother ship as she backs into the harbor and her stern clears for an end-

22

around. She glides for a moment until, with another roar of her engines, her forward gear is engaged, and, churning the waters behind her, she takes an all-ahead two-thirds and begins to move forward, heading for the mouth of the harbor and the night sea beyond.

Commander Raymond Michael Houffman stood on the darkened bridge until his weapon had cleared the harbor. Only then did he descend the hatch to the conning tower. Inside the con, he swept a practiced eye across the area. Just twenty-three feet long and four feet wide, the con contained a helm, two periscopes, a radar mast, torpedo switchboard panels, assorted radar equipment, and the navigators' and quartermasters' charthouse.

Stepping behind the helmsman and taking care not to jar him, Houffman descended through the hatch, just a foot and a half behind the helmsman, into the control room below, where he acknowledged the chief of watch and the other men in control, then headed down the twisting passageway, through the forward battery, and entered the ward room in officers' country. Everywhere he moved through the cramped quarters of the sub, his men gave way to him. It was his weapon and they knew it. How or whether they came back from this, the fourth war patrol, depended on him and his judgments, judgments he would make on the basis of what he knew and when he knew it.

As the sub slipped through the darkness, a melding of sea and sky, on bearing for the East China Sea, one piece of information that Houffman should have known, but didn't, hung buried in a group of messages on a clipboard in the comm shack. Communications officer Mike Bass had picked up the message—including the critical one received by the tender at 1300 hours—late that afternoon. Following operational procedures that had become habit aboard the vessel. Bass had carried them over to the *Queenfish,* hung the board on a nail, and fanned through the messages. The officers would drop by, scan the messages, and initial those pertaining to them; those pertaining to command would require the initials of either the executive officer, or the commander.

But one of the messages was contained on a short sheet of paper that had been buried among the longer pieces of correspondence. Apparently it had gone unnoticed by Bass and others who had fanned through the messages. Had the *Queenfish* been at sea that day as scheduled, they would have received the message directly by radio and would have notified command. *Seafox* and *Spot,* the sister ships that had headed out on schedule the day before, had received that same message directly.

This was the second in a chain of presumably careless, but most certainly costly, mistakes. The first was made by Com-SubPac at the briefing the day before. For some reason, headquarters had failed to pass on to, or even to briefly discuss with, the three sub commanders present the critical information contained in the unread message.

That night, as Commander Houffman squeezed past his men in the passageway, he did what he would do hundreds of times in that last and fateful patrol. He passed within eighteen inches of the clipboard that hung in full view just inside the comm shack. On that board was the message that could—if anyone read it in time—spare the lives of over two thousand men, women, and children in what was to become, and remain, the second-worse sea disaster in history.

Date: March 8, 1945
Place: Aboard the *Awa Maru,* Singapore
Time: 1830 hours

Captain Yoshita Hamamura did not like the decision the young port pilot had made. But it was only one of many decisions that had been made for him by younger men since the *Awa Maru* had left Moji nearly three weeks before. He had liked very little about the whole thing.

Now, with the young pilot standing next to him at the wheelhouse, barking orders into his walkie-talkie, and with the rain sweeping down across Singapore and onto the decks of his 11,249-ton vessel, Hamamura fell into a grim silence. He would not argue anymore. Many things had changed since the war, and he did not know where he or anyone else stood.

Although he had docked at and departed from Singapore hundreds of times in his career as a merchant seaman and had yielded as captain to many older men who knew the harbor and who guided his ships well, he had never seen this young pilot before, and there was something he distrusted about his manner.

He was a product of the war, this man who stood next to him, and he had forgotten the traditional courtesies. When he had boarded the vessel in the rain a half hour before, he acknowledged no one. He climbed to the bridge and, standing inside the wheelhouse, shook the rain from his parka and deliberately polished the steam from his steel-rimmed glasses. Only then did he blink once and nod to the captain, and even before the captain could return this small concession to courtesy, the young pilot embarked on a series of rapidfire questions about the vessel: weight, cargo, displacement, and estimated windward sail area.

These answers and others were noted with a stub of a pencil on a small pad of paper. Hamamura had not known pilots before who needed to do their figures on paper. The older pilots made their answers in their heads. And because they had done this many times before, and had safely piloted vessels in and out of the busy harbor, the answers they made in their heads were the right ones.

As the young pilot worked with the numbers on the pad, Hamamura looked through the wheelhouse windows at the city beyond. The colors that clung to the harbor and rose to the forested heights of the peninsula were washed and blended by the rain, which ran in rivulets down the glass. Hamamura was reminded of the finely brushed, suggestive wash drawings and watercolors that he had seen in the museum in Tokyo before the war. When he was a younger seaman, he had not often admitted that he admired such things, but now, with age, it was possible to say these things about paintings, about books he had read, about music he had heard. The hard thing these days was to find someone to listen.

With the war, a kind of lunacy had descended upon his country, and the talk was of battles and little else. There had been years of arguments between the people who wanted war in his country and those who did not. It was an ancient argument and often took on the bitter tone of the argument he had with the young pilot when he had finished his figuring. The pilot told the captain that they could ease out under their own power, that they had enough steerage to avoid the freighter berthed at the next slip, that they would not need the assistance of the harbor's tugs, which were, according to him, otherwise occupied in more important war efforts.

The captain quietly suggested that the pilot return to his figures, that perhaps in adding one to another—considering the dampness of the pad and the shortness of the pencil—he had made a perfectly understandable error. He told the pilot again, that the wind was gusting unpredictably and that, because they had offloaded tons of airplane parts, bombs, tanks, and some relief supplies the day before, the ship was light and riding high in the water, exposing many hundreds of square yards of sail area on the port side. He told the pilot, again, the direction of the tide; that, should a gust blow the bow of his vessel into the freighter as they eased out of the wharf, the damage would be considerable; that, since the damage would be the responsibility of the pilot, the situation merited the pilot's reworking of his figures.

"Captain, are you questioning my authority in this harbor and now on your ship?"

"My able fellow seaman," the captain said quietly, "I am only questioning your addition." But that was only the beginning of the argument.

As night fell across the port, and with the diesel engines screaming against repeated orders of full-ahead, stop, full-ahead reverse, the pilot was able, somehow, to jockey the 502-foot length and 66.3-foot width of the *Awa Maru* out of its berthing space and clear of the freighter. The operation took nearly two hours, the wind-blown bow clearing the stern of its smaller neighbor by no more than 24 inches.

The gray-haired captain of the *Awa Maru* had said nothing more to the pilot during the two-hour embarrassment. Rather than witness the accident they only narrowly averted, the captain alternated between closing his eyes and counting the number of times the pilot was forced to wipe the steam from his glasses as his contradictory orders reached a near-frenzied pace.

The captain did not allow it to show in his face, but, just before the pilot had left the bridge to descend the ladder to the pilot boat that met them at the mouth of the harbor, he was pleased to hear the voice on the walkie-talkie order the young pilot to report immediately to the harbor master.

Captain Hamamura would have one less problem when he returned to Singapore in two weeks.

For the first time since the *Awa Maru* had undergone refitting in Moji, where the deck armaments had been removed, the purser's cabin and vault rooms enlarged, the officers' quarters expanded, and the first-class passenger compartments modified, he felt safe. Though they had maintained the itinerary they had originally filed with the Swiss intermediaries and had otherwise conformed to the conditions of the treaty on the southern leg of their journey, Captain Hamamura had been all too aware of the six thousand tons of war materials they had carried to Takoa, Hong Kong, Saigon, and Singapore. He did not believe that carrying war materials was part of the treaty agreement. With the last of that unloaded, and now carrying only the remaining five hundred tons of relief supplies that they would unload at Djakarta and Bangka Island, he felt reasonably confident.

As long as he kept the *Awa Maru* on the changed route and schedule he had filed with the 3rd Regional Sea Transport Command in Singapore only that afternoon, and conformed to the conditions the warring governments had set—radioing in at designated noontime positions and illuminating at night the huge white crosses painted on both sides of the stack and on the hull fore and aft—there would be, he felt, little trouble. He knew enough to keep the ship in deep water to avoid the coastal mines.

Though the two-hour delay in leaving the dock at Singapore did not help, the almost twenty knots they were making through a calming sea would soon make up the difference. The lightened load helped.

What concerned the captain was not this trip southward. What concerned him were his orders to return to Singapore.

He had not been told the nature of the cargo they would be loading in Singapore for the last leg home. Nor was he given a passenger list. Instead, when he had filed the changed itinerary at headquarters that afternoon, he was told rather abruptly that this matter was a war concern and, as such, warranted a top-secret classification. Then he was told to save any further questions for Lieutenant General Kawasuki Kodamo, the officer in charge of passenger and cargo selection, when he returned the *Awa Maru* to Singapore on March 24, 1945.

There was some reason why his government had chosen this huge cargo and passenger liner for this mission. A much smaller vessel could have handled the meager two thousand tons of relief supplies she had carried. Nor did the additional six thousand tons of war materials they had unloaded in Singapore tax her capacity.

Whatever the purpose for their return to Singapore, it had stirred a flurry of encoded messages. He had heard through the waterfront grapevine that more than three thousand messages had been received concerning the passenger list alone. If, as he was led to believe, they were to carry wounded soldiers home, there would not have been so many messages on the subject.

No. There was some other reason for choosing the capacious *Awa Maru*. Just as there was another reason for the radically modified compartments and cargo holds, the three enormous safes that had been winched aboard at Moji, and all the secrecy that surrounded the operation.

27

According to the changed itinerary, once they left Singapore on the final leg to Japan, they would take the shortest route home. They would make course through the Formosa Strait, hugging the Chinese mainland, heading straight to Moji. It was to be fast and direct. He knew there was never any intention of adhering to the original itinerary, which put them through mine fields east and north of Formosa. That, he supposed, was one of the games.

Captain Hamamura had not wanted this war. He did not believe that the emperor had wanted the war either. And now, with the air of desperation that seemed to cling to those involved in the war the past few months, he liked the war even less. The division that had always separated the civilians from the military in his country had grown to chasmlike proportions.

Secrecies once intended to cloak Japanese war operations from the enemy now were invoked more freely and served to conceal operations from those the militarists considered untrustworthy.

It was this policy that led to excluding Captain Hamamura from any information on the upcoming Singapore operation. To Hamamura, it seemed an insane policy, for the burden of safely piloting the *Awa Maru* home still rested on his shoulders. As captain of the vessel, he was responsible for it. He, more than anyone else, needed to know what she carried. He would talk to this Lieutenant General Kodamo when they returned to Singapore. He would be polite, but he would find out who and what they planned to load. If there were risks, he wanted to know them. Lieutenant general or not, a captain was still the sole authority on his vessel.

Captain Hamamura felt that he had been quiet too long. If, for example, he had insisted on a tug in Singapore instead of allowing the young and foolish port pilot to make his own mistakes, they would not have had to wrestle with his ship for two hours and risk the damage that only good fortune had prevented. He would be polite, but he would not be quiet when he returned to Singapore.

He would not risk the *Awa Maru* to any more of this lunacy.

III

Date: March 27, 1945
Place: Aboard the U.S.S. *Queenfish*, at sea
Time: 1000 hours

Torpedoman third-class Carl Boldern was approaching the longest hour of his lookout watch atop the shears that cool, cloudy morning. Clutching the periscope with one arm while training a pair of heavy 7 x 50 binoculars on an empty horizon is, at best, tedious work. The first three hours of a watch like that are bad enough; the fourth is interminable.

Before he had .climbed up, he had been briefed on the critical areas of the search: the seas to the horizon for smoke of a ship or the shears of another submarine. He was not to overlook the skies, for they were crossing a likely aerial supply route and could be spotted readily from above.

Some things worked against Boldern's concentration on his duty. It was not easy to support a pair of binoculars with one hand over a prolonged period of time, looking all the while at a great expanse of nothing. The roll of the seas from the northwest made necessary a constant adjustment to keep the binoculars trained on the horizon. Though he had learned to move his body in time to the gathering swells, to become a part of the movement of the sea, in the end he began to feel it; his muscles ached, his wrists were tired, and his eyes didn't want to focus anymore.

And it was easy to forget about why he was there in the first place and what he was looking for. The wind, the way the sea moved, and the quiet made it difficult to concentrate. Sometimes Boldern had to shake himself from daydreams, to bring himself back to what he was doing. When things happened, they happened fast. If something was spotted and a dive called, those on the deck who didn't make it through the hatch in time didn't make it at all.

29

The other thing working against torpedoman third-class Boldern was his age. It had worked against him from the beginning. When war had broken out, he was in Long Beach, California, dozing through his first year of high school.

He had wanted to go to sea since he was ten, and when the war came, the stories of bombs, torpedoes, and ack-ack guns were irresistible. He wasn't going to let the fact that he was only fifteen years old stop him. He doctored some papers and reported downtown to the naval recruiter. Now, three years later, he was one of the youngest seasoned war veterans aboard the U.S.S. *Queenfish*.

There had been problems. It had not been easy to live in close proximity to others while pretending he was three years older than he really was. He had sometimes been the butt of jokes. But, all in all, this was where he wanted to be.

He had been calmly watching the speck on the horizon grow in size until the realization bolted through his consciousness. He began, sputtering, to say it all at once, then recovered, got it together, and called to the bridge: "Aircraft approaching off the port bow." The deck officer swung to action: "Where away?" Boldern called back, "Ten o'clock coming in low."

When things happen on a submarine, they happen fast. Scrambling, those on the deck got off the deck quickly. Boldern, his age this time working in his favor, was the third man down the hatch. He was through the con and control and heading to the forward torpedo room with the ring of the diving siren still in his ears.

The *ahooga* of the diving siren had caught RM3 Merville Easter with his pants down. Literally. He had retreated only moments before to the one-holer that served as the after-torpedo-room head, and had been deep into reading *Northwest Passage,* a book he had bought from a boatswain aboard the *Picuda* while in Camp Dealy. He had been questioning whether he too could have survived the march the book described by chewing on a friend's head, stuffing it neatly into a knapsack, and moving on.

For RM3 Easter, poised as he was on the aluminum can, it was not the best of times. Curiously, he had been caught enough times in that unlikely position that he had begun to suspect a conspiracy. It wasn't that Easter spent any more time in the head than anyone else, it was only that he seemed to time it wrong. It had become a pattern. Pharmacist mate

"Doc" Tobey had once suggested that they move the sonar equipment into the head so that Easter could man his battle station from within.

"It'll never work," Easter had told him. "If I'm wearin' that headset while I shit, think of the concussion. I'll blow out my eardrums."

At twenty-five, RM3 Easter was considered one of the old men of the boat. He had been aboard the *Trigger* before joining the *Queenfish,* and he had seen all kinds of action. But each time the siren sounded and the scramble began, he performed his job—and performed it well—by operating partly out of habit and partly out of the flow of energy that abject terror provided him. Fear, he knew, was what you could imagine. And he imagined the worst. He envied those aboard who could imagine nothing and who, like young Boldern, knew no fear.

He had once asked Boldern if he was worried that the officers were making a mistake by pursuing a small freighter escorted by a convoy of enemy destroyers—to pursue that when they had not surfaced the night before and would not be able to surface again until dusk, twelve hours later.

"What do you mean?" Boldern had asked.

"I mean, do you think the officers are making a mistake?"

"The officers?" Boldern asked.

"Yes."

"I don't know. I mean, I never thought about it like that. What the officers do is their business," Boldern said.

"But they're committing you to take a certain action. It may be a mistake."

Boldern thought about that for a minute. "I don't think so."

"You don't think they're committing you to take action?"

"I don't think they're making a mistake."

"How come?"

" 'Cause they're officers. Officers are smart. They know about a lot of things. Don't you think so?"

"Don't I think what?"

"That officers are smart."

"Sure, Carl, I think they're smart."

"I think they're smart too," Boldern concluded.

In the control room, Easter assumed his position behind chief of watch Roy Bicca. Bicca was getting verbal rechecks from the men who were in their compartments preparing for

31

battle assignments. The illuminated rig-for-dive panel showed all dashes, indicating the shut positions of valves, hatches, and vents. Each had to be verified separately by voice reports.

"Con, bridge." Bicca was on the comm line. "On course two-four-seven, all-ahead standard. Ready to submerge."

From above, the answering call from the officer of the deck: "Clear the bridge, clear the bridge. Dive, dive."

And with the dive comes the wait. When the depth is reached and neutral buoyancy regained, after the stern and bowplanesmen have assumed a one-degree-down bubble, a quiet descends on the vessel.

Easter was no stranger to those tense periods of silence, when there was nothing left to do but wait and see, first, if you had been spotted, and second, whether you would begin to take a depth-charge attack. He had been through many. There had been times in the last patrol when he had felt certain that those charges would find the sub. He had watched lightbulbs pop with the concussion, grease fittings explode into a stream of water; he had felt, on one occasion, the concussion work at the fillings of two back teeth.

Once, being pursued by a destroyer after three fish went astray, missing their target, they had dived. At a depth of fifty feet, they had heard first the click of the detonator, then the blast. The explosion must have been beneath them. The blast blew them to the surface like a cork. Apparently undamaged, they sought cover again on a quick dive to the deep. They did not stop until they had reached four hundred feet, hoping they hadn't damaged the air flasks and could blow out the ballasts to stop the descent. By the time they leveled off and began a slow ascent, they had exceeded maximum operational depth.

This time they waited only half an hour, then ascended to a periscope depth of fifty-seven feet. With the all-clear, they surfaced into the sunlit morning.

In the forward torpedo room, sitting on a torpedo skid, seamen Garrabaldi and Costello had resumed their game of acey-ducey and one of the ongoing arguments they had been waging since the second patrol; this time it was back to whether the Italian women in Detroit were better lovers than the Italian women in Chicago. Since each of them could call on a host of real or imagined pieces of evidence to support his contention, it was not an argument the rest of the crew minded. It beat their frequent and heated discussions over which city produced the best salami.

Machinist mate Rico Perez sought to slip past the two Italians unnoticed, but Garrabaldi looked up.

"Where you going, Que Pasa?"

The potbellied little machinist mate out of Phoenix pretended not to hear.

"How do you do it, Que Pasa?"

Perez, still heading out, smiled sheepishly.

Costello picked it up: "Jesus, Que Pasa, you're not going back to sleep!"

"No," said Garrabaldi. "He's only going to rest his eyes. Hey, Roy. Have you ever seen Que Pasa sleep?"

Roy Bicca, chief torpedoman, was explaining to Carl Boldern the intricacies of the gyro steering assembly on one of the Mark XVIII torpedoes. Not looking up from the exposed assembly, he answered. "I never see him. Only hear him. Night and day since Guam."

Perez had nearly reached the hatch to head through officers' country to the crew's quarters. He had a standard reply that he used with various inflections.

"Shit," he said.

Costello wouldn't let it go. "Wait, Que Pasa. Really. How the hell can you put in so much sack time?"

"You got somethin' better to do?"

As Perez stepped over the combing, he had to squeeze past cook Robert Klaus coming aft. Klaus was a good cook, rising to moments of sheer genius. The doughnuts he had made the night before had been generally accepted as one of those moments.

If submariners had a tendency toward a short lifespan, they ate pretty well while they were around. A good cook went a long way in compensating for some of the other shortcomings aboard a sub. Klaus had been the cook aboard the *Queenfish* since New Hampshire, a position he maintained by feeding officers and crew the kinds of things they wanted to eat in a way they wanted to eat them. Commander Houffman would let only one man, Robert Klaus, cook his snack-time speciality: a crisp bacon and radish sandwich. Klaus wore that chore like a badge, and served up the sandwich in battle or not.

"Hey, Bicca," he said. "You're never going to believe this. Somebody ate the thing!"

"What thing?" Roy Bicca, still working the assembly, had turned one shoulder so that Boldern could study what he was doing.

"The damn doughnut," Klaus said. "The one we was pitchin' at Old Ox last night."

Bicca looked up. "Jesus. Somebody ate the thing? How do you know?"

"Well, I left it on the table last night and this morning it was gone. Somebody on the 0400 watch, for Christ sake!"

Costello, who had started to defend Chicago women again, stopped and turned to the cook. "What doughnut's this?"

"Well," Klaus began, "you know Easter, right? Anyway, a bunch of us was off watch in the mess last night, eatin' up the rest of my doughnuts. One had fallen on the floor and been kicked around for a while when Easter gets this idea. He says he'll cover anything up to five bucks that he can ring that doughnut three out of five times on Old Ox's big toe."

"Ox's toe, for Christ sake?" Garrabaldi was incredulous.

"Jesus," Costello said.

"Well," Klaus continued, "you know Old Ox, right? I mean, none of us was too keen on him takin' off his shoe and crusty sock in close quarters, okay? But we figured it was an easy five, so we covered the bet.

"But what Easter knew and none of the rest of us did was that Old Ox could fold down four toes so that his big toe pointed straight up and out like a long, quivering cucumber. I kid you not. Anyway, Old Ox could sense where that doughnut was going like his toe had a life of its own, and sure as hell, that doughnut encircles his big yellow toenail and drops home three out of three tosses.

"So, we pay up. I'm the last one out and I remember seein' that doughnut on the table as I leave. Now, I don't think anything more about it until I'm makin' the 0430 coffee and I'm lookin' around and it's gone. My guess is that it was somebody on the 0400 watch."

As Klaus was explaining the incident, torpedoman Carl Boldern was taking a renewed interest in the inner workings of the torpedo gyro. Bicca turned to Boldern and said, "Hey, Carl, you were on the 0400. Did you notice . . ." It took a moment for Bicca to comprehend the look on Boldern's face. When he did, he stood up. "My God, Boldern, you didn't eat the thing?"

"Hell no! Oh, no. Hell, no . . ." But it was too late. "Well, how the hell was I supposed to know, for Christ sake? It was just sittin' there. I mean . . ."

Prospective Commanding Officer Steve Trevor, his big hands encircling a cup of black coffee on the ward-room table, looked up as the lanky commanding officer dropped into the seat across from him.

34

"Skipper," said Trevor, "you've got a war-is-hell look on your face."

Commander Houffman, who had brought his coffee with him, took a long, slow sip.

"Steve," he said. "They got it all wrong. It isn't war. It's waitin' that's hell. And I'm sick of it."

"Nineteen days, right?" Trevor knew exactly how many days they had been out, but he sought to bring Houffman out of his reverie.

"Yeah," Houffman said to his coffee, "but who's counting?"

"Anything from Ultra?" Trevor was referring to incoming messages from ComSubPac, sometimes helpful, sometimes infuriating. Since the Americans had broken nearly fifty percent of the Japanese code, headquarters could often place a Japanese convoy and learn what it was carrying and where it was headed. Since it had not broken the balance of the code, headquarters was wrong just as often as right. But being half wrong half the time did not prevent ComSubPac from issuing cooperational directives with the kind of certainty that comes from conducting war from the rarified atmosphere of a plotting room in Pearl.

"Nothing," Houffman said. "Of all the times I dreaded hearing from them, I'd welcome damn near anything at the moment. We haven't spotted so much as a puff of smoke in two weeks."

"How about Seafox?" Trevor asked. Spot, the third component of the wolfpack, was already back in Guam. She had engaged a heavily escorted convoy ten days before and had expended, without much success, her complement of torpedoes. For her, it had been a short patrol.

"I haven't heard a thing from Seafox," Commander Houffman said. "She's evidently doing as well as we are. If we don't get—"

Ensign Delward T. Diefenbaker had been standing outside the ward room, unsure about how he should approach the two officers inside.

"Diefenbaker," Houffman said. "Have you got something?"

Diefenbaker, one of the youngest officers aboard, squeezed into the ward room. All apologies, wagging his head first to Houffman, then to Trevor, he obviously had something on his mind. This was his first patrol; likely, it would be his last.

Not accustomed to the company of what he considered high-ranking officers, the pudgy Diefenbaker, his red cheeks aglow beneath clear plastic glasses, was not sure whether he should deliver his message upright or sitting down. He made several contradictory moves before Trevor invited him to sit down.

"Skipper, sir. I don't like to bother you on a matter like this, and normally I would go through the chain of command, but you see, Lieutenant Bass . . . he was on watch last night and he's, well, unavailable right—"

"He's in the sack, Diefenbaker," Houffman said impatiently.

"Yes, sir. And in light of this thing I have only recently uncovered—"

"Which you're going to tell us about, right?" Houffman said.

"Yes, sir. It's something I just discovered in the radio shack. I haven't talked to anyone about it yet. But I thought you should know."

Trevor looked away, then moved his hand across his face. Houffman leaned back in his seat and said, "Just go ahead and tell us what you found, Diefenbaker."

"Yes. Of course, Captain. I think some of the crew are engaged in making illicit alcoholic beverages. I discovered—"

"Is that booze?" Trevor asked innocently.

"Yes, sir. I discovered the makings for a pretty crude but effective still. I wouldn't have noticed it, but it was in the radio shack, back behind—"

"Diefenbaker," Houffman interrupted. "Exactly what are the makings for a 'crude but effective still'?"

"That took a while to figure out, Skipper, but there was a silex, some rubber stoppers, a hotplate, and a coil of aluminum piping. My guess is that they've been distilling the denatured alcohol for the torpedoes."

"That seems," Houffman said, "a pretty fair assumption. What have you done with this device?"

"I haven't touched a thing, sir. I knew you would want to take a look at it, so—"

"So you came right here to tell me."

"Yes, sir. I realize this is a serious matter, so—"

"Thank you, Diefenbaker."

"So I sensed that . . . Uh, yes, sir. Would you like anything further on this, Skipper?"

"Yes."

"Good. I'd be more than happy to show you the evidence so that—"

"Diefenbaker," Houffman said quietly, "I'd like you to gather it all together and throw it overboard."

"Overboard?"

"Yes, Diefenbaker. If you go up on deck, you'll notice we're surrounded by water."

"Yes, sir. What I meant—I thought you would want to preserve the evidence. I have a good idea who's responsible for this, and—"

"Thank you, Diefenbaker," Houffman said.

"Do you want me to bring the men here?"

"What I want you to do," Houffman said, leaning forward, "is to go to the radio shack, gather up the thing, and dump it overboard. Then forget about it. Are there any questions?"

"No. No, sir. I'll go do that right now."

"Thank you, Diefenbaker."

The thing that happens to men who choose to fight their wars from within the belly of a submarine—men like Commander Houffman and Lieutenant Commander Trevor—had not happened, and probably would not happen, to men like Ensign Delward T. Diefenbaker. There were some men, for example, who could never pass through a hatch without banging their knees.

Houffman and Trevor waited for the thump and groan as Diefenbaker passed from officers' country to the forward battery before allowing the smiles that had been building for the past few minutes. The incident had opened Houffman to talking.

"You been through anything like this before, Steve?"

"Well, there's always something new. But this one's been around since before they made torpedoes," Trevor said.

"The thing that bothers me aboard subs," Houffman said, pushing his coffee away, "is how difficult it is to keep a secret. I believe in this eleventh commandment: What the officers don't know won't hurt them. But you have to really work at not knowing things you're not supposed to know. If you noticed, I don't make many inspections." Houffman paused, ran a hand through his gray hair.

"You know," he continued, "there's a lot of sharp guys on this boat of mine. And they're not all officers. And most of these guys—I mean the sharp ones—wouldn't last three days in peacetime. They haven't got the patience for it. For them, regulations were made to break; it gives them something to do between engagements.

"I'm not saying I condone all of their actions, but if I don't know about them, what can I say? Right? But, Steve," Houffman leaned forward, "not knowing is getting to be harder and harder as this war drags on."

37

"And," Trevor volunteered, "the Ensign Delward T. Diefenbakers of the world don't help."

Houffman laughed. "They don't help worth a damn. But these guys—this crew—I didn't put them together and fight ComSubPac to keep them together because I like the way they follow regulations. I did because I like the way they fight. When they dog off, they know *when* to dog off. But in the fight, Steve . . ." Houffman seemed to think about that.

"Listen," he went on, "you've got to see these guys work. Some of 'em are mean, some are angry, some are goof-offs, but in the fight, when it counts, I wouldn't trade this crew for any other, Pacific or Atlantic."

"Would you admit to some prejudice?" Trevor asked.

"Yeah. Okay. I know that sounds like some kind of a PIO news release, but a crew like this decays in a hurry. They begin workin' on each other, first kidding each other, then more serious. Soon there'll be arguments. Next, the fights start. Then you haven't got a crew at all. All you got are problems.

"And if we don't find something for this crew to work at—something Japanese and floating—and soon—we're going to have eighty-three problems. Steve, these guys are hungry. And they damn well better be fed before they start devouring each other."

Trevor knew that while the captain spoke of the crew, he was also speaking of himself. There's a fragile relationship between crew and captain, and circumstances, whether in the control of the skipper or not, can alter that relationship. While Trevor had not experienced it, he knew that there could be near-mutinous conditions aboard subs when that relationship broke down. Only a few months before, when a crew had gotten wind of the fact that their captain had volunteered for an untested mine-detection mission using a new piece of sonar equipment, half the crew refused to board the vessel. Trevor knew it wasn't so much the mission as the command that brought the crew to revolt. Somehow, that skipper had lost control. The fragile relationship had been shattered.

And, probably, what was hardest on that relationship was inactivity, the kind of malaise that settles on a crew that has nothing to do but wait. In some respects, ennui was worse than syphilis, and just as contagious. It was the fear of what prolonged inaction could do to the crew of the *Queenfish* that now worked on Commander Houffman. Trevor could see it

38

move, periodically, across his face. He could see it even now, in his retreat to silence.

Respecting that, Trevor took the silex off the hotplate, refilled their cups, and waited.

"You know, this may be it for me." Houffman had a way of emerging from his thoughts as though the person he was talking to had been a party to them. "Someday I want to fly that flag, Steve. It's been what I wanted since I was a kid, to be a flag officer. I won't admit this to everyone, but this war—well, hell, there's nothing to admit. As bad as this sounds, it's an opportunity.

"What I do here is going to follow me. I've got three fairly respectable patrols behind me. You and I both know that kind of thing leads to making flag rank." He paused. "With one to go, one stinkin' patrol to go. And, you know . . ." Houffman fell back into thought.

When he started again, he spoke to his cup of coffee. "Ever since that business at Guam, the U joint, the delay, ever since then, I've had this sinking feeling. . . ."

"I hope you don't mean that literally." Trevor had been watching the muscles that tensed and relaxed at the back of the skipper's jaw. When he had first met Houffman, he had been taken aback by his youthfulness; now, he could not even recall that image. It was as though he had watched Houffman grow old in the two weeks of this patrol.

"I'm not sure I can tell you what I mean. A feeling, you know? Call it paranoia, short-time fever, personal problems. But, Steve." He looked up. "I want a target. And I don't want any problems. There may be a few noses bent out of shape over this, but when we make contact, I want it done. I want you to handle the fire control party. I want maximum effort on anything we get."

"Sure, okay, Skipper." Trevor started to stand up, but Houffman had something else.

"Steve, it's bothering Edwards again, isn't it?"

"What?"

"His stomach."

"Well, he's not talking about it, but yeah, he's pretty sick." Trevor stood up, then turned back to Houffman. "I thought you didn't know about that, Captain."

"Steve, you've been on one of these things long enough to know that God and your skipper know everything."

IV

I mean, that's the way it was. Look, I spent a good part of that war floating around in those damn sewer pipes, and, up until the end, the least of our worries was finding something to shoot at, for Christ sake.

Even the last year of the thing aboard the Queenfish. I mean, shit. For three patrols, all we had was targets. It was the shootin' 'em down and gettin' away with it that was the problem. I mean, you didn't just float up to anything you sighted and start unloading fish. You had to think some, take your best shots at what you considered would hurt the Japs most, then run. More than not, anything worth sinking was pretty well covered, escorted, and if you weren't already running by the time the last of the fish had left the tubes and before the first had hit home, you're going to be swallowin' water, lots of it.

So, on those early patrols, you took what they called the best targets of opportunity. The Navy had those kind of phrases, like opportunities and optimum targets, so that you had the feeling it was one big game, like the winner would advance to "Go," collect two hundred dollars, and get three hotels on Park Place. There's a hell of a lot of PR bullshit in a war, where words are twisted around to have other meanings, and pretty soon everyone is talking about war like there were no people involved, and what you thought you did was one thing, what they reported you did, another. Like, have you ever read one of these citations they issue? I mean, what the hell. There you were on deck, a Nip destroyer off your bow, zeros screamin' in, and you're tryin' to find a hatch before someone below dogs it on you, 'cause your boat's going under whether you're in or out; and comin' down the ladder, not knowin' whether you've been hit or not, there you are, feelin' the warmth of your own urine fill your socks. You learn later that what you had really done was to "boldly defy severe air and surface opposition in an aggressive and tena-

cious manner." You could have sworn they scared the piss out of you.

And even when they convinced you that you were in a game, and you played it that way, you really weren't, and almost paid with your life. I remember the skipper, Houffman, got us into one of those kinds of things once.

One morning we spotted this big-bellied Jap flying boat just after we had come to surface to charge batteries. It was flyin' low, the engines sputtering like it was out of breath. Sure as hell, it circles us and lands, just outside of torpedo range. But it's sittin' there, fatter 'n a Christmas hog and helpless, dead ahead. So I'm on lookout, the captain's on the bridge, and I hear him yell down into the conn, "Hey. I'm going to be the first skipper to shoot an airplane with a torpedo!"

Well, we all thought that'd be somethin', you know. I mean, how are they going to write that up, right? So, still on the surface, we start edgin' toward this big tub of a plane. Just as we get in range, the little slants inside crank the thing up; it sputters, taxis off, and dies again. So we started to head toward it again. Well, we just get it in range again, and the slants crank it up again. It moves off, sputters, and dies. Everybody on board's got it figured this is an Abbott and Costello movie, right? So we're heading for it again, when the skipper, who's been grinnin' like a kid in a whorehouse, gets this radar report of a blip off our stern. I turn and look aft and there, bigger'n Sunday, is a torpedo wake comin' on us like Gang Busters.

And the old man, he's not smilin' anymore, but yellin' at the top of his lungs, "Right full rudder, right full rudder!" And I'm watchin' that thing close—I mean close—slantin' along our port side. We get just enough rudder into it for that beauty to skim by, damn near peelin' paint. You could have read the numbers on the exploder cap as she went by.

So we dived in pretty short order. But that was only the beginning, for Christ sake. We had no juice, right? We had only just surfaced and hardly had time to breathe, let alone take a charge. So there we sat with—what?—ten, eleven hours of daylight left before we could dare surface again. No power, damn little air, and everything shut off. There we wait. Knowin' it's only a matter of time, that the destroyer, or whatever it was, was sittin' up there waitin' for us. As soon as we came up for air, she'd blow us out of the water.

We tried movin', but all she'd make is dead slow. We tried that off and on all day. Otherwise, it was still. Dead quiet. At 2000 hours, we eased up to periscope height. We used our

41

wide-angle periscope, took a quick sweep, and dropped it. Nothin'. We took a longer sweep. Still nothin'. We surfaced.

I remember bein' in the forward torpedo room when the hatch there was undogged and swung clear. And as the cool night air swept across us, I was lookin' straight up at a field of stars. I could have been in heaven—and don't think that didn't cross my mind.

When the navigator took a fix, we learned we had drifted miles from the attack sight in an undersea current that I still say my prayers to when I think anyone is around to listen.

No. Up until that last patrol, we had all the targets we could shoot, and then some. For a while, you could walk across the decks of Jap vessels from the Ryukyu Islands across the East China Sea to Shanghai and never get your feet wet.

But when we headed out of Guam on that fourth patrol, it was a different story. Remember, this was in '45. We had mined the hell out of those waters for better'n a year. What the mines didn't get, the subs got, and what we didn't get, didn't float. By that time, we had got to know what kind of a weapon we really had in those subs. We could do things with 'em nobody thought possible. But that kind of schoolin' came slow.

It took half the war to discover that the sub wasn't the defensive weapon the Navy designed it for, and that, quite by accident, it was hell on merchant shipping. So, somebody back in Washington had to shuffle his ethics around a little bit, to make it all work out. When war broke out, we were all playing the ships-of-war games: that what you did was play fair and only shoot at other war ships, and what you didn't do was shoot unarmed merchant vessels. It was exactly what John Wayne would do, and therefore it was absolutely moral.

When it became clear that being absolutely moral was going to absolutely lose the war for us, they did what they do in Washington. They called a meeting.

Somebody stood up and said that, as near as he could tell, he thought Japan was an island. When somebody else agreed, he took it to step two. Since Japan was an island—and a pretty small one—they had to cart in a whole lot of what they needed from countries around. Because what they had in raw materials wouldn't sustain them.

They needed to import, and that, he said, accounted for all the shipping Japan seemed to be doing. He had heard an Edward R. Murrow report on it once. Someone else stood up *and said that while he wasn't sure where Japan was, he had heard the same report. And, since he was a high official in Washington, he had an idea.*

Why not stop the shipping to wherever this Japan was? That, he said, would strangle the island's economy and end the war in the Pacific. They voted on that, and agreed to win the war in the Pacific. But they were still uncertain about the propriety of shooting down unarmed merchant ships.

When someone else pointed out the prospect of either doing that or losing the war, they had another vote. It was agreed. They would shoot down unarmed merchant ships, but call them something different. They thought awhile, until someone in the back of the room stood up and said, "Why not call them war-supply vessels plying the Pacific on a treacherous mission to feed the ravenous appetite of Japan's vicious war machine."

That brought down the house. One more vote and they had a policy.

I mean, why not, for Christ sake.

Even the most casual student of history must question the logic that led Japan to engage and then occupy so great a part of the world as she did following her diversionary attack on Pearl Harbor.

While no one doubted the need for raw materials in conducting a war on the scale that the emperor had in mind, and no one doubted Southeast Asia's abundance of those materials, one would have to question whether she was chewing a great deal more than she should have bitten.

What began as the Greater East Asia Co-Prosperity Sphere, the title Japan affixed on the aggregate of her Asian conquests, turned, in the closing days of the war, into perhaps the most tangle-footed logistical nightmare in the annals of war.

In the few short months following Pearl Harbor, Japan softened, then seized the Philippine Islands, Guam, Borneo, Hong Kong, Bangkok, and Malay. By March, all Indonesia and New Guinea lay open to Japanese occupation. She had been pressing her demands in China for years, and, in keeping with her appetite for new territory, she continued to press China's troops in the inland reaches where, entrenched, they held out, tying up more than six divisions of 120,000 Japanese troops. But, in Japan's mind, it was worth it.

The Japanese firmly believed they would share the world with the Nazis.

United States policy, as reflected in a brief telegram to then Secretary of State Cordell Hull from one of his State Department advisers, Joseph W. Ballentine, confirmed that fear:

November 22, 1941: "You might say [about the Japanese] that in the minds of the American people, [one of] the purposes underlying our aid to Great Britain is that the American people believe that there is a partnership between Hitler and Japan aimed at dividing the world between them."

That assessment predated Pearl Harbor. The attack cinched it.

In Japan, junior members of the Imperial Cabal were outlining just such an Imperial plan, dividing the world with Hitler. It was but one of a range of far-reaching goals that motivated Japan's dedication to war. The inner sanctum of Japan's madness in those days was clear—two worlds was indeed the goal of World War II. But that, according to Japanese thought of the day, was only a start.

There would be another war. Hitler and his half of the spoils would be dealt with then.

According to this plan, the United States would remain "nominally independent" after her surrender and would retain sovereignty east of the Rockies, but the Alaska Government-General of Japan's Co-Prosperity Sphere would include Alberta, British Columbia, and the state of Washington. The scenario would conclude with World War III, the final war, this one with Germany. Out of it would rise the Japanese Empire, a monolithic state with Emperor Hirohito at the helm, culminating, according to Japanese theorists, in a single, harmonious Japanese world dedicated to the pursuit of aesthetics and appreciation of nature.

Could you fault a country with goals like that?

In a word, yes. Goals, however lofty, that are predicated on death and destruction—in the end, regardless of the means—often lose sight of the people they are intended to serve.

Hirohito led his people toward these goals from the cloistered vantage point of the Imperial Palace. He had inherited from his great-grandfather a singular view: rid Asia of white men. Unlike the Imperial generations that preceded him, Hirohito was to take on that task with personal relish.

This was not in keeping with the contemporary, fashionable view of Hirohito as a helpless, benevolent man who, despite his real desires, was placed at the disposal of a strong military clique of ruthless fascists. Rather, the emperor was a man who skillfully manipulated his countrymen for twenty years, preparing them for the task of conquering the world at whatever cost—to Japan or to the world.

The campaign had been meticulously planned. Long before the attack upon Pearl Harbor, the plan began to take hold in the 1920s at Nanking; the plan was still operative decades later, with a secret scheme to devastate the U.S. Navy at Pearl Harbor—a plan made more than a year before the attack.

In Nanking, according to a panel of jurists comprising the International Military Tribunal for the Far East, the Japanese army of occupation was responsible for the deaths of 200,000 men, at least a quarter of them civilians, and the rapes of 20,000 women. A third of the city was destroyed by fire, and a deed was perpetrated that was to be repeated again and again in the Japanese territorial conquests throughout Asia. Everything of monetary and aesthetic value was stolen from Nanking, from the dead, the dying, and those who were spared. Everything.

In the six months following the attack on Pearl Harbor, the Philippines, Borneo, Singapore, Sumatra, Java, and a dozen other areas of immense natural wealth fell to Japan, and the systematic collection of a wealth that would one day stagger the world began. The troops' dedication to the emperor was such that objects of value seldom found their way into the private knapsacks of the foot soldiers. Rather, the great bulk of the booty—rugs, paintings, pianos, antiques, screens, chests, gold, silver, and jewels—was loaded into official Army warehouses. Although some high-ranking officers were able to keep small fortunes in jade and porcelain and silver, most of the plunder was later sold and the money was used to defray overall Army expenses.

Could this accumulated wealth be considered the spoils of war? Or was it the ransom for war? After the war, Hirohito survived prosecution as a war criminal, over many protests, in the then-widespread belief that he was a mere puppet of the malevolent militarists, an unworldly innocent who spent his time sampling the fragrance of flowers in his formal Imperial Gardens. But he survived to carry out his unwavering intention, in war or in defeat: to make out of his country one of the strongest powers on earth.

Today, based in part on Hirohito's cruel and calculated approach to achieving Japanese supremacy, his country is the third industrial power on earth, with industrial holdings in every corner of the world; an economic policy in which accumulations of great wealth were ripped from other lands to feed the unquenchable appetite of a nation bent on expansionism.

The questions remain. Were Hirohito and his top advisers looking beyond defeat before they began the war? Were they willing to face the high cost of sacrifice? Did they deliberately throw the more than four million Japanese men, women, and children who died in the war into the furnace of postwar industrialization?

Or were they a small land of ninety million people, a land without enough resources to feed them? Were they pressed by a nationalistic Imperial policy to react to the severe trade restrictions applied by the United States and Great Britain?

In any case, without the natural resources that Southeast Asia could bring to Japan, Hirohito would have never begun his daring attack on the United States.

In 1937, Sumatra was the world's second-largest producer of tin; Bangka Island was the third largest. Sumatra could boast of gold, oil, coal, iron, and oil refineries. Java rivaled her neighbor Sumatra with abundant supplies of gold, sulfur, oil, phosphates, lead, copper, manganese, and oil refineries. On Bangka Island, a few miles off the coast of Sumatra, there was such a prodigious quantity of tin that the sea surrounding the island was said to be choked with it.

Perhaps World War II was not a war at all, but only one battle in a continuing war that Japan, through ingenuity, determination, religious fervor, and cunning, is winning. If that's the case, she won the war—the one we thought she lost—by the wealth she gained through looting and pillaging her conquests, a wealth she shipped to her homeland three decades ago in the holds of numerous merchant vessels, some as large as the *Awa Maru*.

By the time the U.S.S. *Queenfish* and the *Awa Maru* sailed in 1945, most of Japan's merchant marine fleet lay in the depths of the seas she once commanded. Without a conduit for supplies, the homeland and all her far-strung possessions were being systematically starved of food, medicine, and vital war materials. The fate that had long ravished those 170,000 hollow-eyed men in her prison camps was now being applied to her own people, in their own land.

Further crippling her ability to bring in food and supplies through shipping lanes was an incredibly effective Allied aerial mining attack. The over-all effect of the mines had an economic impact equal to the effect of all bombing and incendiary raids carried out by the U.S. 21st Bomber Command.

An estimated forty percent of Japan's shipping losses were attributed to aerial mines. The Japanese were forced to avoid shallow areas, to reroute shipping to deeper waters, thereby exposing their vessels to direct torpedo attacks by U.S. submarines. The rate of attrition was enormous.

In the closing stages of the war, fleet-type submarines like the deadly U.S.S. *Queenfish* were hard pressed to find targets. Growing bolder and bolder, some sub commanders were pressing their vessels into extremely shallow reaches where maneuverability was limited and detection was likely.

The reports of the results of this blanket sea blockage began funneling out of Tokyo:

MINING OF WATERS ACTING AS VIRTUAL SEA BLOCKAGE

ALUMINUM, COAL IN SHORT SUPPLY. OTHER ESSENTIAL WAR MATERIALS URGENTLY NEEDED

RESULTS OF MINING OPERATIONS MORE CRITICAL TO FUTURE GOOD HEALTH OF JAPAN THAN BOMBING OF OUR FACTORIES

PROPORTION OF SHIPS SUNK: FOR EVERY ONE SUNK BY SUBMARINE, SIX WERE SUNK BY BOMBS AND TWELVE WERE SUNK BY MINES

HARBORS REMAIN BLOCKED. MINESWEEPING FACILITIES IN SHORT SUPPLY. MORALE OF SHIPS' CREWS AND MORALE OF TROOPS ON BOARD TRANSPORTS DETERIORATING DANGEROUSLY

As targets of opportunity decreased dramatically in the final months of the war, so did the amount of tonnage sunk. According to Commander J. S. Gabbett, Royal Navy Intelligence officer, East Indies Station, the following month-by-month account of tonnage sunk by mines in Japanese industrial ports demonstrates the effectiveness of Allied efforts to halt shipping:

March 1945	—	810,000/tonnage sunk
April 1945	—	785,000/tonnage sunk
May 1945	—	560,000/tonnage sunk
June 1945	—	325,000/tonnage sunk
July 1945	—	260,000/tonnage sunk
August 1945	—	180,000/tonnage sunk

According to *Offensive Mine Laying Campaign Against Japan*, a document published by the Department of Navy, 1969, a Japanese Navy captain, Captain Tamura, was questioned on the impact of Allied mines. He said:

There were no mine technicians in Japan comparable to those in America.

We forced shipping through, regardless of the knowledge that it was dangerous. If we suspected mines were in certain areas, we stopped shipping one day . . . pending minesweeping operations, but then started again, realizing full well that the ships would be lost.

We would leave the decisions for a ship to go through mine fields or follow a certain course to the Area Commander or Port Director, leave it to them to route the ships.

In the beginning, we had half regular Navy and half reserves; the manpower losses were terrific, so we replaced them [the reserves] with regulars . . . but even the regulars had difficulty, and there were many changes in Commanding Officers . . . the situation was very bad and we used the most competent personnel available.

Toward the end, the Japanese were able to equip most of their remaining merchant ships with sonic detectors; this program began in 1942. But it was not nearly enough. And Japanese degaussing equipment was not available in sufficient quantity to prove effective. (The degaussing equipment was used to neutralize the magnetic field around a ship, thereby permitting it to pass a mine without triggering the magnetically sensitive needle that would detonate the explosives.)

Lack of mine countermeasures, lack of personnel, and lack of materials in Japan became so acute that it was necessary to delegate the responsibility for sweeping to a special torpedo attack unit originally organized for suicide work in the Ryukyu Islands.

By April 1945, steel output in the Japanese Empire had dropped from four to five million tons, at the beginning of the war, to one million tons.

"Submarine warfare affected everything in the Japanese economy," Admiral Teijiro Toyoda, the Minister of Munitions, recounted. "Original plans called for all steel and coal from Kyushu to be shipped through the Inland Sea to Osaka . . . aerial mining made it impossible . . . near the end of the war, transportation facilities were barely sufficient to carry adequate food and salt.''

As Allied victory over Japan became more and more certain, the West began to learn some chilling truths about the character of its enemy: his absolute, almost religious dedication to his emperor, to his homeland, to his people, and to his belief that honor and social concern were served by what the Japanese called the "Glorious Death," that of suicide.

By the early months of 1945, four million Japanese had been killed in the war. If the emperor ordered it, the Japanese people were prepared to lend their remaining eighty-six million bodies to the carnage. Every man, woman, and child.

It was, as we were to learn, no idle threat.

V

Date: March 27, 1945
Place: Aboard the *Awa Maru*, Singapore, the return
Time: 1000 hours

A bandy-legged man in cotton shorts threaded his way
through the crowded passageway of "A" deck, off the first-
class cabins. Since few of the passengers yielded to his
passing, despite the load of luggage he strained under, his
headway was slow, impeded by the exacting care he took not
to bump any of those whom he passed. He knew that these
were respected persons of high station and that it would be
unforgivable for a steward to inconvenience them in the
slightest. So, he worked at it like a problem, waiting sometimes for minutes, until a group broke up or someone shifted
his weight enough for him to inch by, or someone else moved
to flick an ash over the rail.

It wasn't any of this that bothered him. He had been a
steward all his adult life—twenty-two years at sea—and these
inconveniences were small things that one accepted graceful-
ly. It would be better when he found the cabin where the
luggage belonged and could rest his arms. So, while he would
like the group that now blocked his way to yield and allow
him to pass, he would not ask or clear his throat or otherwise
make his presence known. That was part of being a ship's
steward, and he was one of the best. Captain Hamamura
would tell you that, if you were not one to believe the words
of a steward.

No. It wasn't the waiting that bothered the arm-weary
Mitsuma Shimata that morning aboard the *Awa Maru*. It was
the other thing. A thing vastly more important.

Until they had left the homeland on this voyage that had
taken them to Singapore, southward to Bangka and Djakarta,
and now back to Singapore, he had been chief steward, and

50

as chief steward he would not be carrying luggage at all but instead would be directing those who did.

He had been a good chief steward, appointed by the honored Captain Hamamura himself, and he resented the younger, less experienced man who, only days before this voyage, had taken his place. It had not made any sense. In Moji, Shimata had discovered that they had relieved many of the stewards he had hired much earlier, and, incensed, he had taken the problem to the chief of crew. A man in military uniform was in the chief's quarters. He told Shimata that he was the new chief of crew and that he could explain why many of the old stewards were no longer working.

"It is because, my good Shimata, you are no longer chief steward."

Shimata could not believe it. "If Captain Hamamura is still the captain of this vessel, I am still chief steward," Shimata told him. It had come out quickly and in anger, but he felt confident of his base of power and knew that Captain Hamamura would have none of these changes.

"Captain Hamamura," the man in uniform told him, "is, for the moment, still with us. You, sir, are hanging by the silken thread of a worm. Should you want to pursue this discussion any further, you shall not be hanging at all."

It had not been like Shimata to seek a private audience with Captain Hamamura, but since this matter was of grave importance and reflected on his family, and since he knew that the captain would brook none of these changes, he sought and won five minutes with the captain in his quarters. The meeting took thirty seconds.

The captain told him of his new position as common steward. He told Shimata that it was unfortunate, but, as regrettable as it was, the decision was out of his hands. While the captain was on board, however, Shimata could serve as his tiger, his personal steward. As Shimata was taking his formal exit, Hamamura said:

"My good Shimata. There are many changes taking place in these troubled days. There will be more changes. Things will turn worse as these days darken. But take it all, Chief Steward Shimata, as one who shoulders a plow in a field of rocks. If one serves the harness, the rocks will yield, first to the blade, then to the harvest."

Shimata, now inching ahead under his load of luggage, thought of those words again, as he had done many times in the past five weeks. He was not sure what they meant, but they seemed to be good words and worth committing to memory. He had a good memory for words. There had even been those in school and later who believed he could speak English because of the words he memorized. His trouble was knowing what the words meant.

Though he had not minded being tiger to Captain Hamamura, it was beneath the station to which he had risen. And when the captain was off the ship, as he was that morning, Shimata was called on to be a common steward and to do these things he had once ordered others to do. It was that, and now his slow progress through the people who jammed the first-class passageway, that bothered former Chief Steward Mitsuma Shimata.

For each of three days, Shimata had expected to sail, and now, as the late morning sun rose high off the harbor, things still did not look promising for departure. The winches continued to strain under the weight of the lead, tin, medicine, rubber, and rice they lifted into the forward holds. The stevedores, shirtless in the morning heat, were forced to work through the crowd that jammed the wharf.

For three days they had come like refugees, packing their possessions high on their backs, pulling themselves up the gangplank; men mostly, but some women and children. Some of those who had managed to pass through the maze of identity checks set up along the pier were given permission to move along only after an exchange of yen, an exchange that grew at each checkpoint. Then they were stopped and turned away by six fully armed Japanese soldiers posted at the top of the gangway.

There had been arguments, and those who tried to recover their money at the checkpoints were driven off by other guards. Yesterday there had been a violent scuffle. A man in civilian clothes had ordered the Japanese soldiers at the top of the gangway to let him pass. He had shouted at the soldiers and told them his name. He had told them that he was vital to the continuation of the war, that he would have them face a firing squad if they didn't back off and allow him through. When he told them his name again, the soldier nearest him pushed his rifle barrel into his stomach and told him, again, to leave. The man in civilian clothes lost his temper and, when he shouted something about the homeland, someone standing near him tripped; some blows were exchanged, a shot was fired. The man, his face and shirt bloodied, was lifted over the guide rope. The woman with him screamed. From where Shimata had stood, he wasn't able to see the man and how it would be when he struck the dock three stories below. He could see the backs of the Japanese soldiers as they looked down. He watched their backs for a long time and noticed that others along the gangway also were looking down. After a while, they didn't look down anymore, and the soldiers returned to checking the papers.

It was Shimata's guess that nearly two thousand passengers and crew were already aboard. The first-class cabins, which had accommodated sixty passengers in somewhat spartan conditions on earlier voyages, now were berthing eighty. And that number was growing. While most were in civilian clothes, he had recognized one general who had been aboard another ship with him. He had heard that there were high-ranking members of the Ministry of Foreign Affairs aboard, as well as some admirals and flag officers.

Elsewhere on board, the already crowded conditions were growing worse. In the past three days, each time that Shimata had been called upon to run an errand that took him through the lower decks, he was startled to see how many more passengers the ship was attempting to accommodate. People jammed every inch of the vessel. Straw mats were spread on hatches and in walkways and spilled into the main dining area. People and their possessions cluttered companionways, extending out through what had been the second-class promenade, the smoking rooms, and the dark-wooded tea rooms. The lounge had become an open dormitory of wall-to-wall bedding. Hammocks were swung from the enclosed portion of the promenade. It had been difficult for the stewards to move through the tangle of humanity to serve dishes and drinks and to administer to the perpetual flow of complaints.

Only this morning, one of the clumsy young stewards who had replaced one of Shimata's better men had tripped over a bed roll while working his way up from the pantry to "A" deck. He had lost a tray, a floral china tea set, and, abruptly, his job.

Corridors and stairwells were serving as makeshift living quarters, though occasional and perfunctory attempts were made to keep them clear. Even the lifeboats and riggings served as temporary storage areas. Out on the open deck, free now from gun emplacements, whole populations arose in something like a tent city; lean-tos, pup tents, bed rolls, and sleeping mats accommodated the masses, while overhead, the winches continued to swing pallets of cargo into the open holds.

The carnival-like mood that had initially swept through the *Awa Maru* as they began loading on this second stop in Singapore was gradually replaced by mounting tension as more passengers found their way onto the crowded ship. Shimata didn't like any part of this. His was an orderly, deliberate world, of things done and services rendered with a kind of precision. He did not like all this crowding, and the shouts and demands those on the lower decks made to him as he sought to perform his duties were insulting to him. Those who shouted did not know that he should have been chief steward and, as such, should have been afforded greater respect. And even now, as he toiled up the central staircase with possessions of still another first-class passenger, they couldn't have known that he was not a common steward at all but the personal steward of Captain Hamamura, once he returned to the vessel.

This misunderstanding did not please Shimata at all. He took pride in the quality of service he had rendered in a lifetime as a ship's steward—a lifetime that had almost been brought to a close on three separate occasions. He did not know for sure, but Shimata felt certain that he was the only seaman to have survived the sinking of three ships on which he had served. All had been torpedoed out from under him. And all within the past two years.

These discourteous people could not have known how difficult it had been for Shimata to board still another ship in these perilous days. As Shimata saw it, to continue to serve a ship flying the Japanese flag these days was an act of extreme bravery. His wife and children knew that; he had made sure of that. And those who scoffed at what he claimed was courage, who said that he continued to go to sea not out of bravery but out of a need to make a living, did not really know Mitsuma Shimata.

There were many positions open to a man of Shimata's talents. While he didn't know exactly what those positions would be, he felt certain of them and feeling certain, he spent little time delving into alternate occupations. But, for example, weren't people always telling how well he spoke the English words?

When the war was over and this place called America was occupied, perhaps he would move his family there. Perhaps he would be a translator for the natives. He knew many of the words already. He would spend some time while he was off watch in trying to find out what these words meant.

So let them shout and demand. They could not know who he really was. Most of those who insulted him were only second-class passengers anyway, and you could not expect much from them.

Still, it would be better when Captain Hamamura returned; he had left early that morning. Shimata did not like this thing of being a common steward.

Waiting in the outer office of the 3rd Regional Sea Transport Command, Captain Hamamura was offered very little to distract him from his gloomy thoughts. From where he was sitting he could watch the steady stream of military visitors who won a salute and immediate access to the office behind the double oak doors. The one saluting and granting access was the little aide-de-camp who had told him, without looking up from the Tokyo *Shimbun* he was reading, to sit and wait.

Hamamura had been waiting for over two hours to see Lieutenant General Kawasuki Kodamo. Each time the office door swung open, he had a glimpse of the lieutenant general behind his barren desk. Sometimes he would rise to greet the incoming visitors; sometimes he would not. Each time, the aide-de-camp would firmly close the door before he could hear the lieutenant general speak; then he would fix the captain with something just short of a glare, and sit down. When he read the paper, Hamamura noticed that he moved his lips.

The outer office had been stripped of furnishings. Hamamura occupied one of three hard-back chairs that faced an official, full-length portrait of Emperor Hirohito, the room's only concession to decor.

The aide-de-camp occupied a fourth chair, behind a spindly desk that faced out into the room. The desk was bare save for a pen holder out of which rose a' tiny Japanese flag. Though facing Hamamura, the aide steadfastly disdained eye contact with the aging captain.

So, Hamamura was left with the portrait. He did not mind looking at the likeness of the emperor, whom he admired and respected, but it was one of those badly done oils that had been painted under the direction of the Royal Imperial Portrait Art of Illustrious Figures Committee, and, as a result, it had suffered numerous and obvious alterations. Apparently, the artist had intended to portray the emperor on horseback, then was directed instead to pose him standing in the Imperial Gardens. The result was a vast, empty foreground filled in arbitrarily with camellias and azaleas and what was either a very thick vine or some exterior plumbing from the Imperial Palace.

In any case, the emperor's benevolent gaze did not hold Hamamura's attention for long. When he was finally invited through the doors, a half hour later, Hamamura rose slowly, his legs stiff from the long wait. Before entering, he glanced at the headline of the newspaper the aide-de-camp was reading: VICTORY HOPES HIGH DESPITE SEA BLOCKADE.

Lieutenant General Kawasuki Kodamo did not stand as Captain Hamamura entered his sparsely furnished office, but merely nodded his head in response to the captain's low and courteous bow. Nor did he offer to pour tea from the serving tray on the low table to his left.

The lieutenant general had the broad, flat face and thickened physique of a provincial. Captain Hamamura had heard that he came from one of the outlying villages in Hokkaido and had risen to power in the military chiefly through his reputation for ruthlessness, earned in some of the early engagements in the China War near Nanking. Short and squat, the general carried the nickname "the tank."

He pointed to a chair and the captain sat down. The lieutenant general swiveled his chair to the tea serving, poured one cup, and sipped noisily. He did not turn back, but instead gazed through the french windows to the city and the harbor below. When at last he spoke, Hamamura knew there would be no formalities to this meeting.

"You are the Hamamura of the *Awa Maru*." Though it was a statement rather than a question, Hamamura nodded. "You have sought this meeting with me, and you will very briefly tell me why."

When Hamamura suggested that there were some things that the lieutenant general, as officer in charge of passenger and cargo selections, should know about the already strained capacity of the *Awa Maru,* he was met first with stony silence and then a wave of the hand. He continued:

"I'm certain the honorable general, so widely and rightly heralded for so many victorious land battles, has not had the time or the inclination to turn his attention to the sea and sea craft. But there are limits to what a ship can carry, sir, and the *Awa Maru* has already seriously taxed those limits; yet, the loading goes on. At last count there were nearly two

56

thousand passengers aboard, and still they come. The cargo has brought the ship dangerously low to the sea, and still it comes. I'm certain—"

The general spun from the window and faced the captain. "Just what makes you certain, Hamamura?" The words were clipped, bitten, and delivered with force.

"I'm certain," Hamamura said quietly, "that, once you know the facts, you will end the loading."

"Hamamura, I have not yet begun the loading! We will sail tomorrow, I with you. But we shall continue to load today and tonight. We will continue to board those passengers who can best serve the war effort. Now, I have many things that urgently deserve my attention, and this is not one of them."

Hamamura made no move to leave. "As captain of this vessel, sir, I ask you to reconsider. In the event of an emergency at sea, we could not get to the lifeboats. Drills are out of the question. You have the lives of—"

"As captain of that vessel, Hamamura, you are nothing but a pilot, a spare part that can easily be replaced. We have not chosen this ship of yours because you are its captain, nor because we want to make everyone comfortable on the trip to Moji."

"But, General, it isn't a matter of comfort. I do not come here to tell you of comfort, but—"

"Then just what brings you here, Sea Captain? Is it the grip of fear?"

Hamamura, stung, stood up sharply. "Yes, it is fear, General. Fear that my ship is in jeopardy. Fear of lunacy in high places!" The last Hamamura had not meant to say, but it came out in anger.

For a full minute the general did not move. When he spoke, he spoke slowly, pinching off each word as though the bitter taste of it tore at his lips. "If you were not a civilian, Hamamura, you would be hung and quartered for that remark. Since you are a civilian, you may live to see Moji. You *may* live. But I would not risk it further."

He allowed the words to hang for a moment, daring a retort. When they were met with silence, he turned back to the window. On the streets below, the distant cry of a fish vendor calling out his price for dried squid echoed upward; somewhere more distant, the hollow sound of a wooden flute set the vendor's price to music.

"Hamamura," the general began, "I am going to tell you what you need to know. *Only* what you need to know. And

57

you need only listen. And listen well. Your ship is crucial to the war effort. It has been guaranteed safe passage. Otherwise it would never get through.

"The enemy, Hamamura, has stupidly granted this safe passage by formal, written agreement, through the Swiss government. They are compelled to stand by it, for this treaty is before the eyes of the world.

"For our part, we did what we said we would do. We took their shipment of relief supplies from Nakhodka and delivered it to the points we said we would deliver it to in our itinerary. The eyes of the world cannot deny this.

"And now, Hamamura, comes our part. And, in a token way, yours. If, as you say, there are now two thousand passengers aboard, there are only a few more remaining. I shall board tonight. One of the last to board will be a vice-minister. He will board early tomorrow morning.

"In the meantime, between late tonight and early tomorrow, there will be the loading of a most critical cargo. You need not be entrusted with the nature of this cargo, but you will conform to the instructions on this message."

The general reached into the drawer and extended what appeared to be a radio dispatch. It was addressed to the captain. Hamamura began to open it.

"Spare me your reading it here, Hamamura. But understand this, Captain: once that cargo is loaded and secured, any man, woman, or child, passenger or crew, captain or deckhand, caught in, near, or around Cargo Hold number four, the vault room, or the purser's cabin will be shot. Not talked to. Not questioned. Shot. So, Captain, if, as you say, you value the lives of your passengers, make your restrictions crystal-clear, make them early, and make them stick."

Outside, Captain Hamamura pulled his hat lower to his eyes as he headed into the sun, down through the crowded streets of Singapore toward the harbor. He would walk. It would be good to fill his lungs with fresh air, to expel the black anger that filled his chest. He tried not to think of the meeting.

Very little had changed about the crowded city since its occupation by the Japanese. The colors, the smells, the music, the character of those he passed, the rhythm of the streets, the eclectic quality of the architecture—all remained as they had been. It was a city beyond the vagaries of politics. It was a port city in the most vibrant sense of the word. The Japanese had come, and now they could be seen uneasily filtering through the streets—their uniforms setting them apart—in groups of six to ten; soldiers, airmen, sailors; collected, reassured, together.

Before the Japanese, there had been others. After them, there would be others. But Singapore—the smells of spiced meat and fish and exotic herbs, of wood, bamboo, of rain somewhere in a distant jungle—remained.

Hamamura, passing two fishwives engaged in a loud and heated argument just off the open market, at first did not notice the woman who had moved up on his left and matched his stride. She wore a shawl and a brightly colored madras but was, he noticed only after she began to speak, Japanese.

She said quickly and furtively, "Sir, I know you to be the captain of the *Awa Maru.*"

Hamamura did not answer. Someone was trying to ease a cart brimming with coconuts through the crowds on the street. Hamamura was forced to wait until the vendor, swearing at the crowds, pushed it clear. As he moved forward, the woman was still at his side.

She spoke in a formal manner. Though she could be heard clearly, she spoke quietly. She was not a girl of the bars. Tall, attractive, Hamamura thought she might once have been a geisha. And she knew his name.

"My husband is a military man, an officer, a proud man, sir. He would not permit this. But I know of no other way."

"You know of no other way for what?"

Hamamura and the woman were stepping around a man clad in soiled white cotton who sat on a blanket amid a sea of brightly polished copperware. Behind this blanket and seated against a wall, another man blew a flute over the flat head of an undulating cobra that had emerged from a basket between his knees. Nobody seemed to notice.

"Please let me say, Captain, that I approach you with the utmost timidity. It is only urgency that forces me to speak." She was, perhaps, in her middle thirties, but she had not forgotten her early training. Her hands moved easily when she spoke, and she walked smoothly. She did not engage Hamamura's eyes, but trained her own downward. "I will try to tell you all of it, though please know that it is hard for me to speak.

"My husband's rank is high enough for him to have learned of your ship and the many who seek refuge on it. He knows of what is to come if we remain in Singapore. He believes that there will be no other ships home. We have tried to board your vessel, but we have been turned away. It is in desperation that I offer you this."

She extended an envelope full of currency to the captain. Hamamura stopped and turned to the woman; her arm still extended, she did not look up.

"I can't take that," Hamamura said.

"But it is all that we have."

"Even if I took it, I could not get you and your husband on my ship."

"But you are the captain, sir."

"Increasingly, I have had my doubts about that." Hamamura and the woman began to walk again. "I'm sorry. I think you are right about this being the last ship home. But there is nothing I can do."

She reached out and touched his arm, stopping him again. This time she looked up, directly into his eyes. Her arm remained on his. "I will give you anything I have, Captain." Then, in a whisper, "It is seven days to Moji, and seven nights." She let the meaning of her words hang in the air.

Hamamura turned his head away. They had reached the foot of the wharf. In the far slip, the *Awa Maru* loomed over the smaller vessels surrounding her. The crowd that had jammed the pier when he had left this morning had dissipated. The winches remained, but the loading had stopped.

When he told the woman, again, that it was impossible, that he could do nothing, she took the news quietly and did not argue further, nor did she look up again. Bowing, she turned and disappeared up the street.

Before Hamamura was allowed to board his own vessel, he had to show his identification to the soldiers who guarded the head of the gangplank. They looked at his picture, then at him, then again at the picture. They talked through a walkie-talkie, then joked with each other until the verification was made and the voice on the instrument said it was permissible for the captain to board.

By the time he reached his quarters, moving silently among the passengers that jammed the ship, ignoring those who called to him, it was noon. He had not had breakfast and would not have lunch. He remembered the message that the lieutenant general had given him before he had left the headquarters. He pulled it from his shirt pocket. It was from the office of the Ministry, East Asian Imperial Affairs. It was directed to him for immediate action. A copy had been forwarded to Officer in Charge, 3rd Regional Sea Transport Command, Singapore.

1. Be advised that, due to the strategic and highly secret nature of cargo to be onloaded aboard the AWA MARU in the night and morning hours of 27 March 1945 and 28 March 1945, Captain Yoshita Hamamura is instructed to restrict passenger movement aboard the vessel from 2300 hours on 27 March 1945 to 0600 28 March 1945. Passengers and crew assigned to other than first-class areas will be confined to their quarters during those times. Cargo Hold 4, the vault room, and the purser's cabin will thereafter remain off-limits to all personnel.

2. Separate single-room accommodations will be prepared for Lt. General Kawasuki Kodamo, Officer in Charge of Cargo and Passenger Selection, and Vice-Minister Hiraka Kawibashi, East Asian Imperial Affairs. Ship's officers now occupying cabin 14 and cabin 17 on "B" deck will be berthed elsewhere.

The dispatch was signed "Vice-Minister Hiraka Kawibashi, Administrator of Procurement and Under-Inspector of Internment, Co-Prosperity Sphere."

VI

Date: March 27, 1945
Place: In a jungle clearing, somewhere north of Singapore
Time: 1200 hours

The black man was bound securely to the tree in the jungle clearing. Stripped to the waist, he stood, eyes transfixed in shock, clad in loose-fitting khaki trousers. The sun washed across his damp chest, lending shadow and form to his prominently displayed rib cage, heaving now in sustained panic. Below it, his badly swollen belly ballooned against the drum-taut skin that contained it.

Those of the men facing him who could rouse enough interest to look at him at all followed the black man's eyes as they darted first to the Korean camp administrator the prisoners called "Chisel," who stood impassively to his left, then beyond to the Japanese man in the clean white shirt—a shirt already wet with sweat—then back to the group of ragged, hollow-eyed men.

The prisoners stood quietly. The speech of the young man in the white shirt was broken only by the angry buzz of the flies that fed, almost unmolested, on the faces of the men he was addressing.

They had been called from their work on the road to stand in the sun in this fetid clearing. It was a welcome chance to rest.

Chisel had ordered the American prisoners out of the detail, leaving the Aussies and the British to continue the work. He did not like to see the prisoners idle. The generators had been brought in again, and, if they did not break down, and if they could get fuel for them, he could work the men in the dark under lights. It was not good to have the prisoners stand idly in the sun with all the work ahead. He wanted the Japanese man in the white shirt to finish what he had to say and turn the men back to him. But he knew the importance of the man, so he remained quiet.

It was an effort. He was already impatient for the return of his authority. Perhaps he would use the wire whip this afternoon. It was important that the men know how well he'd learned to use it.

The eyes of the black man darted again to the Japanese man in the white shirt as he resumed his talk. He spoke in English, a language the black man did not understand.

"We—all of us, you see—are the same. We are all similarly constituted. I am Oriental, you are not; he is black, you are not; but in one respect, all of us, you see, all of us are the same."

His words were chosen deliberately and, though delivered with a heavy accent, were weighed, precise. His neck was short, thick, and muscular; his head shaped from it, an extension, a part of it. The sweat on his shaved head gleamed on either side of the ragged scar that traversed it, an umber worm that crawled from the crown of his head down to a point just above the left eye. Curiously, the scar provided a counterpoint to his otherwise youthful, regular features.

He had already told the men that he had studied medicine for two semesters in a university in Evanston, Illinois, ten years before, and had thereafter gone on to graduate with "extreme honors" from a university in Tokyo. His talk today concerned, he said, the displeasure he had incurred while in the American school. He said that he had been offended by the actions of some of his classmates during his stay in the United States; they had repeatedly discredited him for his nationality, and his roommates had called him the unflattering name "Yellow Peril." This was an unforgivable slander, he said. He told the group how he had worked hard in the American school and later in Tokyo and that, through it all, he had remembered.

"So that you have cause to remember," said the man in the white shirt, "today I will surgically demonstrate our similarities; that at the core of our humanity, we are the same, regardless of our skin color or racial distinctions."

He told the men how he would show that the inherent supremacy of the Japanese was something other than biological.

But first, there were other things he wanted them to know. He told them his name, Hiraka Kawibashi, and that, although

63

he held high office in the ministry, they were welcome to call him by his nickname, "the Scar." He hastened to assure the men that the scar that adorned his head and served to identify him was many years old and no longer provided him any discomfort.

"It would please me," he said, "if I could tell you that I won the scar in a glorious contest of war with your countrymen. But it would not be the truth. And truth is the cornerstone of my talk today.

"No. I confess that the scar was the product of a mild disagreement between friends, and therefore it is of no concern to us today."

He told the men, instead, that he brought good news from home.

"In your country, there has been much concern over the lack of food and medicine in prisoner-of-war camps such as these. And, you'll be pleased to know, they have taken positive action. In an agreement between your government and mine, thousands of pounds of food and medicine packaged by the Red Cross have been delivered to this camp, like dozens of other camps for which I am responsible."

Some of the men, for the first time, looked up.

"I know it will please you to learn that these packages, even as I talk, are being distributed to needy camp administrators and their families. Chisel, here, whom you all know and love, will receive his allocation at the end of the day.

"It grieves me that there will not be sufficient supplies to benefit you directly, but you can be certain that the improved morale of the camp administrators will work in your favor.

"So much for the good news."

The man in the white shirt then told the column of men who stood before him that this, regrettably, would be his last inspection of the men and facilities at this camp, for he would be leaving in the morning for his homeland.

"Since there is an outside chance that some of you may live to see yours, I wanted to make a final and lasting impression on you, to indelibly impress you with what this war is all about. Hence, I have chosen our frightened and unfortunate black man here."

When the man in the white shirt turned to the black man and smiled, the black man nervously returned it. The man with the scar then rested a hand on the black man's trembling shoulder as though to ease his fears.

"But, lest you think I have chosen this man because of the

dark color of his skin, rest assured that my demonstration would be just as effective using any of you here. As I said, biologically there is no difference.

"When you recall what I am to do, please accept it and this lecture in the light in which it is delivered. I am not a cruel man. I am a Japanese man. As prisoners, all of you, in the eyes of my culture, are dead; the day you permitted yourselves to be captured is the day you surrendered your flesh. It is the day your spirit died.

"And years from now—should you see those years—some of you will understand what this war has been about. You will understand about the Japanese. You will understand that it isn't biology which sets one man apart from another. It is this spirit—that which you have surrendered—which dominates, sets one person, one race, above another. If that spirit is untarnished, and if the race is pure—whether it takes one battle or more, one war or more—victory will come. One day it will come.

"No, it is not a matter of flesh."

The black man, attempting to read the man in the white shirt by the pleasant, even tone of his voice, again affected a nervous smile as the Japanese man unsheathed a long and slightly curved hand-made knife that he carried at his belt. The handle was of rayskin and a silk cord hung from it. The single-edge blade gleamed.

The smile was still passing across the face of the black man as the doctor neatly inserted the knife just below the swollen navel. Effortlessly, in a single movement, the Japanese man brought the knife up to the sternum. He was careful to avoid staining his shirt, and he stood to one side when he severed the pulmonary artery.

Chisel watched the operation with mild interest and only glanced at the object of the dissection, which he was ordered to pass among the men. It had been nearly an hour and he was eager to get the men back to work.

The last man to receive it held the warm organ for a moment, then let it fall at his feet. Like the rest, he didn't look at it. It was quiet in the clearing. There was only the sound of the flies.

Authority was returned to the man they called Chisel and the men were marched out of the clearing and back to the jungle for work on a road that led to nowhere. The disemboweled body of the black man, hanging suspended from the ropes that had contained him, was left behind.

What had begun as a trickle of information concerning the unspeakable treatment of prisoners of war in the deep-jungle Japanese encampments through Southeast Asia grew, in those closing days of war, into a torrent of accounts of atrocities, torment, and torture—slave-labor teams racked with malaria and malnutrition; men driven to the ground in endless, back-breaking labor; days that would begin at dawn and end four hours before the next.

What the Japanese lacked in the wholesale technology for the extermination so mercilessly employed against the Jews in Germany, they made up for in the conditions in which they forced men to work, to live, to suffer, and to die.

As the Allies gained a stronger and stronger hold on the sea lanes, as more and more of the Japanese Navy was lost to the voracious appetite of the American wolfpack operations patrolling the deep, conditions at the camps worsened. Food, once parceled out in carefully measured packets to ensure minimum daily survival, was reduced to a handful of polished rice infested with maggots—the larvae providing the protein, perhaps the most nourishing element of the ration. Medicine to cure the jungle diseases—malaria, cholera—that sometimes leveled a camp came in quantities too small to do more than ease a chill of a camp administrator.

Accounts of mistreatment of American and Allied prisoners of war began to reach the neutral Swiss government in a barrage of telegrams hammered out in the thousands by the U.S. State Department. The intelligence network in Southeast Asia was in full swing by now, and the worst fears of the Allies were realized, then recounted in verifiable detail to the Japanese through the Swiss.

When Japan addressed these messages at all, the reply was often an exercise in the oblique:

The Swiss legation in Tokyo forwarded a preliminary reply from the Japanese government in response to one of the messages urging action. "Concerning special circumstances prevailing in areas which have, until recently, been fields of battle" and concerning the "manifold difficulties which exist in areas occupied by the Japanese forces, or where military operations are still being carried on," the Japanese were, in essence, they said, unable to afford prisoners of war with the treatment they would be assured of in a behind-the-lines, peaceful camp.

The U.S. government fired back the response:

"The government of the United States has taken note of the statements of the Japanese government. The government of the United States points out, however, that the regions in which Americans have been taken prisoner or interred have long ceased to be scenes of active military operations and that the Japanese holding authorities have, therefore, had ample opportunity to establish an orderly and humane treatment program in accordance with their government's undertakings."

These, then, were the conditions that set the stage for the voyage of the *Awa Maru*.

The governments of the United States and Japan began negotiations a full year before the *Awa Maru* finally set sail from Moji with what must be considered a hopelessly inadequate supply of emergency medical and food supplies. But the principle was there and would serve to boost the morale of prisoners in the outlying POW camps throughout Southeast Asia.

What would not become clear until later was why the Japanese agreed to consider delivering medical supplies at all, and why they selected the largest cargo-passenger vessel available to them to run the relatively small quantity of emergency supplies. Altruism? Humanitarianism? Abiding concern for their captives' welfare?

Doubtful. Doubtful, even at the time, to the diplomats serving the United States, who would play a vital role in clearing the way for a Japanese vessel to pass safely through waters controlled by the U.S. Navy.

In the course of these negotiations, U.S. Secretary of State Cordell Hull resigned. He had carried a good deal of the burden of Japan's invasion of Pearl Harbor on his shoulders. Hull had advised President Franklin Roosevelt that Japan's aims were based on need, not militarism, that Japan sought oil, and that while she might attack the Philippines, she certainly would not risk an attack on the United States.

Joseph Grew was a career diplomat, a dean of the foreign service. He had been ambassador to Japan when Pearl Harbor was attacked. Grew's advice to Hull was based on his close association with all the wrong people in Japan—those who didn't recognize the strength of the militarists in the country or the long-range intention of the emperor.

When Hull resigned in October 1944, Grew took over as acting Secretary of State. Grew once again played a part in a State Department miscalculation: permitting the *Awa Maru* to sail as a hospital ship. By the time the deception was realized, the real intention understood, the political die was cast and all but one option was closed—one too desperate and too politically suicidal to seriously consider: the deliberate sinking of the vessel.

The tangled chain of events leading to the decision to let the *Awa Maru* pass safely began more than a year before the ship's embarkation. On January 15, 1944, Leland Harrison, minister in Switzerland, complained to Secretary Hull:

"Representatives of the Swiss Government entrusted with the protection of American interests in Japan and Japanese-occupied territory have not been permitted to go to every place [POW camps] without exception, with no interviews allowed, without witnesses."

A few days later, Hull replied:

"The government will, among other things, promptly implement the provisions of Article 86 in respect to the activities of the government of Switzerland as protecting power for American interests in Japan and Japanese-controlled territory and will make it possible for the government of Switzerland to give to the government of the United States assurances to the effect that Swiss representatives have been able to convince themselves by the full exercise of the rights granted under Article 86 that the abuses set forth have been completely rectified."

On midnight, January 28, the War and Navy departments issued a joint press release. The text of the telegram was released to the U.S. press on February 11:

The United States government, until now, has refrained from publishing in this country the facts known to it regarding outrages perpetrated upon its nationals, both prisoners of war and civilian internees, by the Japanese.

The United States government hopes that, as these facts are now again officially called to the Japanese government's attention, government will adopt a policy affording to United States nationals in its hands the treatment to which they are entitled, and will permit representatives of the protecting power to make such investigations and inspections as are necessary in order to give assurances to this government that improved treatment is in fact being accorded to American nationals.

In such case, this government would be in a position to assure the American people that the treatment of American nationals by the Japanese authorities had been brought into conformity with the standards recognized by civilized nations.

The Japanese government almost never responded to such direct and indirect appeals for her to abide by the agreement to which she was a party when the terms of the Geneva Convention were ratified on July 27, 1929.

For more than four years, Japan had been in receipt of the first telegram from the United States government offering to supply food and medicine to the prisoners of war held captive by Japan. The United States' offer included a guarantee of safe passage of any Japanese ship so engaged. The offer had been accepted and executed several times in the course of the war, but, for over a year now, a year of severe depletions in the camps, no major relief ship had sailed.

Quite unexpectedly, on May 10, 1944, the silence was broken. Secretary Hull received a message from Switzerland that was to open the book on the *Awa Maru* incident:

The Japanese government is prepared to comply with the request of the United States government to render facilities in regard to the transport of relief goods and letters sent to American prisoners of war and internees via Vladivostok, Russia, under the following conditions:

1. The Japanese government will, as a rule, send a Japanese ship to Vladivostok, Russia, once a month in order to transport the relief goods and letters sent from the United States by a Soviet ship, provided that the United States government obtains the consent of the Soviet government to the entry of the Japanese ship into the port of Vladivostok.

2. The quantity to be transported shall be decided and notified by the Japanese government upon consideration of the capacity of the Japanese ship sent for the purpose.

3. The governments of the interested countries shall give a safe-conduct for the navigation of the Japanese ship to be sent for the transport of the goods and letters.

4. The country sending relief goods shall pay all the dues, rates, and other public charges to be levied at Vladivostok on the Japanese ship sent for the freight of the relief goods from Vladivostok to the port of destination in Japan and the cost of the loadings to and landing of the Japanese ship and the warehousing of the relief goods.

5. In cases where the Japanese government sends

relief goods and letters to Japanese subjects held by the United States government, the United States government shall take the necessary steps for the transport of them to be effected by a route and method similar to these about to be adopted.

Moreover, presence of Japanese Consular service is necessary for Japanese ships to enter port and take delivery of supplies. Should, however, the Soviet government find it difficult to accord to the above proposal as a result of negotiations, the Japanese government would agree to make delivery of supplies at the alternate port city of Nakhodka, provided the American government obtains consent of the Soviet government to the following:

a) That two members of the staff of the Japanese Consulate General at Vladivostok be given facilities for traveling to Nakhodka and be permitted to stay for a necessary period of time and to discharge their official duties relating to entry and correspondence.

b) That the captain and senior officers of the Japanese ship be permitted to go ashore and communicate with said Japanese Consular officials.

c) That on the arrival of the Japanese ship at port, she should be given first priority in entering port, enabled to load supplies without delays, and allowed to leave that port without any impediment.

d) That indication of safe course of the ship will be followed and all other facilities for transport of supplies be accorded to the Japanese ship.

As regards to relief supplies and correspondence presumed to be now lying at Vladivostok, the Japanese government will take delivery of them to aggregate amount of 2,000 metric-weight tons at Vladivostok or Nakhodka, whichever port is agreed upon, by a single voyage, if possible.

When this surprisingly detailed piece of communication arrived at the State Department, a meeting of senior staff members was immediately called. Because intelligence at that stage of the war in that location had still not gained enough momentum to accurately read Japan's intention, its input into the meeting was nominal. By the time a strong intelligence network was operational and Japan's intentions were accurately understood, the United States was publicly committed to this "act of mercy." Who, after all, could fault a nation for agreeing to make such a humanitarian effort on behalf of the request of a "belligerent nation"? And, whatever Japan's real intentions, could the United States refuse an opportunity to relieve, if only nominally, the suffering of its own POWs? At whatever cost?

In the meeting, Secretary Hull overrode some of the suspicions of two senior staff members. The message that Secretary Hull forwarded to the Japanese confirming the right for her so-called hospital ship to travel unmolested, almost without limitation, demonstrates how one man—again misreading the character of the Japanese government—could indeed make the same mistake twice.

The dispatch read:

The port of Vladivostok as a transshipping point for supplies sent from the United States for distribution to Allied nationals in Japanese custody desires to cooperate in this humanitarian undertaking.

It is willing to carry out the transfer of relief goods presently at Vladivostok, either at the border railroad station in Manchuria or the Soviet port of Nakhodka, as the Japanese government may prefer.

Notification of date of departure from sailing ports, as well as from Japanese ports, should be made to the United States government, which will inform the other interested governments.

In order to ensure the safety of the Japanese ship during the course of its missions, notifications of sailing dates and noontime positions should be received at least seven days prior to the date of departure, together with a complete description of the ship and detailed information as to the course to be followed by such ship.

Notification came. An itinerary for the *Awa Maru* was set by the Japanese government, an itinerary that would put the ship on its return voyage through some of the most heavily mined waters in the East China Sea. Not Allied mines. But Japan's own minefields north of Formosa, off the Ryukyu Islands.

The itinerary submitted to the Allies called for the *Hakusan Maru* to onload the Red Cross supplies at the Russian port of Nakhodka, from there to return to Moji, Japan, where the goods would be transferred to the *Awa Maru* for its journey south.

A dispatch forwarded through the Swiss government to the

Japanese Foreign Office by the U.S. State Department acknowledges, in full, the itinerary submitted by Japan:

This safe conduct is based on the following schedule: leaves *Moji* afternoon February 17, passes 31 degrees 12 minutes north latitude 126 degrees 58 minutes east longitude about noon February 18, passes 26 degrees 17 minutes north latitude 122 degrees 29 minutes east longitude noon February 19, arrives *Takao* forenoon February 20. Leaves *Takao* forenoon February 21, arrives *Hong Kong* afternoon February 22. Leaves *Hong Kong* forenoon February 23, passes 16 degrees 2 minutes north latitude 110 degrees 37 minutes east longitude about noon February 24, arrives *Saigon* afternoon February 25. Leaves *Saigon* forenoon February 28, passes 4 degrees 10 minutes north latitude 105 degrees 32 minutes east longitude about noon March 1, arrives *Singapore* forenoon March 2. Leaves *Singapore* forenoon March 8, passes 2 degrees 28 minutes south latitude 109 degrees 10 minutes east longitude about noon March 9, arrives *Surabaja* afternoon March 10.

On homeward voyage, leaves *Surabaja* forenoon March 11, arrives *Djakarta* afternoon March 12. Leaves *Djakarta* forenoon March 18, arrives *Muntok* [Bangka Island] afternoon March 19. Leaves *Muntok* forenoon March 23, arrives *Singapore* afternoon March 24. Leaves *Singapore* forenoon March 28, passes 7 degrees 52 minutes north latitude 107 degrees 37 minutes east longitude about noon March 29, passes 12 degrees 11 minutes north latitude 111 degrees 4 minutes east longitude about noon March 30, passes 16 degrees 53 minutes north latitude 114 degrees 37 minutes east longitude about noon March 31, passes 20 degrees 28 minutes north latitude 119 degrees 32 minutes east longitude about noon April 1, passes 26 degrees 4 minutes north latitude 122 degrees 63 minutes [subject to later correction] east longitude about noon April 2, passes 30 degrees 41 minutes north latitude 126 degrees 30 minutes east longitude about noon April 3, arrives *Miture* afternoon April 4, arrives *Moji* forenoon April 5. [Miture could not be identified under that name. Presumably, it is one of Japan's offshore islands.]

The itinerary confirmed, the United States dispatched an admonition to the Japanese that could have been prophetic:

The American government draws attention to the necessity for strict adherence to the ship's schedule and course as proposed by the Japanese government and agreed to herein.

It is expected that there will be no—repeat no—deviation therefrom, except for reasons beyond the vessel's control.

In such case deviation becomes necessary, notice of such revision in schedule as may be required should be communicated to this government by the Japanese government by the most expeditious means possible.

Japan, of course, had no intention of conforming to the itinerary originally set. The *Awa Maru* would not traverse Japan's own minefields. If, on the basis of the itinerary, the United States Navy considered the area off the Ryukyu Islands free of mines, and accordingly began sending ships and submarines through the area, that of course was its own hard luck.

It was on that final night in Singapore, under floodlights and in strict secrecy, that the Japanese military themselves undertook the loading of a cargo that would make King Solomon's bones rattle.

VII

Date: March 28, 1945
Place: Aboard the *Awa Maru*, Singapore
Time: 0500 hours

Former Chief Steward Mitsuma Shimata was beginning to regret the day, almost six months before, when he had signed onto the *Awa Maru*. At first, things had gone well. Serving under Captain Hamamura on the relatively new ship had been rewarding. As the ranks of competent seamen were being rapidly depleted by the war and by the rumors and fears that swept Japan, Shimata's fortunes had risen.

But his fortunes had begun to change on this voyage. First, there was the indignity of being reduced from chief steward to a captain's steward. Then, with the crowds, and in the captain's absence, serving as a common steward. And then the final indignity, the circumstances that had culminated in his presence at the rail of "A" deck at five o'clock in the morning.

The day that had begun with hauling luggage and taking abuses as a common steward had not improved when the captain returned at noon. The captain, in a black and uncommunicative mood, had told Shimata that he would not require his services until they were at sea. He was, instead, to report back to the chief of crew.

The day that had begun with hauling luggage and fielding abuses had ended that way. And it had ended late. So tired was he that he had almost sacrificed his ritualistic tour of the deck.

For many years now it had been his habit to make a counterclockwise walk around the main passenger deck, on whichever ship he was serving, just before retiring. It gave him a feeling of proprietorship. But more, he attributed his survival of the three sinkings to this ritual. It had not been his idea but had been told to him by an old naval officer whom he had talked to as a child. "Sleep above the water line when you can," the officer had said. "But when you can't, and must sleep below, sleep with that deck and the walkway in your dreams. Walk the deck before sleep, and you shall wake to sleep again." Counterclockwise had been Shimata's idea, and he treated it as a religion.

When he returned from his walk last night and descended the stairwell to his quarters, he found that they were occupied by four infantry lieutenants. His gear, they said, had been moved to the cook's quarters.

But the final indignity had not been sleeping with pot-and-bottle washers and galley help, but sleeping directly under the 320-pound aspiring sumo wrestler who served as the crew's mess cook. Working the night shift, the cook had descended on the upper bunk at 0455 hours. With a great crashing and heaving of springs, the bunk above him gave, then held, suspending the 320 pounds of flesh no more than six inches above Shimata. At 0457 hours, the cook began to snore.

After being driven from his quarters, such were Shimata's gloomy thoughts as he leaned on the rail, absently watching the loading operation below, that he did not notice the figure who had descended the ladder behind him and took his place near him on the darkened and deserted companionway.

Since sunset the day before, there had been a strange pattern to the loading operation. Curiously, the winches, which had been idle since noon, started up again after dark. This time they began unloading the sacks of rice they had onloaded only that morning. The sacks were pulled out of the holds and swung to the wharf, where stevedores stacked them in long rows. This continued for four hours; then the wharf was cleared of all personnel.

Then, at 2300 hours, just as Shimata was moving around the stern boom rigging on his counterclockwise walk before turning in, before he learned they had changed his quarters, the cargo lights flooded the deserted wharf below. Beyond, on the road leading to the head of the pier, a string of trucks that had been holding in a long line, waiting there in the dark, started their engines. Their headlights formed an illuminated snake that wound up the hill, arched to the south, disappeared behind a warehouse, and emerged on the other side. He could not see the end of the line of lights. The gate that had secured the wharf was swung clear by two armed guards, and the convoy headed out onto the dock. Moving past the line, on the left, was a black 1941 Chrysler sedan. It pulled up and stopped just below Shimata. Its license plates were official, but Shimata could not read the numbers. It flew a Japanese flag on each fender.

The first half-dozen trucks were personnel carriers, and, when the soldiers, fully armed and in combat fatigues, briskly took positions at intervals along the dock, Shimata feared an air attack. He considered breaking for the gangway and fleeing. He'd be damned if he'd go down in a ship again.

But before Shimata had taken any action, some of the soldiers removed their shirts and began stacking weapons. Those near the Chrysler remained in place. They snapped to attention and saluted the man who emerged from the rear of the car. The man was in civilian clothes, and, from above, Shimata could see the scar that ran the length of his shaved head. He moved up the gangway and into the ship.

For half an hour last night, Shimata had watched the secret and heavily guarded loading operation; the shirtless Japanese soldiers, serving as longshoremen, labored under the floodlights, sweat gleaming on their backs as they strained under the weight of the endless stream of identical wooden boxes that they pulled from the trucks.

And later, off and on through his restless night in the new and cramped quarters below, Shimata awoke to hear the roar of the winch engine, the grind of the windlass, and the distant shouts of the soldiers. Throughout the night, when he wasn't considering the depths to which his fortunes had sunk, Shimata tried to figure out what was in those boxes. He assumed that they contained medical supplies, since they were each marked with a painted red cross, but he did not know what kind of medicine weighed as much as those boxes must have weighed.

Each of the boxes was no larger than one cubic meter, yet it took four men to move a single box from the truck to the loading pallet. The winch would groan mightily under the strain of lifting only four of the boxes at a time. Whatever medicine was being loaded under this unprecedented security, those boxes seemed to weigh as much as the lead and tin they had onloaded two days before.

When he reached the rail this second time, just before dawn, he noticed that they had finished loading the wooden boxes and now were winching long steel containers directly off a flatbed truck. Once, the sling gave way as the load swung up and teetered just over the deck. The steel case slid, tilted, but hung. They eased it carefully to the deck.

"The defecators, those ignorant defecators!"

The voice, at Shimata's immediate left, startled him. He had not realized that there was someone standing next to him at the rail, and, with the lights flooding the scene below, it was hard to make out the figure of Captain Hamamura.

"Forgive me, good Captain. I did not see you. Is there anything you need?" The figure did not move.

After a moment, Hamamura said quietly. "To end this lunacy, Shimata, to end this interminable lunacy!"

Shimata did not know what he meant, so he waited for the captain to make his order clear. The soldiers on the deck had unhitched the sling from the steel case and were maneuvering it into the hold. The captain did not speak until the container slid out of sight into the dark below.

"Look at them," he said in disgust. "Look what we have now. Now we have these military incompetents serving as stevedores. And, if we survive their clumsy mindlessness, they shall soon be at the helm!"

It was still not clear what the captain wanted Shimata to do, so Shimata smiled and bowed slightly.

An Army sedan that moved from the head of the dock toward the loading operation created some confusion among the soldiers. Some of them continued with the loading, others turned and saluted the car. The driver brought it to a stop behind the Chrysler, then scurried around and opened the rear door. He stood, holding the door with his left hand, the right cocked in a rigid salute.

No one emerged. Those who had been working in the vicinity of the car had stopped, waiting for the passenger to exit. They waited a long time before the passenger inside began to make his way through the open door. He did it piece by piece, one limb at a time. When at last he pushed off the seat in an attempt to stand, he careened sideways into the open door and fell forward. He grabbed the private around the waist and clung there. The private, deciding that this action did not constitute a return of his salute, and sagging under the weight of the lieutenant general, held his salute. When the squat little man fell to his hands and knees on the dock, clear of the car and the private, those assembled snapped to attention and saluted.

Lieutenant General Kawasuki Kodamo appeared, for a moment, as though he would acknowledge the honors by dipping his head in a bow. Instead, he vomited on the dock before him.

For a moment, nobody seemed to know quite what to do. Finally, three soldiers broke rank to raise their fallen leader to his feet. As they moved toward the gangplank, the lieutenant general suspended among them, they were joined by another passenger who emerged from the back seat of the sedan.

As she moved clear of the car, Shimata could see that she was tall, attractive, and that she moved with grace. She wore a brightly colored madras and a shawl that shielded but did not conceal her face. She was Japanese. As she moved up the gangplank a few paces behind the foursome, Shimata thought that she carried herself like a geisha.

As the sun rose, easing first through and then over the blanket of mist that clung to the harbor, it rose on a clear day. Only a thin trail of high cirrus clouds washed the sky to the south.

But the weather check Captain Hamamura had made just before the *Awa Maru* was to cast off on the last leg of its journey home confirmed the sense of impending danger he had felt the day before. There was weather to the south and it was moving in, which was exactly what Captain Hamamura did not want.

The vessel that had sailed into the Singapore harbor three days before had presented a sharply different silhouette from the ship that now stood, loaded beyond capacity, at dockside. Since she was well below her full draft level of 30.5 feet, she rode with the water line high on her steel-plated hull. Hamamura was not sure how much over her normal cargo capacity she bore, but the bottoms of the white crosses fore and aft on her hull, which were high above the water line when she had moored, were now dipping beneath the oil-slickened water at the slip. While he conceded that the cargo had been fairly distributed within the six holds, he was anxious to find out how she rode when under way. He feared that even in calm seas, the fantail would be awash at speeds of 10 knots or more. He doubted that she could take much more than 14 or 15 knots, well short of the 20.8 knots that she was normally capable of making.

But that was in calm seas. If they could outrace the weather moving in and did not encounter other storms, it would be all right. But, should the low weather front to the south overtake them, he was not sure how she would ride. He hoped that he would not have to find out.

But how or whether she would take the seas was only a part of what concerned Captain Hamamura that morning. He did not know the exact contents of the carefully concealed material loaded the night before, but he did know that the enemy's intelligence network was not blind, and he also knew the Japanese procurement policies in Indonesia. One who made his living sailing those waters could not avoid hearing about the wealth of gold, platinum, silver, diamonds, and other treasures that had been collected and freely shipped to Japan for years. Freely, that is, until things this past year got tough.

It did not take the mind of a seasoned espionage agent to guess that whatever had been loaded last night had been accumulated in procurement centers for months, waiting for the next—if not last—ship home. And whatever it was that warranted such elaborate security measures must have been worth endangering the lives of the 2,009 passengers and crew—at the last and final count—who were now aboard.

What Hamamura did not know, he did not care to hear. It was none of his business. Whatever was in the three carefully constructed safes in the newly reinforced and expanded purser's cabin and vault room, whatever was in cargo hold 4, whatever was contained in the heavy Red Cross boxes, was of no interest to the captain. So it was with the other crates they had onloaded just before sunset, the ones with the English letters marking the long crate *A* and the shorter crates *B* and *C*, the crates they so carefully stored in his own sitting room just off the bridge. Whatever warranted a twenty-four-hour guard who would not even acknowledge his passing was the business of the Japanese government, not his.

Just getting the ship home would be enough to occupy his mind. He would not think about the secret loading the night before. He hoped the enemy would do likewise.

The selection of the *Awa Maru*, the largest and fastest of Japan's remaining passenger-cargo vessels, a ship that was half as tall as the Empire State Building, was itself an exercise in deception.

This was the *Awa Maru:*

Length:	501.9 feet
Width:	66.3 feet
Speed:	20.8 knots
Six cargo holds	
Gross tonnage:	11,249 tons

What did the *Awa Maru* carry on her departure from Singapore that clear but threatening morning of March 28, 1945?

Although the Allied intelligence network was strong and building, it did not know in detail what the vessel carried. It did know that it contained thousands of tons of strategic war materials—lead, tin, rubber, iron—that could prolong Japan's futile struggle for an estimated six months.

And there was strong evidence that the secret loading comprised an unprecedented payload of precious metals, perhaps the highest payload on any one ship traveling those waters since the beginning of the war.

As sources later revealed, intelligence at the time, despite its startling findings, was far too conservative. The *Awa Maru* carried not only the highest payload of the war but the highest payload of precious metals, currencies, and securities ever.

Ever.

Some five billion dollars' worth!

Here, then, according to a host of sources questioned in detail after the war, is what the *Awa Maru* carried:

Titanium: 800 tons.

Tin: 3,000 tons.

Tungsten: 2,000 tons.

Brass/bronze: 500 tons.

Quicksilver: 2 tons.

Lead: 2,000 tons.

Ivory: 5 cases.

Rubber: 3,000 tons, in bales.

Iron: quantity unknown.

Gold: 40 tons.

Platinum: 10 tons.

Silver: quantity unknown.

Diamonds: 5 cases, 150,000 carats.

Mixed jewelry: 40 cases, value unknown.

Antiques and artifacts: quantity and value unknown.

Paper currencies and securities: unknown number of waxed paper bales, various nationalities and denominations, value unknown.

The fossil remains of the Peking Man, of priceless anthropological value.

Sources for this detailed account of the contents of the *Awa Maru* were obtained, in the years following the war, from:

1. A high-ranking Japanese Intelligence Department staff officer.

2. Two officers in the Yokosuka Navy general headquarters.

3. A Japanese national serving in the area headquarters of the South Sea Islands' Expeditionary Force.

4. The minutes from a sensitive Japanese National Assembly meeting.

5. Protected, high government sources in the United States, Formosa, Japan, Hawaii, and the Philippines.

When one talks of the contents of the cargo on the *Awa Maru* and arrives at a value of somewhat near five billion dollars on today's market, it is easy to lose perspective. When we speak of billions, we are usually referring to national debts or distances to stars. It's a figure few can grasp. So, let's take only one aspect of what was contained in the cargo holds of the *Awa Maru*—the gold.

Concealed in Red Cross packages, gold was loaded that night before embarkation. Forty tons of it. Nearly one million troy ounces. At today's prices, the gold alone would amount to over $170 million. That's ten times more than all the mines and fields of Alaska yielded in 1940; about two-thirds of the entire annual production currently being mined in the United States; five times more gold than was brought out of the Homestake Mine in South Dakota in 1974 (Homestake is the largest gold mine in the United States).

Some of the most valuable cargo loaded aboard the *Awa Maru* carried no price tag—the art and artifacts of the countries Japan plundered and occupied for almost a decade.

The last item to find its way aboard the vessel, the one stored in the captain's sitting room and guarded around the clock, was the fossilized remains of the famed Peking Man, the most valuable anthropological discovery in history. Lost in China in the early days of the war by the Americans, the bones, taken from foot lockers and carefully packaged and sealed against the elements, had worked their way across China, then south to Singapore. They were loaded that night in crates marked A, B, and C. Believed to be the remains of a humanlike creature that lived more than half a million years ago, the fossils were first unearthed in a limestone quarry near Peking in the late 1920s. So valued are they that a standing reward has been posted for any information leading to their whereabouts. That reward, posted recently by Chicago stockbroker Christopher Janus, is set at $150,000.

Selecting the *Awa Maru*, the largest ship remaining to the Japanese, a ship half as large as the ill-fated British superliner *Titanic*, to carry a meager two thousand tons of relief supplies strained credulity. The real mission? To return to the homeland the hoards of wealth and wartime pillage accumulated during years of conquest and occupation, and to return,

81

in particular, those persons vital to the last-ditch effort to prolong Japan's dying influence in Southeast Asia.

It was a different harbor pilot who climbed to the bridge that morning. He greeted the officer of the deck, the helmsman, and the navigator with some civility. When Captain Hamamura emerged from his quarters behind the bridge, the pilot discussed how best to tug the *Awa Maru* out of the slip. This time, there was no question about using the vessel's own power to clear the dock. The tug stood ready behind them.

A British plane, swinging in low over the water only hours before, had laid at least one mine in or near the mouth of the harbor. If it was triggered on the way out, the tug would take the blast. The *Awa Maru*, in tow, would be spared.

There were some advantages, Captain Hamamura mused, to having high-ranking officials aboard.

When they had made it outside the mouth of the harbor, the lines to the tug were cast off.

Hamamura, conferring with the navigator, set a northeasterly course and called for full-ahead from the engine rooms. He felt the shudder of power as the diesels surged and the ship gained momentum through the steady seas. At 17 knots, the shudder turned into an angry, teeth-shattering vibration. Hamamura tried to outspeed it, but he could not bring the ship, low and heavy as it was, to more than 17.5 knots. He settled back to 16 knots and held.

From the port wing of the bridge, he looked aft and studied the wake. The stern was low; the fantail, as he had suspected, was almost awash. But, if they could hold it there, and if they could outdistance the weather front to the south, and if they didn't hit new and turbulent weather to the north, and if they could survive the first test—the critical one—they would be all right.

The test would come soon, Hamamura felt. When the enemy sighted them, it would come. Would they continue to let her pass unmolested? Would they risk the international repercussions that would ensue if they did not?

The Japanese were betting that they would not. The *Awa Maru* traveled under a signed and sealed treaty that permitted her to pass safely. The Japanese were betting 2,009 lives, the cargo she carried, and their best ship that the Allied powers would stand behind the treaty.

Captain Hamamura hoped his countrymen were right. In any case, he would find out very soon.

VIII

Date: March 28, 1945
Place: Aboard the *Queenfish,* on patrol northwest of Formosa
Time: 0800 hours

There are not many places where one can be alone in a submarine, and if, by chance, one finds a place, he should savor the experience. He won't be alone for long. As the patrol approached the end of the third week—three weeks of sighting nothing but an occasional recon plane and an endless expanse of water—one felt, increasingly, the need to seclude himself, to feed on the quiet, on his own thoughts.

Commander Raymond Michael Houffman felt such a need that morning and found such a place forward of the bridge on the cigarette deck. He had taken his coffee up after breakfast and stood, his foot propped on the lower rung of the rail, forearms draped across the upper. He tried not to think of his wife and his problems at home.

It was another fresh but cloudy morning. The seas were steady. The rhythmic purr of the diesels thrust the heavy bow forward at an even ten knots. From where he stood, he could see as well as hear the curve and fall of the wake. One could see for miles. And miles. And that is what bothered him. There wasn't one goddamned thing in sight!

Houffman had not noticed his executive officer approaching and was startled when Edwards extended a clipboard and said, "Skipper, I wanted to bring this to your attention."

Houffman glanced at it and said, "Bill, just tell me about it."

"Well." Edwards took a deep breath, the ridges of a frown working above his eyes. "The first thing is, we've got a quartermaster aboard who can't take a direct order. We've been having trouble with the 20 mm. The deck gun there?" Edwards pointed to the gun below them. Houffman, his back against the rail, did not look around. "And somebody keeps fooling around with it after it's been maintained, and I'm not going to have any part of that."

"How about the gunnery officer?"

"That's who brought it to my attention, Skipper. So, since no one will own up to this thing, I've written out this order and have required everyone in the crew to sign it."

"Edwards . . ." Houffman closed his eyes against the brightness of the morning sun. "Okay, then what happened?"

"Well, that's just the point, Skipper. Jessops—the quartermaster—Stan Jessops refused to sign it. Absolutely refused!"

"Why?" Houffman asked.

"He said that since he's qualified to handle the gun, he's not going to sign any order that tells him he can't touch it. Those weren't his words, Skipper. His words were clearly insubordinate."

"Let me read it, Edwards." Houffman took a minute to read the order on the clipboard; then, managing a straight face, he handed it back to his executive officer.

"Bill," he said, "this Jessops has been around, you know. You're requiring him to sign an order that he's not to touch the gun unless he has the gunnery officer's permission."

"Exactly, Captain. When I told him I was going to bring it up with you, he said that I could bring it up with Nimitz, he still wouldn't sign. He said, and these are his words, 'Throw me in the brig, I don't give a shit.' Then he turned and walked out."

Houffman laughed. It was not the reaction Edwards had expected.

"Bill, don't you see what Jessops is saying? He's telling you that he's going to use that gun if he has to, and if he has to, he's not going to have time to run around finding you or the gunnery officer to sign him out."

"But that's not what I meant, and he knows it."

"But that's what you *said* you meant," Houffman told him.

"So you don't want to see Jessops?"

"Only if he wants to see me."

Edwards, heading forward, passed Steve Trevor without saying a word.

"What did you do to Bill?" Trevor asked.

"He just had a course in journalism. What have you got?" Trevor was carrying a radio message.

"You're not going to believe this one. Mike Bass just received it."

Houffman read the message, which had been in encrypted form. It was from ComSubPac and addressed to all submarines in the Pacific:

> . . . LET PASS SAFELY THE AWA MARU CARRYING PRISONER OF WAR SUPPLIES. STOP. SHE WILL BE PASSING THROUGH YOUR AREA BETWEEN MARCH 30 AND APRIL 4. STOP. SHE IS LIGHTED AT NIGHT AND PLASTERED WITH WHITE CROSSES . . .

"Well, for Christ sake," Houffman said. This was the first message about the *Awa Maru* to reach him, and, clearly it made no sense. "Where do you suppose they mean to place this damn thing?"

"I don't write 'em, Skipper, I just pass 'em along," said Trevor.

"But, who does? I mean, listen to this: 'She will be passing through your area . . .' Where the hell is that? This is the stupidest dispatch I've ever seen. It's addressed to every submarine from Australia to the north of Japan. How the hell are we supposed to know where the *Awa Maru* is?"

"Well," Trevor said, "they're giving her a six-day leeway. That could put her almost anywhere, even if they had her on track. I don't think anyone knows where the damn thing is. Least of all ComSubPac."

But ComSubPac and almost everyone else operating out of those waters did know what the *Awa Maru* was and where she was going. The official story of who-knew-what-when was constructed later by Commander Richard T. Speer, U.S. Navy. The story appeared in a document called "Proceedings," published in April 1974 for the United States Naval Institute.

The author was graduated from the University of Minnesota in 1950 and was commissioned at Officers' Candidate School in Newport in 1952. Earlier, as an enlisted man, Speer had served aboard the *Seafox,* the sister ship of the *Queenfish.* Commander Speer is currently head of Ships' History Branch, Naval Historical Center. Since he has spent his life in the Navy and continues to work under its official auspices, one would expect him to be somewhat less than objective in his reporting. But his chronicle—at least that part of it reported here, which traces the *Queenfish* through the chain of misplaced and misdirected messages that culminated in the first and only message to be read on board by Houffman concerning the *Awa Maru*—appears accurate:

The story begins in mid-1944 when the U.S. government, concerned over the unsatisfactory conditions existing in Japanese prisoner-of-war camps, contacted the Japanese government through Swiss intermediaries for the purpose of furnishing relief supplies to these camps.

With the severing of the sea lanes between the Malay Peninsula and the Japanese homeland, the Japanese government received these initiatives with favor. In exchange for the transfer of a relatively small amount of relief supplies to the prisoner-of-war camps under a guarantee of safe passage, the relief ship could additionally be loaded with thousands of tons of vital war materials and, on her return, transport hundreds of critically needed stranded Japanese merchant seamen as well as a full load of desperately needed raw materials to feed the Japanese war industry.

The evidence of these motivations was the assignment of the huge *Awa Maru* for the delivery of about two thousand tons of relief supplies.

Another, more insidious motivation may be attributed to the Japanese government. The homeward route initially described for the *Awa Maru* took her through waters between the Ryukyu Islands and the coast of China, which U.S. Intelligence sources had known for months were heavily mined.

Richard Voge wrote: "It is impossible to conceive that the authorities responsible for laying out the original route were ignorant of this mined area, and the only reasonable conclusion is that the false route was prescribed as a ruse to convince us that the area concerned was safe for navigation. Had our own intelligence service been less efficient, it probably would have worked, and many of our submarines might have been lured to their doom."

Consequently, in November 1944, the Japanese took delivery of two thousand tons of relief supplies which had been sent from the United States via Siberia. Through an exchange of diplomatic notes with Japan on 13 December 1944, and again on 30 January 1945, the U.S. government agreed that the ship designated by the Japanese for the transport of relief supplies to prisoner-of-war camps in the East Indies would be accorded safe passage.

In early February 1945, the Japanese informed the United States that the *Awa Maru* had been designated to

transfer the relief supplies and furnished a detailed itinerary of her transit to the East Indies and return to the
Japanese home islands.

The Japanese requested and received from the U.S.
government a reconfirmation of the guarantee of safe
passage on 13 February 1945.

In the interim, the U.S. Navy had dispatched a message concerning the *Awa Maru* to all submarines at sea
in the Pacific. Whereas it was standard procedure to
cipher nearly all radio messages, this particular dispatch
was sent in plain language to ensure timely and accurate
reception by its addressees.

The message specified the exact route and schedule of
the *Awa Maru*, gave her description, and directed all
submarines to allow her to pass unmolested. Specific
details concerning her identification were provided:

AWA MARU WILL BE PAINTED WITH A WHITE CROSS
ON EACH SIDE OF FUNNEL. STOP. CROSSES TO BE IL-
LUMINATED ELECTRICALLY AT NIGHT. STOP. WHITE
CROSS ON TOP OF BRIDGE. STOP. WHITE CROSS ON
SECOND AND FIFTH HATCHES. STOP. TWO WHITE
CROSSES ON EACH SIDE OF SHIP. STOP. ALL NAVIGA-
TIONAL LIGHTS TO BE LIGHTED AT NIGHT . . .

As was the case with all important messages to submarines, this dispatch was broadcast three times on each
of three successive nights . . . a total of nine transmis-
sions. Thus, it would seem reasonable for higher authority to presume that the necessary precautions had
been taken to ensure the *Awa Maru*'s safe passage.

It was at this point, however, that circumstances existing on board the *Queenfish* were to provide the first link
in the incredible chain of events which resulted in the
sinking of the *Awa Maru*.

The *Queenfish* was a highly regarded submarine. Commanded by Commander Raymond Michael Houffman.
She had three very successful war patrols to her credit
prior to the *Awa Maru* incident. Houffman was a graduate of the Naval Academy, class of 1932, where he was
a two-time All-America football player and a ranking
intercollegiate baseball player. His class annual described
him as "the ideal classmate."

Following battleship duty, Houffman received submarine training in 1937 and served in the older S-boats for

the next six years, ultimately commanding the U.S.S. S-14 *Panama* in 1942. Ordered to the Portsmouth, New Hampshire, Navy Yard in October 1943, Houffman supervised the fitting out of the newly constructed *Queenfish* and, upon her commissioning in March 1944, assumed command.

By any set of standards, the crew of the *Queenfish* was a superb assemblage of trained submarine professionals. In the words of Captain Donald A. Kemp, USN (ret.) then a lieutenant attached to the *Queenfish* and a veteran of eleven submarine war patrols: "*Queenfish* had one of the truly outstanding submarine ward rooms of World War II in terms of professionalism and sheer experience."

By the time of her fourth war patrol . . . the officers represented a collective total of forty-two submarine war patrols among them . . . an impressive figure even at that late stage of the war.

The enlisted personnel were of similar makeup in terms of experience. Not only was there assigned to the *Queenfish* a significant number of veterans from previous Pacific action, but Houffman had succeeded in bringing nine top-flight fellow crew members with him from the *Panama* when he was detached from the S-14.

What sort of commanding officer was Houffman?

As his performance on the *Queenfish*'s first three war patrols was to attest, Houffman was one of the finest submarine skippers of World War II. He is described by Captain Kemp as ". . . an athlete, capable, aware of his own abilities . . . a master of submarine tactics . . . spent twenty-five hours a day on his job . . . possessed all of the elements of a wartime leader . . . high-strung but sensitive . . . observed everything going on . . . was everywhere all the time, essentially never slept . . . evinced great confidence in his crew. . . ."

In short, Raymond Houffman was the sort of wartime submarine commander from whom great things could be expected.

Houffman was quick to prove himself. After the *Queenfish*'s first war patrol, Houffman was cited for sinking 48,000 tons of enemy ships and rescuing eighteen British and Australian prisoners of war who were survivors of a Japanese ship which had been sunk by U.S. submarine action. For these efforts he was awarded the Navy Cross.

On the *Queenfish*'s second war patrol, Houffman succeeded in sinking 55,000 tons of hostile shipping and for
this action was awarded a second Navy Cross. On his
third and fourth war patrols, Houffman won the Silver
Star and Bronze Star medals, respectively.

The *Queenfish* received the Presidential Unit Citation
for her accomplishments during her first war patrol. This
truly impressive record of performance of duty was soon
to be called into question as a result of the sinking of
the *Awa Maru*.

Returning to the circumstances surrounding the sinking of the *Awa Maru*, it will be recalled that a plain-
language message was dispatched by the Commander in
Chief, U.S. Fleet, on 7 February 1945, which provided
information concerning the *Awa Maru*'s itinerary and
appearance and stipulated that she would be granted safe
passage throughout her transit.

At the time of the transmission of this message, the
Queenfish was at sea en route from Hawaii to Saipan
prior to the commencement of her fourth war patrol.
Houffman relates that atmospheric conditions during the
three-day period of this message's transmission were so
bad that the *Queenfish* was unable to obtain a version of
the plain-language message ungarbled sufficiently to
make sense.

Not much concern was evinced since, throughout the
war, experience demonstrated that almost all messages of
import were cryptographed.

Consequently, a garbled, plain-language message was
not a great cause of excitement on board the *Queenfish*
during relatively tranquil transit from Pearl Harbor to
Guam. Houffman was confident that his communications
officer, Lt. (jg) M.W. Bass, would be able to procure a
copy of it upon arriving in port at Guam prior to
commencing patrol. The first link in the sealing of the
Awa Maru's fate had been forged.

In early March, the *Queenfish* arrived at Guam, where
she received another message which never came to the
attention of the commanding officer. Subsequent to the
initiation of the original message concerning the track of
the *Awa Maru*, the Japanese government dutifully informed the U.S. State Department of a change of the
homeward route, conveniently taking her clear of the
Japanese mine field alluded to earlier.

The revision to the itinerary of the *Awa Maru* was the

subject of a message to all U.S. submarines in the Pacific which was duly transmitted three times nightly during the period 6–8 March 1945.

Throughout this time, the *Queenfish* was in port at Guam, alongside the submarine tender *Fulton*. A plain-language copy of this message which amended the *Awa Maru*'s return track to Japan was received on board the *Queenfish* from the communications section of the submarine tender *Fulton* and was filed.

For reasons still unknown, Houffman was never informed of the contents of this message. The second link in the chain of circumstances leading to the *Awa Maru*'s demise had been forged.

The *Queenfish*'s fourth war patrol was to take her to the area of the Formosa Strait, where she would conduct wolfpack operations in company with the submarines *Spot* and *Seafox*. As was customary, a briefing team from the staff of Commander, Submarine Force Pacific Fleet (ComSubPac), flew into Guam and briefed the three officers on the operations to be conducted. At no time during the briefing was the subject of the *Awa Maru* raised . . . the third link in the chain was forged.

The *Queenfish* departed Guam on 9 March 1945, to commence her fourth war patrol. The ensuing weeks were largely uneventful. At this stage of the war, Japanese shipping was extremely sparse, and the *Queenfish* was chiefly occupied with avoiding hostile aircraft operating out of Taiwan.

On 17 March, the *Spot,* having expended all her torpedoes during an attack the previous night, departed the area to proceed to Saipan for reload. Houffman assumed command of the wolfpack, now consisting of the *Queenfish* and the *Seafox*. The next few days continued to be uneventful.

On 28 March 1945, in order to refresh the minds of the submarine commanding officers at sea, ComSubPac sent another message concerning the *Awa Maru.*

This message in cryptographed form...

And that was the message received on board that morning, the one PCO Steve Trevor handed to Commander Houffman on the cigarette deck, the one that could put the *Awa Maru* anywhere. Anywhere at all.

Wait a minute, for Christ sake; just wait a minute. I want to get something in here, something they never talk about in these goddamn books.

I mean, I've read them all. All the horseshit, right? War at sea, for Christ sake. Great socking battles, ships and guns and boats and bombs and torpedoes and all of it described by some retired admiral who saw it out in a plotting room somewhere. The big scene is when he comes down with chalk poisoning, or some damn thing. I mean, I've read the things.

And the submarine books where you've got some ex-skipper who everyone at the time considered as a candidate for Bellevue, comin' on with his great campaigns, his patrols, like he was the only one around. When he mentions anyone else, he calls them "the men" . . . so you get things like: "So the men, of course, knew I was right when, our torpedoes expended, I elected to drive the sub through the hull of the Jap carrier," and: "Sure, we had our disagreements. But, when we docked in Pearl and the men carried me off the sub on their shoulders, I knew all was forgiven, that they knew I won the war. . . ." Things like that.

And these books always have a kind of apologia in the front. You know. "To the families of the men without whom he would not have won his medals."

And in the opening paragraph, he gets right into his regrets, apologizing for the curious circumstances surrounding the last patrol which permitted him, the captain, to be the sole survivor on the sub, then saying that, while he realizes that may seem strange, he wants to assure the families that "those things happen in war" because—you guessed it—"war is hell."

And in all the books, every one of them, the action described "turned the tide of the war." You know, that goddamn tide has been turned more times than they flush toilets in a dysentary ward.

I mean, Jesus Christ. Have you ever read this Kennedy thing? Skipper of a PT boat, for Christ sake. Won the war, hands down, right? Look. Right out of boot, they give you a test. If you couldn't tell a square knot from a pipe wrench, they gave you a PT boat and sent you out. If you didn't come back, they knew where the enemy was.

But, bad as they are, I read them—the books. All of them. Anything to do with war on the sea. And not one gets into the thing we thought about then. I don't say this thing is uppermost in your mind, but it's there. Anybody who's been to sea will tell you it's there.

The thing that you thought about was the sea.

You had the enemy, sure, but you also had the sea. And anyone who tells you the sea is not a hostile environment has probably never left the farm in North Dakota. It's there, the sea, and it works on you. Always, in the back of your mind somewhere, you're thinking—you're thinking about surviving the sea, you're thinking of swimming on it, drowning in it. It's there, the sea, and it will be there long after the crazy men floating on it quit blowing each other into it.

It's there. It makes its own rules, plays its own game. I mean, shit. Think about it. When a storm hits, the war stops. I mean, that's it. If you're still around when the winds die, you can play war some more. But you do it on her terms. You better do it on her terms.

So, what I'm sayin' is, they don't talk about that much in these war books. They don't talk about it much at all. But we did. We talked about it, we thought about it. If a depth charge took us, or a torpedo, and we made it out—what then? How long can you stay on the surface and survive? How long can you take the blinding sun in the day, the freezing in the night? Till you say "to hell with it." How long until you don't want to survive?

I remember on the first patrol we dragged up an Aussie pilot who had been out there four days. For four days he had been floating around on his own trousers, for Christ sake. You know, he'd swing them over his head, the trousers knotted at the ankles, until he caught enough air in them to hold him up. They'd hold air for maybe fifteen minutes and he'd have to fill them all over again. For four days and nights this guy did that. His buddy, doing the same thing, was lost on the second day out.

From the beginning there had been sharks. One had bumped this guy's leg in passing on the first day. I mean, shit, can you imagine that? On the second day, his buddy starts yelling at him. They had drifted maybe twenty yards apart. This Aussie thought his buddy was pointing out a ship on the horizon. When he turned back to him, he was gone; the water around where he'd been was blood-red and boiling. I mean, Jesus, that would make you think, right?

Anyway, we get him on board after four days. And he's not talkin'. I mean, he's not sayin' a word. They rigged a bunk for him on the reloads in the forward torpedo room, carried him in, and laid him down. He wouldn't eat, drink, or talk about it. He had lain there for two days, on his back, starin' straight up.

I pulled nursemaid duty on the second night. I was reading, sittin' on the skids, everybody else was sacked out, when he spoke for the first time.

"Gov'," *he says. He said it so quietly I didn't know whether he had said anything or not. He was still looking at the torpedoes above him, as he'd been doing since they'd bunked him out. So I leaned over to him, and, just as quiet, with that Aussie accent, he says,* "How high did they get me, Governor?"

"What do you mean?" *I says.*

"My legs. How high did they get me?" *I still didn't get it. He thought about it awhile, still looking up, not blinking.* "I'm talkin' 'bout my legs, Gov'. How much did the sharks get?" *I told him his legs were okay. And still not lookin' at me, I can see he's mad, right?*

"Don't give me any flamin' crap," *he says.* "Tell me 'ow much of my legs those bloody bastards took."

"They didn't take anything," *I tell him.* "Your legs are okay." *But he gets madder yet, so I lay it on the line.* "Look, Charlie," *I tell him,* "I ain't no doctor, but I can tell two legs when I see 'em, and you got both of 'em."

But it's no good. He's got to see for himself. So I pull back his blanket and lift him up so he can focus on his legs. So he's quiet, sittin' up, lookin' at his two legs, right? Blinking now, and seeing his legs like he's looking at them for the first time in his life. I'm about ready to lay him down again when he lets out with a shriek that would curl the toenails on a platoon of cannibals.

I mean, Jesus. People came slidin' out of their racks like we'd been hit by half the Jap fleet. This guy yellin' all the time. We had to get Doc out to sedate the bastard. He couldn't be convinced. Every time he'd look at his legs, he'd see two bloody stumps. I'll bet he sees them to this day.

The sea, you know? It was a part of what you fought when you fought a war on it. I mean, you figure it. You get hit, you make it up and out, how long can a guy dog paddle, right? I mean, this wasn't the infantry. You didn't lay there for a squad of corpsmen to drive up and cart you away in a Red Cross ambulance, for Christ sake. If you made it to the surface, whatever was left of you, that was only the beginning. For you, the war had just begun.

Figure it.

IX

Date: March 29, 1945
Place: Aboard the *Awa Maru,* in the South China Sea east of
      French Indochina
Time: 2200 hours

The woman who responded to Captain Hamamura's knock
showed only a brief flutter of recognition in her eyes as she
stepped back, bowing, to usher him into the quarters formerly
occupied by the ship's navigator, now occupied by Lieutenant
General Kawasuki Kodamo. She no longer wore the brightly
colored madras she had worn when they met in the streets of
Singapore but was instead dressed in a light-colored, brocad-
ed gown cinched at the waist by a black satin obi. Her hair,
piled high and contained with a comb, was lightly lacquered.
She moved back in a series of deferential bows to where the
lieutenant general was seated at a long, low table. The general
did not look up from his reading even when the captain
seated himself on the pillow opposite him. First, there was to
be the ceremony of the tea, which the woman performed on
her knees with a series of smooth, delicate moves.

The general waited for her to finish and to move away
before he looked up from his papers.

"I hope all is well with you and your family, Captain
Hamamura. They look forward to your return?"

"Thank you, General. A family always looks forward to
the return of a man from the sea." He did not think the
general knew, and he did not want to tell him, that his entire
family had been killed in the first American air raid over
Tokyo three years before.

"I am pleased, good Captain, that you have taken time to
come here in response to my request." Though he was
making an effort toward congeniality, a trace of sarcasm
flattened the tone of the general's voice.

"As I am pleased to be here," Hamamura replied.

"Hamamura," the general said, "I would like you to tell me the speed you are maintaining."

"I have set our speed out of Singapore. It is set at sixteen knots; it remains sixteen knots."

The flesh that hung from the cheekbones of the general had taken on an angry flush.

"I understand this ship is capable of making twenty knots. Is that correct?"

"Absolutely, General. Under normal circumstances, she will do twenty."

"Since, Captain, you acknowledged receiving my second message inviting you here, I must assume you did not receive my first, the one sent up with your steward. Is that right?"

"I received both messages, General," Hamamura said quietly.

"Just as I thought, Hamamura. Just as I thought. You will tell me, Captain, why you have elected to ignore a direct order by a lieutenant general of the Imperial Army. An order which required you to increase speed."

Hamamura took a long, slow sip of tea, putting distance between the sharpness of the general's last retort and what he would say. It would not serve anyone to escalate this into a shouting contest. When Hamamura spoke, he spoke quietly.

"You are not, forgive me for saying, General, a man of the sea, and you could not know the conditions under which a captain sets the speed of his ship, but I would like to try to explain them to you. I'll try to be brief. We are carrying far more than this ship is designed to carry. I have mentioned this to you before.

"The speed I have set," he continued, "is not set casually but based on what we can safely maintain during—"

"Are we back to the matter of safety, Captain?"

"I have considered little else, General. As long as the weather holds, the speed of sixteen knots is what we can safely maintain. We are nearly an hour ahead of the posted itinerary, and we are gaining. I expect to hit inclement weather. When we do, we shall lose what we've gained. An increase of speed would be unjustifiable, reckless, and would place an unwarranted strain on the diesels and on the stability of the ship. Since we—"

"I am going to try to hold my temper, Captain, but I'd like you to appreciate the difficulty of that." The general shoved his teacup away and reached for the papers he had been reading when Hamamura came in.

"I have no doubt, Hamamura, that you are a man of the sea

and know—within that tiny world—something about your ship, its safety and capabilities. What you do not know, honorable Captain, is what is contained in this." He slapped the packet of papers he held in one hand with the back of the other.

"These, Captain, are military assessment papers. Since you are a man of the sea, you wouldn't be expected to know such things. Indeed, since they carry the stamp of high security, you would not be permitted to know. But I think it would not be a breach of security for me to provide you a very brief summary.

"Each minute we lose to your concern for safety is a minute that we cannot supply the men who fight this war with the materials and ammunition they need to continue it. And these papers spell out very clearly how important those minutes are. As we talk, Captain, the enemy is amassing their ships for a landing on Okinawa. Our security indicates that they will begin shelling the island shortly, that they will soften a beachhead and land. Our security also indicates that we will, in the end, sacrifice Okinawa, that we are clearly overpowered. But we will make that sacrifice at a high cost to the enemy. Of that you can be assured.

"What we're buying, Captain, is time. Time. The same time you, sir, are squandering with your petty concern over diesel engines!"

The woman, attuned to the tone the conversation had suddenly taken, moved in quickly. She had been trained well. Kneeling, nodding her head first to the general and then to the captain, she poured tea, smiling, looking down, flirtatious. When she rose, she did so in one continuous, liquid movement. By the time she backed away from the table, the general's anger had diminished. She had learned well her lessons in timing, Hamamura thought.

"The reason we are so indebted to time, my able Captain, is the need to prepare ourselves for the final eventuality, the invasion of our homeland by the Allied Power criminals. Once we are prepared—and what we carry tonight will go a long way toward that preparation—then time will once again become meaningless."

"It seems to me, General, that what is important is that we make it to the homeland at all. In my judgment, whatever the need, sixteen knots is the limit at which we can prudently travel."

When the stocky general rose, it was not with the grace of

the woman who had risen earlier. But he did rise quickly. Hamamura joined him.

"Captain, you are an old man. I have wasted too much time in talking to one who can no longer hear. But you will hear this, and you will hear it well: go now to your place of command and make your orders clear. You will increase your speed from sixteen knots to whatever this . . . this obscenity of a ship of yours will do!"

Captain Hamamura made no move to go. "General," he said, "I have listened patiently to you, and now I'd like to say a few things." It would come out now, Hamamura thought. He was finished with his silent rage. He felt an easing in his chest, an easing of the tightness that had been there, he recognized now, for years.

"I am sorry that there were those in our country who permitted themselves to yield to the folly of you and men like you—selfish, military adventurists.

"I am sorry that I and men like me did not, from the beginning, stand up to the bloody insanity of this war.

"I am sorry that so many good men were silent in the beginning. By our timidity, our cowardice, and our silence, we condoned this lunacy, and I am sorry for that. In that respect, I—we—are as guilty as you.

"For me, General, the war ended almost before it began. It ended, my good General, when a bomb flattened my home and the peaceful family in it—the same family you so kindly inquired about.

"I'm sorry that my love for my country and the most honorable emperor who rules it was not strong enough to compel me to speak out—no, shout out—my abhorrence for what we have permitted.

"You're right about one thing, General. I am an old man, many years older than you. And, while age can make it harder for one to hear, it makes it easier for one to speak. The consequences seem less important.

"Finally, General, there is one more thing I am sorry for. I am sorry that you do not realize that you no longer speak to me from a military headquarters but from the confines of my own vessel. As long as we are at sea, I give orders, I do not take them. We will proceed at sixteen knots!" Hamamura turned and started out.

"Hamamura," the general called after him, his voice low, resolute. "You are a traitor and shall be shot in Moji."

Hamamura stopped and turned back. "No, General," he

97

said quietly, "it is not I who is the traitor. Should I be shot in Moji, I shall die the good death; I shall die for the love of my country, my ancestors, and my family, and I shall die for what I believe.

"There is no better death."

When the Allies engaged in all-out war with the Japanese, they discovered that they were locked into combat with an enemy they knew very little about, an enemy whose culture was so different from that in the West that the measuring stick that was used to size up other nations had to be cast aside. Here was a country, a people, with sharply different ideas of good and evil, a country whose politics, religion, and economic life were so bizarre, to the West at least, as to render them otherworldly, beyond comprehension.

In the absence of understanding, the West was quick to arrive at conclusions about their Eastern enemy—conclusions based on Western logic and ideology. Thus was born misunderstanding.

The Japanese, we said, were clearly heartless and cruel. We ignored evidence that they were also extremely generous and caring.

The Japanese, we said, were insolent and overbearing. We tried to ignore the evidence that they were also unprecedentedly polite.

They were, we said, a nation of militarists, of warriors with bloody swords. It was not easy for us simultaneously to accept that this was a nation of aesthetes, of writers, painters, and flower arrangers.

The Japanese, we said, sought and revelled in war. We chose not to acknowledge that they also sought peace, harmony, and quiet contemplation of matters far removed from war.

The Japanese, we said, would follow their emperor, literally, to the ends of the earth; that, to the man, they regarded him as a living, infallible, godlike ruler. In this, and only in this, we were right.

Until we accepted the host of contradictions that were the Japanese, we had to rely on our clichés. It was easier that way. Inaccurate, but easier. They were, after all, our enemies. It is easy to condemn enemies on a wholesale basis.

Learning about so strange a culture was a slow process for those in the West.

As victory over Japan became imminent, as it became clear

that they would not be able to hold their occupied territories and would be driven back to their homeland to stand or to fall, the West tried to come to grips with the terrible possibility that Japan might never surrender, that instead she might stand and fight to the last. To take the war into Japan's cities and countryside would be the costliest exercise in history, to lives on both sides.

Would this culture, with its allegiance to Hirohito, make the final sacrifice? Were they contemplating the "glorious death" on a national scale? Would the emperor ask for his country's suicide? And if he did, would the Japanese comply? Every indication pointed to one inescapable conclusion: the Allies would win the war, over Japan's dead bodies.

Suicide, the deliberate seeking of one's own death, is the final tribute, the last sacrament of the religion of *Giri-ninjo*. From the days of the samurai, this traditional means of death has been used by the Japanese to recover from the humiliation of defeat or betrayal. It is steeped in ritual and is a strong part of the Japanese military character, then as now.

The *gyo kusai*, or "glorious death," is a device that has been used throughout Japan's history to make an apology to the world. The final gesture, if handled ritualistically, supposedly earns points for those left behind in this world and for he who departs to the next.

David Bergamini, writing in *Japan's Imperial Conspiracy*, gave this account of the method employed centuries ago, a method still practiced today:

Six centuries ago, a retainer of the southern dynasty, after surrendering his army to a general of the northern dynasty, had asked his captors to bear witness to the fact that he had surrendered for the sake of his men and not out of fear of death.

Kneeling in front of them, he had deliberately cut open his belly and pulled out his entrails, explaining the while that he was dying by the most prolonged and agonizing method that he knew.

Since this time, the painful ceremony of *hara-kiri* or belly cutting, of *seppuku* or intestinal incision as it was called by the fastidious . . . had been ritualized and observed by every man of honor who wished to "prove his sincerity" before passing over into the spirit world.

As the war turned against Japan, squads of kamikaze pilots, for the most part young farmboys without wartime skills that could aid Japan, were given a quick course in aviation. The course was limited to takeoff and diving skills. There was no need to clutter the minds of these young dedicates with landing techniques. A well-placed suicide crash could sink a destroyer at relatively little cost to the Japanese government. The real bonus, of course, was the honor that farmboy could bring to his homeland and his family.

Because this method of committing the ritualistic deed departed so radically from tradition, Hirohito and his policy makers were pressed into a campaign of selling this updated version of the glorious death to his countrymen. It required some imaginative public relations efforts to make it work. But, work it did.

From the lowest echelon to the highest, suicide was used to pay the final courtesy to the emperor.

As the war drew to a close, War Minister Mitsu, a high-ranking member of the Hirohito regime, carefully drew out the calligraphy that was his memorial. He was clad in a white shirt given to him by the emperor, his belly bound by the traditional white scarf.

He had been drinking sake by the mugful.

His closing sentence, in prose, was, "In the conviction that [our] sacred land will never perish, I offer my life to the emperor as an apology for the great crime."

He laid out the memorials he had written, as well as a picture of his son who had been killed in battle a year before. There, in an enclosed veranda off his bedroom, sunlight streaming through the cracks of the wooden shutters, he assumed a kneeling position. He took a short sword, *wakizashi*, in his right hand, a dagger, *tanto*, in his left. Focusing on an edge of light spilling into the room from a crack in the shutters, he sank the short sword into his well-muscled abdomen below the lowest rib on his left side. The sword had been honed to a razor edge. The sharpness served him well as he wrenched the sword to the right through his stomach and then sharply upward.

There was a formula for a death like this and he followed it to the letter. With blood spilling from the wound, he waited, with a sharpening sense of curiosity, for death to take him.

It was not to be that easy.

With the dagger still in his left hand, he reached around to the right side of his neck, feeling for, then locating, the carotid artery.

His brother-in-law rushed into the veranda and kneeled in the blood alongside him. "May I have the honor of assisting you?" Despite his excitement, he spoke formally, with all the tonal control he could muster.

At last Mitsu shook his head. He sank the dagger into his neck. It missed the carotid artery and instead hit the cervical vein. It would take still more time.

Mitsu began to weave from side to side like a fighting bull about to drop. When at last he sank to the ground, he was unconscious but still writhing. His brother-in-law waited for death to come for almost an hour before he called in a medical corpsman.

With a final shudder, Mitsu succumbed to the less-than-ritualistic plunge of a hypodermic needle.

With the frightening specter of mass suicide confronting the Allies, and with the absolute dedication demonstrated time and again to Emperor Hirohito by his people, the Western powers approached the apparently inevitable Allied landing on Japan with a great deal of consternation. Would the Japanese immolate themselves on a pyre of honor for the sake of their emperor? And would he, in one last reckless siege of madness, spell ruin to an ageless civilization?

For centuries the Japanese had been inculcated with the infallibility of the emperor; there were no laws or moral standards that could be applied to this bespectacled, moon-faced man. He was beyond reproach.

His dictums had set Japan on a reckless rampage of territorial conquest and murder, a conquest that was now drawing to a painful close. Even in those fading days of despair, fervent emotionalism and national pride continued to rise from a proud, honorable people.

Their pride and honor was not diminished by the havoc wreaked by the two great bombs that dropped on Hiroshima and Nagasaki, spelling the end of one war and the irretrievable threat of world ruin should another begin.

For Japan, with pride, honor, and emperor intact, the signing at Tokyo was the surrender only of an approach to a goal it would live to realize.

The postwar battle was on—this one waged with money.

Now she rose from the earth of her small farms like the tiny mustard seed, sprouting a thousandfold to world prominence and insatiable conquest.

On whose wealth was this twentieth-century transformation built? The economic miracle we attribute to this small nation of industrious men may not have been a miracle at all, but rather the carefully devised ambition of a few powerful men who planned, then implemented, the rape of all Asia, a rape that bore the child of economic power.

At the war's end, Emperor Hirohito's family holdings reportedly stood at about 3 billion yen—about $200 million —the bulk of it in undepreciated land, gold, and jewels.

Working hand in hand with the Imperial family and its overflowing vaults were the great cartel families of Japan. These all-powerful industrial families held absolute rule over Japan's foreign trade, heavy industry, and banking.

Billions of dollars' worth of gold, paper currencies, and jewels, stored in vast warehouses from China to Java, found their way to Japan before the war's end, there stored in scattered vaults and backland caves known only to a handful of the Japanese elite.

As the postwar economy took hold, the cartel families broke out of their traditional roles and expanded into electronics, shipping, international banking, machinery, gadgetry, transportation—anything saleable to the insatiable appetite of Western civilization.

The allegiance to the emperor never died—it changed, shifted gears; then that same fervor that had been applied to the emperor was turned to the new ruling power of the island nation: The Employer.

Today, the Japanese could no more live without their televisions, movie theaters, rapid transit systems, motorcycles, supermarkets, and fast-food chains than Americans could; they are wholly a product of the twentieth century.

But we lose sight of the salient point: If the great cartel families of Japan had not accumulated such vast wealth from the plunder of Asia and Southeast Asia, would she still have become the third largest industrial power on earth?

In his treatise, *Japan—The Fragile Super Power,* Frank Gibney noted: "In Japan, the society is the job. The job is the society. Every man who enters a company equally shares in it. What counts is that he works for Mitsubishi. If he works for Mitsubishi, he is a Mitsubishi man. Most of his friends come from Mitsubishi. He drinks with them, golfs with them, but like siblings competing within a family which no one would think of leaving."

The economic and social power that the Mitsubishi company holds today in Japan stems from the contribution it made to the war effort years before. The Mitsubishi company was well known for shipbuilding in World War II and, in a small factory in Nagasaki, for turning out quality torpedoes and small arms.

Immediately following the war, the nation's economy, under the emperor's benevolent policies, fell into the hands of three great cartel families. These three—the Mitsubishi, the Sumitomo, and the Mitsui—were reported to have accumulated large fortunes by the end of the war. (The Mitsubishi company had accumulated a reported $175 million.)

These families and others spawned a growing list of products that were the first to compete with and then to threaten Western markets: automobiles, electronically sophisticated calculators, transistor radios, color televisions. In productivity, Japan's steel plants outpaced U.S. plants; in shipbuilding, Japan stands unchallenged. Her economic march since the war has never faltered.

While Japan controlled the shipping lanes during the early years of the war, from the tip of Java to the Sea of Japan, merchant vessels like the *Awa Maru*, laden with contraband collected by the Japanese procurement agencies, freely routed these riches to the banks and vaults of Japan's most powerful and favored families.

But as the Allies took over the sea lanes, there was no way to continue sending home the hoard of plunder. For almost a year, Japan waited. The warehouses in her far-off procurement points were fairly splitting at the seams with gold, silver, platinum, diamonds, ivory, jewels, artifacts, strategic metals, currencies, and paper securities from all her conquered and occupied territories. Each day, the stockpile grew.

As the heavily laden *Awa Maru* moved up through the South China Sea toward the entrance to the Formosa Strait —maintaining a steady sixteen knots—she carried what is believed to be the most valuable single load of plunder of the war; that loot, in time, would wring victory from defeat.

X

Date: March 30, 1945
Place: Aboard the *Queenfish,* heading for lifeguard station in
       waters off Shanghai
Time: 2000 hours

Old Ox had a lot of trouble with draw poker. Though he
played it with dedication, with passion, he almost always lost,
and lost badly. A part of it was just that—his unbridled
passion for the game. He had solemnly sworn off poker a
dozen times since leaving port twenty-one days ago.

But now it would be different. Under the lights of the
umpteenth running of the Charlie Chan movie in the crew's
mess, just as Charlie Chan's number-two son was being
admonished by his father for consorting with the Dragon
Lady, Ox had filled a jack-high straight flush. Bicca had
folded, but Boldern, Perez, and Easter remained. Ox would
be casual, he would control himself; he would not make the
mistakes he had made in the past.

Boldern, discarding three, was describing an incident
during shakedown exercises prior to the first patrol on the
Queenfish.

"I mean, how was I supposed to know, for Christ sake," he
said. "I had never heard the skipper was so touchy on those
words. He hadn't taken command more than ten days before,
and nobody knew anything about him."

"Where were you when you said it?" Easter asked.

"It was night and we were under lights—on the maneuvering watch. I was on deck with a heaving line when this
smart-ass seaman from the *Sunfish* flips me the bird, you
know?"

"What had you done to him?" Bicca asked.

"I don't even remember. Anyway, he flips me the finger,
right? How the hell was I to know Captain Houffman was
standing on the bridge?"

Easter laughed. "So you yelled to him, bigger'n hell, right?"

"No. It wasn't all that loud, but with the engines going and all the other things going on, I had to make it pretty clear, you know. What else you going to say to a smart ass like that?"

"So you called him a cocksucker," Easter said. "What did the skipper do?"

"You've never seen anything like it." Boldern picked up the three cards Easter had dealt and organized them in his hand. "He was on that deck in ten seconds flat, reading me up and down. It wasn't ten seconds after that, that the Shore Patrol had me off the boat heading for the brig. Five days."

"Shit," said Perez. While Perez could normally convey a lot of expression with his single-word vocabulary, it was unclear whether he was denigrating Boldern, the hand he'd been dealt, or the way in which Charlie Chan was reproaching his son.

"I never did get the bread and water, though," Boldern said.

"What do you mean?" Easter asked.

"That's what the old man told the Shore Patrol—five days, bread and water."

"The thing I could never figure out," Bicca said, squaring off the cards lying face-down before him, "was what he's got against the word *chow*. I can see, maybe, why he'd object to *cocksucker*, but how do you account for the word *chow*? I mean, how could that bother anyone?"

Perez opened the betting by shoving two matchsticks into the pot.

"That's interesting," said Easter, calling Perez's bet by sliding another two matches forward. "If *cocksucker* gets you five days, what does *chow* get you? Ox, the next time the skipper comes through, why don't you—"

When Easter stopped mid-sentence, the others at the table turned to see what he was looking at. It was Ox.

"Oh my God," said Bicca. "Ox has a hand!"

The trouble that Old Ox had with draw poker was his complete inability to maintain composure in the face of a good hand. Three of a kind or better came over Old Ox like a paralysis. The muscles in his forehead closed in concentration; his eyes began to water; moisture appeared on his upper lip. The casual smile he reached for worked in complete disregard to the rest of his face. He was able to hold the smile only at great cost. Muscles trembled in spasms at the corners of his mouth. He shoved fifteen matches into the pot.

"Jesus, Ox," said Easter, folding his cards and tossing them onto the discard pile. "It looks like you got a coronary occlusion, for Christ sake."

"Look at the grip," Bicca said. "Ox, come on, you're crushing your cards."

"Shit," said Perez, folding. Boldern followed.

After Ox collected the meager pot, the color in his face returned, he breathed evenly again, and the sweat on his hands began to dry. It was only money, he told himself.

Quartermaster Stan Jessops came in from watch in the control room. He had to duck under the light of the projector to get to the back table. The card game had stopped; everyone's attention was focused on the Dragon Lady as she moved up a long flight of stairs in a tight skirt.

"The skipper's really frosted," he said. After Jessops' problem with Edwards over the signing of the written order, Jessops had not heard about the deck gun again.

"What's up?" Boldern asked.

"The lifeguard duty off Shanghai. The captain can't figure why ComSubPac assigned *Queenfish* and not *Seafox*. It's two days dead in the water, you know, sittin' there shining a light in the sky, for Christ sake." It was not the first time the *Queenfish* had been called off patrol to serve as a night beacon for a B-25 bombing run.

"Yeah," said Bicca. "I thought we were heading up this patrol."

"I don't get the difference," Old Ox said. "They got war where we're going, same as we got where we've been." Since Ox was dealt two sixes and hadn't improved it in the three cards he drew, he could easily follow the conversation.

"Because," Easter explained, "if the Japs are still floating anything, chances are they're coming through the Formosa Strait with it. In and around the strait has always been the best hunting grounds. Anything to and from Singapore, Hong Kong, Sumatra, Borneo, they pretty well got to use the strait if they want a direct shot. Sure as hell they're not going to be toolin' around Shanghai."

"Well, you never know."

Ox had two ways of summing up a discussion. Either "you never know" or "you can't never tell." This philosophy had never earned him an argument.

"So he's pretty pissed, huh?" Boldern asked Jessops,

who, with two pairs, aces up, was already raking in his first pot.

"Yeah," Jessops replied. "It was the topper, you know. I mean, ever since Guam, the skipper's really been torqued. He's fightin' something. I don't know what it is, but I do know this: he wants action and he wants it bad. And it's more than that. He's worried. Something's up. And then, that goddamned Diefenbaker . . ."

"What did Diefenbaker do now?" Easter cut the cards for Perez. The movie had worked itself up to a shoot-'em-out in a dockside warehouse; Number-one son had taken what he described as "only a 'fresh' wound" in the shoulder.

"Well, Diefenbaker had carried the lifeguard message up for Lieutenant Bass, you know? It was about 1300 hours. We were all in the conn at the time. Well, hell, the old man reads it and hits the ceiling. I mean, he really blows up. So Diefenbaker stands there and waits for the old man to finish chewing out everybody and anybody connected with sending us to Shanghai. Then he turns the storm inside. I mean, it's there, it's just locked up. He's madder than hell, but he's quiet about it."

"What about Diefenbaker?" Boldern asked.

"That's what I'm getting to. He's been waiting all this time. Finally, he asks the captain whether he wants to respond to the message, but the skipper had already started calling out a course change. So, you could tell Diefenbaker didn't know whether to leave or not, and that's when he said it."

"Said what?" Ox still didn't have a good hand.

"Diefenbaker said, 'If you haven't anything further, sir, I haven't had chow yet.' "

"Jesus," Easter said. The game had abruptly come to a stop. "What did that do to the skipper?"

"Well, that's just it," Jessops said. "When he said 'chow,' everyone in the conn froze—officers, men, everybody. We all turned to see what the skipper would do. Well, after a minute, he turned to Diefenbaker and said, real quietlike, 'Okay.' "

"And that was it? Just 'okay'?" Easter was incredulous.

"That's all he said," Jessops replied. "Just 'okay.' "

Date: March 31, 1945
Place: Aboard the *Awa Maru*, approaching the South China coast, southeast of Hong Kong
Time: 2030 hours

107

Captain Hamamura's inspection tour had taken almost an hour. All was not well. From the engine rooms to the crew's quarters on the 02 level, up through the second-class passenger compartments on the 01 level, where he surveyed the two sick-bays, laundry and storage areas, then up again to the main salon on "A" deck, through the dining room, the first-class guest cabins, baths and heads, it was the same. Hamamura saw little that conformed to the health and safety regulations for a large vessel at sea.

Even "B" deck, directly below the bridge and his own quarters, was impossibly crowded. The ship's officers who normally occupied that deck had been moved below to make room for the more than twenty high-ranking officials who replaced them, each toting enough personal gear to supply a small civilization in relative comfort for decades.

Every inch of the *Awa Maru* was jammed with passengers and gear. Stairways and companionways were hopelessly clogged. Lifesaving equipment was inadequate; lifejackets and deflated rafts were being used as bedding and, in order to prevent further misuse, other jackets were locked away. Even in the event that they could be reached, by last count there were only 1,500 jackets for the 2,009 aboard.

The crowded conditions had severely taxed the ship's four galleys. The food-preparation compartments were being manned by off-watch oilers and wipers to supplement the regular personnel. Hamamura feared what an outbreak of dysentery could do to the already overburdened sanitary facilities.

There had been complaints, arguments, and demands from "A" deck's passengers as he made his rounds; complaints about the food, the sleeping accommodations, the lack of fresh water. He had posted guards on the stairwells leading to the first-class areas to keep the second-class passengers from spilling upward. But, judging from the crowds that now occupied the passageway, he suspected that the guards were accepting bribes. Soon the passengers would be moving up onto the officers' deck—maybe the bridge itself. He didn't want to contemplate that.

The electric lights that illuminated the ship and its white crosses at night had already been switched on. Now, as he headed toward the ladder to the bridge, where he would fill out his log, the lights were beginning to work against the deepening dusk. Though the seas were building, he had successfully kept the ship ahead of the following storm. It would be another clear night. It might be different when they neared the coast of China or if the diesels, which had begun to labor, failed to keep the vessel ahead of the storm. So far, there had been no contacts with the enemy.

As Hamamura started to head up the ladder, he recognized the woman at the rail. He turned back and walked toward her.

"I trust you are having a comfortable voyage," Hamamura said. She wore a light coat against the chill, her upturned collar framing her face like a cameo. Without makeup, she looked older than she had in the general's quarters, and somehow more fragile, vulnerable.

"Yes. Thank you, Captain." As she bowed, the lights caught and played in the blackness of her hair.

"Your husband is aboard?"

"Yes, Captain. He is below. But I have been refused permission to see him until we reach Moji."

"The Tank?"

She smiled and looked away. "Yes," she said. "The lieutenant general is very possessive."

"I thought he might be." The captain did not know how to say what he had in mind. "You are . . . you are satisfied with the decision you made which brought you aboard?"

Looking down, she appeared to think about that for a while. "I think, Captain, you and I are different in that respect."

"I would be interested in hearing how you see that difference."

"It is hard to explain, Captain, but I will try. I overheard you and the general in your discussion: it was difficult for me not to listen. You are convinced of your position and stood up to the general, even in the face of—"

"In the face of being shot," the captain said.

"Yes, Captain," she said quietly. The wind had freed a lock of hair, which she brushed back off her forehead. "That, sir, is a bravery that I do not possess."

The captain smiled. "It is not bravery when what one does is easy, natural. Standing up for what you believe is the easy part. The hard part is pretending to believe something you do not. The pretending takes a kind of bravery."

"Then, for me," she said, "I must do the hard part. I must pretend to the general that he pleases me. And that is not easy. But it does not make me feel brave."

"But you are doing this for your husband?"

"Yes," she said, "but it is also for myself."

"But you are convinced it is the right thing?"

"Can prostitution be right?" she asked.

"It can," the captain said, "if one is doing it for the right reasons."

"I guess," she said, turning her eyes away again, "I guess I do not know whether the reasons I have are the right ones."

Captain Hamamura waited as an Army general and two Air Force colonels passed. They did not acknowledge the captain and the woman. One of the colonels was telling a war story. One hand was an airplane, the other a boat. As he passed, he was making the sound of the airplane as it swooped toward the boat. So impressed was the other colonel that he repeated the noise of the aircraft and added to it the noise the bombs made. As the group moved off down the companionway, the general retold the story, using both hands to show the effect of the bombs on the boat.

Hamamura turned again to the woman. "It is hard sometimes to know what reasons are the right ones. Those men who just passed, and your husband, the Tank—they all believe their reasons for fighting this war are the right ones."

"But you do not," she said.

"No," the captain said. "I don't think there are any right reasons for war."

"Then you, Captain, are still in the hard part. It is harder for those who do not believe in this war than for those who do. And if you are in the hard part, Captain, and you are standing by what you believe, then, by your own definition, you are brave."

Hamamura smiled. "What you have said—whether it's true or not, it makes me feel good."

The woman smiled. "It is my training, Captain."

As Captain Hamamura again approached the ladder to the bridge, he met steward Shimata scrambling down.

"Captain, sir. They just sent me to find you, sir. They want you on the bridge immediately."

"Shimata," the captain said quietly, "if you'll step out of my way, I'll go up."

In the bridge, the ship's first officer and navigator were hunched over the shoulders of the radar operator. The first officer spun around at the sound of his steps. "Sir, we've got a contact. One vessel off the bow, range twelve thousand yards, and approaching."

"What about the lookouts?" the captain asked.

"Nothing yet, sir. It's too dark now for that distance, Captain."

"Have you taken action?"

"No, sir."

"Helmsman, maintain speed and course."

"Shall I sound—" The first officer was cut off abruptly.

"Sound no alarms," the captain said.

"Bearing 035° true, and still closing, sir," the radarman called.

Through the intercom came the crackle of the voice of the lookout:

"Surface vessel sighted, seven thousand yards off the starboard bow."

"Is it lighted?" the captain called into the box.

"Negative, sir."

"Identify."

"I cannot clearly tell, can't get a profile. It's approaching almost head-on, sir. It could be a submarine or torpedo boat, Captain. Appears too small for a destroyer."

"Bearing 030° true," the radarman called out. "Now on collision course and closing, speed about twenty knots, sir."

"Helmsman, maintain course and speed. Navigator, she's in good torpedo range?"

"Excellent range, but bad position, sir."

There was no sound on the bridge. The men waited, listening. The next sound could be the last sound any of them heard.

Finally the radarman broke the silence:

"Five thousand yards and still closing."

"I got a visual, sir." The first officer was using the binoculars. The radarman was the only one not looking in the direction of the sighting. There was only the rapidly approaching darkness. "It's an American sub, Captain." Another wait, then. Long, long seconds.

"Veering off, sir," the radarman called.

"Is it an end-around or are they veering?" the captain asked.

The first officer broke in, "They're veering off to the east, sir. We'll starboard them."

The enemy sub passed within a thousand yards, close enough for Captain Hamamura to make out the sail and, dimly against the skyline, some figures on the bridge.

XI

Date: April 1, 1945
Place: Aboard the *Queenfish,* returning to patrol area north-
west of Formosa
Time: 0100 hours

Those of the crew who talked about it later—and most of
them did—said that they found nothing particularly unusual
about the behavior of Commander Houffman that day, the
first day of April 1945.

He had always had that electric tenseness about him, and
while it was clearly visible that day, it wasn't unusual. And
when you considered that he was going into his twenty-third
day of a zero run, the longest span of inactivity any of them
had encountered, what else could you expect?

They said you had to understand about Houffman. He was
an aggressive skipper, and if he was aloof, reserved, and held
himself apart from his men—even maintaining a certain
distance from his fellow officers—it was because he felt that
that was his job. A good commander did keep himself apart.
A position of leadership demanded that, didn't it?

A good leader was a loner, and Houffman was all of that.
He confided in no one on personal matters, and if there was
anything else bothering him, few, if any, heard about it.
Anyway, with all the crap going on since Guam—the bowplane, the delays, the calls from his wife, then more than
three weeks of nothing—and finally this last thing off Shanghai—I mean, what the hell, they said. That kind of crap
would work on anybody.

And this Shanghai deal, they said. Getting called out of
patrol to head all-hell-and-gone up north on a lifeguard
function, for Christ sake. Then getting up there, only to have
the air raid or whatever the hell it was called off. I mean,
Jesus Christ, they said.

So he had been pretty stoked, and coming into that night it

got worse, a hell of a lot worse. But that wasn't a reflection on anything but the way things were. It didn't have anything to do with the captain and his ability to make the right decision, they said.

They agreed with Lieutenant Donald Kemp, who served as torpedo data computer operator that night, when he later described the commander as "a master of submarine tactics ... spent twenty-five hours a day on the job ... essentially never slept ... observed everything going on ... was everywhere all the time. ..."

I mean, that's the way he was, they said. Those of the seamen who talked about it later all agreed: Commander Houffman was a good leader, the kind of guy you ought to have heading up a sub, a guy you had confidence in. Sure, he had problems, but didn't we all?

All right. Maybe he did fly off the handle now and then. And maybe lately there had been a hell of a lot of that. There was no room in his world for mistakes, and damn little for inexperience. Maybe he wanted too much out of his crew sometimes, but you could say this for him: he didn't revel in the chicken-shit of inspections and regulations. If you did your job and didn't make mistakes, that's all he cared about.

Yeah, you could make a good case for the skipper being well steamed that night, they said. Particularly after that attack report from *Seafox*. I mean, Jesus Christ, they said, six damn hours after they found something to shoot at! Hell, we were—what?—maybe an hour, maybe two, from the scene when *Seafox* engages that Jap convoy. And do you think they're going to bring us in? Shit. Darvies, *Seafox*'s commander, he wants it all for himself, for Christ sake. So he waits for more than six hours, until we're hell-and-gone south of there, to tell us he got himself a convoy. I mean, what the hell?

You're damn right the old man was pretty stoked that night. Maybe he was a little more than just stoked. But wouldn't you be?

I mean, Jesus Christ, they said.

1 April 1945.
CONFIDENTIAL
U.S.S. QUEENFISH (SS393) — *Report of the Fourth War Patrol*

TIME: 0115 hours. ENTRY: After passing Tungung within visual distance, fog set in which persisted while we proceeded toward northwest Formosa.

TIME: 0930 hours. ENTRY. Fog lifted sufficiently to sight peaks on Formosa but closed in again shortly thereafter.

TIME: 1200 hours. ENTRY: Position—Latitude 25° 47' North; Longitude 121° 09' East.

TIME: 1300 hours. ENTRY: Dived for trim.

TIME: 1343 hours. ENTRY: Surfaced ... proceeded toward China Coast in vicinity of Tungkuen Light.

TIME: 1700 hours. ENTRY: Surfaced with SD (radar) contact at 14 miles, going away.

TIME: 1852 hours. ENTRY: Commenced paralleling 20 fathom curve to southward below Tungkuen Light in clearing visibility.

TIME: 1940 hours. ENTRY: Received SEAFOX attack report on convoy made at 1300 today. Assigned new patrol stations ... (NOTE: Corresponding confidential report—the 3rd War Patrol, U.S.S. SEAFOX, shows no entry of this delayed radio dispatch to the QUEEN-FISH.)

TIME: 2148 hours. ENTRY: Fog set in after we had passed Turnabout Island. Light abeam to starboard, distance: about 5 miles. (NOTE: Executive Officer Edwards, acting as navigator of the U.S.S. QUEENFISH, and performing his duties under increasing abdominal pains—he would later undergo an appendectomy—fixed a position from this visual sighting of what the Americans called Turnabout Island. Actually named Niu-shan Tao in Chinese, the deserted island had a lighthouse near its summit and was frequently used as a nautical landmark.)

TIME: 2159 hours. ENTRY: Changed course to 225° True, standing toward Ockseau Light.

TIME: 2200 hours. ENTRY: Made contact on single ship bearing 230° True at 17,000 yards range. Manned battle stations, commenced tracking and approach. Sent contact message to SEAFOX.

Commander Raymond Michael Houffman had taken to spending more and more time on the bridge. When it was late and he couldn't sleep, when he ran out of all the techniques that were supposed to make sleep possible, when battle scenes rose up in his mind in vivid detail and he would go through the things he had or hadn't done, correcting things here, adjusting things there, or when personal things made him sorry at first, then angry—when it became clear that these thoughts would continue, he sought the bridge and the quiet he sometimes found there. Like tonight. The fog, the chill of the strait, the feeling he was alone on a blackened sea.

This last, interminable patrol would complete it for Houffman. He and the war were winding down together. He had expected this war to be organized differently; that each successive patrol would offer more action, more opportunities, more decisions; that, coming into this last, he would have been working on, building from, an orchestration of events that would culminate in a dramatic, live-or-die last chapter.

But what Houffman felt that night, hunched against the cold that settled deep within his foul-weather jacket, was a kind of disappointment, a letdown. Twenty-three days of viewing the sea had settled like an undigested potato in the pit of his stomach. He wanted something more from this war before it was taken from him. Something more than returning with empty fuel tanks and a full load of fish.

The two men on the bridge with Houffman that night, Lieutenant (jg) Ivan "Billy" Williams and Lieutenant (jg) Jasper Giacoletti, officer and junior officer of the deck, knew enough to leave him to his own thoughts. When they talked to each other, they talked quietly, in hushed voices.

The moon directly above Houffman sometimes tunneled out of the fog to diffuse an otherworldly light to the mist that clung to and hovered over the water. It was late, quiet. He listened to the muffled throb of the diesels below and the sound the bow made cutting through the water. It was good being there. It eased the anger.

Sometimes, for minutes at a time, he'd forget how badly he needed a target.

Just before 2200 hours that night, he had gone down through the conning tower past CPO Doc Tobey, who was hunched over the radar screen, and into the control room.

Executive Officer Edwards, propped against the torpedo data computer, had been discussing with Ensign Monroe Kurtz the tactical aspects of surface warfare in the North Pacific during the epic battle of the *San Francisco*.

"Still pretty bleak up there, Skipper?" Edwards asked.

It took so long for Houffman to answer that Edwards considered rephrasing the question.

"Yeah, Bill. It's pretty bleak."

"Well, it can't go on forever like this. Skipper." Turning, Edwards resumed his conversation with Kurtz.

On the power phone, Houffman recognized the underlying fear that tugged at the voice of Tobey in the conning tower above him:

"I . . . Sir? I got something here. Captain, I've got radar contact at seventeen thousand yards . . . speed approximately sixteen knots."

The tension came back to Houffman. "Doc, keep tracking. Get me a true speed."

Edwards and Kurtz were looking at him. He said to Edwards, "Tracking party, man your stations." He said it quietly, firmly.

Within a split second, Edwards' words boomed back in an amplified echo over the PA system: "Tracking party, man your stations." That and the sound of the alarm charged the room.

RM3 Merville Easter should have known better. While it was not a national holiday, April Fools' Day was enough of one to make going into the forward torpedo-room head with a copy of Hemingway's *For Whom the Bell Tolls* risky at best. If he had put it together, the pattern of his being in the can and the number of times they had encountered targets on holidays, it might have given him pause.

But he had not put it together. The voice, "Man tracking stations," and the general alarm put it together for him. And put it together all at once, decisively.

What Easter said, then, turned out to be pretty appropriate to the occasion, though he hadn't considered the meaning of his comment before he made it. Startled, the alarm bolting through him like an electric shock, it had come out before he thought much of anything.

"Shit," he said.

Instantly, like Easter scrambling for his sonar station in the conn, everyone aboard—in bunk or out—moved.

Lieutenant Commander Trevor was the first of the fire party to reach the control room. On his heels were plot and assistant plot officers Ivan Williams and Mike Bass.

Houffman called to Trevor as he entered, "Tell that damned *Seafox* what we've got. For the hell of it, let's not make them wait six hours!"

116

Houffman headed through the conn up to the bridge, and when Trevor had seen that the *Seafox* was notified of the radar contact and position, he joined the captain. Trevor recalled later how Houffman looked when he approached him on the bridge:

"He was standing there, still as a stone. You know, just lookin' out. You couldn't see a damn thing. I don't think he heard me come up, because when he spoke he was speakin' to the fog, sort of, or out into the night. At first I thought he was talkin' to someone on deck, but he wasn't. There was something absolutely calm about his voice. I remember him sayin'—I remember his exact words—he said, 'Come on, come on, be there.' "

Seven days later, facing a general court-martial for the action he took that night, Commander Houffman was to file the following confidential written report to his superior officer:

U.S.S. QUEENFISH (SS393)
8 April 1945
In reply refer to SS393/A9

CONFIDENTIAL
From: the Commanding Officer
To: the Commander, Submarine Force, Pacific Fleet

1. On 1 April 1945, the U.S.S. QUEENFISH was conducting an offensive patrol against enemy forces in the waters of the East China Sea in accordance with an approved operation order of Commander Task Force 17.

2. At about 2115 zone time [all times noted are minus 8 zone], while on course 180° True, speed 8 knots, the ship navigational position was verified by visual sighting of Turnabout Island in conjunction with radar ranges and bearings which placed the QUEENFISH 4.9 miles bearing 090° True from this island. At this time, the sky was completely overcast, night-dark, with visibility estimated at about 10 miles.

3. At 2148, a fog bank enveloped the ship, reducing surface visibility to an estimated 200 yards. Continued to plot the ship's position by radar ranges and bearings on Turnabout Island. At 2159, changed course to 225° True, maintaining the same speed of 8 knots.

4. At 2200, radar contact was made on a single ship

bearing 230° True, distance 17,000 yards. The tracking party was immediately called to stations and the course of the ship changed to 050° True at 2210.

During the initial tracking stages, it was determined that the enemy ship was proceeding on courses from 050° True to 040° True at speeds of 17 to 18 knots.

Subsequent tracking prior to attack, however, changed the estimate of enemy course and speed to 045° True, 16 knots. During this phase, a navigational track of the movements of own ship was maintained by a quartermaster who utilized ranges and bearing on Turnabout Island, and plotted the changes in course and speed made by this ship while obtaining position for attack.

AT NO TIME DURING THIS APPROACH PHASE, AND LATER ATTACK PHASE, WAS IT SUSPECTED THAT THE APPROACHING SHIP WAS OTHER THAN A DESTROYER, OR DESTROYER ESCORT, AND THE APPROACH WAS CONDUCTED WITH THAT IDENTIFICATION IN MIND.

The decision as to this probable identity was predicated on the initial radar range at which the ship had been contacted, which corresponded to that obtained many times previously on own and enemy ships of a destroyer or destroyer-escort size.

Having used the radar for navigational purposes day and night for the past two weeks, and having recently obtained ranges as great as 32,000 yards on aircraft, there seemed to be no reason to doubt the efficacy of its operation at this time.

Additional factors which seemed to substantiate the probable identity of the combatant ship were:

—The relatively high speed of 16–17 knots in a dense fog.

—The proximity to the position of a torpedo attack made nine hours earlier by the SEAFOX which would tend to increase antisubmarine measures in this vicinity.

—And the course of the ship on what is believed to be the only route used by enemy shipping along this portion of the China coast.

5. At 2225, transmitted a contact report to the SEAFOX, who was in the near vicinity, including the navigational position and estimated course and speed of the enemy ship. Continued to track, and at 2239 notified the

SEAFOX that QUEENFISH was attacking from the starboard flank. The decision to carry out an attack at this time was influenced by the navigational position which indicated that an anticipated change of course would take place as the enemy ship rounded Turnabout Light. Considering the high speed of the approaching ship, it was unlikely that firing could be delayed until the arrival of the SEAFOX without jeopardizing the chances for a successful attack.

6. As the enemy ship approached the position at which the torpedo attack would commence, that portion of the bridge watch including the junior officer of the watch, after lookout, quartermaster, and commanding officer endeavored to sight the shape of the approaching ship, but with no success.

At this time, 2259, the moon was visible through a partial overcast by the fog blanket which persisted. Surface visibility, about 200 yards.

Trevor knew enough not to try to break through the icy quiet maintained by the lanky man next to him as the enemy vessel was tracked. Trevor had been sitting over coffee in the ward room when battle stations were sounded. After sending that first message to *Seafox*, he had to pass the conning tower and the men on radar and sonar to reach the bridge.

Both Houffman and Trevor knew where the ship ought to be and they strained to see it through the fog. Sometimes the moon would hover above them, filtered, ghostly; sometimes only the light of it worked through the fog, lending a sort of luminescence to the deck below them. Fog is not uncommon that near the China mainland at that time of the year. The late March winds blowing eastward across the vast mainland still carry the chill of winter in them. When they pass over the relatively warm waters of the strait, heavy to patchy fog results.

It seemed clear that the radar had picked up a destroyer, probably one crippled by an air attack and heading for cover as fast as her reduced power permitted. It seemed clear.

Anything else—anything running in less than emergency conditions—would have been groping cautiously through the fog at between eight and ten knots. It seemed clear.

But what seemed clear was not enough. To be certain would take a visual sighting.

Trevor tried looking to the side where the target should be, then back, in the hope that he'd catch movement, a glimpse, something that would register on the wall of a retina. It was an old trick. He saw a darkened hulk vaporize, reappear, then fade again. It was fog. It was an old trick that didn't work.

The tall, lanky man standing next to him, the man who had been silent for so long, spoke suddenly into the night. The words made Trevor jump. They were spoken in a hoarse whisper, flung out, hurled toward that empty place in the fog:

"You Jap bastards—where are you, you lowly Jap bastards?"

It wasn't the content of the words that stung Trevor. It was the way they were said. They came from a part of Houffman he hadn't been aware of, and they erupted in a way that made Trevor feel like an intruder. The way the words were said was a private thing, between one man and his enemy. What made Trevor jump was the hate of it. Trevor had seen plenty of action. But in all of it, he had never before heard the sound of pure and absolute hate.

Something had been bothering Steve Trevor. It had bothered him since coming from below to join Commander Houffman on the bridge. Throughout that part of the tracking operation, as they strained against the fog to see the ship, and as Houffman took information from the conning tower and assembled it in his mind, then barked down orders on the basis of it, something nagged at Trevor. He wanted—needed—some visual confirmation. In those waters at that time, it had to be presumed that it was an enemy ship. It sure as hell scoped like a destroyer or similar-size warship, and it was going like hell, but Trevor wanted to see it. Something made him uncertain enough to want to see it. What the hell was it?

Submarine warfare is much like any other kind of warfare. Opportunities rise and fall. They don't wait for all the facts. A commander works with what he gets, makes his decisions —sometimes on sketchy information, miles short of what he needs—and lives with it . . . or dies with it. A good commander has a second sense about things and works from that, uses that. Trevor had heard about Houffman, and what he'd heard had been good. He had that second sense, that lethal sense of a hunter who knows his game. Like a hunter, the sub commander lives in the mind of his game and knows where it will be—sometimes before it knows itself.

Commander Houffman knew exactly where the enemy ship was headed. They were on a parallel course, now one thousand yards off her track. And, whatever it was, it was overtaking the *Queenfish* at a blistering sixteen knots.

Houffman would have only one chance at it. He felt sure that it would hold its course at steady until it cleared Turnabout Island. Then, it was hard to tell where it might go. He would have to take it before it cleared the island.

What worried Trevor later, when he thought of it, was placing the time when he began reading the decision for attack in Houffman's expression and actions. There is a time when a decision is set, is made, and while it can be aborted at the last minute, something crosses a man's face at the specific moment of decision. What worried Trevor was that, from the time he had approached the commander on the bridge, he had the distinct feeling that Houffman had already made the decision to attack and had been operating on that single premise for some time, and that it would take something definite, absolute, something clear as hell to make him change his mind.

When he spoke, it was obvious that he didn't expect to find that something. His words were whispered:

"Steve, notify *Seafox*. Tell her we're going for attack." He had not turned his eyes away from the dense wall of fog that veiled the target.

As Trevor dropped below into the dim red of the conning tower, the thing nagging at the back of his mind, the thing he couldn't recall, still lingered, afraid to step forward. Like the ship out there in the fog, he knew it was there, he felt it, even though it refused to materialize.

The end-around maneuver was made smoothly and, with the outer doors open to the stern torpedo tubes 7, 8, 9, and 10, the *Queenfish* waited for the advancing target. The men in the conn moved as one, calling out bearings and the ever-changing angle on the bow of the approaching vessel. The target dials of the torpedo data computer were graphically revealing the closing angle of the advancing target and the nearly stationary sub, simultaneously computing the proper gyro angle and the angle for the poised and readied torpedoes. Trevor gathered the information and funneled it upstairs to the one man on the bridge who would ultimately make the call.

"Standby for bearings . . . ."

When radioman third-class Merville Easter, who was working the sonar gear, called over his shoulder, Trevor realized what had been bothering him. A minute or two earlier, as he had passed Easter on his way to the bridge, the sonarman had commented, "Those are some pretty heavy-sounding screws for any destroyer!"

Now, pressing the headphones close to his ears, Easter turned and said directly to Trevor, "I'm telling you, if that's a destroyer, I'll eat it."

"Bearing—mark!"

Just below the conn. in the control room, Chief of Watch Roy Bicca had stopped Ensign Delward T. Diefenbaker just as he started up the ladder to the conning tower. Since they had rigged for quiet, the exchange between them was made in hoarse, urgent whispers:

"Where the hell are you going, Diefenbaker?"

"I've got a message . . . I've got to see the captain!"

"For Christ sake, we're on bearing!"

"I've got to see him! This message. I've *got* to see him!"

"No. You're not going up there now, Diefenbaker."

"But—"

"Forget it. There's too much going on!"

"But—"

"Out, Diefenbaker!"

"Set!"

"But, I got this—"
"Out!"

"Fire one!"
"One torpedo fired electrically, sir."

Stern tubes 7, 8, 9, and 10 were fired at intervals of zero, fifteen, twenty-seven, and forty-one seconds. Serving as approach officer, Executive Officer Bill Edwards pushed the fire buttons as designated, on command. The depth was set at three feet on all tubes. The Mark XVIII electric torpedoes traveled at twenty-eight to thirty knots—about half the speed of the erratic steam torpedoes. But they were decidedly more accurate. They didn't broach. And they slid to the target without a wake of telltale bubbles. The Americans had been using the German-designed torpedoes for more than a year. They worked just fine. If they were on target, the first should find home in one minute fifteen seconds.

In the still of the conning tower, in the control room, in the torpedo rooms fore and aft, and on the bridge, the countdown continued:

"Thirty . . . twenty-nine . . . twenty-eight . . ."

PCO Steve Trevor had returned to the bridge just before the first torpedo struck. "It was eerie," he recounted later. "You could see nothing. I mean, nothing. There was fog and us lookin' into it. The moon—somehow—shinin' down. There we were, tryin' to see. Tryin' to spot the damn ship. There were no foghorns or whistles.

"When the first torpedo hit, you could see the flash through the fog. Nothin' else, just this flash and then, a second or two later—*bam!* I mean, just an incredible noise. It rocked you where you stood. Then, another split second, and—*whoosh!* —you got the same thing through the air.

"Christ! We weren't expecting that second blast. We thought they were unleashing fire at us. Later, we figured it. The first blast traveling through water beat the same blast comin' through the air.

"So, you got this *bam! . . . whoosh . . . bam . . . whoosh!*

"Okay. But listen . . . remember, everything we did that night was predicated on sinkin' a goddammed destroyer. A destroyer is—what?—300 to 350 feet long. Okay. So you set your spread so that you make pretty sure you hit it once . . . I mean, that's what you're after. A good shot will sink her. Well, if you get two fish into her, that's gravy.

"Anyway, we get the first *bam!* Then comes the *whoosh!* Got her! I look at Houffman and he's grinnin' like a Cheshire. Then comes the second *bam! . . . whoosh!*

"Well, goddamn, that was some fire control! I mean, we got two of 'em in.

"No sooner had we thought that, when the third hit . . . and then the fourth. We didn't see those, for some reason. But heard 'em, bigger'n hell.

"We just looked at each other, Houffman and I. We didn't say anything, but I saw it bigger'n hell in his face, and he saw it in mine: Whatever we hit was one hell of a lot bigger than a destroyer!"

In the space of three minutes—from the time of detonation of the fourth and last torpedo—the blip on the radar screen appeared to separate into two parts . . . and then disappeared.

Within three minutes—180 seconds—the target, the ship that was never seen, slipped beneath the East China Sea.

Immediately following the attack, Houffman was caught up in dispatching the appropriate maneuvers; first, to follow up in the attack, then, when the blip on the screen below broke up and disappeared, to return to the sinking site for the rescue of any survivors.

Now, as they headed toward the site, Houffman took out a cigarette and turned to Lieutenant Commander Trevor.

"I got a gut feeling," he said. The light from the match cupped in his hand caught the shadow just under his cheekbones, carving away the boyish expression. He pulled on the cigarette. "I think, Steve, what we got is a freighter. And what worries me . . ." His words trailed off.

Trevor waited. There was the smell of burning oil in the air.

"What worries me is this: if that's a freighter, it's one of Japan's last. Everything else the size of this thing must have joined the underwater fleet long ago. If it's a freighter, Steve, what's it doing out here in fog, at that speed, on a non-zigzag, going along like it didn't have a worry in the world?"

Communications Officer Mike Bass was the first through the hatch; right behind him was Ensign Diefenbaker. Bass did the talking:

"Captain, I think we got a problem." The two men were silhouetted by the red light that seeped from the open hatch behind them.

"Let's have it, Mike." There was a tone of resignation in the captain's voice, an edge of something expected.

"Skipper," Bass began, "Diefenbaker discovered a message on the clipboard in the comm shack that we'd overlooked. He said he tried to get to you during the approach phase but couldn't get through."

"That's right, sir," Diefenbaker said. "I knew you needed to see this, sir, so I tried to get through, but I was stopped by the chief of watch. Now, I have his name, Skipper, and if you want to—"

"Diefenbaker," the captain said, "do you have the message?"

"Yes, sir. But as I was saying, I can get—"

"Then give it to me, and shut up!"

Captain Houffman stepped over near the open hatch. There was enough light to read it. It was a plain-language message from ComSubPac, dated March 6, almost three weeks before.

If any of the officers had read it, no one had initialed it. In the dim light, with the building seas rocking him as he stood, he read only enough of it to get the meaning.

He didn't need to read all of it. The meaning of the message couldn't have been clearer. . . .

God, that's one night I'm not going to be big on forgettin'. When we lost the blip on the scope, the captain calls down for left full rudder. We're heading back, you know? Anyway, when Edwards says to me, "Easter, get on deck and do something useful," I go, right? I put on my foul-weather coat and lifejacket and head up. On deck, Old Ox and some of the others are already there.

Like I say, it's a night I'm not going to forget. I mean, Christ, there we were, creeping up on this scene—right?— and we're using the lights off and on. I mean, with all that fog, we're not too worried about being spotted, you know? But we're not picking up anything but an oil slick. We keep movin' along, real slow.

The wind was picking up, and it was colder than a bone in a snow drift, and I was standin' there on the deck, my line coiled, wonderin' what we were about to get into.

At first, I thought it was the wind or something. I don't know. I just wasn't tuned in to what I was hearing. Then it occurred to me. I wasn't listening to the goddamned wind at all. What I was hearing off in the distance was people. I mean, a crowd of people, like at a football stadium or something, except some of them were screaming in pain, shrieking. As we got closer—you know how noise travels on the water at night—you could hear some of them talking, shouting to each other in Japanese. But still our lights weren't picking up anything, I mean, nothin' but this goddamned white curtain of fog.

Then, all of a sudden, they were all around us. I mean, it was weird. Nothing. Then, all of a sudden, all this humanity, you know?

God. You don't forget something like this. I wake up with it sometimes at night. It's those eyes I see. Can see 'em now. Ever read Edgar Allen Poe? He couldn't make up anything like that night.

Suddenly our lights are reflecting off forty to fifty sets of eyes floating above the water. Goddamned blinking eyes looking at us! Jesus Christ! I stepped back, stumbled over the line, and damn near joined 'em!

Then I began realizing what I was lookin' at. See, these people were covered in oil, and unless you looked real hard, all you'd see were the whites of their eyes, the only part of them that wasn't black, the only part that wasn't covered in oil. Those terrified eyes lookin' at you out of the black of the sea.

After a while, you could see that there was more than that in the water . . . and you'd wished you'd stopped at the eye part of it.

All the debris, all the stuff that floats, had come to the surface. Huge bales, I guess rubber, bobbing along, crates, timber, hatch covers. Funny how you notice things, but there were a whole lot of apples, or maybe oranges or something. It was while I was trying to identify those that I began to notice what else was in the water.

I don't know any other way to say it, but floatin' around with those apples and oranges were parts of people; I mean— well, hell, you can imagine it. . . .

So we started throwing these lines out, sort of casting them out toward those floating eyes. And they'd land. Christ, some of the lines landed right on the shoulders of these guys. They wouldn't grab them. They wouldn't do anything. Just look at us with those goddamned eyes.

I mean to tell you, I started to get really scared. At first I thought it might be just shock . . . that they were just floating zombies from the shock of the thing.

But when I threw a line to a guy below me, almost under the bow, I mean, we were this close, he and I. The ring struck him in the face, and the line lay in the water not two inches from his nose. He had been hanging on to this big bale. Well, I see his eyes. He looks at the line, then up at me. I yelled to him: "Pick it up, for Christ sake!"

Then, lookin' at me—those eyes lookin' at me, right?—he pushes off that bale. And, with his mouth open, he begins inhaling water—choking, coughing—and he goes under.

Now, I don't mean he takes a deep breath and goes under. I mean, he inhales water and goes under. What he doesn't do is come back up.

And that's when I got scared. Lookin' around at all those eyes around me, and me standin' silhouetted on deck. Now, I don't know how much you know about small arms, but it don't take a genius to know there's a good chance they can fire soakin' wet.

If the old man didn't get us out of there pretty soon, they were going to start pickin' us off like pigeons.

About then, I see one of these guys off the port bow raise his arm, waving. I reeled in the line and cast the ring toward him.

By then, the seas were really pickin' up. The deck was wet and it was damn hard to keep my footing. I fell on my ass twice before Old Ox, who was standing next to me, saw my problem and grabbed my line. Together, we brought this guy alongside. By then, the seas were lifting the bow right out of the water. And the wind was goin' like forty.

Well, he went alongside, right below us, then the bow came crashin' down, I mean, right on the guy! Right on him! I don't know how, but he held on.

The next wave picked him up and damn near set him on deck for us.

Well, there he lay, blacker 'n night from the oil, and shiverin' like a rat.

Sometimes you say dumb things, right? Well, there he was, more dead than alive, upchucking oil, his face and head caved in, bleeding, and I bent over this guy sprawled on the deck and said, "Are you all right?"

No, I swear to God, that's what I said. "Are you all right?"

Then, still bent over this guy, I come up with the second bright question: "Do you speak English?" Now, what the hell's this guy going to say to that, right?

But, you know what? He nodded his head. I kid you not. This guy nodded his head.

XII

Date: April 1, 1945
Place: Aboard the *Awa Maru* in the Formosa Strait, eighteen
      miles off the China coast
Time: 2000 hours

When the *Awa Maru* was first officially notified of the large
American naval task force directed toward Okinawa on the
morning of April 1, 1945, Captain Hamamura saw little
reason to believe that the invasion would impede the course
the ship had previously established.

That course led directly from Singapore to a point about
thirty miles from the Chinese mainland southeast of Shan-
t'ou. From there, the revised safe-passage itinerary, which
had been published three weeks before, after their first swing
through Singapore, indicated that the *Awa Maru* would
proceed northeasterly through the Formosa Strait, maintaining no more than twenty miles of distance between the ship
and the mainland. Once through the strait, it was only
fifty-two hours, angling across the East China Sea, to the
safety of the Japanese islands.

It was a course that put plenty of water between the *Awa
Maru* and the American naval armada.

By noon of April 1, the *Awa Maru* had made good time
since leaving Singapore. Despite the pressure on Hamamura
to increase his speed—a pressure he ignored—the ship was
now about one and a half hours ahead of her published
schedule and about twenty-four miles ahead of her itinerary.
It was not a large variance, considering the distance traveled.

At 2230 hours, Hamamura responded to a message calling
him to the bridge. As he reached it, the need for the time they
had gained on their itinerary became apparent. He had
expected to hit fog or weather. It was easy to lose time to
those conditions and, with the load they carried, very difficult

to make it up when conditions cleared. What he didn't expect was to hit fog and weather at the same time. But that wasn't what angered him.

"Executive Officer Yanagihara, you will tell me what speed you are maintaining!" Hamamura's voice cracked sharply against the quiet on the bridge. The executive officer, the first officer, the radarman, and the helmsman had not seen him come up from behind. Startled, the executive officer turned and bowed stiffly.

"Sir," Yanagihara said. "We are maintaining sixteen knots, on orders."

"My orders are for sixteen knots in good weather. Do you find this favorable weather?"

"No, sir."

"And, when I am off the bridge, are you not in command?"

"Yes, sir. Normally, sir. But, I sent a messenger for you—"

"Yanagihara." Captain Hamamura was holding on to a thin thread of control. "Do you need me to tell you there is fog?"

"No, sir."

"Then you will tell me, briefly, why you are maintaining sixteen knots in hazardous conditions!"

"Captain, that is why the messenger was sent. Admiral Toshibo ordered me to maintain speed."

"Who?" Captain Hamamura was incredulous.

"Admiral Toshibo, the superior officer, sir."

"Superior officer! Since when have we had a superior officer aboard my vessel! And what in the name of your ancestor's obscenity is a superior officer?"

"He was appointed, Captain, by Lieutenant General Kodamo. I tried to reach you, but—"

"Appointed! I make the appointments here!"

"Yes, sir. But—"

"The next time any of my ship's officers take orders from . . . appointed military idiots, they will be appointed right off this vessel. And I won't wait for a port! Is that clear?"

"Yes, sir."

"Good. Now reduce speed to—"

"Captain!" It was the radarman. "Sir, I've got . . . I've got contact, I think. No, it's gone. I—wait. There it is again. Yes, sir. Contact at eleven thousand yards off the starboard bow. The weather. It's hard to read, sir. But I definitely have something, bearing 045° True. It appears to be moving on a parallel course to us."

"Hold speed and course," the captain said.

"Sir, contact has turned to the starboard, on course 135° True, speed four knots."

"Continue holding."

It would be a mistake to reduce speed. If this was an enemy vessel, any change in their speed or course might cause suspicion. They were on a protected course, and they were lighted, but even if the fog prevented their lights from being seen, the enemy had been receiving messages on the *Awa Maru*'s passing for weeks. Nonetheless, it was not good to do anything suspicious. They would maintain their speed unless the fog persisted and forced them to reduce speed.

And even the fog, Hamamura noted, was playing games. For minutes, sometimes, it would be clear, the moon bright on the building seas before them; then abruptly it would close in so that he could not make out the deck below him.

What really concerned the captain at 2240 hours that night, the first night of April, was the little general they called "the Tank."

For Hamamura, at least, the game the general was playing was potentially more lethal than the dangers of a ship in fog or what might be an enemy contact on radar.

It appeared that the general would test his command clear to Moji. And, when they made it to Moji . . .

But the captain would not worry about that either. There were many things that could happen between here and Moji.

It was later than usual for Mitsuma Shimata to make his traditional walk around the first-class deck before retiring. And it was slow going. The fog, which would sometimes close in around him, made it difficult to see where he was going. The lights illuminating the ship and the crosses sometimes made a glowing, opaque blanket of the fog, and he had to walk carefully, sometimes holding on to the rail.

By the time Shimata made his way down the two levels separating the first-class cabins from the crew's quarters, it was late. Passengers who had found no other place to bunk had crowded into the stairwells, making it difficult for him to pass.

The four days since they had left Singapore had been filled with mounting tension. The fresh-water supply was low. The heads were not able to accommodate the near-steady stream of passengers who waited in line to use them. Just moving from one place to another became an exercise in frustration. There had been arguments, and more than one fistfight—the one this afternoon, as Shimata understood it, had concerned whether one of the passengers had the right to demand of another the freedom to sleep with his feet in the face of the first.

At about 1500 hours that day, a baby was born to one of the passengers on a cot in the main salon. Suggestions that the woman be brought to the infirmary were discouraged; the infirmary was being used to house members of the 41st Imperial Infantry Regiment, and they would be disinclined to move for such an event, even for the wife of a branch manager of the Mitsubishi bank.

If the hospital ship carried any wounded soldiers on its return to Japan, Shimata did not know on what part of the ship they were being attended. While he had not seen all the loading in Djakarta and Singapore, he had not noticed anyone being carried aboard on a stretcher.

Since entering the shallow waters of the Formosa Strait, and with the increasingly heavy seas that night, some of the passengers were experiencing seasickness, placing a further burden on the already taxed accommodations.

Shimata could feel the damp of the fog even in the crew's quarters as he pulled back the tightly stretched wool blanket that covered the thin mattress on his bunk. The fan against the wall by his head labored against the moist, heavy air.

Shimata was not bothered that night by the light in the passageway that shone in his eyes, nor by the heavy snoring of the cook who slept in the bunk above him. It was late and he was sleepy. Shimata was confident that his luck was still with him.

He had survived the sinking of the *Hyiyo Maru,* the *Teiko Maru,* and the *Tea Maru* within the last two years. Now, shortly before 2300 hours on the night of April 1, 1945, sleep overtook Chief Steward Mitsuma Shimata. He was aboard the *Awa Maru.*

Date: April 1, 1945
Place: Aboard the *Awa Maru* approaching Niu-shan Tao
      (Turnabout Island)
Time: 2300 hours

When the radarman had reported to Captain Hamamura that the unidentified vessel they had picked up on the scope had veered off, had turned away, the captain had crossed to the starboard wing of the bridge. The lights on that side were reflecting off the fog and he could not see through it. He would hold their present speed for another thirty minutes, then have the first officer relieve the lookouts and post the night watch. He would think about what he would do about the lieutenant general in the morning.

The first explosion was below and just aft of where the captain was standing. The glass through which he was looking blew into his face. He did not know whether it was the glass or the brilliant white light of the explosion that blinded him. When he turned to face his officers, he continued to see the brilliant light. He could not see beyond it.

"Helmsman, right full rudder!" He could see nothing but the light that had been the explosion. It continued to move across his eyes in varicolored waves. He had to assume that the helmsman was still there.

"No steerage, sir!"

"Full ahead, reverse." His words were echoed by somebody, and Hamamura felt the answering shudder of the diesels below as they responded to his orders, the twin screws churning against the terrible weight of momentum.

"Sound fire stations. Get me—"

The second blast knocked him to his knees. There was the crashing sound of falling equipment, a distant rumbling, the groan and shriek of tearing metal. He had trouble standing, could not keep his balance.

"First officer . . . first officer! Respond, damn you!"

"Sir!"

"I can't see. Give me a visual report of . . ." Like a dream, he could not make his words work for him, could not make them rise above the shouts and sounds that surrounded him on the bridge. He called out, but there was no sound.

He had found his footing and started to rise, when something heavy and metallic crashed into his left shoulder, knocking him to the deck. He heard the bones in his upper arm and shoulder snap like dry tinder. He was fighting to push himself off the deck with his remaining good arm when the third explosion came. There was the unmistakable answering rumble of one of the boilers far below. There was the smell of burning oil.

He could not tell where the deck was. He had rolled into the corner of something. He could not tell which part of the corner was the deck and which the bulkhead. The feel of gravity was one of his few remaining senses, and that played tricks on him.

If he could stand, if he could find the deck below him, it would be better. He could think then, could get a damage report, could learn whether others had taken control, whether they could fight the fire, whether they could free the lifeboats, whether they must abandon ship.

He did not know whether the ship was listing radically or whether he was losing consciousness. The brilliant lights in his eyes had lost their color, had dimmed, but he still could not see through them. He tried to wipe away the thing that was keeping him from seeing, but there was only warm, wet, open flesh.

He reached out with his right hand, found something solid, and pulled himself up. He could not tell on what he was standing. There was only the sliding and crashing sounds of equipment, gear breaking loose. He held on to the thing that was solid and took a hesitant step forward.

It may have been that there was another explosion. It may have been that he had stepped through something. He was falling. There was nothing beneath him, and he was falling. And that, too, was like the dream, the same dream that kept him from being heard when he called out. It was a dream he had experienced recurrently since childhood.

There had been the river and the long, tall tree on its banks, and how it had looked from the top of it, looking down to the river below. And, with the wind, there was a rushing in his ears as the tree began moving, slowly at first, then fiercely. The tree began whipping, first one way, then the other, until the strength in his hands was torn from him by the wind and his own weight, by the force of the tree as it whipped back and forth, each time leaning lower to the river below. And the falling part. The sensation of it. The weightlessness of the long, slow fall. In the dream, each time, just before crashing into the water, he had awakened.

This time, Captain Hamamura did not.

The first torpex-laden torpedo to strike the *Awa Maru* that night was planted amidships, just below the water line, beneath compartments B8 and B9 in the crew's quarters. The sixteen men who occupied those quarters—deck hands, oilers, machinists—tightly shelved in their bunks, were engulfed in the explosion that tore through the thick hull plates and ripped upward. The force of the explosion brought to them

133

an instant end to the war. Others on board were less fortunate.

That was the first in the tight formation of four torpedoes to find the *Awa Maru*. They would all find their mark within forty-one seconds. Each of the Mark XVIIIs fired by the *Queenfish* at a range of 1,200 to 1,270 yards carried a 732-pound torpedo warhead, torpex more than half again as powerful as TNT. Those sleeping above the first blast never heard the others.

The second torpedo struck forward of the first; the last two, aft. All ripped into the hull of the ship three feet below the water line. Had they been planted lower, closer to the keel, the ship would have broken in two, possibly in thirds.

Instead, she took the crushing blows, groaning and heaving under the impact, and held herself together. At once, she listed to her starboard, still slicing through the blackness of the sea, the momentum carrying her forward. The sea ripped through the gaping wounds in her steel sides, pieces wrenching backward in a shriek of twisting, contorting metal. And she slowed.

Her smooth lines now broken, her flesh open to the rushing sea, she lay completely over, and, in less than three minutes from the fourth and final detonation, she began her descent into the black chill of the East China Sea. Her belly open, she strewed her guts, her cargo, in ragged trail behind her.

Seconds later, her forward speed nearly stalled, her bow pitched high above the water, the stern scraped the ocean floor 210 feet below. Twisting some, as though to right herself, her screws folding under the impact, the keel of the crippled vessel cut into the continental shelf like a great plow, the sediment bursting behind her in an exploding cloud.

Then, quiet. A split second of quiet. And, with a prolonged sigh, her bow settled in the deep.

The *Awa Maru* lay dead in the still.

Shimata awoke sitting on the stomach of the cook who slept in the bunk above him. It was curious but not altogether uncomfortable, sitting there on this man's ample belly. The cook was missing a good part of his right shoulder and most of his head. The interior wall, which had served to support the bunks on which he and the cook had been sleeping, had been blown inward, and now the fan, hanging by its cord, swung freely across the ragged hole that opened onto the lighted passageway. The fan was still working.

There are certain advantages to having experienced three torpedo attacks. After coming to terms with why he was sitting on the belly of a headless cook, Shimata applied all of that experience in the next eventful seconds.

In the smoke-filled passageway, he fought through a group of skivvy-clad men who were stumbling out of their compartments. They were talking excitedly, asking what happened, what the ship had hit, and whether anyone was hurt.

Shimata didn't hesitate. He did not linger. He did not pause to ask questions. He did not inquire about anyone's health. He jammed through the group and headed for the stairs to the 01 level above. Shimata knew that this dazed concern for others would soon give way to panic. He knew that most of those who would die that night would die not in the waters or by fire but under the feet of others in the passageways and stairwells and corridors of the stricken ship. He had been through it before.

He was halfway up the first set of stairs when the second torpedo hit. He was knocked against the bulkhead. The lights had gone out and somebody was pushing him back down the stairs. The panic was on.

Others grabbed at him, but he slipped free in the dark and continued heading up. He knew the ship well and knew that heading up was his only hope. Below him, he heard the belly of the ship erupt as the boilers in the engine room exploded. Now, still heading up, there was fire, smoke, the stench of oil, and screams.

Shimata continued to climb as the third and fourth torpedoes hit. As he fought his way upward, he pulled at anything and anybody that could bring him a step or two higher. Later, he would say he made it to "A" deck and the rail. For now, he did not know why, exactly, but he was under water, a lot of water; he had swallowed some of it, but his lungs, while bursting for breath, for the moment remained clear. He continued to pull upward. If he was still within the ship, he would know when he struck the deck above.

The surprising thing to Shimata as he pulled against the weight of the cold, dark water was how long he had gone without breathing. And now, pulling higher, he did not need air. Instead, he exhaled some, a stream of bubbles flowing up from his mouth. He was elated, giddy with his power. He was feeling good about this swimming around in the dark, about the aimlessness of it; about not needing to breathe. He was not sure whether he was swimming to the surface or into the deep. But it did not matter. Shimata had done all he could do to survive. He wondered if you always felt good just before you died.

When he broke through to the surface, he was sorry, in a way, to see that there was still more life to go before the end.

The first breath came searing into his lungs like so much fire. He was hurt badly.

The second breath coincided with a wave that engulfed him. He began to take in the oil-choked sea around him. Weakened, he dog-paddled, reaching out in the dark for something to grab.

It was cold and the waves were high. He could not see the *Awa Maru*. A wood plank that had broken from below shot up near him like a missile. He grabbed for it, and while the oil on his hands made it hard to grip, he managed to hold on. It wouldn't support him. He went under, swallowed more oil and water, and rose again. Around him, more and more debris kept popping to the surface, some at enormous velocities. He found a large bale that, while it wouldn't take his full weight, took the weight of his chest, and there, for a moment, he was able to rest.

He worried that he would vomit and lose his grip. He held back the oil that wanted to come up from his stomach, forced it back.

That's when he heard the others. There were calls for help, screams. Around him were hatches, barrels, crates. Someone near him in the dark shrieked in pain. Though his eyes burned, they were growing accustomed to the dark and he could begin picking out details: someone's shoe, pieces of deck, a table, bottles, a light bulb, an assortment of cans, and what appeared to be a melon floating not more than two feet from where he clung to the bale. The melon, on close examination, was attached to a neck and shoulders and was supported by a lifejacket.

It was clear enough that night for Shimata to see others around him, the dead, the dying, the dismembered. Later, he would swear that he was able to pick out details like this in the white-capped water because there was no fog.

Many of the 150 employees of the Takoku-Saigu Oil Company and some of those who worked for the Co-Prosperity Bright Metal firm were housed in the infirmary on the 02 level, just above the engine rooms. From the first, there was panic. Everybody tried to make it out to the

136

corridor at once; some were driven back by the acrid, poisonous smoke that filled it. There were two exits and both of them were jammed with humanity, almost from the beginning. Most were fighting their way out; some, hopelessly, were trying to return.

From the start there were fights, pushing, shoving, and as the deck began to tilt crazily, the panic rose.

Those who had been knocked to the deck in the struggle felt the heat of it first; they felt it in their hands as they pushed themselves up. Others, most in bare feet, for some reason did not respond to it immediately. They came to the realization only gradually. The fire below was heating the steel deck they moved on, and each second they were bound to it, each second they couldn't move off it, the temperature rose.

When it became clear that those who were jamming forward, pressing for the hatches, could not stand the heat of the deck long enough to make it out of the infirmary, the course of the panic shifted. Some continued to fight toward the exits by standing on those who had fallen. Others fought to climb on those who were still standing. Still others turned to find refuge on anything that was off the deck: bunks, tables, rigging, bedding—anything that could give them respite from the searing heat.

As the ship continued to list hard to the starboard and the deck was pitched upward, it became increasingly difficult to maintain footing. Everything began to slide across the now-blistering deck. Everything and everybody.

For a few minutes, when the water came, it was better. The rush of water flushed clear the hatches, which were clogged with the dead, the dying, and the fighting, and hissed across the steel deck plate. Steam filled the room like a turkish bath, and the water rose, surging relentlessly through the two hatches. It was knee-high to those still standing, then waist-high, then they were swimming.

It was dark then, and the fight just to remain on the surface was brutal. People clawed, pulled, grasped, and tore at one another in an effort to take one more breath.

Since the ship was leaning radically by then, those still alive but trapped in the infirmary swam on the surface of the rising water, which formed the base of a triangle; the bulkhead and the deck above formed the sides. As the water rose toward the apex, the surface area of the water was reduced proportionally. Those still alive were crammed together, fighting for the diminishing breathing space. The surface was

137

reduced in a kind of mathematical progression to the numbers who sought it.

Then there were those last feverish seconds, when an airlock that had held the advancing flood to within a few feet of the apex suddenly broke. In a final thunder of water and rumble of steel, those who had fought to survive found themselves with no surface at all. Those who had lived through the hell of those panic-stricken minutes, who had clawed their way to still another breath, were finally, irrevocably engulfed.

Forward on the main deck, at first, there had been no panic. There had been the explosion amidships, and those who had been sleeping in bed rolls in the open or under lean-tos, and those who had been sitting in groups, scrambled to their feet. There was a lot of talk about what they had hit, the damage, and whether they were in danger. Someone had told everyone to calm down, when the second torpedo hit. That hit just off the starboard, forward of the bridge. Some of those on the starboard side had been leaning over, trying to assess the damage of the first hit, trying to see where the explosion had been. They were at the rail, leaning over, looking aft when the second torpedo hit a few feet below them.

They took the force of the second hit fully. Those looking over the rail were cut in two. Others took the shrapnel and flying debris from the blast.

A woman, engulfed in flames, ran across the deck. She was tackled and thrown to the deck. But the flames clung to her clothes, her hair, her skin. They tried rolling her on the deck but the flames would not go out. They tried stripping her clothes from her, but they were burned and had to back off. Finally, someone covered her with some bedding and the flames were extinguished. She was charred and smoldering when she sat up and calmly asked if she could please have a glass of water. She did not live to drink it.

By the time the last two torpedoes struck aft, some were already attending the wounded, tying off severed limbs with bedding and belts; a group had gone up to "A" deck to try to free the boats; from storage bins lining the stern, someone else had begun throwing out lifejackets.

To those forward, it did not look like the ship was in danger of sinking. At first. Someone had been trying to gather women and children together on the port side. They would be the first in the boats.

But, as the ship listed to the starboard, it became difficult to stand on the deck. The oil made it worse. Throughout, there were those who tried to take control, tried to organize. There were no announcements from the darkened bridge.

There had been no drills and few knew how to strap on the lifejackets. It was dark, and the list to the starboard worsened, causing people to lose footing, to slide across the oily deck and drop into the water. Soon, those still on the deck could remain there only by holding on to the rails, hatch covers, rigging, the boom machinery, cleats—anything that would keep them from sliding, first to the starboard, then to the stern, as the great bow lifted high above the water.

When there was no doubt that they were sinking, panic took hold. The lifeboats could not be cut down. Those who left then, who jumped to the water and swam away, were spared the fire that would soon ring the oil-slick water around that part of the ship. When it came, it lapped up toward the rapidly descending bow. Many who had waited until they could fit on their lifejackets discovered that they had strapped themselves into their own death sentence. When at last they jumped free, they bobbed immediately to the fiery surface, and, illuminated there, they thrashed against the flames until they were finally consumed.

Without a lifejacket, one had a chance of swimming beneath the surface, beneath the twenty yards of flame. But even then, some came up too soon. Though they had made it beyond the flames, they surfaced where there was nothing to breathe, where the oxygen in the air had been stolen to feed the flames.

XIII

QUESTION: How long were you on the surface that night?

SHIMATA: I do not know. I do not know how long I was there.

QUESTION: Was it five minutes, an hour, two hours?

SHIMATA: Nothing was very clear in my mind. I do not know. I don't think it was two hours. I don't think it was one hour.

QUESTION: Do you think it was less than that?

SHIMATA: Yes. I think it was less than that. I was freezing and my hands and legs were becoming numb. It was hard to hold on to the bale. My body felt heavy. I wanted to go to sleep. I thought that was how it was going to be. That I would sleep, and it would be over. That's when I spotted the ship.

QUESTION: The submarine?

SHIMATA: Yes. But I did not think it was a submarine at first. I saw a large ship between the waves. I thought it was a Japanese destroyer.

QUESTION: What made you think that?

SHIMATA: I think it is what I wanted to see. It had been a Japanese destroyer that had taken me from the water the last time my ship was sunk. I expected it to be the same this time.

QUESTION: When did you find out it was a submarine?

SHIMATA: A big wave came and lifted me way up. From there, I could see that it was not a Japanese destroyer; from there, I could see that it was an American submarine.

QUESTION: Did you swim for it?

SHIMATA: No, sir. I did not.

QUESTION: What happened?

SHIMATA: I don't know if the submarine came to me or the waves carried me to the submarine. The distance between us rapidly shortened, but I did not swim to it. No, sir. I did not swim toward it.

QUESTION: When did you raise your hand?

SHIMATA: No, sir. No, sir. I have heard those stories, and they are not true. I did not raise my hand. I did not want to be rescued. In those stories, they said I raised my hand. I don't know why they say that. I did not raise my hand.

QUESTION: Then how did it happen that you were picked up and put aboard the submarine?

SHIMATA: I don't know for sure. I only know that the waves carried me and the submarine came, and then I was thrown against the submarine by a large wave. I was caught in the chain from the submarine, and I lost consciousness.

QUESTION: What chain?

SHIMATA: Yes. And I lost consciousness.

QUESTION: I mean, what is the chain which you got caught in?

SHIMATA: It was a submarine chain.

QUESTION: A submarine chain?

SHIMATA: I don't want to talk about that anymore. When I woke up, I was on the deck, and I remember somebody was talking to me. It sounded like he spoke in English, but I do not know what he said. I thought it would be better for me if I understood, so I nodded. Then, they did the funny thing.

QUESTION: What funny thing?

SHIMATA: They put steel on my wrists so I could not move my arms. It was funny because I could not have moved if I wanted to.

QUESTION: Wait a minute, Mr. Shimata. Let's go back to where you were in the water, before you made it to the deck of the submarine. You said you could pick out details, you said you could see the advancing submarine. You said it was *not* foggy, is that right?

SHIMATA: Yes.

QUESTION: Yes, it was not foggy?

SHIMATA: That is right. It was not foggy.

QUESTION: Do you realize that the American commander of the submarine filed a report to his leaders in the Navy and he said in that report that it was very foggy?

SHIMATA: Yes.

QUESTION: Do you still believe it was not foggy?

SHIMATA: Yes.

QUESTION: Can you tell me why you believe this?

SHIMATA: Because I was there. When I came up from

under the water, when my eyes could see in the dark, I could see that it was not foggy.

QUESTION: You could see the moon? You could see stars?

SHIMATA: There were big waves. I don't remember seeing the moon.

QUESTION: I'm going to play back on this machine, Mr. Shimata, something you said earlier. "...I could not keep balance for one moment, I was tossed left and right and swallowed salt water every time, almost choking. The surface of the sea was pitch dark and I could not see the *Awa Maru* anyplace. The wind was strong and there was no fog...." Do you remember saying that?

SHIMATA: Yes.

QUESTION: Under the circumstances—you were more dead than alive—under the circumstances, perhaps you were mistaken about the fog.

SHIMATA: Maybe it is so.

QUESTION: Maybe the *Awa Maru* was still on the surface when you looked, but you could not see her through the fog.

SHIMATA: Maybe it is so.

QUESTION: Later, you said, "I heard calls for help, but I could not see those who were calling." Maybe the fog prevented you from seeing these people.

SHIMATA: Maybe it is so.

QUESTION: So, maybe it was foggy that night? Is that right?

SHIMATA: (Answer inaudible.)

QUESTION: I'm sorry, I didn't hear you.

SHIMATA: I said it is not so.

QUESTION: What is not so?

SHIMATA: It is not so about the fog.

QUESTION: What do you mean?

SHIMATA: It is not so what you say about the fog. It was not foggy that night.

QUESTION: You're sure of that?

SHIMATA: I was there. It was not foggy.

QUESTION: But, many others were there. On the submarine they said it was foggy.

SHIMATA: They were under orders to say that. I don't blame them for obeying their orders, but it was not foggy.

So, like I said, when I ask him if he can speak English—him laying there on the deck—he nods his head. I mean, it

142

*was a dumb question, right? I sure as hell wasn't tryin' to
interrogate the guy. I mean, what the hell. What would you
do?*

*Look. Here's this guy shiverin' to beat hell, covered with
oil, bleedin' like a stabbed rat; it just seemed right that
someone talk to the poor bastard.*

*Okay, I knew he was the enemy, but I mean, Christ!
What's he goin' to do, jump up and take over the ship 'cause I
ask him a couple of questions?*

*Well, shit, I never thought I'd hear the end of it from those
goddamned lifers: What was an EM doing interrogating a
prisoner? Did I know I could be court martialed for such a
thing? How would I like to spend time in the brig? . . . and
like that. Shit, they took me up one side and down the
other.*

*I mean, Jesus Christ. I don't like these goddamned Japs
any better than the next guy. But here's a guy—I mean, you
had to see this guy to believe it—who looked about three
breaths this side of checkin' out.*

*So it seemed someone ought to say somethin' to him. I
mean, one-guy-to-another kind of thing. Like "how are you"
or "go to hell" or something. So, I talked to him, right? Asked
him a couple of things, right? Big deal, right?*

*Hell, no. There was going to be none of that. Everybody
was going to play it by the manual. This little guy was to be a
big-deal prisoner of war, right? Well, let them have at it.
When I got the picture, I backed off.*

*So, up comes Old Ox. He's been ordered to handcuff the
guy. I kid you not! Now, I don't know what they thought the
guy could do, you know? Pull a machine gun out of his
skivvies, for Christ sake? But, that's what they had in mind.
They were going to cuff the bastard.*

*Anyway, here's Old Ox, right? And behind him is Garra-
baldi with a BAR, Browning Automatic, you know? I mean, it
was going to be the big scene. So, you know Old Ox, right?
He had no idea how to put on the goddamned handcuffs. And
Garrabaldi's standing there trying to explain it to him.*

*Finally, Ox rolls the poor bastard on his stomach, and he's
got one wrist cuffed, but he can't work the other. So,
Garrabaldi bends over and is trying to help him when the
captain yells down from the bridge, "Watch where you're
pointing that weapon, sailor!"*

*Well, it's true that while Garrabaldi was trying to work the
handcuffs he had forgotten what he was doing with the BAR,
and it could have mowed down half of those on deck. But, he*

looks up, startled. "It's okay, sir," he calls up. "It's not loaded."

Well, the big scene was rapidly going downhill, right? Anyway, when Ox finally gets the cuffs on, Edwards calls from the bridge, "Bring the prisoner aft!"

Well, hell that sounded pretty impressive, right? So Old Ox, not knowing quite how to handle bringing a prisoner aft, seemed uncertain again about what to do. Finally, he reaches down with one of those meaty hands of his, and grabs the little guy just below the shoulder and lifts him straight up off the deck. It's like he's in a butcher shop holding up a piece of meat to see whether it's good or something.

Well, up until then, I thought the guy might have been dead, but when he was lifted off the deck, that pushed his button, you know? I mean, he started talking. Christ, did he start talking! It was like he had this whole thing ready, this kind of speech, and he was going to get it out no matter what, his eyes bigger'n volley balls. Well, whatever he said was in English, but I couldn't make it out from where I stood.

So, Ox, still holding this guy off the deck with one hand, turns and looks up toward the bridge, you know?

"Captain," he calls up. "This guy says we shouldn't be alarmed, but . . ." You could tell Ox didn't know how to finish it.

"But, what?" the captain calls back.

"But . . ." Old Ox says, "but he says he needs . . . well, hell, sir. He says he needs to find a men's room!"

U.S.S. QUEENFISH (SS-393)
8 April 1945
In reply refer to: SS393/A9

CONFIDENTIAL
From: the Commanding Officer
To: the Commander, Submarine Force, Pacific Fleet

7. . . . Although the prisoner indicated by a nod of his head that he could understand English, no coherent information was immediately forthcoming, and he was taken below for medical treatment while the ship was maneuvering in search of additional survivors. Visibility conditions failed to improve, and though faint yells were heard a few times for about 30 minutes following the arrival of the QUEENFISH in the area of sinking, no additional survivors were recovered. The sea conditions were such that it was deemed too hazardous to send men

into the water to forcibly recover survivors or to pick up samples of the debris which covered a wide area.

Most of the debris consisted of large and small rectangular-shaped boxes or bales, of which there were numerous groups numbering several hundred or more, bobbing in the oil-covered water. At this time, the character of the cargo carried by the sunken ship was of relatively minor importance in view of the fact that the prisoner could probably be induced to identify the ship and inform us of the cargo on board.

At 0010, 2 April, having failed to locate or hear additional survivors, departed from the immediate attack vicinity and proceeded to assigned patrol station about 25 miles to the eastward.

8. From 0010, 2 April, until 1548, 2 April, conducted surface patrol in the Formosa Strait with SEAFOX PATROLLING TO THE NORTH OF OUR POSITION. During this period, the fog lifted about 0150, increasing the visibility to an estimated 4 miles; remaining at that limit during the night. After dawn, visibility increased to about 7 miles until another fog bank entered about 1100. . . .

9. Following departure from the immediate attack vicinity at 0010, 2 April, it was some time before coherent information could be obtained from the prisoner. At about 0600, the prisoner identified the ship that was attacked as the AWA MARU. . . .

Everything smelled of fuel oil. Every time Mitsuma Shimata tried to open his eyes, they burned. Before his eyes blurred, he saw that he had been taken to the place on the submarine where the torpedoes were.

His hands were still bound behind him, and he could not rub his eyes. His arms ached, and he guessed he had been there for a long time.

When he heard the man come in to relieve the big man who had taken him there, he opened his eyes and, before they teared, he recognized the man's uniform as that of an American officer. He wondered if this man had come to pull his toenails out, as the vice-minister had said they did with prisoners.

The officer said something to the big man, who then took the metal clamps off Shimata's hands.

He could rub his eyes, and, after a while, with the smell of fuel oil still around him, he could see. It was then that he realized what they had in mind. They were going to light the fuel oil. He tried to get to his feet but was too weak; he had trouble just holding up his head.

When the man in the officer's uniform spoke, it eased Shimata a little. It did not sound like he was angry. The officer looked worried. He tried to speak in Japanese. He looked at a book, and, frowning, tried to make sense, but Shimata did not understand any of the words. That made the man more worried.

When the officer spoke in English, it was easier for Shimata. He thought he understood some of the things he said. At least it was better than when he spoke from the book. He asked his name, and Shimata, understanding that, and with much effort, said it, then said it again slowly, so the man sitting across from him could write it down. Except, he wrote down "Shita."

Then the man asked how his wife was, and Shimata said, "Fine." But the man persisted about his wife. Shimata worried that he had plans to take her to a company of American marines.

The man then drew a picture of a ship and asked again how his wife was, pointing to the picture. After a while, Shimata figured he had his words wrong, that the answer, "Fine," did not fit the question. The worried man made another drawing and some signs with his hands until Shimata understood that he was being asked what his ship was named. He told the man, then told him again slowly, so he could write it down. This man, who wrote things down carefully, looked very worried. Shimata wondered if it was because he had been selected to light the match.

EDWARDS: Wait. Stop right there.

QUESTION: What do you mean?

EDWARDS: Up to this part, I'll go along with what he says. I mean, not the fuel-oil nonsense. That's what we used to wash him off, clean fuel oil. But the rest of it, in the aft torpedo room, my questions from the book, what he said— it's all more or less as it happened.

QUESTION: And the second part of his story? What he said afterwards?

EDWARDS: That's absolute nonsense. I mean, the stuff about the captain.

QUESTION: But why would he say it?

EDWARDS: I don't know.

QUESTION: Would he have anything to gain by saying it?

EDWARDS: Look. There's two Shimatas. The guy we knew in that sub, he was scared stiff the whole time. A frightened little man. After a while, it even got that everyone kind of felt sorry for him. But later, when he got home to Japan and got to be something of a big shot—the only survivor of the biggest sea disaster in naval history, four ships torpedoed out from under him, that kind of thing—it was a different Shimata, and, in my mind, he began making up things. Things that just weren't true. The things Shimata said later are just not accurate. He was a different man when he was with us. When he got back to his own people, he wanted to make himself a hero.

QUESTION: But the details he uses in the second part of the story are pretty convincing, aren't they?

EDWARDS: Well ... no. No, they are not. Like I said. I agree with his story up to here, but none of the second part is true. I've got the actual interrogation notes right here. . . .

When Shimata told the officer with the worried expression the name of his ship, the officer said something to the big seaman and he left.

When a new man came into the room, Shimata could tell by his uniform that he was the commander of the vessel. He said something to the worried man and the worried man left. The commander carried a rolled-up paper. He was angry.

He asked Shimata the name of his ship. He told the commander as he had told the other officer.

The commander said no, it wasn't true. He was very angry. He unrolled the paper. Shimata could see that it was a basic line drawing of the *Awa Maru*, one that the enemy government had issued to help identify it.

He asked if that was Shimata's ship. Shimata told him it was. The commander was still very angry. "No!" he said. Shimata was afraid he would hit him. The officer pointed to the picture, then to the gun batteries the picture showed. The officer did not know that the batteries had been removed from the *Awa Maru* at the port of Moji prior to their departure.

Shimata tried to tell him, but the commander did not understand. According to Shimata:

"That's when the commander said the thing that I remembered. I remembered every word of what he said, and later, it became very important. The commander said this:

" 'This picture shows gun batteries! The ship I sank did not have gun batteries!'

"Later, when the thing about the fog came up, I wondered how he could see that my ship had no guns if he could not see my ship at all."

EDWARDS: That just isn't true.

QUESTION: Why?

EDWARDS: I don't think Houffman talked to the prisoner. I don't think he ever said anything to him.

QUESTION: But wasn't it true that the Allies had published and circulated this drawing of the *Awa Maru* and that it showed the ship with gun emplacements?

EDWARDS: I don't know, but let me tell you why this couldn't be true. For a start, this guy didn't speak that much English. You know how he said he heard the captain say: "This picture shows gun batteries. The ship I sank did not have batteries"? Well, he wouldn't have understood that.

QUESTION: What do you mean?

EDWARDS: He just didn't understand that much English. I was with him then, and later, for a long time. I got a lot of information from him, but it wasn't easy. I used Japanese words, pictures, sign language—everything—to find out what he knew. He just wouldn't understand a thing like that. He knew a few words in English, and some of these he had mixed up. So, he made up all that later. It made him look better to his countrymen.

QUESTION: What did you do when Shimata told you the name of the ship?

EDWARDS: Nothing at first. The *Awa Maru* meant nothing to me. It was only when he drew me a picture of it, when I got the size of it from him, and when he drew crosses on it, that I knew we had a hospital ship.

QUESTION: What did you do then?

EDWARDS: I took it immediately to Captain Houffman.

QUESTION: Where was he?

EDWARDS: He was in the conning tower. I think Trevor was with him. . . .

During those early morning hours following the pickup of the prisoner, Houffman and Trevor had waited in the conn through three cups of coffee and half a pack of cigarettes apiece.

When Houffman had first come down the ladder into the conn, he had handed Trevor the message that Diefenbaker had delivered shortly after the sinking.

"You better read this, Steve." There was a sound of resignation in Houffman's voice.

It was all there. The route, the schedule, the description of a hospital ship called the *Awa Maru*. It directed all submarines to allow her to pass unmolested. Some of the details of identification were provided:

AWA MARU WILL BE PAINTED WITH A WHITE CROSS ON EACH SIDE OF FUNNEL. STOP. CROSSES TO BE ILLUMINATED AT NIGHT. STOP. WHITE CROSS ON TOP OF BRIDGE. STOP. WHITE CROSS ON SECOND AND FIFTH HATCHES. STOP. TWO WHITE CROSSES ON EACH SIDE OF SHIP. STOP. ALL NAVIGATION LIGHTS TO BE LIGHTED AT NIGHT . . .

After Trevor had asked where the message came from, he studied the schedule and made some calculations in his head.

"I don't know, Skipper," he said. "There's a good chance this isn't it—that this isn't the ship we sank. The strait is a hundred miles wide. It could be coming through any part of it. And there's this other thing. . . ." Trevor worked it out again. "If the ship we sank was the *Awa Maru*, it was an hour and a half ahead of schedule."

"We'll know soon enough," Houffman said. Edwards's got the prisoner in the after room."

There was no need to talk about it any further. They waited, smoking cigarettes, drinking coffee, mostly in silence. Long silences between the two officers were not uncommon. They worked well together. There was enough credibility between them to permit times when neither felt the need to talk, to fill the quiet space. Trevor felt that Houffman recognized their growing camaraderie, and, under the strain of the last few weeks, had opened the door occasionally to his inner world.

"Do you think I was right in that, Steve?" Houffman broke the silence between them.

"What?"

"Not sending anyone in. They're going to shit at that at headquarters, you know."

"Probably."

"I can hear 'em."

"So can I. But I think you did the thing you needed to do, and got out. All of it is going to look different from behind a desk. I mean, you went in. The seas were rough. But you got one of them out. You know, what can they say? I wouldn't have given you a nickel for anyone you sent over the side to forcibly rescue one of those guys."

Houffman studied his coffee cup. Trevor, knowing what was coming, waited.

"I don't like it, Steve."

"What?"

"The whole goddamned thing."

"What do you mean?"

Houffman looked up. They were no longer rigged for red, and the light in the conning tower diluted the blue of his eyes.

"I don't know what I mean. I just don't like the whole goddamned thing."

When Edwards burst up through the hatch into the conning tower, he had the look of a man who has seen the sky fall in and has evidence to prove it.

Houffman spoke before Edwards had a chance. "You've spoken to the prisoner and he told you that he was aboard a hospital ship. Is that right?"

"Well . . ." Edwards was taken aback. "Yes. Yes, sir."

"And he told you the name of the ship, right?"

"Right, Captain."

"The name of the ship is *Awa Maru*, right?"

Edwards could only nod in the affirmative.

"Bill?"

"Yes, Captain?" No one in the room moved.

"Thank you."

Edwards looked over to Trevor, then back to the commander. He started to say something, then checked it. Houffman had tunneled into himself. You could see a distance in his eyes, a dissociation. Edwards started out, turned, considered saying something, turned again, and headed down to the control room.

Trevor stood a long time, waiting for a response from Commander Houffman. When it came, it came from somewhere within, somewhere where the controlled part of him was:

"Jesus Hector Christ!"

EDWARDS: Well, as it turned out, the message had been in the shack all the time. And when the prisoner confirmed that his ship was the *Awa Maru,* that was it.

QUESTION: It had been in the radio shack since you left Guam?

EDWARDS: Yes. It was on a short piece of paper, about six inches long. On regular reproducing paper—not Xerox—but faded purple. We used to call it Purple Jesus.

QUESTION: Who was supposed to have read those messages?

EDWARDS: Everyone. I mean, all the deck officers were supposed to have gone over the messages. But, see, when each of us picked up the clipboard and thumbed through it, we missed this short piece of paper that was covered by the others. Just skimmed by it.

QUESTION: Did anyone have to initial these messages to show that they'd read them?

EDWARDS: Well, yes. Normally. See, it was the communications officer's function to get—

QUESTION: Who was that?

EDWARDS: I have it here in my notes somewhere. I'll—

QUESTION: Never mind. I can find it. Go ahead.

EDWARDS: Anyway, it's the communications officer's job —Bass, Mike Bass. That was it. Anyway, it was his job to get these things initialed. They had to be initialed by the captain and all officers of the deck.

QUESTION: Where would they initial it?

EDWARDS: Well, there was a little rubber stamp with boxes for signatures. You signed right on that stamped area.

QUESTION: Was the message on the *Awa Maru* stamped?

EDWARDS: I don't think so. No, I don't think the thing was even stamped.

QUESTION: Was it signed?

EDWARDS: No.

QUESTION: Then what did you do?

EDWARDS: Well, when the captain found out we'd just sunk a ship that had been guaranteed safe passage, all of a sudden it was important for this Shita to tell me about the cargo she carried. I made careful notes. All of a sudden, this cargo was very important.

QUESTION: Shita?

EDWARDS: The steward, the prisoner.

QUESTION: You mean Shimata.

EDWARDS: Yes, Shimata. I keep calling him Shita because, when I first wrote down—

QUESTION: Why was it important to learn what cargo she carried?

EDWARDS: Well, if she carried what I already had begun to guess that she carried, it would put the nature of her safe passage in jeopardy. So, like I said, I took careful notes. It was not easy. This Shita did not speak much English, so I had to rely on my rather limited Japanese and—

QUESTION: Are those the notes you have there?

EDWARDS: Yes.

QUESTION: May I see them?

Personal and Private Notes of Bill Edwards
SUBJECT: The interrogation of Mitsuma Shimata, only survivor of the sinking of the Awa Maru.

With the aid of Japanese English dictionaries was able to obtain information regarding the prisoner Mitsuma Shimata (whose knowledge of English was limited but helpful). He said his age was 46 years old and was a steward first-class. Had a wife and five children living outside Tokyo. Mr. Shimata stated that he and his wife were Buddhist and that his children were Christian (educated by American missionaries). He had studied English.

Prisoner was very eager to be rescued from the water, in contrast to the other members of the crew and passengers of the *Awa Maru*. He further stated that: 16- and 17-year-old boys were being used as aviators . . . B-29 raids are terrorizing Tokyo.

The information concerning the ship *Awa Maru* is as follows: 12,000 tons, diesel-driven, twin screw . . . last of four NTK line sister ships, built at Mitsubishi shipyards in Nagasaki, two years ago. Ship was painted green with illuminated white crosses on each side of the bow, quarters, and topside, forward and aft.

Awa Maru did not zigzag and had no escort. She was proceeding on a straight course for Japan at 16 or 17 knots.

Two American aircraft had sighted the ship earlier during daylight hours, but did not attack. Prisoner saw no other ships while under way. *Awa Maru* was hit by four torpedoes, and she sank stern first.

Prisoner was in his bunk below decks 3/4 aft and was

sucked down with the ship for some depth before he managed to swim safely to surface in the cold water.

Information regarding the cargo:

Much rubber was loaded at Singapore and Djakarta. Tin was loaded at Singapore and lead loaded at Singapore. Rice loaded at Siagon. Many Red Cross packages loaded at Singapore by Japanese soldiers.

Passengers and crew:

Crew	—	120
Passengers	—	1,889
Total	—	2,009

Some passengers were survivors of the ships sunk in SoWesPac. 36 women and 14 small children picked up in Saigon. Others picked up at Saigon and Singapore. No POWs or wounded on board.

Guns and ammunition had been previously removed from the ship at Moji. All passengers were destined for Moji. All hands on board were Japanese.

Shimata thinks the war will be over in two years. Japanese subs no longer any value . . . go to sea and don't come back.

XIV

Date: April 2, 1945
Place: The Formosa Strait
Time: 0015 hours

The explosions had brought them—the grey shark, the hammerhead, and the dreaded great white. And they had come from miles. They didn't feed at first, but circled, stalked, making long, graceful sweeps beneath the clusters of legs above them.

When, finally, one struck, something about the turbulence, the excitement of it, brought the others to life. And there was blood, and the surface churned. When the insanity of it faded away, when the sharks were sated, when one by one they drifted off, the scavengers, the baracudas feeding in schools, darting, slashing, the groupers, the eels.

The four concussions had brought countless schools of silverside to the surface for a mile around, luminescent bellies upward. The scavengers fed on them. And they fed on what the sharks left. They would feed for days before it was all gone, and would be joined by the seabirds when what was left on the surface drifted closer to land. In time, below, there would be only the remnants of that night: a coral-encrusted hulk and a scattering of ocher-white bones.

In terms of total lives lost, the sinking of the *Awa Maru* was the second-largest single sea disaster in history. Of the 2,009 persons aboard, all but one lost their lives.

The sea disaster with the greatest loss of lives was the sinking of the French cruiser *Provence* in the Mediterranean on February 26, 1916. There, 3,100 lives were lost. The famed *Titanic* disaster of April 4, 1912, claimed the lives of 1,517 persons. The torpedoing of the *Lusitania* on May 7, 1915, off Ireland took 1,198.

In terms of the number of survivors, the sinking of the *Awa Maru* is by far the worst of any major naval tragedy on record. In other sinkings with more than one thousand persons aboard, there have always been substantial numbers of survivors. Never before was there only one. In this respect, the sinking of the *Awa Maru* on April Fool's Day, 1945, was the most deadly sea disaster ever.

When Commander Houffman got the confirmation he feared from Edwards' interrogation of the sole survivor, he immediately notified ComSubPac of the details. Upon receipt of the message, Vice-Admiral William B. Garfield, Commander in Chief, ComSubPac, dispatched a reply to the *Queenfish* and her sister ship *Seafox*. The instructions, this time, were clear: return to the scene of the sinking, search for additional survivors, and recover any evidence of contraband cargo.

Garfield's immediate and principal concern was that the Japanese would take terrible action against previously captured American submariners.

In his book, *Sink 'Em All*, Admiral Garfield spelled out his reaction to the sinking of the *Awa Maru:*

> When the staff Duty Officer called me in the early morning hours of April 2 with *Queenfish*'s dispatch reporting the sinking of the *Awa Maru* and recovery of only one survivor, we immediately ordered the *Seafox,* who was patrolling close by, to assist the *Queenfish* in rescuing all possible survivors.
>
> I was gravely concerned about the view the Japanese might take of our apparent breach of faith in sinking a vessel to which full immunity had been accorded, and I was deeply concerned, also, that so fine an officer as Michael Houffman had made such a serious and fatal mistake.
>
> However, my chief worry was occasioned by the fear that the Japanese might wreak barbarous reprisals upon submarine prisoners whom they had captured or might later capture.

QUESTION: You saw the *Awa Maru* sink? You were watching it on radar?

EDWARDS: It took three minutes ... three minutes maximum.

QUESTION: Others said it took two minutes.

EDWARDS: It took three minutes, three minutes maximum.

QUESTION: What did it look like to you?

EDWARDS: Well, that's the funny thing. At least, I thought so at the time. It wasn't until I learned how much she was carrying, how heavy she was, that I understood.

QUESTION: What do you mean?

EDWARDS: Well, as I say, it took three minutes. The blip on the screen first broke into two parts. I'm talking about on the radar. Then, the blip broke up again; this time it showed three pieces, and one by one they disappeared.

QUESTION: What did that mean to you?

EDWARDS: Well, at first I had it figured . . . we all sort of figured . . . that the ship broke into three pieces and sank. But later, I figured it out. See, the torpedoes were set at a depth of three feet. The explosions were probably vented upward, and I don't think any one torpedo could have split the ship at that shallow setting, considering the *Awa Maru* had a draft of thirty feet.

QUESTION: Why the three blips on the screen?

EDWARDS: I think what happened on the radar was that the upper superstructure and stack and bow . . . as each one of these things sank . . . they provided three separate blips. I mean, just that fast: one blip, then two, then the third, and gone. Just about that fast.

QUESTION: Was there a self-destruct device aboard? Was that the reason she went down so fast?

EDWARDS: I don't think so. The four torpedoes exploded in the programmed sequence. I didn't notice any unusual explosion.

QUESTION: And, when you questioned Shimata later, you understood why she went down so fast. Is that right?

EDWARDS: Yeah. Shimata didn't know about the gold, but when he told me about the lead and tin and rubber loaded in Singapore and Djakarta, and realizing how low in the water she sat, that all led up to why she sank so fast. Loaded beyond normal cargo tonnage—overloaded to the extent that her stern was damn near awash.

QUESTION: You said Shimata didn't tell you about the gold?

EDWARDS: No. He didn't know about the gold. He just knew about the loading of over seven thousand Red Cross boxes in Djakarta.

QUESTION: I thought they were loaded in Singapore.

EDWARDS: I mean Singapore. I think Shimata . . . I don't remember all of it, it's been thirty years . . . but I think Shimata said the boxes were loaded in Djakarta, but other sources confirmed Singapore.

QUESTION: But, wait a minute; you said Shimata didn't tell you about the gold. I think you made reference to it in your interrogation notes.

EDWARDS: No.

QUESTION: Let me find it ... here. You've got the word *gold* written in, crossed out, and written again.

EDWARDS: Well, I think that was written later. That had to be written later. I don't think Shimata knew about the gold.

U.S.S. QUEENFISH (S-393)
8 April 1945
In reply refer to SS393/A9

CONFIDENTIAL
From: the Commanding Officer
To: the Commander, Submarine Force, Pacific Fleet
Subject: Sinking of Japanese ship AWA MARU (Continued)

9. ... It was felt that the now exceptional circumstances required obtaining as much information as possible [from the prisoner] and the information resulting from an immediate interrogation and subsequent questioning is submitted as enclosure (a). The apparent veracity of the statements willingly made by the prisoner checked favorably with known information available concerning the AWA MARU such as speed, destination, expected date of arrival, and markings on ship. Particular attention is invited to the statement of the prisoner that the cargo on the AWA MARU included tin, lead, and rubber.

10. At 1548, received dispatch from Commander Submarines, Pacific Fleet, directing the QUEENFISH and SEAFOX to make every attempt to rescue all possible survivors and to recover samples of debris which might indicate character of cargo.

So, we got ordered back, right? Well, when I got the word, I said, "Oh, shit." I mean, it was not where I would choose to spend my afternoon, you know? Jesus, I'll never forget the scene the night before—those eyes, the screams, the people —and here we were going back, really makin' tracks, maybe twenty knots, I don't know.

Look. You don't go through war in one of these sewer pipes without sometimes gettin' so scared your testicles rattle, right? Well, hell, by then, I'd been in—what?—two, three years, and I'd figured I'd seen everything. I mean, like how many times can you shit your pants, right?

But, I'm tellin' ya, with just the thought of goin' back there, of seein' that scene again, and whatever was left of those people after—what?—fifteen to twenty hours—I mean, Jesus Christ. You know?

I remember the whole thing like it was a movie. When the old man cut back the engines, it threw all of us standin' on deck; threw us forward a little, 'til we caught our balance. And then we just kind of coasted in. Nobody sayin' anything. We were just waitin', wonderin' what we were about to see, and wishin' we didn't have to look.

It was pretty late in the afternoon, maybe 1800 hours. The afternoon winds had died by then, and the winds that would pick up later that night hadn't got around to startin'. The water beneath us was just like syrup; I mean, there wasn't a ripple. My brother and I used to go bass fishin' in upper Michigan in water like that; you know, just before sunset? You know how a lake gets? Well, that's how the strait was: cold, still, and quiet. If you didn't know where you were, you'd expect to see a large-mouth bass rise for a fly, you know? The only sound was the sound the bow made slicin' through this gray syrup. Then, pretty soon, we were in the oil slick, still coastin'. If anyone was out there then, they sure as hell weren't makin' sounds about it. About then, we started pickin' up wreckage.

First, a crate, some debris, more crates, a big bale with bands of wire holding it together, the whole thing barely floating, barely showing above the surface ... then, we were in it. Wall-to-wall garbage. I mean, everything for as far as you could see.

Wood, hatch covers, five-gallon containers, rattan tied in bundles, in bunches, like. Tin cans, chairs, and I don't know how many of those big bales, life preservers, crates, boxes, an empty raft—shit, you name it, it was floatin' there.

And not a sound, right? Just slicin' through this stuff like an icebreaker, movin' it aside as we coasted in. And not a sign of anybody, dead, alive, clingin' or not. Not a solitary sign that anybody human had ever been connected with the wreck.

I mean, shit. Think about it. Eighteen hours earlier, the place had been alive, crawlin' with people. And now, nothin' ... nobody. Nobody hangin' face-down in a preserver, nobody dead on a hatch, livin' in a raft. Nobody.

Nothin' but all this garbage floatin' on this dead still slick of oil, with the sun goin' down. . . .

158

U.S.S. QUEENFISH (SS-393)
8 April 1945
In reply refer to SS393/A9

CONFIDENTIAL
From: the Commanding Officer
To: the Commander, Submarine Force, Pacific Fleet
Subject: Sinking of Japanese ship AWA MARU (Continued)

10. ... At 1548 ... proceeded at 17 knots in a calm sea to the attack vicinity, meanwhile directing SEAFOX to join this ship at that location. At 1739, reached position, latitude 25-26.1 N., longitude 120-07.2 E., and detected a large oil slick around which were floating many rectangular boxes and bales similar to those observed immediately following the attack. After considerable physical exertion on the part of the deck force, and utilizing the bowplanes as a recovery platform, three bales were recovered and identified as rubber, each weighing about 175 pounds. Many smaller boxes were observed, of which one was recovered for examination. This box was carefully made up and was found to consist of a five-gallon tin container, covered by wicker or rattan, containing a dark granulated material which could not be identified. No identification marks were on the tin containers. What was assumed to be Dutch markings were stenciled on the sides of the majority of the rubber bales.

11. At about 1815, SEAFOX arrived at the scene and details of the search plan were communicated to the commanding officer by voice. A knowledge of the set and drift of the current observed by both ships during this patrol established the axis of the search plan with the QUEENFISH searching to westward and the SEAFOX to eastward. It was considered highly improbable that anyone could survive in the open water, temperature 56° F., with no protection for this length of time, but a continuous surface search was conducted throughout the night and most of the following day as indicated on the track chart.

Although the fog persisted continuously, no difficulty was experienced in maintaining contact with the oil slick and debris which increasingly covered a wider area of many square miles. Complete negative results, however, were obtained in the search for survivors. No evidence of survivors in the form of lifejackets, lifeboats, rafts, etc.

One junk was encountered, however, at 1040 hours in

latitude 25-32.9 N., longitude 120-09.8 E., and we closed in for inspection, but it contained only five Chinese fishermen and their gear. Considering the suddenness with which the AWA MARU sank, the condition of the sea, and the very few survivors located immediately after the attack, clinging only to bits of wreckage, it is believed that no one survived the sinking other than one person saved by this ship.

I don't know, there was just somethin' about the guy. I mean, what do I know, but ... well, shit. Look at it this way: the war had dragged on for a goddamned eternity, right? We were all pretty sick of it by then. I mean, you can only play the game so long, you know: jumpin' up, soundin' the alarm, runnin' to your battle station. For a while, it's exciting, fun—I mean that—war is fun for a while. But after a while it isn't so much fun anymore. You get sick of it. You want to play something else, right?

Well, we all got that way. And we looked at that knobby-kneed Jap as a kind of a symbol for the way we felt. I mean, shit, here we had been told about our enemy, right? Remember? Big posters of some slant-eyed monster who eats babies for breakfast. Right? You know the kind of thing.

Well, we had been told that. And here was our guy. You know what I mean? He thought everything was great. Big grin spreadin' out across those yellow teeth. We began by givin' him second chances on the depth charges.

Let me explain that.

You know, for some goddamned reason, the government issued these little bottles of brandy in a kind of a punchboard, little cartons. It was our nightly reward when on patrol. When you looked, you could only see the top of the bottle, containing at the most maybe two ounces of brandy. Well, whatever you pulled out is what you got.

Shit, more than not, you'd pull out your depth charge and you'd find it two-thirds evaporated. But, that was it until the next night: what you pulled is what you got. Right? God help you if you tried to take another one.

Well, Shimata the poor bastard, pulled an empty bottle three nights in a row. Empty! None of us—and I kid you not—none of us had ever seen a bottle completely empty before. I mean, shit, if you were really unlucky one night, you might draw half a bottle. Well, like I said, this knobby-kneed little Jap drew empties three times runnin'! The same guy, remember, who was torpedoed out of four ships, right?

Now, he liked booze as much as anybody, and each time he drew an empty, you could see his disappointment. Then he'd begin shakin' his head, sittin' there, shakin' his head back and forth. And pretty soon that grin would start, and before you know it, he'd think drawin' that empty was the funniest thing since Harry Truman. Right?

I guess maybe it was the third time. I mean, it was incredible. You couldn't do that once, let alone three times. Well, he shakes his head, slow like, then pretty soon he starts the laughin' like before. Even he couldn't believe his luck! I guess it was after the third time; we're all sittin' around, and the laughing was over, and when things got settled again, somebody says: "Let him go again."

I don't remember who said it now. It could have been Old Ox. It came kind of quietly. Everyone was sort of still for a minute. And then somebody else says, "What do you mean?" And this same guy, I'm pretty sure it was Old Ox, says, "Let him have another try, for Christ sake!"

Well, you gotta understand what that means. If the old man were sitting with us, he wouldn't get another try. I mean, what the hell. And here we were sitting around that punchboard with our enemy—right?—the guy whose country, probably at that moment, was committing suicide pilots to blowin' up our ships, whose country had murdered thousands of us, friends, brothers, whatever. And, you know what? Sittin' there, we found ourselves nodding our heads, sayin', "Yeah . . . what the hell, give him another try."

I mean, Christ. I don't know. Maybe we were just sick of playin' war.

When *Queenfish* notified ComSubPac of the nature of the cargo they were able to recover from the debris, and when they reported that there were no further survivors, ComSub-Pac notified Washington.

It was a sensitive matter and reaction in Washington was swift. Admiral Ernest J. King, Commander in Chief, U.S. Fleet, wasted no time. He fired off a two-part message to Admiral Chester Nimitz, Commander in Chief, U.S. Pacific Fleet and Pacific Ocean Areas.

The first part of that message went out immediately to the *Queenfish*. She was to return—with appropriate haste—to her port in Guam.

The second part would be hand-delivered at sea by Vice-Admiral William Garfield when the *Queenfish* approached the harbor in Guam. The second part would wait for that.

XV

Date: April 7, 1945
Place: Heading for Guam from patrol area northwest of Formosa
Time: 1000 hours

When the communication was received to return to Guam following their second visit to the sinking site, Commander Houffman acknowledged it and set a direct course for the southernmost island of the Marianas.

Though the reaction from Washington was unusually swift, for Houffman, the reaction from ComSubPac to the *Queenfish*'s message concerning what they had found at the site in the daylight hours of April 2 and 3 was unusually slow. They had departed the site to resume normal patrol areas around Formosa and had maintained that patrol until the message ordering their return to Guam came through the radio shack in the early hours of April 7.

At 1000 hours, shortly after new watches were set and while under way for Guam, Steve Trevor was called to the captain's quarters.

Houffman was sitting on the edge of his bunk, in his skivvies, leaning forward, his long arms draped across his bare knees. Smoke curled up from the cigarette that hung from his hand.

"Those'll kill your game, you know. Suck on enough of those things and you won't be able to walk from one end of the field to the other." Trevor's comment didn't stir Houffman; he remained in thought. Trevor waited for the deliberate pace that Houffman established for the world.

The commander of the *Queenfish* crushed the cigarette out. On a World War II sub, cigarette smoking was restricted, under most conditions, to the few designated areas where the crew gathered during their off-duty hours. Though this regulation was routinely ignored during time of stress, it was, unlike so many other regulations, purposeful. Air was a cherished commodity when submerged; a prolonged dive could develop into an exercise in preserving, uncontaminated, what air was left without depleting the reserve oxygen stored in high-pressure cylinders. There were periods during lengthy depth-charge attacks when there was barely enough oxygen to support lighting a match.

Among the few privileges that befell a commanding officer was smoking when and where he wanted. As he waited for Houffman to speak, Trevor, who would soon assume command of the *Queenfish*, was beginning to wonder if there were any others. The fourth war patrol had ended sooner than either man had anticipated. It was not yet clear whether Houffman or he would take it out on the fifth. In any case, Trevor's day was coming.

"There's . . . I don't know . . . there's something wrong, Steve. You can look at this thing a couple of ways—the way normal people look at things, and the way headquarters looks at things."

Houffman was flexing the toes on his right foot. Both he and Trevor studied the movement as though somehow it contributed to what was being said.

"First, let's look at the sanity of the issue. We're in war. I'm patrolling in known hostile waters. I pick up a contact. It's got a radar configuration of a destroyer at a distance at which one picks up destroyers or DEs. The sonofabitch is movin' flat out, nonzigzag, heading in the approximate direction where Eli Darvies' *Seafox* had engaged a damn Jap convoy a few hours earlier. It's pea soup outside. Nobody sees shit. The convoy's bound to have radioed for help once Darvies commenced his attack. . . .

"I got a time problem. I mean, I can't wait for a week from next Thursday to see what I'll be shootin' at. I've got her on bearing. She's got to hold course until she gets clear of Turnabout Island. Then, there's no telling. So, I make the judgment. I commit."

Houffman stood up, pulled on his trousers, and sat again; there was a feel of finality in the gesture, like completing something.

"Steve, that's how those outside of a loony bin will look at this thing. Now, let's take a look at headquarters.

"This *Awa Maru* is on safe passage. Two warring governments have agreed to let the damn thing pass. Some crackpot sub commander under the flag of one of those governments orders it blown out of the water. . . ."

Trevor waited for more. When it didn't come, he sensed that it was time, that Houffman wanted to hear some words from another source. He eased down on the corner of the bunk.

"You . . . uh, you almost got it figured. But I think you got some other things goin' for you. Your record—if I've got it right—speaks rather highly of you and the decisions you've made in the past. I mean, for a crackpot sub commander, you've done all right.

"The sea bitch you blew out of the water was not exactly doing everything she could to tip us off she was there, you know. I mean, if you were traveling on safe passage in fog, for Christ sake, wouldn't you sound a horn? And Jesus, you saw what she was carrying! You could walk across the strait on all that rubber! God knows what else sank with her!

"You made every effort, short of swimmin' over to her, to identify her. I was there, remember? No idiot, even those at headquarters, is going to try to hang this one on you, Skipper.

"For Christ sake, quit worryin'. When we get to Guam, they'll have a band at the dock. They'll drape you with so much metal you won't be able to walk to the Red Cross barracks.

"Captain, I'll bet the sonofabitch was loaded with nothin' but war supplies. The bale we fished out is all the proof anyone needs. And there must have been a thousand of those. She violated her safe-passage agreement, and she got caught.

"You read the dispatch. That ship was an hour and a half ahead of schedule. That's a pretty fair deviation. And the message mix-up—all right, we made some errors there. You should have had some information to work from. You didn't get it. There are some people on board who failed you in this.

"But look at the message we did get. The one that put that ship anywhere in the Pacific. That's a headquarters screwup.

"Finally, look at what *Seafox* did to us. Had Darvies notified us immediately when they contacted that convoy, we wouldn't have seen hide nor hair of the *Awa Maru*.

"Take it from me, Captain, when we cast a line to the dock at Guam, Nimitz will be there to grab it with one hand. He'll be holding your Navy Cross with the other.

"Would I kid an All-American?"

Date: April 14, 1945
Place: Aboard the *Queenfish,* five miles off Apra Harbor,
      Guam
Time: 1500 hours

It was clear, crisp, and bright. It was a tropical afternoon, and Guam rose out of the Pacific like a giant green sea turtle to sit defiantly on a table of blue, embracing the harbor before it. For the first time since the start of the fourth war patrol, the sun was clearly discernible. The only trace of clouds were those that were poised directly above. They were wispy and white. If there was a darkening on the underside of some of the clouds, it was not visible from five miles out.

The trip home had not been uneventful. En route, the *Queenfish* was diverted by ComSubPac to search for survivors of a downed Navy patrol aircraft. In the early morning hours of April 12, the *Queenfish* located and rescued thirteen exhausted aircraft crew members. They had spent eighty-one hours in a raft. It was a skillful operation. Houffman later received the Bronze Star for his efforts. To the thirteen rescued airmen, Guam appeared as a kind of heaven.

To the tall, lanky man who commanded the boat, who now stood watching the small motor launch pull alongside, the appearance of Guam was something less than that.

When Admiral William Garfield, commander in chief, ComSubPac, climbed on board, Commander Houffman performed the official courtesies. Garfield was grim-faced. He asked for a word alone with Houffman in his quarters.

It did not take long. Ten minutes after he arrived, Admiral Garfield and his motor launch departed. Steve Trevor was alone in the ward room when Houffman came through the hatch.

Trevor had been reading an account in *Coronet* of how a platoon of Marines, driven to avenge the death of their company commander, had all but won the war. According to the article, all that remained for the rest of those fighting World War II was a kind of mop-up operation. The magazine was two years old. When Houffman slid in across from him, Trevor laid it aside.

Houffman was in shock. The pale of his face had given way to a flush that coruscated from his clenched jaw up to his temples. His eyes were vacant, lost to something else. He could not keep his hands still when he brought the coffee cup to his lips.

"Jesus, Skipper. You want something more in that coffee? I've got something in my quarters that might—"

"Steve." Houffman's voice was edged with disbelief. "Steve, they're going to do it."

"What do you mean? What did Garfield say?"

"Steve, they've got it set. They're going to do it."

"What are you talking about?"

"In five days, Steve. They're making me stand a goddamned general in five days."

"Court-martial? They're going to court-martial you?"

"I'm being relieved of command, Steve. They got it all worked out. I face a general court-martial in five friggin' days!"

The silver whistle did not hang from the neck of Marine Staff Sergeant Bernard P. Gunderholtz as he stood in the brilliant sun on the staging area of Apra Harbor just below Camp Dealy. But, otherwise, he looked altogether splendid; tailored, pressed, and shining. He stood a few feet in front of, and facing away from, the six men who comprised his detail. Although the heat and the day-long wait had long since worn away the sharpness of their pressed khakis and had dimmed the mirror shine on their boots, they too looked reasonably sharp. Sergeant Gunderholtz had seen to that. None, of course, matched the military crispness of their leader, who stood locked at parade rest as the maneuvering watch aboard the *Queenfish* cast lines toward the dock.

He would have liked to have worn the whistle. He had considered it a part of his uniform. He had liked the shimmering quality of it and how it looked against his military blouse. It was a kind of medal that he wore with pride. He had even tried it on and looked in the mirror, to see how it looked head on and from the side. But it was too much. It was not in keeping. Reluctantly, he had decided against it.

At 1430 hours, Sergeant Gunderholtz had positioned his detail of Military Police for the arrival of the *Queenfish* and subsequent transfer of the single prisoner aboard to his custody. It was now 1600 hours. But Sergeant Gunderholtz had never, in his entire military career, been late to anything. Since he vested considerable importance in this mission—he had never seen, if truth be told, a bona fide prisoner of war—he had built his day around the event. Necessarily, since they had little choice in the matter, his men were equally committed.

Their day had begun at 0600 hours. There had been a roll

166

call. There was some waiting then, before breakfast. Afterward, they were called out for inspection. There had been more waiting. And then, there had been lunch. After lunch, the detail was called out again. The lieutenant who was to brief them was late. They were told to fall out but to stand at ready. They stood ready until the lieutenant showed up. He briefed them on the transfer and maintenance of a prisoner of war. He was in charge of military security for the post and he read to the men from a large manual. He read them section 183.26, paragraphs 13 and 14, *Military Seizure and Transport of War Prisoners Aboard Small to Medium Sized Floating Vessels in Daylight Hours*. He read the section twice, and had trouble with some of the words. They were told to fall out but to stand at ready. That was at 1300 hours.

They remained at ready until 1415 hours, when they were assembled and marched to the staging area. Where they waited. By 1600 hours, when the *Queenfish* was secured to the dock, everyone but Sergeant Bernard P. Gunderholtz was sick of the whole thing.

When the gangplank was laid and the sub appeared ready for them, he moved his detail of MPs out across the dock. That was the part Sergeant Gunderholtz liked the best. They marched two abreast and their steps sounded loud and hollow against the wood pier. The last two men of the detail stationed themselves at the foot of the gangplank. They stood with their rifles at ready. Sergeant Gunderholtz requested permission to board, then took the remaining four men up the gangplank to the forward deck of the submarine. He approached the officer of the deck.

"Sir," he said. "In accordance with Military procedure for seizure and transport of Japanese prisoners of war, section 183.26, request permission to take, transport, and confine said prisoner, Mitsuma, No-Middle-Initial Shimata, on this, the fourteenth day of April 1945, sir."

"Huh?" The officer of the deck was not sure what this sergeant had in mind.

"Sir," said Sergeant Gunderholtz. Then he said his speech again.

The officer of the deck looked at Gunderholtz, at the detail behind him, and at the two men by the gangplank. "You want the little Jap?" he asked.

"Yes, sir." Already it was not going the way he had hoped, the way it had been spelled out in the manual.

The officer of the deck walked across to the forward hatch

and yelled down. "Anybody seen Shimata?" Sergeant Gunderholtz could not hear the answer. The deck officer shouted back, "Well, how the hell should I know? A guy up here's asking for him." Something else was said below. "Shit," said the officer of the deck. He approached Gunderholtz. "He's cleaning the head."

"Sir?"

"I said he's cleaning the head. He'll be out in a while."

"Yes, sir," said Sergeant Gunderholtz. He executed a smart about-face. "Detail," he called to the four men in formation. *"Pah-a-rade rest!"*

It took Shimata fifteen minutes to finish up below. He came forward, passing to the port side of the sail, wiping his hands on his baggy shorts. He was smiling.

When he approached Gunderholtz and his detail of men, he came in short little steps, bowing, smiling as he moved. By this time the crew had gotten the word on the taking of Shimata and some of them had come up with him. Others came up through the forward hatch. Still others watched from the bridge and the cigarette deck. Boldern, who had been working up on the shearwater, recognized Gunderholtz. "Hey, Sarge," he yelled down. "Where's your whistle?"

Under the cover of the two riflemen at the foot of the gangplank, the four MPs surrounded the little prisoner. Shimata was trying to execute still another bow when the MPs on either side grabbed his arms and yanked them behind him. The action overwhelmed Shimata and, caught off-balance, he stumbled to his knees. Then he was yanked upward, off his feet. One of the MPs was wrestling with a pair of handcuffs; he could not get them open. Shimata's knees were bleeding.

"You need more men, Sarge," Easter called down from the cigarette deck. "Somebody get Ox."

The operation was not going as smoothly as Sergeant Gunderholtz had hoped. There was too little prisoner to go around. All four MPs wanted something consequential to do, and, in an attempt to do it, they got in one another's way. Since they had spent the day, since 0600, being drilled on the importance of the assignment, it was hard to cool their ardor. And, under the increasingly abusive taunts from the crew, there was a need to finish the task quickly.

The bows that the frightened Shimata continued to make were not making things any easier. Even after the handcuffs were in place, he would not hold his head still long enough for them to tie the blindfold.

"Hang in, Shimata," Bicca called from the bridge. "I think you got 'em beat."

"Hey, Sarge," Garrabaldi leaned across Bicca. "You want us to call in air cover?"

They could not get the blindfold tight enough, and when they started to shove Shimata toward the gangplank, it fell down to the bridge of his nose. That seemed to worry Shimata as much as the MPs. But it wasn't until he reached up to reposition the blindfold that it became apparent that the handcuffs had not been secured, that Shimata had been holding them in place out of courtesy.

When he did reach up, the handcuffs clattered to the deck.

Easter began the clapping. He clapped alone for a few seconds. Then someone on the forward deck picked it up. One, two others joined in. Then, it spread. By the time Shimata had been shoved unceremoniously down the gangplank past the two riflemen, the entire crew of the U.S.S. *Queenfish* was applauding, cheering, and calling Shimata's name.

It was difficult, but, as frightened as Shimata was, he was able to turn his head and, before the MPs closed around him, acknowledge the cheers with a brief wave of the hand and a yellow-toothed grin.

That was on Saturday. On Monday, the *Queenfish* was moored to the starboard side of the U.S.S. *Tench*. The U.S.S. *Apollo* was nearby. The *Queenfish* was assigned to refit status. Following is the boat's log:

0800 hours. Mustered crew at quarters. Absentees: None.

0810 hours. In accordance with orders of ComSubPac, Lt. Commander Steve Trevor, USN, relieved Commander Raymond M. Houffman, USN, and assumed command.

0810 hours. In accordance with order of ComSubPac, Commander Raymond Michael Houffman, USN, was detached this date.

0900 hours. SUBDIV relief crew relieved officers and crew of this vessel.

1000 hours. Officers and crew left ship for Camp Dealy for rest and recuperation.

The log was signed "E. F. Pitt, Lt. (jg) USN."

Commander Houffman was to comment later about how

he felt being relieved of command and facing a court-martial for the actions he took on that fogbound night:

"My feeling about the incident was not one of remorse. No, I did not feel that. Rather, my feeling was one of aggrievement. I did not feel that I had been given the necessary information. I can say this: If I knew now only what I had known at the time, I would do it again!"

QUESTION: Steve, if you were making the decision that night, if you were not the PCO but were in Commander Houffman's shoes and had the same information he had, would you have fired the four torpedoes?

TREVOR: Yes. Unequivocally.

QUESTION: Without visual, without seeing it?

TREVOR: Yes. It all added up. The decision the skipper made was one I would have made, given what we knew.

QUESTION: And you had additional information?

TREVOR: You mean the sonar? Okay, yes. I had that, and I didn't pass it on. I remember the sonarman saying something about the heavy-sounding screws.

QUESTION: Why didn't you pass that along?

TREVOR: We were already on bearing, mark. We were already committed, and you got some kid telling you . . . I don't know. It's true. I didn't pass it along. I thought about it since. But, you know, you can quarterback these things years later, and it all sounds different. At the time, it was war, you know? You make decisions on the best available information. I would have made Captain Houffman's decision, with or without what the sonarman said. But it's true: I didn't pass it along.

Camp Dealy, for Christ sake. You know, there's something that always bothered me about that place. I mean, taking R and R there sure beat floatin' around in a war patrol, but not by all that much. I mean, shit. How long can you play horseshoes, right?

But what got to me, got to all of us, was how they distributed the wealth, you know? I'm not talking about booze. The officers—at least those on the Queenfish—*always took care of their men in that respect. You know, they'd see to it that the booze was sent down. It was against regulations, but most of them were pretty square about it.*

170

See, the officers' quarters was up on the hill. And not all that far from the Red Cross barracks. Down the hill was our barracks. The animals, you know? And that, the whole setup, was what used to get to us.

Now, I'm not sayin' all the Red Cross girls came off looking like Veronica Lake, but there were a number of good-lookin' gals, right? Okay. All right. I know what you're thinking. You're sayin' Old Ox in a nursing cap would look good to us in our condition. But believe me, we thought about those girls on the hill. I swear, in the evening when the wind was right, you could smell 'em, you know?

But they were officers, right? I mean, some high mucky-muck gave these girls officers' status. So, they couldn't fraternize with the animals. Whoever set up this hellhole of a rest camp had it figured that enlisted men were all eunuchs, that what really turned us on was a horseshoe pit, right?

Anyway, I think that's how we got our pipeline to the booze. Some of the officers, between midnight romps on the beach, got to feelin' sorry for us. Not all of them. I mean, most didn't give a shit, you know? But some of them got to feelin' pretty bad about a regulation that limited our ambitions to a good stiff game of pocket pool, you know?

So, we'd get deliveries from the hill. A case here, a case there. But never what we really wanted. I don't care how many bottles you put away, Old Ox never looked any better.

Anyway, we were talking about that, the Red Cross girls on the hill, that morning just before lunch, the morning we began R and R. Costello had it figured. He was sayin' that it was bad enough that the nurses were limited to officers, but when one didn't need his privilege, they ought to allow substitution. He was talking about Ensign Diefenbaker.

Roy Bicca had come into the barracks then. He pulled up a foot locker. The look on his face made us all stop talking.

He asked us whether we'd gotten the word, whether we'd heard about the skipper. Now, we had heard about him being relieved by Trevor, but that had been in the cards all along. What we hadn't heard was what Bicca then told us, about the court-martial, about the captain facing a general court-martial that was to begin three days later, for Christ sake. A general court-martial for sinking a Jap ship! Now, can you believe that?

No. None of us could believe that worth a damn, you know? Even when Bicca supplied us with the details: the message mix-up, the treaty, the safe passage, the whole thing.

It added up, all right. How it added up was that they were putting the screws to the old man because they needed somebody to put the screws to. I mean, we got nothin' but steamed about the whole thing. The more we talked, the more steamed we got.

Let me back off a minute, so's you understand. Now, you've probably heard all the bullshit about submariners. You know, you got the old man, the father figure, a Tyrone Power or some goddamned thing. He's a crusty old bastard, right? But, I mean, you know, goin' in, that deep down he's got ... what? ... a heart of gold. Right? I mean, he's the kind of guy who'll turn his wife over to the crew if it's gonna help morale.

And the crew. They're all pimple-faced kids, and none of them could find their ass with both hands, and when they talk about the old man, a kind of hush comes over 'em. Frankly, the old man would be safe to turn his wife over to this crowd. But, that's the crew. You've heard the stories. Seen the movies. At dramatic moments, the old man turns on the sincerity, right?

"Men, you all realize we're trapped here on the ocean floor under four hundred feet of water. And, you realize we all must make a sacrifice ..." You've heard how it goes, right? "And you know what I think of you men ..." His voice might break a little there. "So, it hurts to have to ask everyone under the rank of lieutenant (jg) to quit breathing." And, in unison, they all cheer, "Aye, aye, sir," and one by one, as they each fall over dead, the camera pans in on the old man, right? And you can see in the corner of one eye a big tear wellin' up, but just in time he swallows, shakes it off....

You've seen all the bullshit, right? Well, the way it really was was somethin' else.

Okay. I don't say none of us liked the skipper. I don't mean that, I think most of us ... like I said ... felt he was a pretty good leader and worked harder'n hell to keep us alive. And, from what I've heard, you can draw a commander who didn't know his aft from a periscope well. You know what I mean?

I mean, there are guys like that. And there are other guys lookin' for trophies the old lady can hang up in the den at home, and to hell with what it costs. And to hell with the crew. You know the kind: hears his wife is makin' it with some chief at home, and all of sudden he wants to take his sub up the Yangtze and portage across the Gobi or some damn thing.

So, there was worse things than being issued Commander Houffman. But, I mean, balls, the guy was human. Every one of us got pissed at him sometime or another . . . and there were the jokes. You know, gray hair or not, sometimes the guy didn't look more than fourteen, right?

Look. Nobody was gonna jump up and swallow a torpedo for him, but he was pretty well liked. And when we got the word, most of us sittin' around the barracks in Camp Dealy, for Christ sake, we got pretty steamed.

I mean, what the hell. Here's a big freighter, probably haulin' enough gear to start and finish World War III, smokin' along in the fog, goin' like ninety . . . I mean, Jesus.

Now, I don't mean to give you any of that old-man crap, but, you know, this guy . . . Jesus Christ, this guy's been through it! So we drop a Jap ship, right? So maybe we were not in war? Maybe we were in some other damn thing?

I mean, Jesus Christ. . . .

You know, I got into the sewer-pipe service figurin' I'd escape some of the bureaucratic bullshit you get on a surface scow, right? I mean, what the hell. You figure the percentages we were workin' under to come out alive, that it was voluntary, that you had to work like hell to get on one of these things. You figure all that, and wouldn't you think they'd let you do your job, let you get on with the goddamned thing?

Are you kiddin? They got to haul your CO to court. Right? For what? 'Cause he blew a Jap ship away. For Christ sake.

We'd talked about it some—hell, we talked about it quite a bit. Most of us were . . . like I said . . . pretty steamed. Particularly when we heard that some of us—me, Old Ox, and others—may have to testify. You know? Well, shit. We talked about it. Old Ox had it that the court-martial was nothin' but a formality, to make the Japs think that we really gave a shit, that the old man would come out of it wearin' a medal.

Well, throughout the next couple of days, the brass starts showin' up, right? Admirals, generals, they had everybody who's anybody on the court. If Jesus Christ showed up, he would have been outranked.

It's about then we got thinkin' maybe Old Ox, for the first time in his rotten life, was right. That the powers that be were goin' to showcase the thing, make a big deal out of it so the

173

Japs could say: "There, you see? They had everybody and their mother on the court. They really wanted to get to the bottom of it."

So, if Old Ox was right, the old man would be in and out of that room in ten minutes flat.

But, like I say, Old Ox never had anything right in his life, for Christ sake. . . .

AUTHOR'S NOTE

The following three chapters are, in part, comprised of material that the government has classified secret. At this writing, it is not known, nor could it be ascertained, whether the document in question has been declassified. Since the full transcript of the general court-martial proceedings of Commander Houffman was secured from other than official sources, those sources shall remain unnamed.

Prior to publication of this material, the writer, on January 18, 1977, talked with Lieutenant Commander Kenneth Stein, office of the Judge Advocate General of the Navy in the Pentagon. The purpose of that conversation was to determine the current state of classification on the document then in the possession of the writer.

Following is that conversation:

QUESTION: I'm trying to determine the classified status of a court-martial transcript. This was a trial held near the end of World War II and concerns the sinking of a Japanese merchant ship traveling under safe passage. What I need—

STEIN: The *Awa Maru*?

QUESTION: Yes. Uh . . . I'm surprised you, uh, have that.

STEIN: Didn't you write a letter of inquiry to us about six months ago?

QUESTION: Perhaps my office did

STEIN: I remember that. You asked whether there was any material pertaining to the sinking that was still classified.

QUESTION: What was your response?

STEIN: Well, I'd have to look in my inquiry file.

QUESTION: Okay. Maybe you won't need to. I'd like to determine if the transcript of the trial . . . the court-martial . . . is still classified secret.

STEIN: I don't think so. But I'd have to check in the

archives. I'll tell you, let me look in the inquiry file. I've got it here. . . .

QUESTION: Okay.

STEIN: . . . Maybe this is going to take longer. . . . Are you on a commercial line?

QUESTION: Yes, but go ahead. Take your time.

STEIN: . . . Here, for some reason, I only have noted that the material is now declassified.

QUESTION: Who was the inquiry from?

STEIN: A Mr. —— of the San Diego Union. Is that you?

QUESTION: No. That's someone else.

STEIN: Well, I just have that one note. I can't tell you exactly, but most of this material is declassified. You know, the movements of ships and matters that once were important are not now.

QUESTION: So, this material on the court-martial of Commander Houffman is declassified?

STEIN: Near as I can tell.

QUESTION: Well, I need to make sure.

STEIN: Well, I'd say it was declassified.

QUESTION: Okay. I'll use your name. You're Commander . . . Lieutenant Commander Kenneth Stein, of . . .

STEIN: Office of the Judge Advocate of the Navy.

QUESTION: Fine. I'll be publishing shortly, and—

STEIN: Was there any part of the court-martial proceedings, any information on the court-martial, you needed?

QUESTION: No. I've got it.

STEIN: What?

QUESTION: I've got it.

STEIN: Wait a minute. You've got the court-martial? You've got the document?

QUESTION: Yes.

STEIN: That puts . . . look, I've got to get a reading on that. I'm going to have to get back into the archives.

QUESTION: Why?

STEIN: Well, I'm not sure . . . I guess it's a moot point, if you already have it. You mean, you've got the thing?

QUESTION: I'd like to determine if it's classified or not. I'm going to use it. My hope, of course, is that the material is unclassified.

STEIN: I'd have to check in the archives.

QUESTION: Okay. How soon can you get me an answer? I'm publishing shortly.

STEIN: Give me your name again, and where I can reach you.

QUESTION: (Name and address given.)

STEIN: I'll get back today or tomorrow.

QUESTION: I'd like to know today.

STEIN: Well, I can't promise. I'll look for it now. I'll try to get back this afternoon. Tomorrow, anyway.

Lieutenant Commander Stein did not return that call. Repeated crosscountry calls to his office failed to earn a return call. Without further communication, one is forced to draw his own conclusions. This, right or wrong, is mine:

That the entire document, which carries a SECRET stamp, may well remain classified, though matters surrounding it are declassified; i.e., Lieutenant Commander Stein may be able to release information on the court-martial on a question-by-question basis but is not permitted to make public the entire document. Since all other war matters within that period of time have been declassified and made public, one wonders about the Pentagon's reticence in this matter.

Curiously, the U.S. government is not alone in its reluctance to release information on this matter. The reticence of the U.S. government is matched by that of the Japanese and the Swiss governments. Calls to the Japanese Embassy in Washington, D.C., to gain information on any aspect of the sinking of the *Awa Maru* have been met with stiff resistance.

The last word from that embassy was:

"We do not have any information on the *Awa Maru*."

"Is there someone I can write in Japan?"

"No."

"You mean, you have no information?"

"None."

"You have information but won't reveal it?"

"I cannot answer any more questions."

"You're saying that you will not answer any questions about the *Awa Maru*."

"I will answer no more questions."

A letter addressed to the Embassy of Switzerland, seeking information concerning the part that the Swiss government played in the agreement for a safe-passage status of the *Awa Maru*, was answered by Colonel R. E. Muhhi, defense attaché:

"After having checked all sources here at the embassy, it is

176

unfortunately not possible for me to send you a copy of the desired agreement or to answer your questions."

Apparently, none of the governments in question, for widely different reasons, seems willing to disclose the truth about the *Awa Maru*. The writer believes that the time to reveal the truth has arrived, now that an American salvage team is in pursuit of an agreement with China to recover the mysteries that lie with her.

Those who will be served by revealing the facts will be those with nothing to hide, those who have suffered the suspicion cast over the episode for three decades, be they individuals or be they governments.

XVI

Date: April 19, 1945
Place: Headquarters compound, Camp Dealy, Guam
Time: 0950 hours
Status: The prosecution

The two burly MPs towered over the prisoner sandwiched between them as they traversed the enclosure, heading toward a group of officers nursing the last of their cigarettes. The officers had gathered outside one of the prefabs that formed the perimeter of the compound. As the three passed the flagpole in the center of the enclosure, the little man in the middle stumbled over the cuffs of his trousers. The two MPs waited uncomfortably as the prisoner stooped to roll the cuffs of his enormous khakis up over his boots. Then, recovering whatever military decorum was left in the situation, the three continued across.

Former Chief Steward Mitsuma Shimata fell somewhat short of what the military used as a model for its basic clothing issue. The arms of his T-shirt hung somewhere below his elbows; the remainder had been jammed into his trousers. These were secured in folds by his GI belt and there was enough belt left over to allow some decorative loops and turns before the end of it was lost inside of his trousers. On his shirt, only the top of the letters PW were visible above the belt. (On the second day of the trial, evidently due to the stern admonition of the court, the letters PW, prisoner of war, would be replaced with the more accurate identification CI, civilian internee.)

In Guam, the heat of the day blooms early and stays late; by 1000 hours it's as hot and humid as it's going to get. It was just short of 1000 hours when Commander Raymond Michael Houffman crossed the enclosure. He was alone. The officers who had been waiting outside had finished their cigarettes

178

and gone in. There was nothing unusual about his gait or his posture as he crossed the baked clay toward the building. He had the long, easy stride of an athlete; his crisp white uniform kept his loose-limbed casualness in check.

Steve Trevor, inside, saw his approach and came out to meet him. They met at the foot of the stairs, exchanged salutes, then shook hands. There were several things Trevor had wanted to say to Houffman, but as he stood facing him in the brightness of that morning, just eighteen days after the sinking of the *Awa Maru,* he forgot them all. After a moment of silence, Houffman spoke.

"She's a pretty good boat, you know. Did I tell you I drove her out of the yards?"

"Uh, yeah, I think so. Look, Skipper—"

"So take care of her, okay? If you've got to whore around for targets, do it with a little class. She deserves it. Up until . . . up until recently, she's been pretty good to me."

"This thing, today, Captain, is—"

"And bring her back, will you? Steve, if you lose her to—"

"Goddamn it, shut up, Skipper!" There was no anger in the words. Both men knew it. For a long while neither spoke. Finally Houffman said:

"I understand they got more rank here than they had for the Billy Mitchell trial. Are they all inside?"

"They're inside, Skipper."

"If I'm gonna go, I'm gonna go big. Right?"

"What are they gonna do, Captain? For Christ sake, what can they do? Skipper, this thing is a showcase, an orchestrated piece of naval nonsense."

"You're right. I was lookin' it up last night, Steve. The worst they can give me is a dishonorable and five years' hard labor. And you know how time flies when you're having fun."

"Captain, damn it, it'll be over in ten minutes. They'll run through it and exonerate you. I can't imagine them doing anything else."

"Steve." Houffman looked down at his shoes, banged the dust off them, looked again at Trevor. "Steve, weren't you the guy who said they would be meeting me at the dock with a brass band?"

Trevor mumbled something, looking down.

"What?"

"I don't think I said it would be brass."

The highest-ranking court-martial ever assembled in naval history was confined to a small rectangular room that had once been used as a barracks, a room so narrow that those seated at the long table could not rise without banging their chairs against the wall. The prosecution sat at one end of the table, the defense at the other. Members of the court sat beneath a row of high, screened windows. If you stood up, you could see out across the compound and to the city of Old Guam below. Seated, you could see nothing but the bright white sky. And, in the morning hours, when the sun streamed in through the windows, it was difficult for a witness to see the members of the court across from him.

Just outside the courtroom was the holding room, where Shimata waited with the two Marines. The walls of the courtroom were paper-thin. Both Trevor and Edwards later reported that one could easily hear the secret proceedings inside the courtroom through the walls of the adjoining head; that, sitting on the can, one could hear as much as could the judge advocate inside the room.

Trevor was the first witness called. He was escorted in and took his seat at the green-topped table. He recognized the members of the court across from him: Captain David Evans, brilliant sub commander, one of "us"; Vice-Admiral Paul McLean, cold, aloof; Rear Admiral Robert Warren; Rear Admiral Arlo Smith; Captain Andrew Rizzo; Vice-Admiral Edwin Rundstedt, smiling, friendly; and Captain Otto Zimmerman, the judge advocate.

Earlier, Houffman had pleaded not guilty to all three charges:

1. Culpable inefficiency in the performance of duty.
2. Disobeying the lawful order of his superior officer.
3. Negligence in obeying orders.

The second charge and the third were the most and the least damaging, respectively.

Later, when Trevor was asked to express the mood of the court that morning, he responded without hesitation:

"It's true. There was a distinct feeling that morning when I went in, and there's only one word—a single word—to describe it: grim. The feeling you got that day was that whatever the court would eventually do, it would do it grimly."

It was a grim climate for a trial. The Japanese government had been notified of the sinking on April 17, sixteen days after the event, two days before the court-martial. The Japanese protest, filed shortly thereafter through the Swiss government, left little doubt about how they viewed the disaster:

One. Japanese Government have received communication of United States Government concerning sinking of AWA MARU transmitted by note verbale of Swiss Legation Tokyo, 17th April, stating information that about midnight, 1 April, ... a ship was sunk by a submarine action at a position approximately 40 miles from the estimated scheduled position of AWA MARU. No lights or special illumination were visible at any time. The ship sank almost immediately. One survivor stated that the ship was the AWA MARU.

Two. Prompted by traditional humanitarian principles, Japanese Government complied with repeated earnest requests of United States Government for assistance in transporting relief supplies to United States and Allied prisoners of war and internees in Japanese hands. During November 1944, Japanese Government took delivery of 2,000-odd tons of relief supplies which had been sent from United States to Soviet territory in East Asia to forward same to Japan proper, Manchutikuo, China, and southern areas.

United States Government guaranteed to Japanese Government, by the communication transmitted by note verbale of Swiss Legation in Tokyo on 12 September 1944, that Allied Governments were prepared to accord safe conduct to Japanese ships to be employed in transport of goods between ports under Japanese administration and Soviet port of trans-shipment, Nakhodka ...

The Japanese Government understood from above-mentioned communication from United States Government that these ships would ... be guaranteed not to be subjected to attack, visit, or any interference whatever by United States and Allied forces, either on their outward or homeward voyage, and in reply to Japanese Government's request for confirmation of this understanding, United States Government, through note verbale of Swiss Legation, Tokyo 13 December 1944, solemnly promised that the ships selected to transport relief supplies will not be subjected to attack, visit, or any interference by United States and Allied forces either on outward or homeward voyage connected with transportation of these supplies.

Again, by their note verbale 30 January last, addressed

to Swiss Legation, Tokyo, Japanese Government notified United States Government to utilize for transport of relief supplies a ship plying between Japan and southern areas. Japanese Government had decided to utilize AWA MARU for same purpose and requested United States Government to reconfirm that same ship would not be subjected to attack, visit, or any interference whatever by United States and Allied forces either on outward or homeward voyage.

United States Government, through note verbale of Swiss Legation, Tokyo, 13 February, fully confirmed above-mentioned guarantee.

AWA MARU sailed from Moji 17 February, and, after carrying relief supplies to southern areas, started on homeward voyage.

Since the night of 1 April, however, she was not heard of and all efforts for her search proved futile. Japanese Government inquired of United States Government 10 April. Japanese Government received United States Government's communication referred to in paragraph 1 above.

It has now become evident that AWA MARU sank by a United States submarine in straits of Formosa at midnight on 1 April and that 1,000 and several hundreds of her passengers and the cargoes shared her fate.

· Three. As stated above, United States Government have thrice guaranteed absolute safety of voyage of AWA MARU. Japanese Government notified United States Government of her routes and schedules and these were duly noted by United States Government. She following same routes according to same schedule, wore the marks which had been notified to and duly noted by United States Government, and the marks were illuminated and navigation lights were lighted at night.

That ship was at scheduled position at time of sinking is clear also from a communication received from her on 1 April immediately before she was sunk.

THEREFORE, IT CANNOT BUT BE CONCLUDED THAT SHE WAS DELIBERATELY AND WILFULLY ATTACKED AND SUNK BY UNITED STATES SUBMARINE. RESPONSIBILITY FOR DISASTER, THEREFORE, UNMISTAKABLY LIES WITH UNITED STATES GOVERNMENT.

Four. In spite of United States Government's malicious propaganda distorting fact of the fair treatment accorded by Japanese Government to prisoners of war and civilian internees, the Japanese Government have unflinchingly continued their efforts for humanitarian treatment of prisoners of war and internees in their hands.

The AWA MARU was selected to be employed in such humanitarian service in order to cope with United States Government's ardent desire and in the face of considerable difficulties. The United States force, in violation of United States Government's solemn promise to give her safe conduct, intercepted her on her return voyage and deliberately attacked and sank her.

THIS IS THE MOST OUTRAGEOUS ACT OF TREACHERY UNPARALLELED IN THE WORLD HISTORY OF WAR. UNITED STATES GOVERNMENT ARE TO BE DEEMED TO HAVE ABANDONED THEIR FORMER DESIRE RELATING TO THE TREATMENT OF UNITED STATES PRISONERS OF WAR AND CIVILIAN INTERNEES IN JAPANESE HANDS. JAPANESE GOVERNMENT MOST EMPHATICALLY DEMAND THAT UNITED STATES GOVERNMENT BEAR THE WHOLE RESPONSIBILITY FOR THIS DISGRACEFUL ACT COMMITTED IN VIOLATION OF THE FUNDAMENTAL PRINCIPLES OF HUMANITY AND INTERNATIONAL LAW.

Japanese Government as well as Japanese people are most profoundly indignant of this extremely outrageous incident. They will watch United States Government's attitude concerning this matter with most serious concern.

THEY DO HEREBY FILE THE STRONGEST PROTEST WITH UNITED STATES GOVERNMENT AND DECLARE THAT THEY RESERVE ALL RIGHTS FOR TAKING ANY SUCH MEASURES AS MAY BE PROVED NECESSARY TO COPE WITH SUCH PERFIDIOUS ACTS ON THE PART OF UNITED STATES GOVERNMENT.

I mean, there we were. Me, Old Ox, and a couple of the other enlisted men. Well, I had a pretty fair idea why they called me to appear as a trial witness, what with the sonar report I had given that night. And, maybe the others could give testimony that would shed some light on the events. But Old Ox?

I mean, Jesus Christ. I guess they wanted some guys who were on deck that night, and Old Ox had been the guy to first pick up Shimata. Maybe that was it. But Old Ox? I couldn't get over it. What's he going to tell anybody, right? If they ask his name and rating, he'll give them his age, and probably get that wrong. But we were all on a kind of standby status, to be called at the "discretion of the court," whatever the shit that was. And, maybe Old Ox wouldn't be called. You only had to look at Ox, for Christ sake, and you'd know he couldn't tell you the name of his own government, right? Anyway, there we were, him and me, sittin' there since 0900 waitin' on whatever the hell the discretion of the court was. And Ox, he's scared, you know? He saw the brass troop in, and when he sees they got everybody but MacArthur on the court—and maybe he's comin' later—Ox doesn't know whether to fill his pants or go blind thinkin' on it.

And I ain't any too easy about the whole thing myself, you know? I mean, what do they want from me? If I tell them what I heard on those headphones that night—that what was out there was sure as shit no destroyer—I'm going to sink the skipper, right?

Look at it this way: anybody who has spent more than three days in the Navy knows how a vessel is identified. You got visual. You got radar. You got sonar. Now, if you can't see worth a shit, you got to rely on the other two, right? So, you got radar sayin' one thing, you got sonar sayin' something else. Conflicting reports, okay? One cancels out the other. Without visual, you could be opening fire on the Enterprise, *for Christ sake.*

So, what I'm going to say is going to depend a whole lot on what Trevor tells the court. If he tells them about the sonar report I gave him that night, I'm off the hook. Trevor's going to be the one to sink the skipper. Bad as that is, at least it ain't me who's pulling the cork.

Now, the other possibility didn't occur to me until I got to thinkin' about it there, sittin' next to Old Ox, that morning. What if Trevor hadn't passed on to the skipper what I had heard on sonar?

It was a question I hadn't thought about before, because I couldn't imagine Trevor not passing along the information. I mean, it just wouldn't make much sense. But, if Trevor hadn't passed it along, and didn't tell the court, I was still on the hook. I would be telling the court one more thing the skipper should have known and didn't.

Up to then, I couldn't tell you for sure whether, if it came to me, I would risk perjury rather than sink the skipper. My only hope was that I wouldn't have to make the decision, that Trevor, when he testified, would make it for me.

Okay. All right. I hear you. You're saying, what's it to me anyway? They hang the skipper or they don't, right? You're sayin' I'm not much for this old-man bullshit, anyway. What do I care, you're sayin'.

Well, I told you, this skipper of ours, this Houffman, was pretty well liked. I told you there are commanders, and there are commanders. Right? I told you we wouldn't walk around swallowin' torpedoes for him, but he was a good leader. And now you're sayin' that maybe this was swallowin' a torpedo, my risking perjury to save him.

Okay. Maybe so. I sure as hell didn't need brig time and a bad conduct at this stage of the goddamned war. Shit, I was on orders to rotate Stateside, for Christ sake. So, why would I risk it, right?

It's hard to explain. I mean, you had to be there, you know? This guy, this captain, he put us through it, he brought us back. And, more than once, he saved our collective asses. And, there's this other thing.

As a kid, I grew up in a gang. I mean, that was your life. You were a member of the gang, or you weren't diddly-squat. You did what the gang did and, no matter what, you stuck together. I was a member of it, and later I was the leader of the damn thing. Throughout, in and out of trouble, you hung in. There was the gang, and there was the rest of the world. That's how it was. And you hung in. If it meant getting your ass whomped or not, you hung in. If it meant going to jail or not, you hung in. I mean, that's how it was, and that's how I felt. I think that's how most of us felt. Aboard that sub, it was like the gang. You hung in, no matter what.

So, I was thinkin' on all this, trying to get my act together, hoping to hell I wasn't called before Trevor, hoping that I wouldn't have to lie about the sonar, when Old Ox, sittin' there next to me, starts up. Now, he's worried about all the brass, about what he's supposed to do if called.

I tell him to cool it, you know? Just answer the questions. I tell him it doesn't take being a genius. But he wants to know all of it, so he can get things figured in his muddled head, right? He wants to know from the beginning. So, I tell him he's going to have to take an oath.

"What do you mean?" he says. So, I explain it, right? The thing about Old Ox is you're never sure he understands anything, you know? But, he's nervous. You can tell that,

'cause he looks like he does when he gets a good hand in poker—his upper lip was sweating and he had this kind of numb look about him. So, I try to take him through it.

I tell him he'll have to give his name, rank, and present station, but that stops him. He's in trouble already, right?

"Present station?"

"The Queenfish, Ox," I tell him. "The goddamned sub, remember?"

"Oh," he says. Honest to Christ, I think it was news to him. I was going to tell him he was going to have to know something about where he was on April 1, that they would be asking him that. But Jesus, you know? What can you do? Let it be a surprise. If the court called him, Old Ox was going to be the biggest challenge those spread-assed admirals had in their entire Navy career.

Captain Houffman was damn near the last in. I remember him coming through the waiting room with Trevor. We, both Ox and me, stood up. He looks at me, kind of fixes me with those steel-blue eyes, nods, and heads into the courtroom.

You're going to get on me for this, but—and I ain't going to admit this to everyone—but I mean, him walkin' in there with a kind of determination in the way he carried himself, the kind of cool composure we'd all seen in him when we were under the gun, when we didn't know whether we were going to see another sunrise or the next thirty seconds. And, I don't know, I just kind of felt proud—I hate that word, but it's true—a kind of pride for serving the guy, for being a part of the goddamned crew of the Queenfish.

Okay, all right. I know that sounds like so much bullshit. But to hell with you. That's how I felt. And you can write that down. All Navy crap aside, this guy was our captain. All right, better than that. He was the old man, you know?

I mean, Jesus Christ.

Case of:

Raymond M. Houffman,
    Commander,
    U.S. Navy
    19 April 1945

S E C R E T

RECORD OF PROCEEDINGS

of a

GENERAL COURT-MARTIAL
convened at

Headquarters,
COMMANDER FORWARD AREA,
CENTRAL PACIFIC

by order of

COMMANDER IN CHIEF,
U. S. PACIFIC FLEET AND
PACIFIC OCEAN AREAS

Copy furnished.

A true copy. Attest:

/s/ Otto H. Zimmerman

Otto H. Zimmerman
Captain, U. S. Navy,
Judge Advocate

Q. State your name, rank, and present station.

A. Steve Trevor, Lieutenant Commander, U.S. Navy, U.S.S. QUEENFISH (SS393).

Q. Where were you during the period of 8 March to 2 April 1945?

A. Attached to and serving on board the U.S.S. QUEENFISH in the capacity of prospective commanding officer.

Q. Where was the QUEENFISH during that period?

A. She was conducting an offensive war patrol in the East China Sea area number 11 A and B.

Q. Where were you at approximately 2200 on the night of 1 April 1945?

A. I was in the ward room of the U.S.S. QUEENFISH at that time.

Q. Did you remain in the ward room?

A. No, sir. On receiving word there was a radar contact, I went to the control room with the commanding officer and when tracking stations were called I went back to the officers' country to make sure they got the word. I then went back to the control room where the captain gave me a communication to send to our sister wolf.

Q. Did you remain in the conning tower throughout the attack?

A. No, sir. I sent a message to the SEAFOX for the commanding officer and later he had a conference on the bridge concerning what depth to set the torpedoes.

Q. Was any other matter than depth setting discussed during that conference?

This question was objected to by the accused on the ground that it was irrelevant and hearsay.

The judge advocate withdrew the question.

Q. Did you have any discussion with the captain during the period of conference with him on the bridge on subjects other than torpedo depth setting?

This question was objected to by the accused on the ground that it was irrelevant.

The judge advocate replied.

The court announced that the objection was sustained.

Q. Did you have a battle station on the QUEENFISH during this period?

A. Yes, sir. I was the captain's communication officer handling all wolfpack communications, and when they were completed served as an observer in the conning tower.

Q. Was that battle station within the vicinity from which torpedo fire was directed?

A. Yes, sir.

Q. On the night of 1 April 1945, were torpedoes fired?

A. Yes, sir.

Q. On whose orders were they fired?

A. The commanding officer, Commander Raymond M. Houffman.

Q. What happened to the target at which they were fired?

A. She was hit by four torpedoes, apparently sank in two pieces in about three minutes.

Q. Were any survivors rescued?

A. One man was recovered who said he was a survivor.

Q. Would you recognize him?

A. Yes, sir.

Q. Have you seen him lately?

A. Yes, sir. He is sitting, under guard, in the outer office.

Q. Had you, during the period 8 March to 1 April 1945, seen any dispatches referring to a vessel under the safe conduct which might pass through areas in which the QUEENFISH was operating?

A. Yes, sir. One message came aboard which said generally that the AWA MARU was northward-bound and would arrive at Moji 5 April and that she was plastered all over with lights and white crosses; to let her through. This message came aboard late in March, I would say about the 26th.

[This was the second message which identified the AWA MARU, but did not locate her in the area she would be traveling or any other.]

Q. Do you remember the originator of that message?
A. Yes, sir. Commander Submarines, Pacific Fleet.
Q. Did you at any time talk with anyone on the possibility of encountering that ship under safe conduct?
A. Yes.
Q. With whom?
A. Commander Raymond Houffman.
Q. What did he say?

This question was objected to by the accused on the ground that it was irrelevant and hearsay.

Outside the courtroom, in part to escape Old Ox's continuing questions about what he should say if called, and in part because he had to relieve himself anyway, Easter headed down the corridor to the head. He passed the open door to the holding room. Shimata sat between two MPs. The MPs were talking across him. He did not look up as Easter passed.

At the urinal, Easter discovered that he could plainly hear everything in the adjoining courtroom. As Trevor's testimony continued, Easter finished up at the urinal and seated himself on one of the sinks along the wall. He would wait to hear if Trevor said anything about the sonar contact that night.

Q. Was the identity of the target established prior to firing?
A. No, sir.
Q. Was any attempt, that you know of, made to establish that identity?
A. Yes, sir.
Q. What was done?
A. Note was made of the enemy contact range with radar on this target and the subsequent actions which indicated a warship proceeding at high speed.

Q. What was the visibility?

A. Approximately 200 yards on the surface due to the fog. At times the stars and moon [were] faintly visible.

Q. Did you ever see the attack ship?

A. No, sir.

Q. At the time that you were on the bridge with the captain, do you remember about what the range was to the target?

A. I cannot be positive, but it was about 17,000 yards.

Q. Do you know what the range was at the time of firing?

A. I did not look at the range. The torpedo run for the first torpedo was 1,250 yards. The range would be slightly larger than that.

Q. Was that, to the best of your knowledge, the closest approach to the target prior to firing?

A. Yes, sir.

Q. Were any precautions, within your knowledge, taken to identify the target other than those you have already mentioned?

A. No, sir.

Cross-examined by the accused:

[The reference to the accused is here referring to Houffman's defense counsel Captain Bruno Gorski.]

Q. You have stated that a message was received from Commander Submarines, Pacific Fleet, giving the information on the AWA MARU. Do you know to whom this message was addressed?

A. Yes, sir. The message was addressed generally to all submarines on patrol.

Q. What was the state of the sea on the night of 1 April about the time of the attack?

A. I would say approximately state 2 or 3.

[Sea states 2 and 3 are described in geomarine technology as a wind range from 7 to 16 knots, from small wavelets to cresting larger waves, with frequent whitecapping, from gentle to moderate breeze. By contrast, at the far end of the scale is sea state 10, a hurricane.]

Q. What depth was ordered set on the torpedoes fired?

A. Three feet.

Q. Did you sight any ships or lights prior to the attack on 1 April?

A. No, sir.

Q. Did you look in the direction of the radar bearing of the target?

A. Yes, sir.

Q. On the night of 1 April, prior to the attack did you hear any fog signals?

A. No, sir.

Q. Did you at any time during the period 8 March to 1 April 1945 sight an enemy hospital ship?

A. Yes, sir.

Q. Will you tell the court the circumstances of this sighting?

A. The weather that night was rather an aggravation of the normal monsoon season. It was raining almost all the time, and when it was not raining, sleet was falling, making visibility quite variable. This state of weather had begun about nightfall, the day previous having been foggy with relatively calm sea. I would say the visibility varied from one mile to much less.

Q. When you first sighted this ship, what did it appear to be?

A. It appeared to be a ship on fire.

Q. What action was taken by the QUEENFISH after the enemy sighting?

A. The ship was closed.

Q. Was the ship later identified as an enemy hospital ship?

A. Yes, sir. A hospital ship by the markings, enemy by its location.

Q. What action was taken by the QUEENFISH after the ship was identified as a properly marked hospital ship?

A. QUEENFISH turned away from this ship and allowed her to go unmolested.

Re-examined by the judge advocate:

Q. Are the distances at which fog signals may be heard invariably of the scope of 2 to 3 miles?

A. Not in my experience.

Q. Is the range sometimes less than a mile?

A. Yes, sir.

Q. How was the hospital ship picked up?

A. Visually.

An unidentified member of the court interrupted to clarify a point:

Q. You stated that the target vessel [the AWA MARU] was a war vessel. How was this fact arrived at?

A. I made the assumption due to the fact that the ship was proceeding at high speed in greatly reduced visibility, which would require special instruments to proceed with impunity or a terrific desire to close some scene of action.

Q. Do you know whether or not the target vessel was zigzagging?

A. Yes. During the period we tracked her she did zig.

As the judge advocate finished his questioning, there was some scraping of chairs that could easily be heard in the adjoining head. Trevor had not been told to step down. There would be some further questions from the defense counsel.

While waiting for the questioning to continue, Easter shifted his position on the sink. He had been looking at the bank of mirrors in front of him as he listened to the testimony inside. Gradually, he became aware of the objects that had caught his attention and held it for the past few minutes: two black military shoes positioned under one of the stall doors behind him. He no sooner identified them as shoes than they moved. There was a shuffling and, as Easter turned around, Ensign Delward T. Diefenbaker swung open the stall door and stepped out.

Diefenbaker, clearly startled at finding Easter there, reddened, cleared his throat, and moved quickly on to the offensive:

"Easter, have you any further business in this room?"

"No, sir. That is, I had some business, but I'm finished with it."

"Then, Easter, I suggest you move out smartly. The testimony in that room is classified, highly classified, and I wouldn't want to have to report you for listening in." Diefenbaker had briskly washed his hands in one of the sinks. He had punctuated the last of his words by ripping a paper towel from the rack.

"Unless, of course," he continued, wiping his hands, "you would like to face your own court-martial on this matter. Is that clear?" Diefenbaker chucked the towel into the bin, adjusted his tie, and started for the door.

"That's clear, sir," Easter said.

Diefenbaker swung open the door and was heading out when Easter called:

"Ensign?"

"Yes."

"Sir . . ."

"What is it, Easter?" Diefenbaker was impatient.

"You forgot to flush the toilet."

Re-cross-examined by the accused:

Q. Did not the fact that the ship was enemy, picked up at a range of 17,000 yards, also aid you in your assumption that it was a warship?

A. Yes, sir, a small war vessel.

Q. You have stated that you were not sure of the identity of the target. Were you not reasonably certain of the identity of the target as to type?

A. Yes, sir. There was an additional reason for the assumption, in that an attack had been made on a convoy by the SEAFOX, our sister wolf, about 1100 hours the same day, about 15 miles to the northward of this contact which was heading northeast at high speed.

The witness said that he had nothing further to state.

The witness was duly warned and withdrew.

The court then, at 12:00 noon, took a recess until 1:00 P.M.

You know the Navy, right? Shit, they got us up and out at dawn to testify knowin'—goin' in—we probably wouldn't see that courtroom till God-knows-when. You know, the hurry-up-and-wait thing. The longest smoke break in history.

We'd talked about it, what we'd say: "Where were you at about 2200 hours the night of 1 April 1945?" "In the sack, sir." "And after you heard battle stations called, what did you do?" "Rolled over, sir."

I mean, the whole thing was a farce. They knew goddam well why we sank that Jap ship. Every one of those admirals filing in that mornin' would have done the same thing, if they had the balls.

One of the guys had it figured. He says five-'ll-get-you-ten the brass sittin' in that court right now had it on orders to deep-six that freighter. I mean, figure it. They couldn't let that thing get through. With what she was haulin' home I mean, come on.

So he says the whole thing was programmed, start to finish. Maybe even the old man was in on it. And this thing with the trial is nothing but window dressing. Or maybe the old man was used, was duped into being in the wrong place at the

*wrong time, the power knowin' all along—bigger'n hell—that
any commander worth salt is goin' to drop that ship as she
passed.*

*Who the hell knows. But after all this waitin', who the hell
cares. You know?*

I mean, Jesus Christ.

Q. State your name, rank, and present duty station.

A. Mike W. Bass, Lieutenant (jg), U.S. Naval Reserve,
U.S.S. QUEENFISH (SS393).

Q. What are your duties aboard the U.S.S. QUEENFISH?

A. Communications, sound, and radar officer, sir.

Q. As communications officer of the U.S.S. QUEENFISH
are you the legal custodian of the translations of enciphered
dispatches received by that vessel?

A. Yes, sir.

Q. Do you have with you the file of those translations
covering the period 8 March to 2 April 1945?

A. Yes, sir.

Q. Is there in that file a dispatch from the Commander
Submarine Force, U.S.S. Pacific Fleet, in tenor, "The S.S.
AWA MARU will pass through your areas between 30
March and 4 April northbound, lighted, marked with crosses.
Let it pass safely"? If so, produce it.

The witness produced the dispatch, and it was submitted to
the accused and to the court and by the judge advocate
offered in evidence. There being no objection, that part pertaining to the AWA MARU was so received, copy appended
marked "Exhibit 1."

At the request of the accused, the judge advocate read that
part of the dispatch which referred to the AWA MARU.

The counsel for the accused stated that the accused admitted having received this dispatch.

The accused stated that this admission was made by his
authority.

Q. Do you have any other duties than communications,
sound, and radar?

A. Yes, sir.

Q. What is that battle station?

A. Assistant plot, sir.

Q. Are you on the bridge at your battle station?

A. No, sir.

Q. On the night of 1 April 1945 at about 2200 hours where
were you?

A. I was in the ward room, sir.

Q. Did you remain in the ward room subsequent to 2200?

A. No, sir.

Q. Where did you go?

A. I went to my tracking station, sir.

Q. Why?

A. Word was passed to man tracking stations.

Q. What occurred while you were at your battle station? What did you do while you were at your battle station?

A. I recorded ranges and bearings, radar ranges and bearings.

Q. Ranges and bearings to what?

A. I recorded ranges and bearings that were sent down from the conning tower.

Q. Do you know what those ranges and bearings were taken on?

A. No, sir. I don't know what they were taken on.

Q. Are you in a position to observe the radar scope at your battle station?

A. No, sir.

Q. Are you in a position to hear any orders that may be given to fire torpedoes?

A. I can hear orders, sir.

Q. Did you hear such orders on the night of 1 April?

A. No, sir.

Q. State your name, rank, and present station.

A. William F. Edwards, Lieutenant, U.S. Navy, U.S.S. QUEENFISH (SS393).

Q. What were your duties at that time?

A. I was executive officer and navigator of the ship.

Q. Were you a member of the coding board?

A. My duties required that I decode messages.

Q. Do you have a battle station?

A. Yes, sir, I do.

Q. What is it?

A. Assistant approach officer.

Q. On the night of 1 April 1945 at about 2200 where were you?

A. I was in the control room, sir.

Q. Did you remain in the control room?

A. No, sir. I did not.

Q. Where did you go?

A. To the conning tower.

Q. Why?

A. We had just picked up a radar contact. My duties required that I go to the conning tower at that time.

Q. The conning tower is your battle station. What are your duties at that station?

A. Assistant approach officer, which during a surface approach consists of coordinating the information gathered in the conning tower and transmitting it to the captain on the bridge.

Q. As navigator, what was the position of that approach and attack approximately?

The witness requested permission to refresh his memory from a memorandum made at the time.

Q. As navigator, what was the position of that approach and attack, approximately?

A. The position of the attack was 25° 25.1 north latitude, 120° 07.1 east longitude.

Q. You stated that to the best of your belief the target sank. On what do you base that belief?

A. I observed the pip on the radar screen break in three, and finally the parts disappeared and I observed a survivor, evidently, being lowered through the upper conning tower hatch shortly thereafter.

Q. In your duties as assistant approach officer, are you in a position to hear orders given to fire torpedoes?

A. Yes, sir. The orders to commence firing are given by the captain, and I fire each torpedo from the conning tower from that point on.

Q. On the night of 1 April 1945, during this attack, were such orders given?

A. Yes, sir.

Q. By whom?

A. By the captain.

Q. Did you have any information as to the passage of a ship under safe conduct in the vicinity of your area of operation?

This question was objected to by the accused on the ground that it was immaterial to the issue.

The judge advocate replied.

The court announced that objection was not sustained.

The question was repeated.

A. I had information as to the passage of a ship under safe conduct in any patrol area in the Pacific.

Q. Where did you get that information?

A. I helped decode, read and initialed a dispatch addressed to all submarines, Pacific Fleet, stating that the AWA MARU would pass or should pass through "your area" between certain dates.

Q. Did you have that information from any other source?

This question was objected to by the accused on the ground that it was immaterial to the issue.

The judge advocate withdrew the question.

Q. Did you receive any instructions from the commanding officer regarding that ship, AWA MARU?

A. No, sir.

Q. What was the minimum range to which the target was closed?

A. Approximately 1,200 yards, sir.

Q. Was that in the course of a normal attack?

A. Yes, sir.

Q. Was the vessel identified prior to attack?

A. The vessel was identified to the best of our ability as a destroyer or destroyer escort or similar type vessel.

Q. On what did you base that decision?

A. Upon the high speed of the target, the straight course towards a position at which the SEAFOX had, I believe eight hours previously, attacked a convoy, the initial radar range of 17,000 yards which compared favorably with opening ranges on similar targets.

Q. No visual contact was made?

A. No, sir.

Q. Are you familiar with radar?

A. From a practical standpoint, yes, sir.

Q. You are used to observing pips on a radar screen?

A. Yes, sir.

Q. Are those pips invariably the same for the same size target at the same range?

A. Not invariably, to the best of my knowledge.

Q. Are they positive identification as to the target?

A. No, sir.

Cross-examined by the accused:

Q. Is it not true that the size of the pip on radar is an indication of the size of the target?

A. Yes, sir, it is an indication.

Q. At what range would you expect to initially pick up, by

the SJ Radar installed on the QUEENFISH, an 11,000-ton merchantman?

A. Upwards of 25,000 yards. We have picked up one at, I believe, 32,000 yards.

Q. At what radar range would you expect initial radar contact with a destroyer?

A. Around 15,000 yards.

Q. You have stated that you have testified as to the position of the QUEENFISH at the time of the attack on 1 April. Is this position accurate?

A. Yes, sir.

Q. How was this position obtained?

A. It was obtained from ranges and bearings on Turnabout Island.

Q. What kind of ranges and bearings?

A. Radar ranges and bearings.

Q. Was a navigational plot being kept at the time?

A. Yes, sir. A navigational plot was kept throughout the approach and attack.

Examined by the court:

Q. Who makes the record of tracks and keeps the basic operating plot?

A. I do, sir.

Q. State your name, rank, and present station.

A. Jasper Giacoletti, Lieutenant (jg), U.S. Naval Reserve, U.S.S. QUEENFISH (SS393).

Q. During the period 8 March to 2 April 1945 where were you?

A. East China Sea.

Q. In what?

A. A submarine of the U.S. Fleet.

Q. What submarine?

A. U.S.S. QUEENFISH.

Q. On the night of 1 April 1945 at about 2200 where were you?

A. On deck. I was junior officer of the deck on the bridge.

Q. You were then officer of the deck during the approach on the target, were you not?

A. Yes, sir.

Q. What was the visibility?

A. Two hundred yards.

Q. Was anyone besides yourself on the bridge at this time?

A. Yes, sir. Ensign Kurtz and Captain Houffman.

Q. Did you receive any instructions from the commanding officer about attempting positively to identify the target?

A. No, sir.

Q. Did you have the conn?

A. No, sir.

Q. Were you aware of the possibility of a vessel under safe conduct being in the vicinity of your operating area?

A. Yes, sir.

Q. Had you received any instructions from the captain as to the possibility of contact with that vessel?

A. No, sir.

Q. Does not the commanding officer himself come to the bridge in case of contact with a ship at night on the surface?

A. Yes, sir.

Q. Was not the commanding officer himself still up at the time of the contact on 1 April?

A. Yes, sir.

Q. What was the state of the sea on the night of 1 April 1945?

A. Condition 1.

Q. Did you look in the direction of the radar bearing of the target?

A. Yes, sir.

Q. Did you use binoculars?

A. Yes, sir.

Q. What was the reported initial range of the contact on the night of 1 April?

A. Approximately 17,000 yards.

Examined by the court:

Q. You stated you saw the second hit. Just what did you see?

A. A muffled light for a fraction of a second in the direction of the target on the torpedo run. Just a flash for a fraction of a second.

Q. Did you hear anything?

A. Yes, sir. Distinct explosions. Four of them.

Q. State your name, rank, and present station.

A. Monroe Kurtz, Ensign, U.S. Naval Reserve, U.S.S. QUEENFISH (SS393).

Q. On the night of 1 April 1945 about 2200 where were you?

A. I was in the control room.

Q. Did you remain in the control room subsequent to 2200?

A. No, sir.

Q. Where did you go?

A. I went to the after cigarette deck.

Q. Why?

A. Battle stations surface torpedo was passed and my station was junior officer of the deck.

Q. Did you remain at that station throughout the subsequent attack?

A. Yes, sir.

Q. Did you see any lights in the direction of the target?

A. Yes, sir.

Q. What were they?

A. The second torpedo explosion.

Q. State your name, rank, and present station.

A. Ivan Williams, Lieutenant (jg), U.S. Naval Reserve, U.S.S. QUEENFISH (SS393).

Q. What was your battle station?

A. I'm plotting officer.

Q. On the night of 1 April 1945 at 2200 where were you?

A. I was on the bridge.

Q. In what capacity?

A. I was officer of the deck.

Q. During that watch as officer of the deck did any unusual event occur?

A. Yes.

Q. What was it?

A. I had reported to me a radar contact.

Q. Did you remain on the bridge as officer of the deck?

A. I was relieved shortly afterwards by Lieutenant Giacoletti.

Q. Where did you go then?

A. I went down to plot.

Q. As plotting officer, you are in a position to note ranges to the target, are you not?

A. Yes, sir.

Q. As plotting officer, are you in a position to observe the radar screen?

A. No, sir.

Cross-examined by the accused:

Q. Approximately how long was the target tracked on the night of 1 April 1945?

A. About 35 minutes.

Q. Does not the commanding officer personally come to the bridge on all night contacts?

A. Yes, sir.

Q. Does he personally conn the ship during approaches?

A. Yes, sir.

Q. Does he not personally conn the ship while the target is being closed and investigated?

A. Yes, sir.

Examined by the court:

Q. At the time the torpedoes were fired, what was the range and track angle?

A. Range was about 1,500 yards, track angle was about 89° starboard, sir.

Q. State your name, rank, and present station.

A. Trent Willard, Lieutenant (jg), U.S. Naval Reserve, U.S.S. QUEENFISH (SS393).

Q. On the night of 1 April 1945 at about 2200 where were you?

A. I was in the ward room of the QUEENFISH.

Q. Did you remain in the ward room of the QUEENFISH subsequent to 2200?

A. No, I did not.

Q. Where did you go?

A. I went to the conning tower of the QUEENFISH.

Q. Why?

A. The word "tracking party, man your stations" had been passed. I went to the conning tower to start the TDC until the regular operator could arrive.

Q. What is your regular battle station?

A. Assistant TDC operator.

Q. As TCD operator, are you in a position to hear orders given to fire torpedoes?

A. Yes, sir. I am in such a position.

Q. On the night of 1 April 1945 did you hear such an order?

A. Yes, sir. I did.

Q. Who gave it?

A. Captain Houffman.

Q. Do you stand officer-of-the-deck watches on the QUEENFISH?

A. Yes, I do.

Cross-examined by the accused:

Q. You have stated you were assistant TDC operator on the night of 1 April 1945. What are your duties as assistant TDC officer?

A. I operate the gyro angle setter on the TDC which transmits the gyro angles to the torpedo tubes; I set the speed of the torpedoes depending on the depth set, temperature of the water, torpedo run; set the spreads that are ordered; and relay the depth-ordered set to the depth setter in the torpedo room.

Q. What spread did you set in degrees?

A. One and a half degrees between torpedoes.

Q. What was the total coverage in degrees by this spread?

A. That would be four and one-half degrees.

Q. How many feet along the target's track would this spread cover?

A. At that torpedo run, it would cover approximately 290 feet.

Q. State your name, rank, and present station.

A. Donald Kemp, Lieutenant, U.S. Navy, U.S.S. QUEENFISH (SS393).

Q. On the night of 1 April 1945 at about 2200 where were you?

A. About 2200 I was in the officers' shower.

Q. Did you remain in the shower subsequent to 2200?

A. As soon as the tracking party was manned I proceeded to the conning tower.

Q. What is your duty in the conning tower?

A. I am the torpedo data computer operator.

Cross-examined by the accused:

Q. What estimated target speed did you first obtain when you manned the TDC?

A. My first estimate was about 18 knots.

Q. How long was the target tracked with the TDC?

A. About one hour, as well as I remember, sir.

Q. What was the torpedo run at the time of firing?

A. Torpedo run was 1,200 yards.

Q. What was the approximate position of the QUEENFISH

relative to the target at the time of firing? I mean was the QUEENFISH on the target's bow or beam or what?

A. We were near the target's beam.

Q. What kind of target was indicated by the target information available at the time?

A. From previous experience I assumed it to be a damaged warship.

Re-examined by the judge advocate:

Q. What was the final speed solution for the target?
A. My final speed estimate was 16 knots.

Examined by the court:

Q. Why did you think the target was a damaged warship?

A. Quite a few factors involved. All the merchant ships I have tracked before were 8 or 10 knots. The initial radar range was 17,000 and combined with a speed estimate of 18 knots I assumed it to be a ship that was damaged and low in the water; and also the fact that during this period there was increased air activity. I thought it might be a stray warship that had been attacked by aircraft and was seeking shelter, therefore not zigzagging, and trying to get to a sheltered anchorage as fast as possible. That was what ran through my mind at the time.

Q. State your name, rank, and present station.

A. Elmo Pitt, Lieutenant (jg), U.S. Navy, U.S.S. QUEENFISH (SS393).

Q. What were your duties on the QUEENFISH during this period?

A. Engineering and electrical department head, diving officer, officer of the deck, member of the coding board, assistant censor.

Q. As officer of the deck, have you ever received in your orders, the morning orders or the night orders, any instructions regarding possible contact with the AWA MARU?

A. No.

Q. On 1 April 1945 at about 2200 where were you?

A. On board the U.S.S. QUEENFISH.

Q. Was there anything unusual that occurred on the night of 1 April 1945?

A. Yes, sir.

Q. What was it?

A. Officers in ship's company were called to their battle stations.

When Mitsuma Shimata was called from the holding room, the two MPs escorted him to the door of the courtroom. They remained on either side of the door, allowing Shimata to enter alone. He came in smiling.

He was directed to a seat, and, smiling and nodding to the members of the court, he made his way over to it. The cuffs of his khaki trousers had been rolled up again—to avoid further accident, they had been rolled well above his oversized combat boots. His skinny legs spanned the distance between the two enormous bells of his rolled trousers and the great black boots below.

The judge advocate introduced the interpreter, Joseph R. Beck, Lieutenant (jg), U.S. Naval Reserve.

The interpreter and the witness were duly sworn.

Examined by the judge advocate:

(The following questions and all other questions to this witness were put and answered through the interpreter.)

Q. State your name, residence, and occupation.

A. Shimata, Mitsuma, Tokyo to Akasakaku, Shimmachi, number 2, Fifth Street, steward.

Q. If you recognize the accused, state as whom.

A. No.

Q. Where were you on the night of 1 April 1945?

A. Off Taiwan that night.

Q. In what?

A. On the AWA MARU.

Q. What happened about 2300 on the night of 1 April 1945?

A. I was sleeping at that time.

Q. Did you continue sleeping after 2300 that night?

A. Shortly after 2300 that night was the first explosion.

Q. First explosion of what?

A. Having experienced a torpedo attack before, I knew that it was a torpedo that struck us.

Q. Was there more than one?

A. After the first strike I got out of my room and three more struck in quick succession.

Q. Was there one strike louder than the others?

204

A. To my sensation there was no explosion that was stronger than the others.

Q. After you came out of your room, where did you go?

A. I came up on deck in a shirt, and as the water was at the level of the deck I grabbed a buoy and jumped into the sea.

Q. What happened to you?

A. The boat was tilted up on edge and just as it started to slip down I threw myself off into the water and drifting around among the rafts and debris felt myself sucked up and I came to the surface again and I am not completely aware of exactly what did happen during those few moments.

Q. What happened next?

A. I held to a raft about two meters square from which I was thrown by the rough waves three times before I was saved by the submarine.

Q. About how long was that after the explosion?

A. I believe it was between 25 and 30 minutes after the time of the explosion.

Q. Do you know what submarine it was?

A. I do not know what submarine it was.

Q. Did the AWA MARU have any special markings?

A. They did have special markings.

Q. What were they?

A. There were two white crosses on the sides of the ship and one white cross on the stack, duplicated on either side of the ship.

Q. Were they lighted on the night of 1 April 1945?

A. I went to sleep at ten o'clock that evening, at that time the lights were burning.

Cross-examined by the accused:

Q. How do you know the white crosses were illuminated?

A. The crosses on the funnel had rows of bulbs through the axis of each arm and there was a light directed on each white cross on the side of the ship.

Q. Did you actually see these lights burning on the night of 1 April?

A. I took a walk around the deck at 2200 and at that time I saw that they were burning.

Q. Any white crosses on top of the bridge?

A. I saw none on the bridge.

Q. Any white crosses on top of hatches?

A. There were white crosses on the top deck.

Q. How many?

A. There were ten white crosses on the ship when all were added.

Q. Were all of these crosses lighted up?

A. Seven of these were lighted.

Q. When you were in the water after the ship sank, how far away could you see the submarine?

A. I couldn't recognize it for a submarine or a destroyer, for which I mistook it, but it was a distance of approximately 200 meters.

Q. Did your ship sound any whistles or fog signals on the night of 1 April 1945?

A. As I was asleep I heard no whistles. However, up to 2200 there had been no sounding of whistles.

Q. If the whistle had been sounded would it probably have awakened you?

A. If it had blown I would have heard it at that time.

Examined by the court:

Q. What cargo did the AWA MARU carry at the time she was sunk?

A. At the time she was sunk, the ship was carrying rubber, lead, tin, sugar, and had crews who were returned to Japan after losing their ships.

The official version of Mitsuma Shimata's testimony in the court-martial differs widely from the version he described in November 1963 to the *Bungei Shunjyu,* a Japanese magazine. Considerable time had elapsed, and in the course of that time perhaps Shimata's memory faded materially. Or perhaps, since he was reporting his response to the events to the Japanese, face-saving became paramount.

Translation of part of that article follows:

A full-scale court-martial began after this [on arrival in Guam]. It took place at the headquarters on top of a hill on Guam Island. From the headquarters building, the wide expanse of the ocean was seen. The courtroom contained only several tables. Nimitz [fact error: Admiral Nimitz was not present; Shimata had mistaken Vice-Admiral Edwin Rundstedt for Nimitz], who had his arm in a sling, was there. He was sitting next to the judge. The reddening of the skin behind his ears from drinking impressed me. [The Japanese text does not imply in any way that he had been drinking when he came to the courtroom.]

The trial was held two hours a day and it continued for twenty-one days [fact error: the trial lasted two days]. The interpreter, Captain Riley, was a cheerful man. He was born in Japan. He had a tattoo on his arm in connection with his name "Riley."

I was confronted with Commander Houffman. The heart of the matter was whether the *AWA MARU* was lit that night—the commander denied this—and whether it was foggy. But the sharpest questioning was on whether the *Awa Maru* faithfully executed her task and whether there were any violations of the agreement.

I was questioned about things we did not know about, such as [one line illegible] the numbers and names of the passengers on the return voyage. The questioning clearly showed that the Americans knew about every detail of the activities of the *Awa Maru*.

The reactions of Nimitz [fact error] and the chief judge to my statement concerning the birth of a baby on the *Awa Maru* were impressive. They both said "oh" quietly, and each one made a cross on his chest. The interpreter and I just sat there.

Our testimony was typed up. After twenty-one days [fact error] the record was thick. On the last day of the trial, I asked what would be done about reparation. I was told [it is not clear by whom], "This is wartime and specific arrangements cannot be made. But it is undeniable that the sinking was unlawful. The record will state that. At this time, the papers will be sent to Washington and will be kept there. Probably, reparation will be paid in accordance with the *Panay* incident." [In 1937, a Japanese Navy bomber attacked the American gunboat *Panay*, which was docked in the Yangtzechiang River, and sank her.]

I don't know what kind of penalty Commander Houffman received.

XVII

Date: April 19, 1945
Place: Headquarters compound, Camp Dealy, Guam
Time: 1300 hours
Status: The defense

The prosecution had concluded shortly after lunch on that first day of trial. It had set the stage for finding Commander Houffman guilty of one, two, or three violations of military law. In sinking a ship that he had failed to identify, a ship that was traveling on a safe-passage covenant as a hospital ship, a sinking that resulted in the deaths of 2,008 men, women, and children, Commander Houffman could face a total of five years nine months at hard labor and, what was even worse for a man like Houffman, the ultimate, lifetime humiliation of a dishonorable discharge.

Houffman was an Annapolis man. His world was the Navy. In these proceedings, his career, his lifetime, was at stake. Unless the court fully, unequivocally exonerated Houffman—and made that exoneration crystal-clear in its findings—his reputation would be severely, perhaps irreparably, damaged.

The prosecution argued that Houffman had either disobeyed a lawful order (i.e., he had read and chosen to ignore the dispatch found in the radio shack concerning the amended course of the *Awa Maru*) or, by reason of inefficiency or neglect, hadn't read that which he should have read, and thereby failed to carry out the order to let that ship pass.

Clearly, Houffman, as sole authority of his vessel, caused the sinking of the *Awa Maru*, an action he took without ever positively identifying the vessel, an action he based on the belief that it was a destroyer. Did he act on sufficient evidence? Even if it had been a destroyer, did he determine whether the ship was in fact enemy and not British, Australian, or American?

While the testimony seemed clear that every effort was

made on the bridge that night to visually identify the ship, the facts remain: It was not sighted; it was not identified.

Instead, the action taken that night was based primarily on a blip on the radar screen. In contradiction to what was seen and interpreted on the screen, is what was heard through the headset of the sonar operator. But, so far, the court did not know of the sonar contradiction. The court knew only that, on the basis of radar, and in the absence of reading any coherent messages concerning the *Awa Maru*, Houffman unleashed four lethal torpedoes against an unarmed freighter of unknown nationality.

Critical to one prosecution argument was this: the contents of any dispatch on board the submarine, any dispatch at all, read or not, was the responsibility of the commander. From the prosecution standpoint, it was necessary only to establish that a message concerning the *Awa Maru* and its course was on board. It was on board, and therefore it was an order for which the commander was responsible.

While the men under the commander were fully responsible for informing him of actions, events, written and verbal messages that would effect his decision, he alone must bear the responsibility once that decision is made.

According to the prosecution, Houffman made a decision when there was information on board indicating, clearly, that the decision was a wrong one.

The defense began.

Mike W. Bass, Lieutenant (jg), U.S. Naval Reserve, a witness for the prosecution, was recalled as a witness for the defense and warned that the oath previously taken by him was still binding.

Q. Are you the communications officer of the U.S.S. QUEENFISH?
A. Yes, sir.
Q. Are you the legal custodian of a translation of an official dispatch, date and time group 010535, received by the U.S.S. QUEENFISH from the U.S.S. SEAFOX?
A. Yes, sir.
Q. Produce it.

The witness produced the official dispatch, and it was submitted to the judge advocate and to the court and by the accused offered in evidence. The judge advocate objected on the ground that it was immaterial to the charges and specification. The accused replied. The court announced that the objection was not sustained. There being no further objection, it was received, and is appended marked "Exhibit 2".

EXHIBIT 2: (The message from SEAFOX to QUEEN-FISH was sent more than 6 hours after the fact.)

From: SEAFOX
To: QUEENFISH
AT FIVE HUNDRED ZEBRA FIRED SIX FOR ONE HIT IN DAY SURFACE ATTACK IN FOG ON SEVEN SHIPS THIRTEEN KNOTS WESTBOUND CONVOY AT POSIT 18 MILES ZERO SEVEN ZERO FROM TURNABOUT. BUSINESS PICKING UP DOWN HERE DURING DAYLIGHT HOURS ONLY. TRYING TO REGAIN CONTACT FISH ONB EIGHTEEN TIME 011140.

Examined by the judge advocate:

Q. State your name, rank, and present station.
A. Glen Regan, Lieutenant (jg), U.S. Naval Reserve, communications watch officer, staff, Commander Submarine Force, Pacific Fleet.
Q. Are you the legal custodian of an official dispatch, date and time group 170600 of April, received by the Commander Submarine Force, Pacific Fleet, from the U.S.S. SEAFOX?
A. Yes, sir, I am.
Q. Produce it.

The witness produced the official dispatch, and it was submitted to the judge advocate and to the court and by the accused offered in evidence. The judge advocate objected to the introduction of this dispatch as evidence on the ground that it relates to events which occurred after the sinking of the AWA MARU and are therefore out of the providence of the charges and specifications. The accused replied.
The court was cleared. The court was opened. All parties to the trial entered, and the court announced that the objection was sustained.

[Because the contents of this message from *Seafox* to ComSubPac was not made a part of the court record, one is left to speculate on whether the dispatch was damaging, and to whom. Clearly, it did not relate in time to the sinking of the *Awa Maru*. The dispatch was received by ComSubPac after the *Queenfish* had arrived in Guam. But did it relate in another way? Most probably. An attempt was made to introduce it by the defense. All the points raised in court and elsewhere about the *Seafox* and its commander, Eli Darvies, went unanswered because no one on the *Seafox* was ever called to testify! The question remains: *Why?*]

Q. State your name, rank, and present station.
A. William Kaltenbrunner, Lieutenant Commander, U.S. Navy, U.S.S. HOLLAND.

[The following testimony of Lieutenant Commander Kaltenbrunner establishes the route and route changes of the *Awa Maru*. The reader is referred to the accompanying nautical charts. (See pages 212–213 and 226–227.)]

Examined by the accused:

Q. What are your assigned duties on the U.S.S. HOLLAND?
A. Navigator.
Q. Have you made a true plot of the first announced track of the AWA MARU in accordance with the first dispatch quoted in the first specification of the first charge?
A. I have, sir.
Q. Will you indicate that track to the court on the chart?

(Indicated on H.W. Chart No. 5951, 1st Edition, March 1944.)

A. The black line starts at *Moji*, then down through the February 18 noon position down to the February 19 noon position along the west coast of Formosa to *Takao*, arriving at *Takao* on the A.M. of the 20th. Departing *Takao* A.M. 21 February, departed *Hong Kong* on the 23 February, and through the noon position of February 24th. From the 24th position down to *Saigon*. From *Saigon* down through March 1 noon position to *Singapore*. Arriving at *Singapore* on A.M. of 2 March. Departed on 8 March for *Surabaya*. Arrived at *Surabaya* on P.M. of 10 March, departing *Surabaya* on 11 March A.M. and proceeding to *Batavia*. Arriving *Batavia* A.M. 12 March, departing on 18 March and heading for *Muntok*. Arriving *Muntok* on 19 March, departing 23rd for *Singapore*. Arriving at *Singapore* 24 March, departing *Singapore* on the A.M. 28 March, to the noon position of 29th to the noon position of 31 March to the noon position of 1 April to the noon position of 2 April to the noon position of 3 April. From here it was to go to, according to the dispatch, *Miture*. Arriving *Miture* to *Moji*. That's the first route.

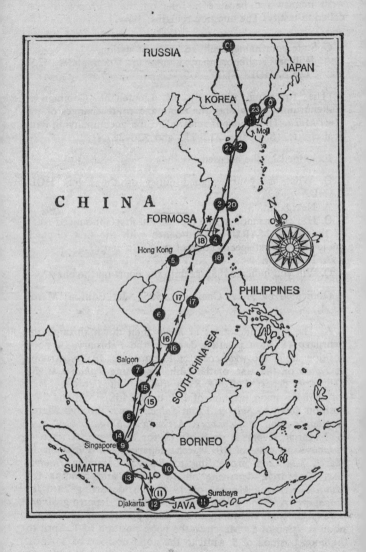

RUSSIA

JAPAN

KOREA

23 0

Mo1

22 2

CHINA

3 20

FORMOSA

*

18 4

Hong Kong

5

18

N

PHILIPPINES

17

17

6

16

16

Saigon

7

SOUTH CHINA SEA

15

15

8

14

Singapore 9

BORNEO

10

SUMATRA

13

11

Surabaya

Djakarta 12 JAVA 11

SAFE PASSAGE ITINERARY OF THE AWA MARU

THE JAPANESE GOVERNMENT HAS DESIGNATED THE PASSENGER-CARGO VESSEL AWA MARU AS A RELIEF SHIP FOR TRANSPORTATION OF RELIEF SUPPLIES TO ALLIED PRISONERS OF WAR INTERNED AND IN JAPANESE CUSTODY.

THE AMERICAN GOVERNMENT GUARANTEES THE AWA MARU SAFE PASSAGE AND NOT SUBJECT TO ATTACK WITHIN THE LIMITATIONS OF THE FOLLOWING ITINERARY AND SCHEDULE OF PORT DESTINATIONS:

① RUSSIAN PORT OF NAKHODKA, NEAR VLADIVOSTOK, U.S.S.R.

⓪ NOVEMBER, 1944 ... KOBE, JAPAN ... HAKUSAN MARU PICKED UP P.O.W. RELIEF SUPPLIES (2,200 TONS) AT NAKHODA, U.S.S.R. AND RETURNED TO KOBE, WHERE THEY WERE TRANSFERRED TO THE AWA MARU OR WENT TO MOJI AND TRANSFERRED THE RELIEF SUPPLIES AT THAT PORT. *

① FEBRUARY 17TH, 1945, AFTERNOON ... AWA MARU DEPARTS FROM MOJI, JAPAN

② FEBRUARY 18TH, NOON ... PASSES 31 DEGREES 12' NORTH LATITUDE, 126 DEGREES 53' EAST LONGITUDE

③ FEBRUARY 19TH, NOON ... PASSES 26 DEGREES 17' NORTH LATITUDE, 122 DEGREES 29' EAST LONGITUDE

④ FEBRUARY 20TH, FORENOON ... ARRIVE TAKAO (SOUTHERN TAIWAN)
FEBRUARY 21ST, FORENOON ... DEPART TAKAO

⑤ FEBRUARY 22ND, AFTERNOON ... ARRIVE HONG KONG
FEBRUARY 23RD, FORENOON ... DEPART HONG KONG

⑥ FEBRUARY 24TH, NOON ... PASS 16 DEGREES 2' NORTH LATITUDE, 110 DEGREES 37' EAST LONGITUDE

⑦ FEBRUARY 25TH, AFTERNOON ... ARRIVE SAIGON, VIETNAM
FEBRUARY 28TH, FORENOON ... DEPART SAIGON

⑧ MARCH 1ST, NOON ... PASSES 4 DEGREES 10' NORTH LATITUDE, 105 DEGREES 32' EAST LONGITUDE

⑨ MARCH 2ND, FORENOON ... ARRIVE SINGAPORE, MALAYA
MARCH 5TH, FORENOON ... DEPART SINGAPORE

⑩ MARCH 9TH, NOON ... PASS 2 DEGREES 28' SOUTH LATITUDE, 109 DEGREES 10' EAST LONGITUDE
(*DID NOT PASS THIS POSITION)

⑪ MARCH 10TH, AFTERNOON ... SCHEDULED ARRIVAL AT SURABAYA, JAVA
NOTE: ACCORDING TO SHIMATA (SURVIVOR) THE AWA MARU DID NOT MAKE THIS SCHEDULED STOP BUT WENT DIRECT TO DJAKARTA FROM SINGAPORE, ARRIVING MARCH 10TH, FORENOON. (SEE ITINERARY CHANGES)
MARCH 11TH, FORENOON ... SCHEDULED DEPARTURE FROM SURABAYA

⑫ MARCH 12TH, AFTERNOON ... SCHEDULED ARRIVAL DJAKARTA, JAVA
MARCH 13TH, AFTERNOON ... SCHEDULED DEPARTURE FROM DJAKARTA

⑬ MARCH 19TH, AFTERNOON ... SCHEDULED ARRIVAL AT BANKA ISLAND, PORT OF MUNTOK, SUMATRA
MARCH 23RD, AFTERNOON ... DEPART BANKA ISLAND

⑭ MARCH 24TH, AFTERNOON ... ARRIVE SINGAPORE (SECOND VISIT)
MARCH 25TH, FORENOON ... DEPART SINGAPORE

⑮ MARCH 29TH, NOON ... PASS 7 DEGREES 52' NORTH LATITUDE, 107 DEGREES 37' EAST LONGITUDE

⑯ MARCH 30TH, NOON ... PASS 12 DEGREES 11' NORTH LATITUDE, 111 DEGREES 4' EAST LONGITUDE

⑰ MARCH 31ST, NOON ... PASS 15 DEGREES 63' NORTH LATITUDE, 114 DEGREES 37' EAST LONGITUDE

⑱ APRIL 1ST, NOON ... SCHEDULED TO PASS 20 DEGREES 38' NORTH LATITUDE, 119 DEGREES 32' EAST LONGITUDE

⑳ APRIL 2ND, NOON ... SCHEDULED TO PASS 26 DEGREES 4' NORTH LATITUDE, 122 DEGREES 53' EAST LONGITUDE

㉑ APRIL 3RD, NOON ... SCHEDULED TO PASS 30 DEGREES 41' NORTH LATITUDE, 129 DEGREES 30' EAST LONGITUDE

㉒ APRIL 4TH, AFTERNOON ... SCHEDULED ARRIVAL AT MITURE (CANNOT FIND ON ANY MAP)

㉓ APRIL 5TH, FORENOON ... SCHEDULED ARRIVAL AT MOJI (PORT OF DEPARTURE AND TERMINATION)

MARCH 3RD ... JAPAN SUBMITS ITINERARY CHANGE AS FOLLOWS:

⑪ MARCH 10TH, FORENOON ... ARRIVE DJAKARTA INSTEAD OF SURABAYA (PROBABLY ONE DAY LATE DEPARTING SINGAPORE ... NOTE: NO CHANGE SUBMITTED FROM ORIGINAL ITINERARY REGARDING ⑬ AND ⑭

⑮ MARCH 29TH, NOON ... PASSES 6 DEGREES 40' NORTH LATITUDE, 107 DEGREES 40' EAST LONGITUDE

⑯ MARCH 30TH, NOON ... PASSES 12 DEGREES 50' NORTH LATITUDE, 111 DEGREES 05' EAST LONGITUDE

⑰ MARCH 31ST, NOON ... PASSES 17 DEGREES 42' NORTH LATITUDE, 114 DEGREES 00' EAST LONGITUDE

⑱ APRIL 1ST, NOON ... PASSES 23 DEGREES 05' NORTH LATITUDE, 117 DEGREES 14' EAST LONGITUDE

✱ APRIL 1ST, 2300 HOURS ... AWA MARU ATTACKED AND SUNK 25 DEGREES 25'1 NORTH LATITUDE, 120 DEGREES 07'1° EAST LONGITUDE

(11 MILES E. TURNABOUT ISLAND OR NIU-SHANTAO)

NOTE: LOCATION OF NAVIGATIONAL FIXES NOT RELEVANT TO THE STORY HAVE BEEN DELETED*

213

Q. Where were they to be on the first of April, there?

A. Noon position on 1 April, south of Formosa.

(H.O. Chart No. 5951, 1st Edition, March 1944, was submitted to the judge advocate and to the court and by the accused offered in evidence. There being no objection, it was so received, and is appended marked "Exhibit 3".)

Q. Have you made a true plot of the announced amended route of the AWA MARU as specified in the second dispatch quoted in the first specification to the first charge?

A. I have, sir.

Q. Will you please indicate that route on the chart to the court?

A. The second route is indicated in the blue pencil. It runs along the same track as the first route, down to *Takao*, arriving at *Takao* and departing the same time. Arriving *Hong Kong* and departing the same time. Arriving and departing *Saigon* the same time. Arriving *Singapore* and departing the same time. At *Singapore* bypass *Surabaya* direct to *Batavia*. Arrive *Batavia* on 10 March, departing 18 March. It was to depart on 18 March by the first route also. And going from *Batavia* to *Muntok* arrive A.M. 19th, departing A.M. 23 March and proceeding to *Singapore,* arriving P.M. 24 March, departing A.M. 28 March. From here to the noon position on the 29th of March up to the noon position on the 1st of April. From the 1st of April it goes, on the dispatch it gave the next noon position on the second of April as this position here, which is obviously an error in transmission or an error in receiving. Because it would be impossible to make a day's run from this point to up here for the noon position of 3 April. The latitude was given at 17 and was evidently meant to be 27, which was the position here for 2 April. From there it went to *Miture,* which I couldn't locate. The dotted blue line indicates the track as specified in the specification. The solid blue line from noon 1 April until arrival in Japan indictates the track with the 10-degree obvious error corrected.

Q. What does the red line on the chart indicate?

A. It indicates what the actual track was as far, to the best of my knowledge whatever, according to the information we had, and it follows the same as the blue line up to the position on the first of April. And from there it runs from the noon position, which we presume the ship went through to the position of the attack.

214

Q. Now referring to the other chart, the large-scale track of the AWA MARU is as specified in the specification?

A. It is.

Q. Is the blue line a true track of the amended announced route as specified in the second message quoted in the specification?

A. Yes, sir.

Q. What is the red line?

A. The red line is what the actual track was, which is run from the noon position of April 1st. It coincides with the blue line up as far as noon April 1st. From there it goes from noon April 1st to position of attack by QUEENFISH here. (Indicated on H.O. Chart No. 3176, 7th Edition, November 1937.)

Q. What is that position?

A. Latitude 25 degrees 25.1 minutes north, longitude 120 degrees 07.1 minutes east.

At this point the accused addressed the court as follows:

The navigator of the QUEENFISH had testified that that was the position.

Q. Where is the estimated position where the AWA MARU would be if she followed her amended announced track?

A. That position would be right here, which is 179.2 miles from the noon position on 1 April, which is figured at a run of 16 knots for 11.2 hours.

Q. What is the distance between the actual position where this ship was sunk and the position where the AWA MARU should have been if she had followed her amended announced route?

A. This distance here on the chart, which is 32½ miles.

[NOTE: This indicates that the AWA MARU was approximately 1½ to 2 hours ahead of her amended schedule.]

(H.O. Chart No. 3176, 7th Edition, November 1937, was submitted to the judge advocate and to the court and by the accused offered in evidence. There being no objection, it was so received, and is appended marked "Exhibit 4".)

Q. What was the current?

A. I didn't plot the current at that time, sir.

At this point the accused addressed the court as follows:

May I respectfully invite the attention of the court to my

interpretation of this 16 knots as a speed in advance of 16 knots.

Examined by the court:

Q. Do we have information as to where the ship was actually at certain times and dates along these tracks?
A. To my knowledge, no, sir.
Q. As far as you know, no one saw this ship before?
A. No, sir.
Q. This is all theory?
A. Yes, sir. I put this in as what I thought would be the logical route between these points.

Cross-examined by the judge advocate:

Q. At what time have you indicated the attack and sinking of the AWA MARU?
A. At 2311 minus 8 time on 1 April.
Q. How many hours remained until his rendezvous at his next noon position?
A. 12.8 hours.
Q. How long have you been navigator of the HOLLAND?
A. About five months, sir.
Q. If, as navigator, you found yourself with a certain distance to run in 12 hours and 49 minutes to go to a designated spot, would you not recommend to the commanding officer a change of course and speed to arrive at that spot at the time?
A. Yes, sir.

Re-examined by the accused:

Q. Will you indicate again the position where testimony in this court has been given that the AWA MARU was sunk?
A. (The witness indicated the position.)
Q. Will you indicate the position 25 degrees 25.1 north longitude, 120 degrees 07.1 east.
A. (The witness indicated the position.)
Q. That is a true position?
A. Yes, sir.

At this point the accused addressed the court as follows:

Those positions are true plots and indicate a definite 32-mile variation to where the ship was and where it should have been. The only guesswork on this chart is in having the red line, which is our estimated true track of the ship, follow the blue line, which was the announced track up to this point. We assume that the ship did follow the route that she said that she would follow and be at that position at the time she said she would be. We don't follow that she passed through this point. But up to this point she followed the position. We do hope we have introduced sufficient evidence.

Q. State your name, rank, and present station.
A. Mark Slovik, Quartermaster second-class, U.S. Navy, U.S.S. QUEENFISH (SS393).
Q. Were you on board the QUEENFISH on the night of 1 April 1945?
A. Yes, sir. I was.
Q. Was a torpedo attack made on a ship that night?
A. Yes, sir.
Q. Where were you stationed during the approach and attack?
A. Battle station quartermaster on the bridge.
Q. What was the state of the sea?
A. One sea, sir. Visibility 200 yards.

Q. State your name, rank, and present station.
A. Edward Keen, Coxswain, U.S.S. QUEENFISH.
Q. Were you called topside following the attack?
A. Yes, sir.
Q. Did you rescue any survivors following the attack?
A. Yes, sir. I helped pull one out of the water, sir.
Q. I show you over in this corner some substance; do you recognize it?
A. Yes, sir. That's what we pulled out of the water. That's the rubber and the can we pulled out of the water.

The bales of rubber and the can of black unidentified substance were submitted to the judge advocate and to the court and by the accused offered in evidence. The judge advocate objected on the ground that this material had never been established as coming from the ship that was sunk the previous night. The court announced that the objection was sustained.

William Edwards, Lieutenant, U.S. Navy, a witness for the prosecution, was recalled as a witness for the defense and warned that the oath previously taken by him was still binding.

Examined by the accused:

Q. Is that the position which you previously testified was the position of the attack?

A. I believe it was 25 degrees 05.1 north, instead of 25 degrees 25.1.

Q. Is that the position which you previously testified?

The witness requested permission to refresh his memory from a memorandum.

The judge advocate stated that he had no objection to the witness inspecting the memorandum.

The request of the witness was granted. Having inspected the memorandum, the witness was asked if he could now testify of his own knowledge.

The witness replied in the affirmative.

Q. Is that the position which you previously testified was the position of the attack?

A. I was wrong. It's 25 degrees 25.1 as indicated on the chart.

Q. Please tell the court what you know about this current.

A. Previous to the time of attack and including the night of the attack, the northeast monsoon was in effect and the set was to the southwest. Shortly thereafter the transition period set in as predicted in sailing directions and the current was confused until it finally settled in a northeasterly direction, the southwest monsoon then being in effect.

The court, then at 5:00 P.M., adjourned until 8:15 A.M. the next day, Friday, April 20.

The enlisted-men's club, such as it was, opened its doors at 1700. It featured a pool table, six balls, three and a half cue sticks, and no chalk. A thick, barrel-chested islander, on U.S. government payroll, was placed in charge of the concession stand: beer, soft drinks, cigarettes, and, when he hadn't eaten the supply himself, candy bars.

Easter and Old Ox arrived at 1705, shortly after the court had recessed for the day. Already, the club was filling. The man Easter was looking for came in shortly after he and Ox had found a table by the pinball machine.

When Yeoman Arnold B. Wainwright looked at you, it

was always a little upward and to the left. His glasses were as thick as the bottom of a Coke bottle and lent to his eyes a dim, refracted look that never seemed particularly on target. When Easter called to him, he seemed to home in on the sound of it, then threaded his way through the crowd. He was carrying a beer. He stopped only when his legs bumped the table at which Ox and Easter sat. Easter found him a chair, and he looked upward and a little to the left of it before sitting down.

Wainwright took his position of court orderly very seriously. As he viewed it, his selection was based not only on his intellect but on the trust vested in him by the government in matters of security. Yeoman Wainwright, who normally served as clerk in the motor pool, was one of the few enlisted men on base who held a Secret clearance and could type.

"Arnold. Arnold. It's good to see you," Easter said. "Let me freshen that beer." Beneath the table, Easter poured a small amount of Canadian Club from a pint bottle he carried in his jacket into the mouth of Wainwright's beer.

"What do you want, Easter?" Wainwright said.

"Arnold. You view everything with such suspicion. I just wanted you to join Oxford and me in a few boilermakers and some lighthearted conversation."

"What do you want, Easter?" Wainwright took a sip from his beer. Someone had punched up Glenn Miller's "String of Pearls" on the juke box, but one of the speakers rattled every time a bass was sounded.

"All right, Arnold. I admit that I want to ask you a couple of questions, but it—"

"About the trial?"

"Well, only in general. What I—"

"No," Wainwright said. He started to stand up. Easter restrained him with a hand on his arm.

"Now, Wainwright. Please. Please, sit down. Please let me explain. I thought we could chat as good friends. But perhaps you're right, Arnold. Let's approach this differently."

"I'm not telling you anything about the trial." Wainwright looked upward and to Easter's left. He took another sip from his beer and looked away.

"Arnold, that's Canadian Club. I have a fifth of it in my—"

"No."

"Now, please hear me out, Arnold. You know how edgy Old Ox here gets when he hears 'no' all the time. I don't think he means to, it's just that he gets uncontrollable sometimes.

219

So please hear me out. All I want is a 'yes' or a 'no' on two questions. That's it."

"String of Pearls" ended in a long, low rattle. On the pinball machine, someone had trapped the steel ball between two pegs, and the lighted numbers on the board marched in a staccato of bells to the finish line of "Indy Speedway."

"What's in it for me?" Wainwright asked.

"Like I say," Easter said. "Just like I say. There's a fifth of Canadian Club in the barracks. And, there's the other thing."

"What other thing?"

"Well, I think I can get Old Ox to control himself. I'm sure of it, Arnold. I'm positive I can keep Old Ox from rising up and crushing you with one of his big meaty hands."

"You just want 'yes' or 'no,' and that's it? Two questions?"

"That's it, Arnold. That's all I want."

"Where's the fifth?"

"Arnold, for Christ sake, trust me. You give me the answers. I'll get you the fifth. We're friends, Arnold. I like intellectuals. You can trust me."

"What questions?"

By the time the sailor at the pinball machine had moved the numbers past the finish line and racked up a two-digit number on the counter for free games, Easter had his answers. All the answers he needed from Yeoman Arnold B. Wainwright.

Yes, they had completed the prosecution testimony early that afternoon and had already begun the defense, which would continue tomorrow. And no, no one, no one at all, had mentioned the sonar findings that night. Not Trevor, not Edwards. Not anyone.

That meant one of two things: either the court-martial was a preconcluded exercise in international public relations, that there was never any intention of finding anyone guilty of anything, and the conflicting sonar report was not to be discussed, or—and this was the conclusion that bothered Easter—Houffman had arranged to call Easter in his defense. And, if he was asked about sonar, Easter now felt certain that he was expected to lie.

Date: April 20, 1945
Place: Headquarters compound, Camp Dealy, Guam
Time: 0815 hours
Status: Defense continues

The grim mood of the court, which had been evident on the first day, was not dispelled on the second. It was still not clear whether the members were assembled merely to ritualize the deed or whether they intended to draw blood. But what was clear was the speed at which they were hearing testimony. In a single day they had heard out the prosecution and some of the defense.

If the unrelenting pace continued, whatever was to happen on this, the second day, would happen in a hurry. The court, operating on the premise that the Japanese might already be punishing submariners held prisoner, were eager to arrive at a conclusion that would stem the tide of international wrath being heaped on the Americans for the deed committed that fogbound night.

Judging by the testimony thus far, speed, rather than a complete exposition of events, seemed to be the governing factor. Whether this worked in Houffman's favor or against it remained to be seen.

On April 20, 1945, former Chief Steward Mitsuma Shimata—the sole survivor—was recalled to testify for the defense.

The interpreter and the witness were warned that the oaths previously taken by them were still binding.

Examined by the court:

The following questions and all other questions to this witness were put and answered through the interpreter.

Q. You stated yesterday that the ship was carrying passengers. How many passengers was this ship carrying?
A. There were 1,700 passengers, not including 80 passengers who were riding first-class.

[Sources later put the figure, passengers, and crew at 2,009.]

Q. Who were the first-class passengers?
A. These 80 first-class passengers were made up of captains and chief engineers of merchant ships which had been sunk, and the Foreign Department officials who were aboard to administer the Red Cross supplies.
Q. Did the AWA MARU have any prisoner-of-war supplies on board at the time she was sunk?
A. They did not carry any Red Cross supplies at the time of being sunk.

Q. State your name, rank, and present station.

A. Michael Denn, Captain, U.S. Navy, operations officer, Commander Submarine Force, Pacific Fleet.

Q. As SubPac combat intelligence officer, have you any official intelligence concerning the voyage during which the Japanese ship AWA MARU was granted safe conduct?

A. Yes, I have. We received information through the Commander in Chief, Pacific Fleet, concerning the loading of the AWA MARU.

[This information had been reported by the Commander, Naval China, who reported that they received it from a French source. They stated that upon the arrival of the AWA MARU in Saigon, she unloaded 600 tons of ammunition, about 2,000 bombs, and 20 planes in crates. It was stated that this cargo was unloaded by the Japanese military. A subsequent report stated that she also unloaded 500 tons of medical supplies and 1,000 tons of preserves (food supplies).]

Examined by the court:

Q. How much preserves?

A. A thousand tons of preserves, and added that when she departed Saigon she still carried a mixed ton of munitions and medical supplies. That is all.

Re-examined by the accused:

Q. I show you here a map. You will note on this map a hatched portion, hatched in green. Does this portion hatched in green indicate anything to you? (An area encompassing the mine fields between Formosa and the Ryukyu Islands.)

A. Yes, it does. That is an area which, from captured documents, we have learned is restricted to enemy shipping, that is, enemy ships are not allowed to enter that area.

Q. Did you say enemy ships are not allowed to enter?

A. Japanese ships themselves are not allowed to enter.

Q. Do you have any intelligence as to the reasons for this restriction?

A. No exact intelligence, excepting that the presence of a group of floating mines near that area indicates that it is probably mined.

Q. I show you here a black line which it has been previously testified was the first announced track that the AWA MARU would take upon returning to Japan. Do you notice anything peculiar about this track?

A. Yes, the track as shown there takes the AWA MARU directly through that area which we consider to be mined.

Q. As combat intelligence officer, is it the practice of the Japanese to arm all their ships except hospital ships and ships granted safe conduct?

A. Yes, it is.

Q. You have stated that you have knowledge of certain information received from CincPac concerning the cargo loaded and unloaded in the AWA MARU in Saigon. Was this information delivered to the commanding officer of the U.S.S. QUEENFISH?

A. No, it was not.

Q. As operations officer for Commander Submarines, Pacific Fleet, would you route one of your forces through one of your mine fields?

A. No, I would not.

Q. Did you see a dispatch amending the route of the AWA MARU which would have followed the black line pointed out to you on the chart?

A. Yes, I did.

Re-examined by the court:

Q. Have you any information as to the loading of the AWA MARU on her return voyage?

A. No, sir, we have not.

[This answer supposes that the sophisticated Allied intelligence network at that late stage of the war did not have observers in major ports and did not know precisely—or even roughly—what the AWA MARU carried on her return voyage.]

Q. State your name, rank, and present station.

A. Edward Albrecht, Commander, U.S. Navy, commanding officer, U.S.S. SPRINGER.

Q. How many years experience have you had in submarines?

A. Seven years this June.

Q. How many war patrols have you completed?

A. Eleven, sir.

Q. How many war patrols have you had command of a submarine?

A. Five, sir.

Q. As an experienced submarine officer, if you were making a relatively high speed of 16 knots and you had poor visibility, about 200 yards, would you consider it necessary to zigzag for your own protection when passing through waters in which enemy submarines would be encountered?

A. No, sir.

Q. As an experienced submarine officer, if your ship was on the surface at night with visibility of about 200 yards, would you consider closing a ship which might be a warship; would you consider closing such a ship to a range of about 1,500 yards adequate to effect identification with a visibility of 200 yards?

A. No, sir.

Q. Will you please tell the court the service reputation of the accused as regards efficiency and performance of duty?

This question was objected to by the judge advocate on the ground that it was improper and irrelevant. If it is mitigation it is improper at this time.

The accused made no reply.

The court announced that the objection was not sustained.

The question was repeated.

A. He is an aggressive, efficient, and conscientious submarine officer.

Q. What is the service reputation of the accused as regards care in obeying orders?

A. His reputation is to take great care and to make every effort to carry out orders in detail as to spirit and letter.

Examined by the court:

Q. State your name, rank, and present station.

A. Otto Zimmerman, Captain, U.S. Navy, commanding officer, U.S.S. APOLLO, temporarily attached to Commander in Chief, Pacific Headquarters, for additional duty in connection with general court-martial.

Q. Are you the legal custodian of a deposition executed by William B. Garfield, Vice-Admiral, U.S. Navy?

A. I am.

Q. Will you please produce it?

A. Here it is.

The witness produced the deposition of William B. Garfield, Junior, Vice-Admiral, U.S. Navy, and it was submitted to the judge advocate and to the court and by the accused offered in evidence. There being no objection, it was so received, and is appended marked "Exhibit 5 (1)", "Exhibit 5 (2)", "Exhibit 5 (3)", and "Exhibit 5 (4)". The judge advocate read the deposition.

[The following written deposition of Admiral William Garfield has been amended to the question-and-answer format.]

Q. Are you in the United States Navy? If yes, what is your full name, rank, and present duty?

A. Yes, William Bryant Garfield, Jr., Vice-Admiral, U.S. Navy, Commander Submarine Force, Pacific Fleet.

Q. Do you know the accused? If yes, state his name and rank.

A. Yes, he is Commander Raymond M. Houffman, U.S. Navy.

Q. Were you the Task Force Commander having operational control of the U.S.S. QUEENFISH during the fourth war patrol of that vessel, from 24 February 1945 to 14 April 1945?

A. Yes.

Q. Did you issue to the commanding officer of the U.S.S. QUEENFISH, prior to 1 April 1945, any orders concerning attacks on unidentified vessels? If yes, what were these orders?

A. Commander Houffman under date of 6 March 1945 was issued Operation Order No. 57-45, signed by me, in which he was directed to conduct his patrol in accordance with Commander Task Force 17 and in accordance with additional instructions as issued by his Group Commander. He was further directed to attack enemy forces encountered, including merchant shipping, and not to attack Chinese fishing vessels. My Operation Order 57-45 told him of submarine areas and area restrictions. It directs that attacks should be made on all surface vessels encountered inside submarine patrol zones excepting hospital ships, ships given safe conduct, and Russian shipping. It further directs that submarines be certain of its enemy character before attacking. Standard Operating Procedure No. 1, in defining the various areas into which the Pacific is divided, definitely states in which areas targets must be identified before attack is made.

[In brief, he had orders to attack all ships encountered within his submarine patrol zone, except, of course, hospital ships and those granted safe conduct and not to attack Chinese fishermen or unidentified submarines.]

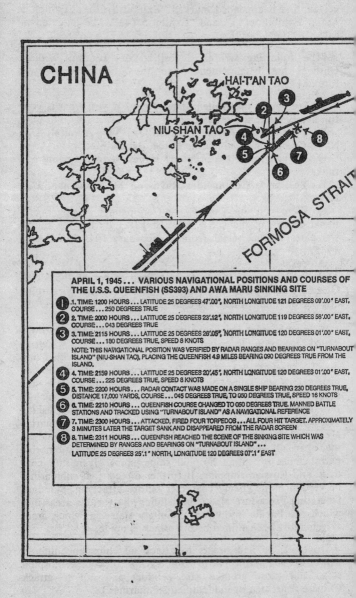

CHINA

HAI-T'AN TAO

NIU-SHAN TAO

FORMOSA STRAIT

APRIL 1, 1945 . . . VARIOUS NAVIGATIONAL POSITIONS AND COURSES OF THE U.S.S. QUEENFISH (SS393) AND AWA MARU SINKING SITE

1. TIME: 1200 HOURS . . . LATITUDE 25 DEGREES 47'.00" NORTH LONGITUDE 121 DEGREES 09'.00" EAST, COURSE . . . 250 DEGREES TRUE

2. TIME: 2000 HOURS . . . LATITUDE 25 DEGREES 23'.12" NORTH LONGITUDE 119 DEGREES 58'.00" EAST, COURSE . . . 043 DEGREES TRUE

3. TIME: 2115 HOURS . . . LATITUDE 25 DEGREES 26'.05" NORTH LONGITUDE 120 DEGREES 01'.00" EAST, COURSE . . . 180 DEGREES TRUE, SPEED 8 KNOTS

NOTE: THIS NAVIGATIONAL POSITION WAS VERIFIED BY RADAR RANGES AND BEARINGS ON "TURNABOUT ISLAND" (NIU-SHAN TAO), PLACING THE QUEENFISH 4.9 MILES BEARING 090 DEGREES TRUE FROM THE ISLAND.

4. TIME: 2159 HOURS . . . LATITUDE 25 DEGREES 20'.45" NORTH LONGITUDE 120 DEGREES 01'.00" EAST, COURSE . . . 225 DEGREES TRUE, SPEED 8 KNOTS

5. TIME: 2200 HOURS . . . RADAR CONTACT WAS MADE ON A SINGLE SHIP BEARING 230 DEGREES TRUE, DISTANCE 17,000 YARDS, COURSE . . . 045 DEGREES TRUE, TO 050 DEGREES TRUE, SPEED 16 KNOTS

6. TIME: 2210 HOURS . . . QUEENFISH COURSE CHANGED TO 050 DEGREES TRUE. MANNED BATTLE STATIONS AND TRACKED USING "TURNABOUT ISLAND" AS A NAVIGATIONAL REFERENCE

7. TIME: 2300 HOURS . . . ATTACKED, FIRED FOUR TORPEDOS . . . ALL FOUR HIT TARGET. APPROXIMATELY 3 MINUTES LATER THE TARGET SANK AND DISAPPEARED FROM THE RADAR SCREEN

8. TIME: 2311 HOURS . . . QUEENFISH REACHED THE SCENE OF THE SINKING SITE WHICH WAS DETERMINED BY RANGES AND BEARINGS ON "TURNABOUT ISLAND" . . .

LATITUDE 25 DEGREES 25'.1" NORTH, LONGITUDE 120 DEGREES 07'.1" EAST

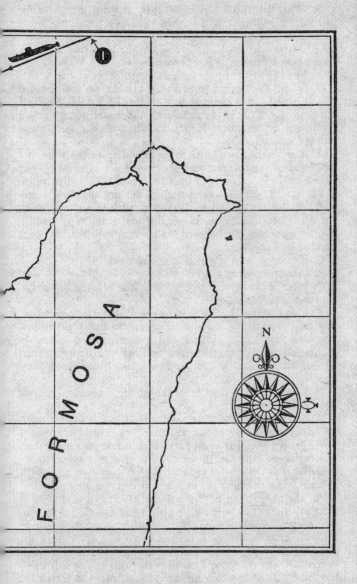

Q. Was the U.S.S. QUEENFISH assigned a submarine patrol zone on the night of 1 April 1945?

A. Yes.

Q. Is the position latitude 25-25.1 N., longitude 120-07.1 East inside a submarine patrol zone?

A. Yes.

Q. Were the orders concerning attacks on unidentified vessels issued to the commanding officer U.S.S. QUEENFISH prior to 1 April 1945 sufficiently adequate to cover all conditions of visibility? If not, in what respect were these orders inadequate?

A. They were considered to be adequate at the time, but this incident has proved that they were not adequate. They have now been amended. Operation Plan 1-45, under which U.S.S. QUEENFISH was operating, did not specifically prescribe action to be taken regarding surface vessels which could not be identified on account of low visibility and which might reasonably be believed to be hospital ships or ships granted safe conduct.

Q. How long have you known the accused?

A. About six years.

Q. What is the service reputation of the accused as submarine commanding officer?

A. Commander Houffman has a splendid service reputation. Not only is he a fine example of an officer and a gentleman, but his record as an officer and a commanding officer in submarines proves that he is a fearless and daring leader, whose attacks are skillful and aggressive to the highest degree.

Q. What is the service reputation of the accused as regards obedience to orders?

A. So far as I know, Commander Houffman's service reputation as regards to obedience to orders is perfect; I have never known anything about him which would indicate that he has ever been guilty of the slightest degree of disobedience.

Q. What is the service reputation of the accused as regards to care in ascertaining his orders and carrying them out?

A. My observation of Commander Houffman is that he is most careful in ascertaining his orders and carrying them out. Of necessity, a submarine command officer is pretty much on his own after he leaves port, and there has never been the slightest question of his failure to properly interpret his orders. On the contrary, I recall with pride the speed, intuition, and skill with which he carried out orders to search for and rescue a number of Allied prisoners of war who had been left adrift in the South China Sea by the sinking of the Japanese transport in which they were embarked. Due to his initiative and to his skill in searching the assigned area, numbers of survivors were rescued and brought safely into port who would otherwise have been lost.

Neither the judge advocate, the accused, nor the court desired further to examine this witness; the witness resumed his seat as judge advocate.

Following the reading of endorsements that substantiated Houffman's unblemished war record to date, his character, his willingness to obey orders, and his honors and citations, the defense rested.

XVIII

Date: April 20, 1945
Place: Headquarters compound, Camp Dealy, Guam
Time: 1030 hours
Status: The arguments

The prosecution, apparently confident that it had its case won, summed up its opening arguments in ten minutes that morning, the second day of the trial.

There was little else to say: the deed had been committed and admitted. But were there orders on board that prohibited the action? Was the commander responsible for those orders? Were the orders clear and precise?

The answers to the first two questions were clear. Certainly the third was debatable. At least one of those orders, the one dispatch that failed to delineate area, was not clear and precise. But, taken together, the judge advocate believed that the facts presented proved a prima facie case and warranted a finding of guilty on all three charges.

The defense saw it another way. There were a host of mitigating circumstances. The defense arguments that day touched on them:

This trial is the result of the sinking of a Japanese ship which had been granted a safe conduct for the purpose of carrying prisoner of war relief supplies, the safe conduct was guaranteed by the United States Government for that humanitarian purpose. That this question is included in this trial may be demonstrated by the charges and specifications, in each specification the act allegedly done by the accused is in effect that he did sink the said AWA MARU.

There has been, up to the close of the prosecution's case, no evidence introduced before this court that the AWA MARU had ever carried prisoner of war supplies.

230

There is a burden upon the prosecution to prove in the minds of the court beyond a reasonable doubt on every material allegation in the specification. When the prosecution failed to prove that the AWA MARU was a vessel carrying prisoner of war supplies, the accused might well have stopped at that point and expected an acquittal because of the failure of the proof.

However, this case is so important, the accused exceeded himself on this parallel. He had carefully attempted to identify the vessel before attacking it under his general orders that unidentified vessels should be attacked, except hospital ships and safe conduct vessels.

Also because it was evident that the Japanese government had taken advantage of the safe conduct given the AWA MARU, if that be the ship which was sunk, to transport war supplies and materials and passengers vital to the war effort, all of which in direct contravention of the recognized rules for the conduct of safe passage ships. There has often been mentioned from time to time in the trial, and the court I am sure knows, in fact it is in the deposition of Commander Submarine Force, Pacific Fleet, that all unidentified vessels with the exception of hospital ships and safe conduct ships were to be sunk, sometimes called unrestricted warfare.

Such warfare is commonly accepted in international law by a custom. You need only to recall the arming of merchant vessels in World War I which was followed by the declaration of unrestricted submarine warfare as a retaliatory measure. In this war and when all of the wartime nations are belligerents, the question of neutrality does not enter into the consideration unless they are excepted by international agreement or are safe conduct ships.

All the ships sailing the seas are belligerent and may be attacked, and ought to be attacked. That that is the modern trend is perhaps best illustrated by a report to the Commission of Jurists, of the Hague 1923, not a doctrine accepted by the nations of the world but proposed to the Commission of Nations. It is my personal opinion of the recognition of the warfare and reprisals carried on in the first World War, which had to do with the new weapon of war, the airplane, and it says, "Belligerent aircraft whether public or civil within or in sight of the jurisdiction of an opposing belligerent, or

231

within or in sight of the area of operations of an opposing belligerent, may be dealt with without warning as aircraft of war." There is no distinction between civil and military aircraft now. Hospital ships and a safe conduct or cartel ship such as the AWA MARU are exceptions.

The Hague Convention of 1907, Article 5, in part says, referring to hospital ships, "The ships and boats above mentioned which wish to ensure by night the freedom from interference to which they are entitled, must, subject to the assent of the belligerent they are accompanying, take the necessary measures to render their special painting sufficiently plain," ratified by the U.S. and Japan.

In other words, gentlemen, the burden is laid upon the safe conduct ship to make her identity known. They suggest for normal times, white crosses and the like, of such painting which may be seen at night. The rules suggest for normal times that the cross be illuminated, and the reason for the illumination is to make the character plain. It is believed that during periods of low visibility whether by day or by night, the discharge of the burden lies upon the safe conduct ship.

She must make her special character known. There is a method understood by all persons who are seafarers that goes by the name of International Rules of the Road, under reproduction in Navy Regulations on page 769 and provides that steam vessels in inclement weather or fog under way as follows: "Steam vessel under way (a) A steam vessel having way upon her shall sound, at intervals of not more than two minutes, a prolonged blast."

There is no evidence produced by the prosecution that this vessel or ship sounded her whistle, but there is positive evidence that established that no whistle or other fog signal was sounded by the ship in question sunk on 1 April 1945. And, bear in mind, gentlemen, the burden is laid upon the safe conduct vessel to make her identity plain. That is, assuming that the ship sunk was the AWA MARU, and that ship was under safe conduct on the night of 1 April 1945.

There is another consideration. The character of a safe conduct ship has been defined many times. I will refer to Oppenheim on International Law, of the 5th edition, to speak of international law. Referring to cartel in safe conduct ships, "They must not do any trade, they are in particular not allowed to carry ammunition or instruments of war, except one gun for firing signals. They must be furnished with a proper document declaring that they are commissioned as cartel ships.

"They are under the protection of both belligerents, and may neither be seized nor appropriated. They enjoy this protection, not only when actually carrying exchanged prisoners or official communications, but also on their way home after such carriage and on their way to fetch prisoners or official communications. They lose it at once, and may consequently be seized and may be appropriated in case they do not comply either with the general rules regarding cartel ships or with special conditions imposed upon them." There are many cases that deal with cartel ships who lose their character of safe conduct.

Inasmuch as the AWA MARU was loaded with tin, according to the prisoner, at the time she was sunk, she rightly lost her guarantee of safe passage. Tin was used as a munition of war in the 1800s.

It doesn't have to be done by the government intentionally, it doesn't have to be done by the owner, if their person is responsible for loading aboard an exchange or cartel ship contraband goods, the character of the ship is destroyed, it is no longer a cartel ship.

At the beginning, when it looked like the Japanese would at least agree to the transport of prisoner of war supplies, as shown the chart, "Exhibit 3," the proposed route for this cartel ship led through a Japanese minefield, obviously a ruse of war to entice United States shipping and submarines to believe that those waters were safe for navigation.

They left it in as long as possible and only amended their route to go around the minefield when it was necessary for their own ship to travel through it; only then did they inform the United States. Treachery on the part of the Japanese government is apparent. It is a serious thing to charge a nation with a deliberate violation of well recognized laws and customs, especially in the matter to which the individuals who depend to a large extent upon these supplies.

It reminds me of an Indian in Oklahoma who was encountered by a friend of his one day. The Indian was carrying a rifle down the street, obviously angry. His friend inquired where he was going, and Joe Fish, the Indian, stated that he was going to kill a white man named Sam Cook. His friend said, "Why? Why are you going to kill Sam, Joe?" And Joe replied, "He steals my land." His friend said, "Well, Joe, you originally had 320 acres of land, years ago, and Sam stole 160 acres from you and you did not get mad about that. A few years later you got into another deal and he stole half of what you had left, and now, the third time, you want to kill him. You did not threaten to kill him the second time and now the third time, he steals 40 acres from you and you're going to kill him. I do not understand." Joe Fish replied, "The first time a white man steals from the Indian, that is his fault. The second time the white man steals from the Indian, that is the Indian's fault. But the third time the white man steals from the Indian, something has got to be done about it now!"

The Japanese had their first trial and it was their fault, when they sunk, deliberately and premeditatedly, the U.S.S. PANAY in 1937. They had their second chance at Pearl Harbor, and they took a third chance when they used a supposedly safe conduct ship as a ruse of war and for the transportation of contraband tin, lead, and rubber, and it was time something was done about it.

It was only the fortuitous circumstances that the Japanese ship neglected to perform her duty of making her character plain by sounding the proper fog signals as required by the International Rules of the Road, that tore from the Japanese the fruits of this latest treachery.

If it please the court: The accused is being tried on three charges. There is a single specification under each charge. It is apparent that the same series of acts forms the basis for each specification and, accordingly, that the specifications have been preferred to cover the exigencies of the proof.

I shall now discuss each specification separately and will show, I believe, that none of them has been proven by the evidence introduced before this court.

With reference to the specification under charge 1, an essential allegation of this specification is that the accused "failed to make proper investigation, identification and observation" of a ship contacted and later sunk on the night of 1 April 1945. The defense contends that a proper investigation was made, that the ship was identified as well as it could be under the circumstances, and that, while the ship was not seen, it was approached to as close a range as it was safe to do so, without undue hazard to the submarine of which the accused was in command, and that every reasonable and proper effort was made to observe it.

This contention is supported by the following facts which it is believed are amply supported by the evidence:

1. The ship attacked was closed from a range of 17,000 yards to a range of 1,500 yards for identification and observation, before it was attacked.
2. The ship attacked was tracked by radar for about an hour before being attacked and much information was obtained concerning it.
3. The information obtained concerning the ship before it was attacked indicated it was a destroyer or a small war vessel.
4. The accused believed it was a destroyer, a small war vessel, throughout the approach and at the time of the attack.
5. A range of 1,500 yards was as close as the type of ship the accused believed the target to be could be approached without undue and extreme hazard to own ship.
6. Every possible attempt was made to observe the target visually throughout the approach and attack, but it could not be seen.
7. If the ship attacked had been sounding fog signals, these signals would have been heard before the range was closed to 1,500 yards and the alleged peaceful nature of the target known.

Referring to the above, little discussion is needed of the first two points. The evidence is contradicted that the target was picked up at a range of about 17,000 yards and was closed to about 1,500 yards before the torpedoes were fired. The TDC operator testified that the target was tracked for about an hour, using the TDC; the target was tracked by plot for a somewhat shorter period.

That the information available to the accused indicated that the target was a destroyer or a small war ship is clearly shown by the following:

a) A ship of about this size, i.e. a destroyer, will normally be picked up by a submarine's radar at a range of about 17,000 yards. A large merchantman will be picked up at a much greater range.

b) The high speed of the target, initially determined to be 18 knots, this being later reduced to 16 knots just before firing, is characteristic of a destroyer or war vessel, which, probably having radar, could safely proceed at this speed in the visibility existing.

c) The heading or course of the target was toward the general vicinity of an attack made earlier in the day by the U.S.S. SEAFOX. This, in view of the frequent practice of the Japanese to send anti-submarine vessels to the scene of a recent attack, indicated that the target might well have been a destroyer or other small anti-submarine vessel.

d) The fact that the target was not zigzagging strongly supports the theory of a destroyer or anti-submarine vessel losing no time, that is, steering a straight course at high speed, for the scene of a recent attack. The fact that the target was not zigzagging in no sense indicated that it was a hospital ship or a ship granted safe conduct, since any high-speed ship might well consider its speed and the existing poor visibility sufficient protection against submarine attack.

The following uncontradicted facts show that the accused himself believed the target to be a destroyer or small war vessel:

a) The depth setting of 3 feet in a force 1 or 2 sea. The testimony indicates clearly that this shallow a depth setting would be used only against a destroyer or other light-draft vessel.

b) The spread used covered only about 290 feet of target length. This is slightly less than a target length of a destroyer or destroyer escort. It is much less than the length of a large merchantman. Such a narrow spread would be employed only when firing at a destroyer or vessel of similar length.

The following considerations indicate the extreme risk and undue hazard to which a submarine on the surface in poor visibility would be exposed if it approached too closely to an enemy destroyer or similar anti-submarine vessel:

a) The well-known vulnerability of a submarine on the surface to attack by gunfire, ramming, or torpedo fire.

b) The fact that, since the target was not visible, a ramming or "turning toward" maneuver by the target would not immediately be detected by radar alone.

c) The probable speed advantage of the enemy vessel.

These considerations, together with the testimony offered by two experienced submarine commanding officers, show that close approach to a target believed to be a destroyer or anti-submarine vessel would not only be highly imprudent but unjustifiably dangerous to the submarine. In this particular case, the QUEENFISH would have had to close the target to about 200-yards range to definitely identify it visually. As brought out by the evidence, this is considerably less than the arming distance of her torpedoes. Thus, if she closed to this range she could not act offensively with torpedoes if the target proved to be an armed enemy ship and would be relatively helpless if detected.

Ample evidence has been offered that every possible attempt was made to see the target visually during the approach and prior to the attack, and that at no time was either the ship or any lights seen.

It is firmly established that the ship sunk was not sounding fog signals in the poor visibility, about 200 yards, which existed prior to the attack. Had it been sounding such signals, they would have been heard well beyond the 1,500-yards range to which the target was finally approached. This is a matter concerning which I am certain the court will take judicial notice.

The points just discussed clearly indicate that the specification of the first charge has not been proved.

However, as an additional defense, the accused further contends that if the AWA MARU was attacked by the accused, she was not improperly attacked, as alleged in the specification, but properly attacked and sunk. The AWA MARU repeatedly violated her safe conduct on her voyage south. On her return passage toward Japan she carried no prisoner of war supplies, but was loaded to capacity with tin, lead, and rubber, all materials vital to the prosecution of the war, and had on board about 1,700 merchant seamen passengers. The assistant coun-

237

sel for the accused has shown that by reason of the above and other acts, the AWA MARU lost her safe conduct and her guarantee of safe passage.

This being so, her character became the same as that of any other Japanese merchant vessel, and if she was attacked and sunk, the attack and sinking was proper and lawful, and her sinking is an important stroke toward the winning of the war against the Japanese.

The portions of the specifications of the first charge which counsel for the accused strongly contends are not proved are vital to the specification. If the court considers that any of the allegations discussed is not proved beyond a reasonable doubt, the specification fails and the accused should be found not guilty.

Now referring to the specification of the second charge, the accused contends this specification is not proved for the following reasons:

1. That if the order specified was disobeyed, the accused disobeyed it unintentionally and not willfully.
2. That the orders issued to the accused by his Task Force Commander concerning attacks on unidentified vessels were not adequate to cover the situation of very poor visibility.
3. That the order received was "let pass safely the AWA MARU carrying prisoner of war supplies" and not "let pass safely the AWA MARU." If the accused disobeyed an order, even though not willfully, it was the order "let pass safely the AWA MARU," which was not the entire order he received. In other words, it is contended that the phrase "carrying prisoner of war supplies" is a vital and essential part of the order.

The accused admits that he willfully attacked a ship on the night of 1 April 1945. However, he willfully and intentionally attacked a ship he believed to be a destroyer or small warship. The evidence introduced and the discussion under the specification of the first charge further show that he had ample reason to believe the target attacked was a destroyer. If the accused attacked the AWA MARU he did so certainly not willfully, but unintentionally and as the result of a mistake in identification, unavoidable under the circumstances.

Thus, when the accused was ordered to "let safely pass the AWA MARU carrying prisoner of war supplies," if he sank this ship unintentionally and by mistake, it cannot be said he willfully disobeyed this order. If an order was disobeyed, it was not done deliberately or knowingly or willfully.

The Task Force Commander of the accused has testified, by deposition, that his orders to the accused relative to attacks on unidentified ships were not adequate in that they did not specifically prescribe the action to be taken regarding surface vessels which could not be identified on account of low visibility. The ship attacked by QUEENFISH on the night of 1 April was such a ship. The Task Force Commander has since issued additional orders clarifying this situation.

This point is stressed because it shows that the orders which the accused had previously received concerning attacks on unidentified ships ... must be considered sufficiently specific or adequate by the Task Force Commander himself. It can most reasonably be inferred that this admitted inadequacy and indefiniteness no doubt affected the accused in his decisions and actions. Furthermore, the orders under which the accused was operating at the time not only justified him but also, it is contended, required him to attack unidentified surface ships which he had reason to believe were enemy and which he could not identify in poor visibility conditions without unduly hazarding his ship. This the accused did, after making every reasonable effort to effect identification, with the result that the Japanese are deprived of a much needed cargo of rubber, tin, and lead, plus a large number of personnel highly valuable to their war effort.

The argument supporting the third point, while admittedly somewhat tenuous, is believed to have validity. The whole order received was "let pass safely the AWA MARU carrying prisoner of war supplies." No such ship passed the vicinity of the QUEENFISH on 1 April. But there did pass near the QUEENFISH the AWA MARU not carrying prisoner of war supplies, but loaded with war supplies and seamen. If the accused failed to let any ship pass safely, it was this ship. Continuing, if he disobeyed any order, it was "let pass safely the AWA MARU not carrying prisoner of war supplies." This is not, however, the order specified in the specification under question.

Finally, referring to the third charge and specification

239

thereunder, the accused contends that he did not neglect, but did proceed with due and full caution and circumspection in the identification of the vessel contacted and attacked on the night of 1 April 1945.

As previously shown in the discussion of the specification of the first charge, the accused closed the ship contacted to 1,500 yards in an effort to identify it, meanwhile striving to sight it in the existing visibility. It has also been shown that it would have been very hazardous for the QUEENFISH to approach closer, under the circumstances, to actually effect visual contact, which would not have been made in excess of a range of about 200 yards. At this range the submarine would have been relatively helpless both offensively and defensively should the target prove, as was believed, a warship or even an armed enemy vessel. Further, the target was tracked for nearly an hour in order to obtain full information on its course, speed, and zigzag plan, if it proved to be zigzagging. In addition, the target was closed to a range at which fog signals could have been heard had they been sounded. All the above unequivocably prove that the accused exercised all due caution and circumspection and made every reasonable possible effort to identify the aforesaid vessel.

The accused had indoctrinated his officers to call him immediately on any ship contact. When a ship was contacted, he invariably took the conn, personally identified the target, if possible, and made decision whether to attack or not to attack. Under such a procedure, which is the general practice in the submarine service, it is not necessary that any officer other than the commanding officer be informed concerning expected or possible contacts.

The AWA MARU relied on the following in order to obtain immunity from attack:

1. Special markings, allegedly illuminated at night.
2. Predisseminated information on her track.

The first was nullified when she steamed into a fog where her markings could not be seen except at a very close range and when she failed to sound proper fog signals. The second was nullified when she got more than 30 miles off her preannounced track.

In conclusion, the service reputation of the accused as regards efficiency in the performance of duty, obedience

240

to orders, and care in obeying orders is of the highest order and leaves nothing to be desired. With such an enviable reputation to uphold, it seems incredible that he would in any way sully it by any of the acts or omissions alleged.

Before closing, there are two final points to which I respectfully invite the court's attention. The first is the relative youth and inexperience of the QUEENFISH officers, a fact which must have been obvious to the court as they appeared here as witnesses.

The second point is the relatively long periods of time which elapsed between the receipt of the first announced and also the amended route of the AWA MARU and the date she sailed through the patrol area of the QUEEN-FISH. The message listing the first announced route was last received on 8 March 1945. In one case there was an elapsed time of 24 days, in the other case 27 days, before the AWA MARU actually sailed through the QUEEN-FISH patrol area.

"A naval court-martial has an enlarged jurisdiction over that of a civil court. A naval court-martial sits also as a court of honor and, accordingly, may find upon the question of honor. It is a peculiarity." (Winthrop.)

This case involved not only the honorable conduct of the accused but touches the honor of the nation. The United States engaged its honor to guarantee the safe passage of a Japanese ship for the purpose of transporting relief supplies for prisoners of war.

Had the Japanese been successful in their attempt to use the humanitarian instincts of the United States to further the war effort against our country, the United States would have been dishonored. Happily, such was not the case. The omission to sound fog signals during low visibility, the one item neglected in the carefully laid plan to profit from the good will of the United States, proved a trap that deprived the Japanese of a ship, the contraband goods, and the seamen passengers.

Section 434 Naval Courts and Boards reads as follows: "The court does therefore most fully and honorably acquit." This form should be used only in extreme cases in which not only have the requirements of a "full" and "honorable" acquittal been fulfilled, but in which the court wishes to place the highest stamp of approval upon the actions of the accused in connection with matters covered by the specifications. The use of this form of acquittal might, for example, be justified in the case of an officer charged with unbecoming conduct in battle if the court wished to make it a matter of record that, far from considering the conduct of such officer censurable, it both approved and commended his conduct.

The accused stands charged with essentially conduct unbecoming in battle and so meets that requirement and upon the evidence adduced respectfully requests the finding of most fully and honorably acquitted of all charges.

The court then, at 12:03 P.M., took a recess until 1:00 P.M., at which time it reconvened.

Present: all the members, the judge advocate and his counsel, the reporter, the accused and his counsel.

No witnesses not otherwise connected with the trial were present.

The judge advocate made the following closing argument:

The judge advocate has covered, in his opening argument, the elements of the charges and the points of proof made by him. He will not reiterate them here.

Counsel for the accused stated in his argument, in effect, that the AWA MARU violated her duties under international law, and therefore was liable to seizure or sinking. The accused is not being tried for breach of international law, which can be decided in other courts, but for specific breaches of military law.

Counsel for the accused stated that the supposed wrong by the AWA MARU, which by the evidence has been shown as not being known to or suspected by the accused until *after* the sinking, gave our government the right to violate the guarantee of safe conduct given that vessel and the Japanese government. The standards of ethical conduct to which I have been trained have taught me that a wrong does not authorize retaliation by a wrong. My country's standards have been the same.

Counsel for the accused stated that the accused's orders permitted and directed him to sink all unidentified ships *except* hospital ships and ships under safe conduct. The AWA MARU was a ship under safe conduct and was not identified until after the sinking.

Counsel for the accused at several times stated that the

accused believed the ship to be such-and-such and attempted to identify her. Belief as to her identity was not enough. He was required by his orders and the information he had received to know what she was.

The trial was finished.
The court was cleared.
The judge advocate was recalled and directed to record the findings.

XIX

Well, Jesus. About mid-morning, Old Ox and me got the word, right? The defense and prosecution were summing up. No further witnesses would be called, and we were free to go back to camp. I mean, just like that, you know?

Now, I'm not sayin' I was lookin' forward to going before the court and tellin' them I couldn't tell what I was hearing on the headphones that night, that it could have been a destroyer or a porpoise in heat for all I knew. But them not calling me at all? I mean, that had to be some kind of trial they were having in there. I mean, figure it.

Can you tell me why the goddamned Navy spent all the time and money training a sonar operator for identifying the type of vessel by sound, if it didn't really make a damn? So, they conduct a trial and they talk about radar. They call thirty guys to tell the court what the hell radar was and how it worked and what they saw on the scope that night. They call in another thirty guys to tell them it was foggy, right? To tell them we couldn't see diddly-squat. So, what's left? It didn't take a vice-admiral to figure that one out.

But, okay. It was clear what the court had in mind from the beginning. It was a two-day piece of diplomacy. You know. Gather together some high military mucky-mucks, hear all the evidence they wanted to hear, everything that conformed to what they had in mind in the first place, and get the results out on an international cable so the Japs would cool on any ideas they might be having for a POW roast. I mean, it was a script, you know? Why else would they bang through this thing in two days?

So, that was okay with me. I didn't like the idea of facing that court with a pack of lies anyway. And Old Ox? He couldn't get his lumbering ass out of that waiting room fast enough. So, everybody was happy, right?

It was going to end just like in the picture shows:

After careful deliberation by the highest-ranking military tribunal ever assembled, the court, after soberly considering all the evidence, finds that the defendant, Commander Raymond Michael Houffman, did what he was supposed to do and ordered that goddammed ship blown clean out of the water. And, while the court sincerely regrets the loss of the high-ranking Japanese military and civilian dignitaries, it can't for the life of it figure what the hell they were doing there in the first place. Therefore, be it resolved that Commander Houffman, who took every conceivable step to identify said vessel as something other than what it sure-as-shit looked to be, shall hereby be fully exonerated from any blame in the incident, and shall, instead, be awarded the Nobel Prize for Peace. The crew, which so diligently served its commander, shall receive the coveted Cut 'Em Loose Award, and shall have, commencing immediately, unrestricted access to the nurses' barracks for seven nights running.

And everybody goes off into the sunset with a gathering chorus of "Glory, Halleluja."

Right?

Wrong.

I mean, dead wrong. They found him guilty, for Christ sake. They found the old man guilty as charged.

Guilty.

But, of what?

Nineteen days after the American invasion of Okinawa, four days after the death of Franklin Delano Roosevelt and the assumption to the presidency of a Missouri haberdasher, and seventy-seven days before the explosion of the atomic bomb over the city of Hiroshima, Commander Raymond Michael Houffman was found guilty of negligence in obeying orders, the least severe of the three charges.

The man who, in substance, was responsible for the deaths of 2,008 Japanese men, women, and children aboard the *Awa Maru*, a responsibility he assumed when he ordered the attack on an unseen vessel on that fog-shrouded first night of April 1945. It was a deed that violated an international treaty. For that, for what the court considered his negligence, he was sentenced.

He did not lose his life.

He did not go to jail.

He did not receive a dishonorable discharge.

He did not lose pay.

245

The commander of the U.S.S. *Queenfish* was instead sentenced by this highest-ranking court in military history to receive a letter of admonition. A letter!

Admiral Nimitz was furious. And for all the wrong reasons. What bothered the admiral is that the court did not provide enough latitude, a harsh enough sentence, for him to review and reduce it. He could not go on record for compassion.

Yet, in finding Houffman guilty, the court had cast a stigma on Houffman, on the submarine service, and on the government of the United States.

By choosing a middle course, the court had really chosen the worst course.

Commander Houffman had not been tried under the laws of war. Though he was accused of an offense that violated these laws, the United States Navy, in direct contravention to the terms she subscribes to under the Uniform Code of Military Justice, failed to try him under these laws or subject him to the punishment provided by them.

The United States is a signator to the Hague Convention of 1907. So too is Japan. Both have agreed to abide by these rules of nations that concern treaties and the customs of war recognized by such treaties.

Much like the Geneva Conference, the Hague Convention governs behavior between warring nations who are solemn signators to its provisions. When a general court-martial exercises jurisdiction under the law of war, it may adjudge any punishment permitted by the law of war. Most of the offenses under the law of war are punishable by death.

Insofar as the provisions of the law of war have been incorporated in treaties and conventions between nations to which the United States is party, they have become part of the supreme law of the land. That is, they take precedence over national and military law.

Such treaties cover the treatment of hospital ships.

The principal offenses against the law of war are:

—Killing of wounded
—Refusal of quarter
—Treacherous request for quarter
—Maltreatment of dead bodies
—Ill treatment of prisoners of war
—Firing on undefended places
—Abuse of the flag of truce

—Firing on the flag of truce
—Misuse of the Red Cross emblem
—Poisoning of wells and streams
—Pillage and purposeless destruction
—*Bombardment of hospitals*

In essence, Commander Houffman was responsible for violating an international treaty. The parties—the United States and Japan—had agreed, by lending their signatures to the Hague Convention, that violations of the terms of these solemn agreements shall constitute an abridgement of international law. And shall be tried accordingly.

A violation this grievous was sure to be considered a capital offense.

It is still unclear why Commander Houffman did not stand trial under the law of war. It is curious that the United States, so rightly vociferous about Japan's violation of international agreements pertaining to the treatment of her POWs, should refuse to practice what it preached, should fail to live up to its own agreements.

The decision was reached at the highest level of U.S. government. Those who were a party to protecting Commander Houffman from the stricter penalties that could have been imposed for the violation of an international treaty were:

Chester Nimitz, Supreme Naval Command in the Pacific

Ernest King, Commander in Chief, U.S. Fleet, and Chief of Naval Operations

Joseph Grew, Under Secretary of State

Henry Stimson, War Secretary

James Forrestal, Navy Secretary

Harry Hopkins, presidential envoy to Franklin Delano Roosevelt

Franklin Delano Roosevelt, President of the United States before April 12, 1945

Harry S Truman, President of the United States after April 12, 1945

In the years following the trial, Commander Houffman, his career surprisingly undiminished, perhaps even enhanced, by the events, was subsequently promoted to the rank of rear admiral.

On April 14, 1949, the United States officially admitted to the government of Japan its responsibility for the sinking and agreed to settle the claim of the *Awa Maru:*

UNITED STATES OF AMERICA
and
JAPAN

Agreement for settlement of the AWA MARU claim (with Agreed Terms of Understanding). Signed at Tokyo, on 14 April 1949.

Official texts: English and Japanese
Registered by the United States of America on 3 June 1951

ÉTAS-UNIS D'AMÉRIQUE
et
JAPON

Accord relatif au règlement de l'affaire AWA MARU (avec protocole interprétatif). Signé à Tokyo, le 14 avril 1949

Textes officiels anglais et japonais.
Enregistré par les États-Unis d' Amérique le 3 juin 1951

No. 1215 AGREEMENT BETWEEN THE GOVERNMENT OF THE UNITED STATES OF AMERICA AND THE JAPANESE GOVERNMENT FOR SETTLEMENT OF THE AWA MARU CLAIM. SIGNED AT TOKYO, ON 14 APRIL 1949

WHEREAS the Government of the United States of America and the Japanese Government reached an agreement during the recent hostilities that the Japanese Government would provide vessels which would transport supplies for the relief of Allied nationals in various areas of the Pacific then under Japanese control and the Government of the United States of America would guarantee the immunity of vessels on such missions from attack by Allied forces on both the outward and homeward voyages; and

WHEREAS the Japanese passenger-cargo vessel AWA MARU was sunk on 1 April 1945, while homeward-bound from such a mission; and

WHEREAS the Government of the United States of America acknowledged responsibility for the sinking of the vessel and assured the Japanese Government that it would be prepared after the termination of hostilities to consider the question of indemnity; and

WHEREAS the Government of the United States of America and the Japanese Government sought to reach an equitable and mutually satisfactory solution of this claim; and

WHEREAS General of the Army Douglas MacArthur has extended his good offices as intermediary between the Government of the United States of America and the Japanese Government in an effort to facilitate agreement.

The undersigned, being duly authorized by their respective governments for that purpose, have reached the following agreement through the good offices of the Supreme Commander for the Allied Powers.

Article I

The Japanese Government, mindful of the equities of the situation they have developed since the inception of the occupation of Japan under General of the Army Douglas MacArthur and in appreciation of the assistance—direct and indirect, in goods and services—received during the post-surrender period from the Government of the United States of America, waives on behalf of itself and all Japanese nationals concerning all claims of any description against the United States Government or any United States national arising out of the sinking of the AWA MARU.

Article II

The provisions of Article I shall bar, completely and finally, all claims of the nature referred to therein, which will be henceforward extinguished, whoever may be the parties in interest.

Article III
The Japanese Government will, in consideration of the special nature of this case, endeavor to provide adequate treatment in way of solatium for the families of those who perished in this disaster as well as for the owner of the vessel.

Article IV
The Government of the United States of America expresses its deep regret for the sinking of the AWA MARU and its sympathy with the families of those who perished in the disaster.

Article V
This Agreement shall take effect as from this day's date.

EXECUTED in duplicate, in the English and Japanese languages, at Tokyo, this fourteenth day of April, 1949 (24 Showa).

(SEAL)

For the Government of the United States of America:
William J. Sebald
Acting United States Political Adviser for Japan
For the Japanese Government:
Shigeru Yoshida
Minister for Foreign Affairs

Attest:
Douglas MacArthur
General of the Army
United States Army
Supreme Commander for the Allied Powers

So, that was the beginning of it, you know? I mean, I spent three years in subs in that war, in and out of every kind of thing you can imagine, and do you think anyone asks you about that? Come on. What they remember is that you were on the sub that sunk a floating hospital, right?

"The Queenfish," they'd say. "Oh, hell yes, I remember that. You're the guys that downed a shipload of wounded,

250

right? And weren't there American POWs aboard, or something? Jesus. You guys must have been crazy. Sure. I remember that. Your skipper took a general court-martial for the thing. Biggest sea disaster in history, right? Women, children. How many were there? A couple of thousand? And you left them all in the water but one. Broke a treaty or something, right?"

So, you'd get that, you know. Everybody had a memory for things like that. And they'd add to it, you know. Pretty soon, it wasn't a Jap ship at all but the British Red Cross, or some damn thing.

But it could have been worse. The news that got back home on the sinking was pretty sketchy at first. And, after the court-martial, when it was pretty clear what we'd done, other events were shoving the story off the front pages. I mean, big events, like the goddamned atom bomb and, not long after, the Jap surrender. And, it was just before the court-martial that Roosevelt died, you know, and you had Truman and the transition, and all that was pretty good-sized news, right?

So, the publicity we got on the thing could have been a lot worse. But, for those of us involved, that was the beginning of it. "The Queenfish?" we'd say. "Oh, yeah, I heard about that. No. Hell no, never served on her. No, I was aboard the Triton. Let me tell you about the time . . ."

It's like I say. We never made a pact about what went on that night; we didn't all get together and say we weren't going to talk about it anymore, that we'd clam up on the whole thing. We didn't do that. We didn't have to. None of us was going to bring up a thing like that.

But, when we got together, we'd talk about it some. At first, anyway. You know, you'd meet a guy you remembered. And he remembered you. And pretty soon you'd start talking about the Queenfish and whatever happened to old what's-his-name, and do you remember the time . . . But it would come back to that night. Eventually, it would come back to that, and you'd talk about it. You tried to work out between you what happened then, and later, at the court-martial. And you got to thinking, right?

It was one hell of a coincidence, you know? Us being there at that particular time, at that particular place. The only sub in the Pacific who hadn't got the word on the passing of the Awa Maru. Nine messages sent on the thing, and the only one that got through to the captain was the one that didn't give her track. And the Seafox. We were passing within a few goddamned miles of the convoy she engaged. And she didn't notify us. Instead, she lets us go by. She doesn't say a word for six hours. All the time we're heading for the Awa Maru. She says nothing until we have passed the course the Awa Maru had set, until we had overshot the track. By then the Awa Maru was almost on top of us. Then the Seafox tells us. Right? So, we turn, make a couple of maneuvers, and bingo. Contact, dead ahead. Right?

Now, we notify Seafox. We tell her what we've got on the radar. Does she warn us off, does she say, "Cool it, guys. You got a hospital ship comin' through that area"? The hell she does. And we don't hear from her for the hour we track that Jap ship. Not a word. When we shoot her down, that's when we hear, right? "Nice work," she says.

I mean, come on. That's one hell of a coincidence, you know? And then, within our own boat, there were a lot of things that made you wonder: a message on a short sheet of paper that was never read, a sonar report—mine, for Christ sake—that was never passed along. And earlier, on Guam, a briefing that didn't, we're told, mention the Awa Maru.

Now, maybe you could buy all that as just a big tangle of coincidences if the ship we sunk was some ordinary scow. But, she wasn't. The Awa Maru and what she carried that night meant one hell of a lot to the Allies. If she had gotten through, it would have meant one hell of a lot more.

All right. I hear what you're sayin'. You're sayin', Whose side are you on, anyway? What's it to you? You got a Jap ship loaded to the gunwales with gear enough to start and finish a brand-new war, jammed with everybody but Hirohito, truckin' enough gold to pave the United States. You're going to let that go? You're sayin'. Like hell, you're sayin'.

Okay. I hear you. But, goddamn it, listen. I served my country in that war, and, as a private citizen, I've served her since. For a reason. Because I believed—continue to believe—in the principles of the country, right? The principles, you know? Now, we made a mistake when we signed that treaty allowing Japan to use her biggest ship to cart a handful of Red Cross supplies so she could carry back everything that wasn't nailed down. But, that was a mistake some bumbling under-secretary made going in. But, we signed, for Christ sake. It was a treaty, and we signed it.

So, here she comes, headin' home, fatter'n a Christmas hog. We've seen her load, and we know what she's got. We want her so bad we can taste it, right? But we can't just float up and blow her out of the water. World opinion wouldn't hold still for that. So, maybe, the State Department sits down with the Department of the Navy, and they work it out, right? What it's got to be, they say, is an accident. We got to have us one big accident, they say.

They could arrange that in one of two ways. They could tell the captain and perhaps one or more of the senior officers aboard the Queenfish to make a mistake, to seek out the Awa Maru one foggy night, and have at her. Difficult, but possible.

Or, you could arrange to keep certain information from the Queenfish, and have her in the area when the Awa Maru arrives. Have them meet at night, and, if it's in the strait at that time of the year, five'll get you ten, it will be foggy. Then, hope for the best. If the sub identifies her and veers off, nothing's lost, right? If the sub doesn't see her, doesn't identify, she's as good as dead.

So, the deed gets done. Now what? In either case, they got to try the skipper. Even if it's some kind of rain dance, they've got to do something. World opinion, again.

So, you haul out some admirals. You have something that looks like a trial and you render a verdict. Guilty, right? All you've ruined is one career. And maybe, later, you can fix that. Let me ask you something. The captain, Houffman, remember? How many court-martialed Navy officers ever make it to rear admiral? Think about it.

Now, I don't know whether anybody will ever know what the hell really went on that night. But I'll tell you this: you've got a lot of guys on that sub who have been carting around the ghosts of 2,008 people ever since. Guys who gave up mentioning the name of the sub they served for fear somebody would start up again: "The Queenfish? Wasn't it the Queenfish that torpedoed that unarmed hospital ship . . ."

No. I don't have the answers. I don't even have all the questions. But the thing that began that night has worked on me. It made that war and the other wars that followed a lot harder to understand. Like I say, before that night, before things got mixed up, it was an easy war to understand—all the good guys were bunched on one side, all the bad guys on the other. The good guys were fighting for all the right principles, and the bad guys, they weren't worth a damn.

Like I say, they were all midgets, had a bad case of the jaundice, and talked funny. You couldn't trust guys like that. They would say one thing and do another.

We were the good guys. We kept our word. Not countin' what we did to the Indians, we hardly ever broke a treaty.

I mean, Jesus Christ.

EPILOGUE

The men who fought that last great war are older now. And still it excites them. When they talk about it, they are fearful that their listeners will turn away or yawn or miss the important parts, so they talk apologetically, embarassed, a little, that it still excites them.

Increasingly, they talk about it to younger men, men who lived through or fought other kinds of wars. These later wars, the ones that the younger men remember, were different. They were described by certain lines drawn by politicians in smoky rooms, imaginary lines etched across the fields of battle. Winning these wars was impossible; losing, inevitable.

It was not nearly as good talking about these later wars, and the older men, realizing that, talked about their war apologetically. But they had been stirred by the things they had seen, and talking about it made it so they could see it again, as though they were there again. And they talked hurriedly, in a tangle of words, many of them meaningless to the younger men, hoping to say it all, to remember the good parts again.

Many of the men who would have remembered the last great war, the one that ended more than thirty years ago, had died. Many of their friends, those who would understand, were gone. Some had died in battle, but most had fallen much later from heart attacks, fattened bellies, martinis, wives and ungrateful kids, or from smoking too much. There were fewer around who would listen, so the war was talked about less.

That, and because it was harder to remember things as older men, their stories became less clear in the telling. Sometimes the names and places would be wrong and it would become apparent only at the conclusion of the story, when suddenly none of it made sense.

"Wait . . . wait," they would say. "Maybe that was before Okinawa. Yeah, sure, that must have been long before the invasion . . . or was that . . . wait, let me get this straight. It's been a long time."

More often, the older men found themselves saying, "It's been a long time." Even those who had made notes of it, at the time and later when they had thought it all through, how it all happened, where the battles were fought and who won, even those who made notes made mistakes. Sometimes they couldn't find their notes.

"Wait . . . this can't be right. No. There must be a mistake in this."

It's hard to be precise about a war nobody talks about anymore.

And feelings about things were different, then. In the great wars, one did not question the motives of his country. Patriotism was a word still being used. That, too, made it harder to discuss. When motives were discussed, even in retrospect, there was resistance from these older men. It was all right to talk of the enemy's improper motives, of other nations' perpetrating evil, but it was not a good thing to talk about America in that way. Even after all the time that had passed, even when we later learned, painfully, how America could be, and was, in many cases, wrong.

Too, it was hard to talk to men who had fought that great war from within the confines of an undersea war machine that would never be used again. Though the newer machines were given the same generic name, they were not really the same thing at all. The nuclear submarines were a different thing from the machines that prowled the seas in wolfpacks in the great second war. It took a different kind of man and, mostly, it couldn't be compared.

And the obsolescence of it all made it even more difficult to discuss. There were procedures and equipment and philosophies that made talking about it cumbersome. It took explaining everything. It was a foreign language that nobody spoke anymore, and nobody really cared to.

A book like this one, which talks, in part, about men who fought a war they no longer remember clearly, from within the steel bellies of machines that no longer exist, will not always please those men. Each remembers different things about it.

There will be some stirring in the ranks:

"My God. That's not how it went. To begin with, Trevor

255

wasn't on the bridge with Houffman when they went to battle stations. He was in the conning tower with Edwards . . . no, wait, Edwards was in the control room and old Billy Williams . . . yeah, Billy was in the control room when Trevor and Mike Bass—remember Mike Bass?"

And there will be other problems with a book like this.

It would be better if we could determine whether the United States government, acting through the State Department and through the good offices of the United States Navy, did or did not deliberately order the sinking of the *Awa Maru*. We know some things for sure: That on April 1, 1945, a Japanese hospital ship on safe passage, laden with contraband, was sunk by a U.S. submarine. We know that ship contained a wealth of riches ripped from other lands, enough strategic materials to seriously prolong the war. We know, or strongly suspect, that American intelligence knew what she was carrying.

We know that subsequent to the sinking, the commander of the sub was tried by a military court and found guilty . . . guilty of the lesser of three relatively mild counts on which he was charged. And we know his punishment: a letter of reprimand. We know that he was not tried under the rules of war—under the auspices of the Hague Convention. We further know that the reprimand had little, if any, damaging impact on his subsequent Navy career, and that he now holds the rank of rear admiral (retired).

Taken together, these facts seem clear. If it were enough to merely juxtapose facts. But that is often misleading. One must, to be fair, establish causality, how or whether one fact bears on another.

With the evidence at hand—considerably more evidence than was at the disposal of those who tried the commander in those few weeks after the sinking—one is still unable to reach a definitive conclusion on whether Commander Raymond Michael Houffman acted under orders or not, whether he deliberately sank the *Awa Maru*, fully knowing who she was and under what conditions she sailed.

But when all the material is taken together and studied, it is extremely doubtful that Commander Houffman could have perpetrated the deed on orders from above without sharing his intentions with some or all of the senior officers aboard the *Queenfish*, particularly officers like Prospective Commanding Officer Steve Trevor and Executive Officer Bill Edwards.

The court-martial testimony and the subsequent, extensive interviews with Trevor and Edwards are conclusive: If Commander Houffman was a party to orders from above, he did not share them with anyone aboard the *Queenfish*, at least not with anyone who is willing to talk about it now, more than thirty years later.

Presuming that Commander Houffman committed an innocent, if tragic, error, that he issued that order in the belief that his target was an enemy ship of war, would this not close the book on a government conspiracy? Wouldn't it be safe to assume that the United States government could hardly be held responsible for deliberately violating a treaty, deliberately sinking a hospital vessel, if it was, after all, an accident?

But let's take a look at one possibility:

The bowplane incident in Guam delayed for twelve hours the departure of the *Queenfish* on her fourth patrol. Her sister ship and member of the pack, the *Seafox*, under the command of Eli Darvies, had earlier headed out toward the East China Sea, with the third component of the pack, *Spot*.

The delay was significant in that *Seafox* and *Spot* received the final, complete message of route change and description of the *Awa Maru* directly, while at sea. The *Queenfish*, on the other hand, took possession of the message through the Communications Section of the sub tender *Fulton*, to which she was tied. When the message was brought aboard the *Queenfish*, it was on a clipboard containing a host of other messages on standard-size paper. The significant message was on a short sheet, buried in the stack.

If that were the only message *Seafox* received pertaining to the *Awa Maru*, her description and route—and, clearly, it was not—then it must be presumed that *Seafox* knew exactly where the *Awa Maru* was and when and where she would pass.

The final message that both *Queenfish* and *Seafox* received on March 28 did not spell out the amended route of the Japanese ship.

On April 1, when *Seafox* engaged the enemy convoy, she did not comply with procedures established for wolfpack operations. She did not immediately notify *Queenfish*. Had she done so, Commander Houffman would have headed toward the convoy, which was then only a few miles from her position as she headed from the Shanghai area on return to her patrol area. Had *Seafox* done so, there would have been a

257

lot of sea between the *Queenfish* and the northbound *Awa Maru*.

Instead, the *Seafox* notified *Queenfish* more than six hours after the engagement. Upon receipt of the message, *Queenfish* simultaneously was assigned new patrol stations. That and subsequent maneuvers put her on an intercept, almost collision, course with the *Awa Maru*. When contact was made, the assumption that the blip on the radar was a warship heading for the attack site was strengthened. The blip looked like a destroyer and, heading as it was for the scene of a recent attack, it was acting like a destroyer.

Again, Commander Speer of the Naval Historical Center:

On 1 April 1945, the QUEENFISH received a message from SEAFOX at 1940 hours which reported an attack conducted by the SEAFOX against a Japanese convoy at 1300 hours that day.

Houffman was later to be critical of this turn of events. A basic tenet of wolfpack operational doctrine was to inform fellow submarines immediately of initial contact gained upon the enemy in order to bring augmented, coordinated force to bear as quickly as possible. *The more-than-six-hour lapse between the time of the attack by the SEAFOX and its subsequent contact report was to have a significant impact upon the fate of the AWA MARU.*

Houffman states: "Had SEAFOX let us know immediately when she had contact on the convoy, as she should have, we would have headed for that spot immediately. Had she let us know, we might have been 100 or more miles away from the AWA MARU and never made contact with her."

But the *Seafox did* make radio contact. It came more than six hours later.

And it was because of the timing of that contact that the *Queenfish* intercepted the *Awa Maru*. A contact that was to result in her sinking!

Of course, if this had been intended, if *Seafox* had made the delayed contact with the *Queenfish* on orders from ComSubPac or above in an effort to engage the *Queenfish* and the *Awa Maru*, it would have done so without any assurance that the *Queenfish* would not visually sight the *Awa Maru*, note her lighted crosses, and veer off.

But those who could have issued such an order would have known that the visibility in those waters at that time of year was generally poor. Fog was the common factor. Patrols had gone a month or more off Formosa without sighting the sun.

And those who would have issued the order that put the *Queenfish* and the *Awa Maru* on an intersect course could not have known that Commander Houffman would act on the belief that it had contacted an enemy destroyer. But they could have known that the *Awa Maru* was so low to the water that it looked like anything but what it was, a large cargo-passenger ship; that it was traveling fast; that it was not employing foghorns or whistles. And that it was heading to an area where an engagement was reported and to which a destroyer, seeking to render assistance to an engaged convoy, would bear.

It was not perfect, but if it was planned on the chance that an accident could occur, the chances were pretty good that such an accident would happen. It was one of the last chances to stop the *Awa Maru*. And if there was an accident, the consequences of it would fall to one man: Commander Raymond Michael Houffman.

Then what? Considering the gravity of the event and how that event impinged on the United States government and its treaty relationship with its adversary concerning the passing of this ship, a speedy court-martial would be in order.

But why the highest-ranking court-martial in naval history? Could it be that this was a conspiracy, a military secret maintained to the highest level; that the members of the court were a party to this conspiracy and were entrusted with this information by virtue of the high rank they held?

If that were the case, how then would they find the defendant? It would be difficult for them to render a verdict of not guilty, even though they may have—certainly would have—sympathized with Commander Houffman. They were pressed to signal Japan, by virtue of their verdict, that this was an accident that could have—should have—been avoided and that Houffman, not the government, was responsible for it. They could not risk the Japanese retaliating on American POWs.

Therefore, the verdict: guilty. But, because of their sympathy, they would find him guilty of the lesser charge and sentence him accordingly. Under normal circumstances, that charge and that sentence, however minor, would in effect have ended his career in the Navy.

But Commander Houffman instead was promoted to rear admiral.

Had Commander Eli Darvies of the *Seafox* testified in the trial, these questions could have been aired, the controversy cleared. But if this was indeed a conspiracy and Darvies had belatedly contacted the *Queenfish* that night to comply with specific orders from above, the *Seafox* commander would be the last person the court would want to hear from.

If there was a conspiracy, this is a more likely scenario than one that involves officers and possibly crew of the *Queenfish*. It would have involved one man, the commander of the *Seafox*, acting on one set of secret instructions.

If it failed, if the fog broke that night and the *Queenfish* sighted the Japanese vessel and veered away, allowing her to pass unmolested, the exposure to the conspiracy would have been limited to those at the highest level of government who would have issued the order and to the one man who would have necessarily carried it out: Commander Eli Darvies.

But it did not fail.

Finally, this: When *Queenfish* made contact with the *Awa Maru* at 2200 that night, an hour before it fired its torpedoes, it immediately contacted the *Seafox:*

". . . contact on single ship bearing 230° T at 17,000 yards range. Manned battle stations torpedo, commenced tracking and approach."

On receiving such a message describing contact of an unknown vessel near where the hospital ship was to be—within a few miles of where it *knew* it should be—would it not be reasonable for the *Seafox* to fire back a message to *Queenfish* cautioning her against shooting down a hospital ship on safe passage traveling in the near vicinity?

She did not then contact the *Queenfish*. Nor did she contact the *Queenfish* for the hour that she tracked the *Awa Maru*. Instead, the *Seafox* acknowledged the dispatch and quietly headed toward the scene of the impending disaster.

The next communication between the two submarines came again from the *Queenfish* to the *Seafox*, just before the attack.

At 2308 hours, the entry in the *Seafox* log describes the final communication, again from *Queenfish* to *Seafox:* "*Queenfish* reported attack completed and ship sunk with four hits. Quick work . . ."

Some of these questions might have been aired if Commander Houffman had taken the stand in his own defense. He did not. Later, he talked about that.

"I wanted to take the stand because I thought that I was being unjustly accused of something," Houffman said. "Under the circumstances, I thought I shouldn't be the fall guy. However, my counsel said no, and that was that."

AFTERWORD

At this writing, the *Awa Maru* rests on her side, some thirty-five fathoms beneath the surface of the East China Sea, an encrusted testament to the days of all-out war. Obliterated now are the white crosses that once marked her purported mission of mercy.

She lies in the still, a huge and ghostly wreckage, home for a variety of marine life dodging easily through her torn and darkened hulk. She rests on a thin layer of silt that blankets most of the debris around her. Only on close inspection will the specter of a human bone reveal itself, an eerie fragment of one of the 2,008 persons who followed her to the chilly depths more than thirty years ago.

Inside, and still sealed against some of the ravages of time and sea, are the contents of three specially constructed safes in an expanded, reinforced vault room. Within these safes and six capacious holds fore and aft lies the answer to the intrigue and mystery that have circulated above her for more than three decades.

The cause for all this concern?

The bounty. Five billion dollars for anyone who can find her and salvage the contents—the biggest undersea treasure of all time, a treasure that has never been revealed or even acknowledged by the Japanese government and, until recent news stories and now this book, never fully discussed in this country.

When news of a secretive, decade-long effort by a group of American diving and salvage experts to recover the treasure finally broke in a San Diego newspaper on November 17, 1976, the headline story was carried worldwide on the international wires.

What gave the story added significance were those who sought the huge treasure: astronaut-aquanaut Scott Carpenter; Jon Lindbergh, son of the aviation pioneer and well known in his own right as a salvage expert; Dr. George Bond, head of the famed Man-In-the-Sea Sealab experiment in extended undersea living conducted off La Jolla, California; former Sealab aquanaut William J. Bunton, one of the nation's leading diving experts and the driving force behind the *Awa Maru* venture.

What came to light in this and later stories was the delicate nature of the operation headed by Bunton and the Hong Kong-based corporation he set up to implement the recovery. For four years, Bunton, his corporation, and his team of experts have sought to win permission from the People's Republic of China to conduct a joint-venture salvage operation in their territorial waters. It's been a test of forbearance.

Assisting them in their proposal with China is top-ranking China expert Dr. Harned Pettus Hoose, a former counsel to President Richard M. Nixon prior to and after his historic China visit in 1972, culminating in the Shanghai communique establishing the prospects for normalizing Chinese-U.S. relations.

Since Dr. Hoose undertook to explore the matter with high-ranking Chinese officials, he has stressed the necessity of patience and perseverence in dealing with the People's Republic of China.

When the so-called Chinese moderates arrested the so-called radicals, including Madame Mao, Hoose reported that his contacts now suggested that circumstances for a contractual salvage agreement could be close at hand.

For four years, the reports from China to the American team have indicated progress, a progress measured differently by the Chinese and by the Americans, but nonetheless progress.

"Increasingly optimistic" is the term Dr. Hoose has applied in the past to the painfully slow considerations given the American proposal by the Chinese.

But in business matters, as in many other things in China, nothing happens all at once. William Bunton and his team have learned this lesson many times over in the past years.

When Bunton was invited to meet members of the PRC Trade Liaison Office at a private dinner party at Hoose's Brentwood home, Bunton expected a call from China by the end of the week; that was more than three years ago. Since then, and in large part because of his association with Dr. Hoose, Bunton has become more circumspect, more philosophical about China and the way the Chinese operate.

The advice Hoose has dispensed to Bunton over the years,

and to a host of representatives from various U.S. and international corporations and governmental institutions who seek—and pay for—his counsel, is weighted by his considerable experience. If his advice is sometimes painful, it is always complete, factual, and honest. The counsel ranges from how to negotiate delicate contractual matters, to where not to point a set of chopsticks (at anyone, ever). Aside from the serious aspects of trade negotiations, he is also quick to advise those who want a continued business relationship with China to avoid staring at the hostess's feet. There's a delicacy here that is the Western equivalent of staring at the breasts of a woman.

Hoose's counsel is delivered in doses, with considerable humor and with a genuine feeling for the people of China that could come only from one born and raised among them.

Amid a splendid array of Oriental art and handsomely carved furnishings, Hoose appears to relish discussing the nuances of Chinese culture and the varying philosophies between the youngest nation and the oldest. Throughout his discussions, Hoose reflects on the meaning of time, what time means to the Westerner and what it means—if it means anything at all—to the Easterner.

Consider a Chinese painting. Typically, the painting will comprise the brushed suggestions of a man, a mountain, and a tree, all set against a vast, uncluttered background.

"Yeah, well, it's nice," the Westerner might say, "but what the hell's all that empty space?"

"That's not empty space," the Chinese would say.

"Well, it looks empty to me," the Westerner replies.

"That's because, my good man, you cannot see all the thoughts that fill it."

It is the completion of thoughts like these, thoughts that take an Eastern sense of time, for which Bunton and his American team wait.

QUESTION: Wait a minute. Before we end this thing, let's talk about the sinking site. We're publishing some pretty good numbers here. Couldn't anyone with a rowboat and compass go out and find the *Awa Maru?*

BUNTON: No. What we're revealing is the U.S. Navy's reported sinking site. The latitude and longitude are in error.

QUESTION: How do you know that?

BUNTON: The reported site, and fifty square miles surrounding it, has been thoroughly searched over the years, surreptitiously, by several well-financed salvage groups. But to no avail.

QUESTION: Are you saying the U.S. Navy deliberately falsified the sinking site?

BUNTON: No. After sinking the *Awa Maru,* the *Queenfish* entered what was thought to be a fairly accurate position in their log. They reported that to ComSubPac. It's the position that's shown in the general court-martial transcripts, the *Queenfish's* fourth war patrol report, and other naval publications and documents.

QUESTION: That doesn't make much sense. Why can't it be found where it was said to have gone down?

BUNTON: Frankly, that question bothered me for years. After analyzing all the entries in the *Queenfish's* log, I discovered . . .

QUESTION: You saw the original log?

BUNTON: Yes.

QUESTION: Where?

BUNTON: In the classified Naval Archives in Washington, D.C., in 1966. I transcribed all the key entries made on April 1, 1945.

QUESTION: How did you get into a classified area?

BUNTON: I got in. It's not important how. After studying the log's data, correlated with other information I had accumulated over the years, and with the cooperation of a highly placed officer who had access to the *Queenfish's* navigational equipment, I discovered why the *Awa Maru* would never be found anywhere near the reported sinking site.

QUESTION: Who is the officer who assisted you?

BUNTON: I can't name him.

QUESTION: Was he one of the nine officers aboard the *Queenfish* that night?

BUNTON: I won't answer that question.

QUESTION: And you discovered the error?

BUNTON: Yes. It was a small error, but meaningful. The radar bearings as generated by the ship's gyro compass caused the *Queenfish's* dead-reckoning position to be significantly different from the true position. Remember, the weather during the fourth war patrol had been overcast or cloudy for weeks. This prevented the navigator from shooting morning stars or taking afternoon sun lines. Without routine celestial navigation, you're at the mercy of radar and cannot positively update navigation fixes which subsequently are fed into the ship's dead-reckoning equipment. This combination, bad weather, slightly erroneous radar bearings on Turnabout Island, and the inability to obtain visual navigational fixes on more than one known landmark, created an error factor that placed the critical location now in question beyond the reach of even modern search techniques. Keep in mind that when the *Queenfish* sank the *Awa Maru* and reported the position, as they knew it, no one ever dreamed how vital the true location would one day become. And, of more importance, what an error of only a fraction of one degree in either latitude or longitude, or both, can mean in searching square miles of open sea.

QUESTION: So, by having that error factor, you know precisely where the *Awa Maru* is?

BUNTON: Yes.

QUESTION: And a treasure estimated sometimes as high as five billion dollars?

BUNTON: Yes.

QUESTION: I don't want to appear cowardly, but we ought to make it clear, right?

BUNTON: Make what clear?

QUESTION: That you know the error factor and I don't.

BUNTON: Okay.

QUESTION: Look. There are people who would declare war for less. I'd like to be able to walk the streets. Could you say something more convincing than "okay"?

BUNTON: I know the error factor. The writer does not. How's that?

QUESTION: You may have saved my life.

A NOTE TO THE READER:
AN UPDATE

As this book was being readied for publication, the Associated Press, Tokyo Bureau, released this story dated May 3, 1979:

TOKYO (AP) The recent discovery and partial raising of a Japanese ship, the *Awa Maru,* torpedoed by the American submarine *Queenfish* April 1, 1945, in the Taiwan Strait may solve one of the lingering mysteries of World War II.

Among the questions are whether the 11,219-ton cargo-passenger ship, on a mercy mission under agreement with Allied powers, was carrying contraband and a fabulous treasure including diamonds and gold bars when four torpedoes slammed into its hull . . .

China said last week that its salvage workers recovered remains and belongings from the ship about 11 miles off Fukien province off southern China. The ship, broken in two parts, was discovered two years ago by a Chinese salvaging firm in about 190 feet of water.

China has promised that the remains and belongings from the *Awa Maru* would be returned to Japan. By some estimates, the *Awa Maru* carried a treasure worth more than $10 billion.

Further reports that day confirmed that the Chinese had discovered the wreckage in May 1977 but had not publicly revealed their find until now.

Then, on May 23, this:

TOKYO (AP) China has recovered the remains of 158 persons from among the more than 2,000 who died when an American submarine torpedoed and sank the Japanese merchant ship *Awa Maru* returning from a mercy mission near the end of World War II.

Kazuo Maruyama, a Japanese official just back from Peking, said he was told the Chinese recovered the remains and personal belongings in a 1977-78 salvage operation that raised part of the cargo-passenger ship from its watery grave ...

He said the Chinese told him none of the remains could be identified. He said the recovered personal belongings included baggage tags, currency, bank books, watches and children's dolls ...

But of the treasure? Nothing. On October 26, Richard Hughes, in an article in the prestigious *Far Eastern Economic Review,* revealed still more detail:

The fate of jewelry and gold bullion worth US $200-300 million, looted by the Japanese army in Malaya and Indonesia and sunk aboard the fake hospital ship *Awa Maru* off the China coast on April 1, 1945, remains a haunting mystery. More than three months have now passed since the Chinese fulfilled their May pledge to restore "the remains and belongings" of 158 (pretty precise) recovered bodies of the 2,000 fleeing Japanese aboard the 11,219-ton cargo passenger vessel.

Welfare Minister Hashimoto led a mission, including 10 members of families of the dead, to Shanghai in July and received the bodies and "384 pieces of personal belongings, including name tags, rusted military swords, shoes and fountain pens, in 13 boxes."

A correct half-hour Japanese ceremony was held the same week at the Welfare Ministry head office, and relatives of the deceased were allowed to "inspect and identify" the remains and belongings. Another ceremony honored the remains when some were placed in a cenotaph at Zojoji temple in Chiba and others in the Tomb of Unknown Soldiers at a Kudan park.

All this detail was reverently reported in the Japanese press, with Hashimoto's reiterated expressions of gratitude to China and pledge of Japan's continued work for peace.

On the hard news side, China's Vice-Minister of Communications Peng Dequing told Japanese reporters that salvage operations by 700 workers in more than 10 boats had been in progress since May 1977 and that no treasure had been discovered—yet. Search for the two missing welded steel, wardrobe-sized safes, which contain an estimated two tons of bullion and precious stones, would continue, if necessary, until next year.

Instructively, that news item was played down in the Japanese press coverage. The media leaders have obviously agreed to build up and polish their Japanese version of the sinking. Their news backgrounding was an explicit denunciation of Washington and the US Navy and an implicit warning of hardening misrepresentation of history.

The facts—confirmed and unchallenged by international sources at the time and fully reported by the world's No. 1 salvage authority, octogenarian Captain W. Doust, in his classic, *The Ocean on a Plank* (1976)— were that the *Awa Maru* slipped out of Singapore just before Hiroshima, after having been craftily disguised as a hospital ship by Japanese army leaders, who secreted the looted treasure aboard. All Chinese labor was suddenly expelled from the passenger ship's dock and only Japanese soldiers were used for reconstruction and the loading of 7,000 tons of commandeered rubber, quicksilver and other metals—as well as the loot.

A pious application for a safe-conduct permit was granted by the International Red Cross in Geneva (which Tokyo had not previously recognized during the war) for the *Awa Maru*'s direct return to Yokohama via the then Formosa Straits with non-existent hospital patients, doctors and nurses.

Correctly suspicious, the US despatched two submarines to shadow the ship, brilliantly illuminated and carrying the necessary Red Cross flags and markings, and —justifiably, according to international law—torpedoed it when in early morning it suddenly switched from its approved course in the direction of Shanghai (then still held by the Japanese).

It is unclear whether Hughes is paraphrasing Doust here or is himself misinformed. There is no evidence to indicate the *Awa Maru* veered off course to Shanghai or materially altered her prescribed route in any way. The report continues:

Now the Japanese press suggests and repeats that the *Awa Maru* was a mercy ship—never a hospital ship— which had been carrying relief goods to interned Allied prisoners of war in Southeast Asia, and which a US sub-marine callously torpedoed in abrogation of the Geneva permit . . .

In retrospect, the real tragedy is that Captain Doust, who had been informed by Rear-Admiral William Sullivan, chief of US naval salvage, of the precise location of the wreck, was denied proper support from the British Admiralty for immediate and doubtless successful re-covery of the ship and the two safes. That was 30 years before the Chinese at last started to nose around the now corroded and wide-swept wreckage.

If they ever do find the treasure, they are now legally entitled to keep it—even if the Japanese finally reverse their new line and claim sincerely that the loot is theirs and far more valuable than invisible hospital beds.

So, the mystery lingers. Questions, international bickering remain. Now, more than 35 years after the sinking of the *Awa Maru*, the fog persists . . .

INDEX

Aerial mines, 47
Agreement for settlement of *Awa Maru* claim, 248–50
Albrecht, Edward, 223–24
Aleutian campaign, 12
Allied Powers, Supreme Commander of, 250
Apollo, U.S.S., 169, 224
Apra Harbor, Guam, 165, 166
Associated Press, Tokyo Bureau, 267
Author's note, 174–77
Awa Maru
  aboard, at Singapore, 24
  afterscene of sinking, 154
  cargo of, 80–81
  claim of, 247
  description of, 79
  disaster of, 134–39
  first alarm, 110–11
  in Formosa Strait, 128–31
  itinerary change, 213
  itinerary for, 71
  life-saving equipment of, 108
  loading at Singapore, 74–82
  mission of, 230
  and Niu-shan Tao, 132–39
  passenger cargo vessel, 249
  report on attacking, 117–19
  report on sinking of, 144–45
  safe passage itinerary of, 213
  salvage of, 262–68
  searching for debris of, 159–60
  second alarm, 129–30
  at Singapore, 50, 74–82
  sinking of, 256
  sinking site, 226
  and South China coast, 107–11
  in the South China Sea, 94–103
  special markings, 240
  special message concerning, 87
  torpedo attacks on, 133–39
  width of, 26

Ballentine, Joseph W., 44
Bangka Island, 27, 46

Bangkok, 43
Bass, Mike W., 20, 23, 89, 116, 194–195, 209
Beck, Joseph R., 205
Belly cutting. *See* Hara-kiri
Bergamini, David, 99
Bicca, Roy, 31–32, 122
Boldern, Carl, 29, 34
Bomber Command, U.S. 21st, 46
Bond, George, x, 262
Borneo, 43, 45
British Admiralty, 270
Bronze Star, 89
Burgel Shunjyu (magazine), 206–07
Bunton, William J., x, 263–66

Camp Dealy, Guam, 5, 166
Cargo Hold number four, 58, 61, 79
Carpenter, Scott, x, 262
China, 43
  and partial raising of *Awa Maru*, 267–68
Chisel (Korean camp administrator), 62–65
Commander, Submarine Force Pacific Fleet. *See* ComSubPac
Commander Task Force, 17, 225
Commission of Jurists, 231
Commission of Nations, 231
Communications officer, 20
Communication Section, 20
ComSubPac, 8, 11, 16–17, 35, 90, 265
  intelligence officer of, 222
  message from, 85
  plain-language message from, 124–125
Cook, Sam, 234
Co-Prosperity Bright Metal firm, 136
Coronet (magazine), 165
Court-martial, general
  accused, 229
  argument, 230–43
  court, 229
  defense, 208–18, 220–29

273

ABOUT THE AUTHORS

W. JOSEPH INNIS was born in Chicago in 1937 and moved to Southern California following high school. He earned a B.A. in Journalism from San Diego State University and after three years in the U.S. Army in France returned to work as a political editor and writer for several California newspapers. In 1969, he moved to Mexico and earned his M.A. in Fine Art from Instituto Allende, San Miguel. His sculptures and paintings have won many awards and have appeared in one-man shows and group exhibitions in three countries. Currently in San Diego again, he is working as an artist, teacher and novelist.

WILLIAM J. BUNTON was born in Pennsylvania in 1933 and was raised in Detroit. Enlisting in the Army in 1950, he served two years with the 187th Airborne Regimental Combat Team in Korea. Shortly after being discharged in 1953, Mr. Bunton migrated to California and pursued a career as a deep-sea diver which eventually led to the position of diving supervisor for the prestigious Naval Undersea Warfare Center in San Diego. He was selected to participate in the now historical U.S. Navy's Sealab Project in 1964 and was officially certified as a "U.S. Aquanaut." In the following years, Mr. Bunton continued his career in experimental diving, underwater photography, teaching, writing and equipment development. In 1973, possessing certain key information (secret to this day) as to cargo and the sinking site of the *Awa Maru,* he commenced a six-year effort for exclusive salvage rights that have continued through the writing of this book. Mr. Bunton is presently working on a sequel to *In Pursuit of the Awa Maru* which will reveal the post-World War II story of the greatest treasure hunt in the history of underwater salvage.

We Deliver!

And So Do These Bestsellers.

Join the Allies on the Road to Victory
BANTAM WAR BOOKS

These action-packed books recount the most important events of World War II. Specially commissioned maps, diagrams and illustrations allow you to follow these true stories of brave men and gallantry in action.

☐	12657	AS EAGLES SCREAMED Burgett	$2.25
☐	13643	BATTLE FOR GUADALCANAL Griffith	$2.50
☐	*12658	BIG SHOW Clostermann	$2.25
☐	13014	BRAZEN CHARIOTS Crisp	$2.25
☐	12666	COAST WATCHERS Feldt	$2.25
☐	12916	COMPANY COMMANDER MacDonald	$2.25
☐	*12927	THE FIRST AND THE LAST Galland	$2.25
☐	13572	GUERRILLA SUBMARINES Dissette & Adamson	$2.25
☐	12665	HELMET FOR MY PILLOW Leckie	$2.25
☐	12663	HORRIDO! Toliver & Constable	$2.25

*Cannot be sold to Canadian Residents.

Buy them at your local bookstore or use this handy coupon:

Bantam Book Catalog

Here's your up-to-the-minute listing of over 1,400 titles by your favorite authors.

This illustrated, large format catalog gives a description of each title. For your convenience, it is divided into categories in fiction and non-fiction—gothics, science fiction, westerns, mysteries, cookbooks, mysticism and occult, biographies, history, family living, health, psychology, art.

So don't delay—take advantage of this special opportunity to increase your reading pleasure.

Just send us your name and address and 50¢ (to help defray postage and handling costs).